This compilation of short stori[ ] characters and reader on a journey beyond and between the veils of reality. They are meant to be - each and individually - either philosophical, deep, touching, thrilling, and heartwarming, or any random combination of those descriptions, and more, all at once. The intention of this book is to expand upon the two previously published books of poetry, *Mr. Swan's Poems* and *After The Flight*, to take the reader onto a journey into deeper rabbit holes and on longer and more drawn out rides that the short story format allows for.

All of these short stories are original works. The date of the final draft of this compiled, completed work was Saturday, June 20, 2015.

ISBN #978-1-329-24011-7

Cover art, book layout, and design were done by Michael DeBenedictis. The author picture was taken by Michael DeBenedictis on March 27, 2015, a week after a drastic haircut.

NOTES

NOTES

A Walk In Stitch's Park

(2/19/2015)

I

It is entirely possible to lose yourself in the crowd and become invisible by your own willpower, not completely of course, but little by little. He'd done it before, many times over - all through his grade school and high school years, especially - and it had become a trick he routinely pulled of at the coffee shop just one town over, over a coffee and sandwich, when he felt like being around people, but not necessarily with them. A hermit wasn't the right word to describe him, but sociable wasn't exactly correct, either. He spent more time in his head than anywhere else, where the storms and winds were always getting kicked up in controlled and uncontrollable ways, while everything seemed completely placid on the surface of his face to look into his eyes. For this reasons the contents of his bookshelf, and formerly his guitar, were his best friends. Not to be pitied was he, however, as he had designed his life this way.

Peace of mind, for him, was different things during different seasons. In the winter it was people-watching at coffee shops while searching for that illusive muse of inspiration, reading, and writing at home, whether on his laptop or his faux-leather bound folio. In the spring, summer, and fall it was going on walks in the parks - his town and New York seemed to share the idea that maintaining national parks was a good thing for the human psyche - more writing, and reading. If you were to compare him to a butterfly he was always either within retreating proximity back to or halfway in the cocoon. Even at work at the manufacturing plant he most enjoyed getting his work assignment for the day, getting down to it, and being left fairly alone, to pop in and out of others' individual company throughout the day, lest he get too stir crazy.

For this reason he felt, on this day, the reason to go for a walk, again, by himself. It was a nice fall day - not too hot in the sun and not too cold in the shade - and he was feeling sociable, with nature at least. He got into his sedan, a moderately stylish and practical car for a bachelor in his thirties, and drove to the park with nothing but an open mind set upon himself, as far as accessories were concerned. Upon arriving the parking lot was fairly filled up, but it was well spread out park with at least two or three different trails, both coming and going, so he would still be able to be by himself and still around people every so often when they passed him. Getting out of his car a slight, welcoming breeze, that cooled the mildly warm air, made its presence felt comfortably.

Walking towards the trail's beginning, and end point simultaneously, he walked past the mildly cobwebbed and half-full bins of trail maps, as if one really needed to do anything more than keep walking another five or ten minutes to get back on track again, let alone coming close to anything remotely called lost. Passing the small, cabin-like bathrooms and an outdoor water fountain that was just too outdoorsy and dirty for him to drink from, beyond these he entered the forested beginning of the trails. From here you could see the river that swept throughout the park, separating the two greater trails reachable from different sides of the bridge above them.

A few hundred feet into the trail he passed a couple on their way toward the parking lot, having finished their walk. Both were in their twenties, a handsome guy and an equally attractive girl, wearing appropriate athletic shoes, cargo shorts or jeans, and t-shirts with unzipped hoody sweaters topped with baseball caps. He nodded, smiled, mumbled the obligatory *hello, nice day*, and went on his way. *A couple*, he thought, *how sweet*, but not the arrangement that worked for him. An old friend of his had once said that no woman wanted a project, that they wanted a man with goals who was on his way toward something, and complete enough to not need fixing. He was still convinced he was still in project phase, and didn't have the energy for a girlfriend or potential mate for life. Even though coupling seemed to be human nature he didn't really find himself in a frenzy to do so. Still, he felt no different than anyone else or like he was on the fringes of human nature. Today, it was him and the river, and everyone else were simply passers-bye, background characters in the sight of his view on this walk.

It was a nice day and he'd enjoyed, as he usually did, the range of views. There were the pathways cut through and around and beside cut-out stone cliffs, the overhead panorama of the steps of other trails and the tranquil, babbling river below, the forest, and trails across the river of the other trail system a few streets up from the one he'd walked on today - the one he'd walked other days. He enjoyed the walks over the novelty-sized bridges over creeks you could either step or leap over without much effort, as well as the wooden stairwells - complete with handrails - build to accommodate the fact no trails were bulldozed and all of nature's rises, falls, and cliffs were undisturbed in the creation and connecting of these systems of trails. He was a good twenty minutes in and had a lot more of the five mile or so long, in complete tally, course to still enjoy. His mind was already wandering and wondering about, as he was guiding his physical body around the twists and turns.

On previous walks he'd seen deer in passing, squirrels climbing the walls of projecting - what passed for - cliffs, and other signs of natural life that made him smile. As he came up to what looked like a cave with a sheered off top and steps of stone he crunched through leaves and disturbed some said wildlife. *Sorry*, he thought, *didn't mean to scare you off. I was just passing through, carry on.* Bending forward to walk through the doorway into this stone cave - instead of taking the other trail around to the left with the view overlooking the river and other trails each step of elevation down over the ledge - he felt the breeze kick up, thought he saw a shadow in the sky above a cloud, and it was as if he was being watched from below. Even though there were no clouds in the sky and no one else he'd seen walking below he felt this, but brushed it off as nothing. Being in nature like this, though not quite the wilds of wilderness he felt like an adventurer discovering new things about himself, nature, and like he was in a way throwing himself into the pool of the natural world. That said, he shrugged it off and entered the cave and looked ahead to the sand (where exactly it came from he never could figure out nor was curious enough to remember to ask anyone, anyway) on the scrub-grassed ground covered with leaves, with parallel stone walls on each side, leading to an uphill walk and more stone steps. These lead to a stone stairway down out of this cave back to the trail, where the left route would have taken him before.

II

Walking on, through the cave he felt the coolness of the walls around him blocking out the breeze and felt the quite, noise engulfing ground take in some of the reflective sounds of the leaves crunching. Looking up, the sky seemed different, however, not like he could describe how, but it was either way. The weather forecast hadn't predicted any ulterior-motived weather patterns, so he brushed it off. He continued onto the next stone stairway briefly up, and then quicker down toward the exit of this passageway. *It's like a jungle gym for adults, sort of*, he thought.

Unbeknownst to him, just as he was exiting the stone cave passageway a character with a somehow darker energy passed by the maps, the outhouses, and the water fountain. Hiding most of his head and face under a hoodie jacket and covered with worn-in jeans, black boots, and a tail ending in an arrowhead-like point. Mild protrusions shown sticking up and out, if one cared to look close enough, at the tops of his hood. There was a mild red tint to his face, as well, but it was of a hue close enough to flesh-pink that one wouldn't have noticed unless they paid close attention to this detail. The former man had just passed through the cave and - unknown to him, a passageway into a different, parallel world that existed just beside his own - into this red-tinted man's world. The red-tinted man, sensing a stranger had passed into his domain, was on his way to greet him. To those friends and accomplices - all of the same shade of mild evil - who knew him by name, he was known as Stitch.

Upon exiting the cave, the man, who's name was commonplace - yet one that set him apart from others by all accounts where identification was concerned - Michael, felt like something was different. Maybe the sun had gone down or maybe the sun had passed behind a cloud or bunch of clouds that had assembled, secretively and inconspicuous, as they are known to do. Ignoring the change as nothing more than the not so Indiana Jones-like adventurer he became upon entering the park trail, he walked on.

The sky seemed different however, a different hue or shade or intensity behind the veil of blue…something. He couldn't figure out what it was, but he could feel it, all the way down here from the ground. Walking on he observed another couple in the distance. Walking, not quite a bit faster, but definitely a bit more fragile, as if something were ready to break-out from underneath or around him for some reason, he felt a bit safer knowing there were others here, as well. Maybe they were sensing the same thing. At first they seemed, at eyeball's shot guess, five hundred feet or so away, another couple. He wouldn't be alone in what he now considered a strange place for too long, even if for the few seconds he would be united, by merely sharing the same relative space in the trail, as they passed each other. Blinking, he looked around at the trees and bushes and shrubbery around him. *Am I seeing this*, he wondered to himself. It seemed darker, a deeper shade of green that in the shadows almost appeared purple for some reason. And it appeared that when he took notice they almost seemed to be in the process of coming to an immediate stop, as if they were on the move or quivering for some reason.

He looked up ahead the trail to try to set his eyes on something normal to ease his mind, at the couple walking toward him. They now seemed about three hundred feet away. Either they were walking fairly quickly or he had lost himself in a daydream-like trance in the trees and bushes. He was prone to having the ten mile stare into thin air as he contemplated life way too deeply and became lost the world, and this could have been a moment as such, no different. *Is that the sound of something shuffling along the ground*, he thought. Returning a shooting glance at the bushes and grass it appeared as if they suddenly, like children running and playing a game they possibly shouldn't be, had just stopped dead still, as if caught in the act of something and were trying to still themselves from a fairly steady rate of shaking. This time they were a bluish shade in the places shadows prevented the sun's rays from hitting. Looking upward at the trail the couple now, was it possible, seemed to be, now, six hundred feet away. Closing his eyes and stopping in his tracks he counted to ten. Opening his eyes they appeared about two hundred feet away. *This can't be happening*, he thought. Still, he kept walking on. There was an intersection of trails that veered off and back towards the parking lot just past where he had first distanced the couple ahead of him.

Now having made his way a further up the trail, halfway from catching up to Michael, Stitch was speeding up his pace. As he fast-walked he looked part straight ahead and part down at the ground twenty feet ahead of him. Raising his head to the sky he stopped, closed his eyes temporarily - the exact moment Michael had begun to feel someone watching him or at least sensing him from somewhere around or above, or below - and smiled a grin that only a devil could love. He raised his arms to the air, as if in homage of something unknown to everyone else, palms up and hands in a claw, and muttered a prayer in Latin. As he spoke the sky grew paler, grayer with a shade of sinister pink, and then purplish to blue. The tree branches swayed a bit, the breeze picked up, and the bushed and shrubbery began to sway. As if seeing Michael through a blurry crystal ball Stitch could see him walking, as if he was just above and behind him, and what he saw pleased him. It was the perfect setting to introduce himself. Uttering one last Latin prayer, most likely not condoned or approved of by the Catholic church of old or new, the couple approaching Michael nodded their heads in approval of something.

As Michael approached the couple, now consistently making their way towards him at a rational rate of time and speed, they came into focus. Similarly dressed like the previous couple, but in hoodies both of theirs' up, they seemed to have a reddish-pinkish skin hue and protrusions sticking up in a - could that really be a - point at the top, front of this hood. Now more than mildly scared, and not doing the best job of physically showing to be keeping it to himself, Michael was within twenty feet of them. As he passed them he approached with his head more down towards the ground, but not so low he couldn't peak out at the corner of his eyes. It was a clear path, free of all protrusions and anything else other than fallen, spare leaves. He'd realized, without looking up and based on the shadows left on the bushes and reflections off the water far down below, that the sky had become an unnatural shade darker. As the couple passed they stared directly at Michael, not taking their eyes off him, as their heads moved to keep him in a straight-line sight. Pretending not to see this, but again not doing a good job at showing that it didn't affect him physically, he passed, walking noticeably faster.

"Careful walking that fast, now," one of the two mouthed, "while you're not looking where you're going." Both of them smiled in a way that made no one feel comforted and snapped their heads forward. Genuinely shaken, Michael looked back to make sure they kept on going away from him and didn't look ahead. A creeper vine started growing from under the surface of the ground and formed a hook of a tree root in his path. Turning his head back towards his direction of walking Michael tripped. Luckily, having already been in pre-panic mode, or something approaching, that his senses were on even more alert and he threw his arms out in front of him. Catching himself in a runner's stance, before the starting gun went off, he saw the cloud of dust he kicked up and could have sworn he heard a laugh, or a breeze blowing through a very strange arrangement of trees that sometimes is known to sound the same.

Stitch, having just finished a hearty laugh, having witnessed the scene from above and behind, lowered his arms, faced forward, and walked on faster to pursue Michael quicker.

III

As Michael walked he thought he should have brought his phone. That could have told him the time, so he could gauge if time had passed at a regular, rational rate of speed, as well. That might have cleared his mind or it could have confirmed the exact opposite. *Best not to think about it*, he thought. He was near the turn around and was now in a full on fast-walk.

All around him he heard the sounds of shin-high bushes getting disturbed by lighter or heavier boots, depending on how far whatever they were from the trail or back in the words. He heard the snapping of a branch occasionally. Not realizing how fast he was going he reached the turn around point and took that trail. Now some of the noises sounded further behind him and even newer, stranger ones sounded closer. It would be, if his guess was right and if the rules of time and space were still in tact, twenty minutes to get back to the parking lot.

Now having cut the distance between them even more Stitch was on the hunt. Getting another genius idea, based on the dark twinkle in his eyes he stopped, did his homage to the sky, again, and turned his hands in the air, as if turning a radio dial. His vision was thrown back up above and behind Michael and his face shown another smile no one would find comforting.

Remembering he brought his I-Pod with him, as he did on occasion, loaded with meditation-enhancing music that almost made his regular walks feel like a walking prayer, he pulled it out of his pocket, put the ear buds in his ears and turned it on. *This will block out the worst of the creepy stuff, at least*, he thought. Upon hitting play the screech and piercing whistle, with undertones of an inhuman scream hidden under radio static, that hit eardrums was horrendous. He immediately removed the I-Pod and ear buds from his body as far as he could in a single motion and threw them far as he could down towards the river. As he peered over the edge of the precipice to the trail below he suddenly saw the same couple that told him to watch his step. They were standing still and glaring at him with their entire face and expression. Horrified, he stepped back from the edge towards the forest side of the trail as he could, half thinking he knew and half wondering what could be just beyond arm's reach, and was now at a quick jog.

Stitch, smiling and pleased, finished his homage and went back to his fast paced walk. His face now read steady, focused, intent determination. He stared ahead, and nowhere else, and knowingly had picked up his pace, too.

Michael thought he heard branches being broken and ventured, with all the bravery he could, to look over the edge of the trail onto the now - if it were even possible to rate which side of the trail was - scarier lane. He peered over the edge and saw the lower realm couple scaling the side of the cliff of roots, shrubs, dirt, and trees. Returning to the mildly less scary lane of the trail he returned to his jog pace, but with a barely subtle, obvious and blatant hint of an almost-sprint type run.

Stitch was now smiling as he increasingly fast-walked into near-jog pace. His tail whipped in the breeze trailing behind him and his hood threatened to fall off, pulled back in the wind, now. His hands, now more clear of the sleeves of his hoodie, appeared to be human hands, but with that pinkish-red hue and the fingers resembling claws that ended in sharper than normal nails that came almost to a point.

IV

Having been going at a good pace the entire time, and having sworn he heard - he didn't yet dare turn his head around to confirm it by sight - the other-worldly couple behind him, having scaled the cliffside apparently, he was a hundred feet from the entrance and exit of the trails. He could see the parking lot in the near distance. Now, thinking it would be a good gauge to decide how fast to approach his car, should he really have to start booking it, he looked back. The couple was not there, but he heard distant crashed in the woods and swore he saw - as if it couldn't get much worse - the back leg and tail of a bluish, purplish tiger or jungle cat diving back into the woods. All around the general area, and wider, of the creature's point of re-entry from where it came there were what appeared to be eyes peeping and blinking open and looking at him every twenty or so feet. Sometimes, in pairs, they seemed to be following his movement as Michael was still - not realizing it - in a fast run at this point.

Reaching the wooden, decrepit map rack, he now noticed it was even more run-down looking. Appearing to have become moldy, beyond splintering apart, and with gaping holes and cracked on the surface. The paint appeared faded and dull gray. The cobwebs had spread significantly, and small spiders now seemed to come out of holes in the wood, upon his approaching the stand. Not until now realizing he completely blew by the water fountain and bathroom cabin he looked back. The cabin was in the same condition and the doors swung back and forth on their hinges on both the his and hers side. From his vantage point he saw that the pipes were rusted, the mirrors broken, the floors swabbed with mud, and the state of the toilets and the sinks, and the water in them, was even worse. The water fountain appeared tilted to a side, had sprung a weak leak, and was now even more so in state that he wouldn't approach it - as if it was possible, before - as it was.

Turning his had back towards the direction he was running he observed the parking lot and stopped. His mouth stood agape, eyes wide, and he stood still. To his sheer amazement his car was the only one there. The parking lot pavement was cracked, broken, and scrub grass and weeds covered the green islands between the sides of the parking lot. The paint delineating each spot was either faded or gone. He hadn't been in the park an hour. It was impossible that everyone could have left in that time.

Behind him, as if it couldn't get worse, he heard the same laugh as before in the trees, carried upon the wind. This time he knew it wasn't a freak occurrence of wind blowing across just the perfect arrangement of exactly the right size branches and leaves, distanced the exact range apart to create something that sounded like laughter. It was the real thing. He didn't need to conjure the image in his mind of whatever it was laughing at him to realize it was exactly what Stitch was doing.

"Ha ha ha ha!", the voice went on, "It's only you, me, and my two friends. Their names don't matter, but you shall learn mine, and we shall come to meet."

Running to his car as fast as he could Michael heard the voice fading out as it laughed, as if it were the exclamation point to his brief monologue. Reaching his car Michael reached into his pocket for his keys. Pulling them out he hit the open button on the fob and listened for that blessed beep he so dearly wished to hear. It didn't come. What came was the same ear-piercing, laugh-laden radio static that came from his I-Pod. Falling to his knees he covered his ears and dropped the keys. Upon hitting the ground the keys and fob shattered like glass before his eyes. *Plastic isn't supposed to do that,* he thought, but then again everything that comprised, up to now, the second half of his walk shouldn't have either. Again, that laugh from the woods came back.

"You'll have to make your way back to your own world before you can go home, again," the voice said, with an evil, sneering satisfaction that wasn't even being masked, "and I believe you know the way." *Do I know the way*, thought Michael. *When did everything start getting weird*, he thought. Then he realized it...the miniature Temple of Doom. "That's right," the voice said on cue, "and I'll be waiting for you."

V

Thoroughly scared to point of approaching last-ditch bravery, or just the idiot's glass is still half full, I swear it is, because it just has to be panic he looked around. He knew this wasn't his world. It was dark, shadowy, and everything was in a downward spiral in the life cycle. Everything seemed to crawl - from the shrubs to the skies - and even the shadows were becoming thicker, if that was even possible to comprehend. Being a fairly lapsed, but not so far removed he'd forgotten what it was to be, Catholic, he suddenly remembered something. He had a rosary in the glove compartment. It was a panic-reaction fueled response, but it seemed to be his last shot at this point. He saw a fairly large tree branch a few feet over and then looked back at his passenger window. He looked back and forth at the two one more time and decided. *Sorry, car*, he thought, as he took a few steps over to the branch, picked it up, returned to the car, and smashed in the window. *Apparently that still works, here*, he thought, *wherever this is.*

The crash was loud and would have been even more audible if - and before everything else had happened he wouldn't have believed this could - the echo didn't seem to have been absorbed into the atmosphere that seemed heavier and heavier, like it was living on the world around it, even thought it knew it was unsustainable. Using the mini-battering to break out the last few remaining triangular shards around the edge of the window he made a safer sized hole to breach. Reaching in, opening the glove compartment, and grabbing the pouch with the rosary - which he held in his tight grip of a fist - he went back towards the trail with a look of determination and focus that would have shocked even Stitch. Michael had grabbed a little something else, as well, as a back-up insurance policy of sorts, if it came down to it.

Upon passing the map booth he didn't even notice its decrepit wood, cobwebs, and spiders. Upon passing the bathroom cabin he didn't even notice its still-swinging doors or apparent lack of upkeep inside. Upon passing the water fountain he didn't notice the puddle now having collected around its general vicinity. He did however notice the eyes in the woods around him, he heard the brush of attached living and detached fallen leaves on unseen boots, and the occasional snap of a branch. On his near-march back into the woods he looked left and right as he moved forward. His look and the full force of what was behind it - combined with the power of the rosary he simultaneously removed from its pouch and placed it around his neck like a necklace - seemed to make the eyes retreat as he passed, only to appear again once he was a good distance away.

Stitch, now standing at the exit of the cave Michael had come out of from his own world to enter into his, stood. Wringing his hands he had a cringe on his face, sensing something different about Michael, but not quite knowing what it was. Now sending his vision above and in front of Michael, Stitch observed the rosary about his neck. Michael hadn't realized it amidst his intense focus, but it was slightly glowing. *Good play*, thought Stitch. Having been tuned into the woods by now Michael returned his though right back. *I know*, he sent back and smiled internally to himself. Set aback, Stitch's cringe turned into a defensive straight-lined mouth, and then a challenging scowl.

Making his way past all the turns and twists in the trails beyond all the cut-out cliff stone, over the novelty wooden footbridge, up and over the wooden stairway around the cliffs, and towards the cave he stopped. He heard a growl, like that of a jungle cat to his right. Looking in that direction he saw a shadow-infested outline of a face emerge and take form in the mass of leaves it was pushing through. Noticing a sprig of hairs jutting from around its nose, a slightly drooling mouth, and teeth beginning to bloom from behind its opening jaws, as the moment began to increase in intensity, Michael responded.

"No!" he shouted and threw the rosary case at the face, "you will not!" Upon finishing his follow-through he saw track-marks in the air behind the rosary. It was glowing and leaving sparkler-like trails behind it. Before he wouldn't have believed it, but now he'd believe anything - even that he could face Stitch with only a little bit of faith and a rosary that hadn't been prayed upon in years, that was suddenly glowing. The face retreated back into the woods with a yelp as the rosary case flew into the hole the face backed up into. In a flurry of shuffled shrubbery, leaves, and branches behind the façade, the end of a tail and a back-legged paw - more like a claw, in appearance - flitted out and went the same way the face did.

Immediately snapping his head forward he walked confidently, in long strides, continuing his march towards Stitch and only God knew what would happen next. Bringing his right hand up to the crucifix he wrapped his hand around it. His left arm still swung and his legs followed the motion of his arm. His eyes never left a forward-staring position. As he rounded the final turn in the trail and could see his own personal Temple of Doom up ahead he heard a rustling in the wood on both sides. It was up ahead about twenty feet and he figured he had time, even if it was only split-second time. He reached into the pouch of his hoodie and grabbed an extra surprise he took from the glove compartment. It was a small bottle of water with an embossed image of the Virgin Mary on it, in genuflection that Stitch could never reproduce. It had never been opened once, but he figured holy water didn't have an expiration date.

As he kept his same military march pace he saw and heard the two bodies - he knew what they were by the same in-tuned inner voice that not only felt, but also heard Stitch's thoughts - within a few feet of the trail. The shrubbery and branches, though already on a fast track to death, didn't have a chance of even enjoying a few last moments, even knowing the inevitable. Just as the bodies - those of Stitch's unnamed counterparts - had half of their bodies through the now fully-grown and overgrown wall of foliage, Michael had twisted off the cap of the bottle and dumped the bottle out into his prayer-cupped hands. As Evil Thing Number One and Evil Thing Number Two - one was demon-like female and one a demon-like male - emerged from both sides completely and were less than ten feet away, Michael scrubbed hands together and brought them up and forward towards each of his attackers. *God, I hope this works*, Michael thought, *it has to.*

They both thought in sync, Evil Thing Number One and Evil Thing Number Two. The thought was in Latin, it was heavy in consonants, with the vocalization pounding upon hard letter sounds, and the thought thudding with booming bass. *No you don't*, thought Michael just as hard and direct right back at them, in his head, as he screamed a war cry that would've sent flocks of Stitch's pet wildlife running. With his hands ready to grab at whatever part of their arms, shoulders, face, or upper torso he could, Michael fearlessly ran at the two minions as fast and daringly as they at him. As the two minions ran at

Michael, arms and claws out as to grab him in tandem, their faces changed from anger and rage to shock as they came within a foot of him. Upon Michael placing his hands on the shoulders of their hoodies and grabbing onto them they turned to their version of white with fear. The holy water was soaked up by their clothing and burned their skin. As Michael felt them try to push themselves off of him with their claws - not even noticing that his hoodie had been pulled open and ripped up into shreds in the front where their claws had sawed through in the scuffle - he held on harder. Jarring them and pulling them closer to himself, sensing that he was winning by a long shot, he projected a though to them as he continued his war cry. *You will feel this, you will feel all of this*, he battering rammed the inside of their minds.

What Stitch saw, from above and in front of Michael, had him fuming. Angrily, he scowled and let loose a roar that Michael could hear outside of his body and feel inside his head, even though it hadn't been projected between their minds. Evil Thing Number One and Evil Thing Number Two were, in reality, play-acting the Wicked Witch's melting job. They were evaporating into thin air in a pasty, dusty mist that flecked on Michael's skin and clothes, but then simply evaporated into thinner air with no trace. As the minions decomposed before his very eyes and began to slump bodily over, lower and lower to the ground, Michael lowered himself with them till he was on his knees holding nothing but a handful of an empty hoodie in his right and left. His war cry having been war cried-out, and his two opponents no longer before him, he stood up and made his way towards the cave exit. His stare was locked onto Stitch the entire time.

VI

Not having had a plan he had at all knowingly formulated his head up to this point he marched on toward Stitch just the same. Stitch simply stood still by the exit, not quite blocking it, but not quite standing beside it, beckoning Michael to simply pass on beside him. Reaching a spot about ten feet away from him Michael stopped and took in Stitch's appearance. The horns on his forehead were ram-like and pointier at their end. His hands were the same as his minions, but sharper and pointier at the nails. Stitch threw back his head in a rage-filled roar and ripped off his hoodie. The human-designed shirt, with a Johnny Cash silhouette and the words "Ring of Fire" and something else appropriate, seemed to fit him well. Returning his face to look straight at Michael, Stitch ceased his roar and smiled that discomforting smile.

"Impressive…so far," said Michael. His face didn't waver from its sheer, razor-edged focus.

As Stitch spoke out loud, something in Latin, he projected the subtitles into Michael's head. *You, too, but you have seen nothing, yet*, were the words.

"Then show me," challenged Michael. Stitch's face became snarled as he charged towards Michael, making him attempt to backpedal, but not being able to fast enough. Stitch, noticing the glow of the rosary, but not taking it too seriously, grabbed Michael by the throat and picked him up off the ground. With his feet two feet above the dirt below him Michael kicked his feet. Fear had returned slightly, but hadn't quite gripped him body and soul.

You will know what I can do to those that think they can merely enter my world and do as they please, Stitch projected, as Latin streamed from his curled, fang-filled mouth and lips. *Yes, kick, shake, and quiver all over. That's exactly what I want you to do. And that idol of yours, ha*, he said, reaching for the crucifix.

Stitch was apparently able to get this up close and personal to him, even with it on. *Last ditch is last ditch*, Michael thought as he grabbed the crucifix, shoved it in Stitch's face, and said a prayer of his own, but in English. Feeling searing heat and sensing his flesh begin to smoke Stitch realized the crucifix was not only imprinting, but penetrating his skin. Recoiling and letting go of Michael's neck, Stitch, this time, backpedaled and brought his claws to his face. Michael, falling to the ground, did not land in runner's position, but rather on his back with a thud. Protecting the back of his neck with his arms he was able to see Stitch recoil and smiled, until he landed, and then cringed with a groan.

Getting up immediately, Michael prepared to straighten out his hoodie, and noticed the tears and rips. Lifting his head back up he put his hands on the front of his hoodie and took it off. His shirt, underneath, was ripped through, as well, and he observed proof that he had - though not having realized it nor felt it in the moment - bled more than a little bit onto the shirt. Walking towards Stitch Michael held out the crucifix and came closer and closer to him as he backpedaled, sensing what was coming ever closer.

Making not so much yelping whines, so much as retreating, desperate growls, Stitch stood up straight, from a crouched position, and Michael backed him up against a tree. His arms and claws up and beside his head, Stitch snarled and barked. Though his speech was still in Latin Michael didn't think he needed to the subtitles to understand what it meant. Still, Stitch projected his words into Michael's English.

Go! Leave this place! Stitch motioned his head towards cave exit Michael had entered this world through.

"Oh I will," Michael said with a sneer on his face, "and I'll make sure no one else ever finds there way here, again. That way you'll be left to die off along with everything else here. I just need to get one thing." Stitch's head tilted in confusion at these words.

As Michael turned to get Evil Thing Number One and Evil Thing Number Two's clothes Stitch began to move forward, away from the tree. Sensing that Stitch moved Michael whipped around, crucifix emblazoned out front, screaming his war cry, and yelled. Immediately Stitch backed up, this time completely against the tree, arms at his side, with an angry, but defeated, sour look on his face. *So be it, then. Take the rags. Then go*, projected Stitch.

Having turned dropped his arms down to his side, Michael, still clutching the crucifix hanging around his neck securely, let it go to drop against his hoodie, and went over to the pile of clothes. Wrapping them in a bundle he felt them. *Good, there's still some left, even if I need to wring these out*, thought Michael. Making his way back to the cave exit he stared and glared at and through Stitch, not loosening his gaze. Stitch held the same defeated, bitter, not wanting to admit defeat, look.

You will never harm another person, ever again, projected Michael, as he then turned toward to cave exit. Just before he went through with his bundle he projected one last thought for Stitch to ponder. *And I will leave you more alone than you've ever made anyone else feel, forever and ever.*

VII

On his side of the world, again, and standing up straight, Michael looked around. The sun, though it had partially gone done, was still seen shining traces of the daylight leftover, the breeze was blowing - even in the tunnel of the cave with its top sheared off - and the sound of everything echoed properly. The shadows fell proportionately and everything was back to normal. He yelled out a hearty hello and smiled as he heard the echo, as proof of his return to his world.

Immediately, he turned, held onto the shirts and hoodies that were still, amazingly, soaked in even the most minimal amount of holy water, began scrubbing the rock and stone surfaces around the cave exit inside and out, and moved onto entrance to do the same. If he'd had Stitch's vision - in the immediacy and necessity of cleansing the gateways into his world - he'd have witnessed a wondrous thing. With every swipe of the minion's hoodies soaked in the holy water upon the rocks and stone the rock and stone on Stitch's side of the wormhole crumbled off. Swipe by swipe on Michael's side of the rock and stone its doppelgangers fell away from the entrance into and exit out of Stitch's house of horrors, evil opposite mirror-land. Stitch was watching, the entire time, with a look of horror on his face, until he could take it no longer and fell to his knees to attempt to pick up the rubble and place it back to from where it fell, all the while roaring in sheer anger. On top of blessing the now destroyed - from Stitch's view - entrance to and exit from the other world, Michael thought of one more thing.

"Sorry, rosary," he said as he grabbed it both hands, stretched it taut, and gave it a pull that ripped in half, careful to be ready to catch any spare beads that could fall. With two lengthy pieces of rosary he looked the entranceway to Stitch's world and the entranceway into the cave itself. At each end, in the dirt, using a bigger stick as a makeshift shovel, he dug into the ground a hole big enough to shove the stick in vertically and potentially, completely bury it, and dropped in one length rosary and packing the dirt back in. He buried the other half, with the crucifix on it, at the now former entrance into Stitch's world.

Stitch, on his side of things, was in complete shock at what had happened. Having given up on picking up rubble and trying to place it back into where it fell from he began, he began to feel a heat emanating from the arch that he had figured out used to be the doorway unknowing mortals from Michael's world stumbled over into his playground through. Putting his claws to the stone in the archway it burned, so much that he roared out loud in pain, first, and then secondly, in acknowledgment that Michael had sealed the doorway shut forever, just as he said he would, leaving him more alone than Stitch had made anyone else ever feel.

When Michael was done wringing out Evil Thing Number One and Evil Thing Number Two's clothes, after he thoroughly cleaned the cave entrance and exits with the holy bleach, he wrapped the clothes up in a bundle and walked out the cave by way of its entrance. Stopping, after having gone about twenty feet, he turned around to take a look at what he himself and a multitude of others had never even possibly considered could be there. Shuddering, a cold chill running down and up his spine, even in the warm - for a later afternoon breeze, now - he turned away from the cave with the bundle of clothes in hand.

As he walked toward the dual-purpose park entrance and exit he enjoyed the gentle, lapping sound of the river. He enjoyed the tranquil sound of the wind blowing through the proportionately grown and still leaves and shrubbery. He took closer notice of the rise and fall of his way up over and down the wooden stairway and appreciated the humble, novelty footbridge over the creek. He was more impressed not with the way the stone seemed to have been cut, but had just eroded over time, to make way for the path to wind around and through it. When he passed the water fountain - solid, straight up and down, and watertight - he reconsidered it, pushed down the lever, and took a drink. Passing by the bathroom cabin he opened both the his and hers doors to see that it was well maintained and in working order. Coming up to the map gazebo he observed that it was in tact, only mildly cobwebbed, and the paint proportionately faded and chipped from the elements. Throwing the bundle of clothes in the wire garbage can he made his way to his car.

Stopping at his car the thought hit him. As he routinely reached for his key in his pocket en-route to his car they were not there. Panicking, he stopped, flitted this way and that way, and forth and back over the distance between the map stand and his car - the entire time searching the ground like a hawk. After not finding a single sign of the keys he turned toward his car, with his head hung low as his spirits were. *How could I go that deep into hell, come back out, and not be able to get into my own car,* he thought with an audible sigh. Then, all around behind him he though he heard - and felt, somehow - multiple sounds like a poof of smoke mixed with the sound of a zippo lighter flicking open. As he turned around he witnessed what he had heard and felt. The transparent, half corporeal, and half spirit bodies of an entire demographic of adults and children were standing before him - some having already appeared and the last few blipping into appearance. With his mouth not agape and his eyes not bugged-out wide - as he had a brand new, significantly wider range of faith in what could actually happen as long as you simply believed - he observed.

"Whoa," he spoke, almost under his breath. All of the spirits before him, smiling the entire time, then - in unison - pointed in the direction under car and directed their eyes that way. Taking in the sight, first, of the their one, collective act, and then, secondly, following the direction they were pointing he turned his body with his head. Underneath his car, right where - in Stitch's parallel world - he'd dropped them, and they'd shattered like a glass version of his world's plastic ones, he found them un-shattered and whole. Bending down to pick them up, gently, so as to make sure this was all real, he then stood up and turned around. One of the spirits, the one the rest all seemed to be watching as he moved, and as they parted in Exodus wave-like fashion for, approached him and stopped three feet away from Michael. He smiled.

"We made sure they were right where you left them," the spirit said in about as peaceful a tone Michael had ever heard, "so you could find them easier." With that, as Michael was now back to standing with his mouth agape and eyes wide, the spirit walked walk into the crowd of his own kind. In kind, as well, the rest of them turned and walked towards something only they could see, as they faded into the late afternoon, early evening night. In the background the river babbled on gently, to confirm that everything was back to normal, as a car with its headlights on drove in the road just beyond the parking lot entrance.

The Carousel
(2/21/2015)

I

Mark Atticus, yes he was almost, but not quite, named after a Harper Lee
character. It was his great-grandparents' fault, but how would they know
somewhere down the line of history an Alabama-born author in the 1950's
would write about a local lawyer in a racially fraught 1920's landscape, raising
two kids. Either way, it was a good icebreaker and topic of opening, foot in the
door, conversation that kept him from retreating back into his introverted foot
in mouth shyness. He was normal, by all terms and definitions of the word he
was familiar with, man in his early thirties, raised in a Northeast Ohio. Not
being the rugged one his father and grandfather were he was glad to have been
spared, at no insult to anyone else based on their geographic birthing, in the
northern part of the state rather than the heavily farmed southern parts. He was
always much more suburban than rural. He didn't even care much for walks in
the park, for that matter. It wasn't that he spat upon nature and its abundance -
which he was convinced would someday take back the paved, civilized land we'd
completely upended - he just enjoyed the tranquility of the solitary, loner,
bachelor life. Consequently, he was a fan of Neil Young and "Loner" seemed to
be his mantra.

Upon coming to, however, he found himself reclined upon a larger than
necessary, child's variety carousel that was for some reason built in the middle
of a natural, park preserve field. The sun was shining, the breeze was nice, and it
was good day weather-wise. He woke up because the iron handrail he was
reclining against had caused enough of a sting of pain in his back to wake him
from the near hibernation-level sleep he didn't know he'd even entered into.
Placing his hands behind him as he blinked his eyes and pushed himself into a
sitting position, he held himself upright by the handrail and looked around. Far
too confused to be set off into panic mode, he thought to himself *where am I?*

Noticing he was dressed in a business-type suit - not a fancy one, but a working
class one that Franz Kakfa's Gregor Samsa could have appreciated - from work.
Ridiculously, given the situation, he patted the back of his pants to make sure
his wallet was still on him, just incase he had to drive somewhere and didn't
want to become victim to a random cop stop, simply for them to practice their

license and registration, please act. As he was doing so, and began to laugh at himself for the futility of his ever-cautious personality - that never ceased to amaze him and pop up at all the strangest occasions - he heard a low rumbling coming up from the ground.

Starting to jitter in his seat with his arms and legs scrabbling for a hand and foothold, he saw something approaching from the distance. It was bathed in shadow, seemingly in front and beside it for a distance that seemed to never end, but allowed the sun to peak over top, however. Relaxing, from confusion, and figuring that panicking never really helped anybody in any situation, no matter how out of the ordinary, he stopped jittering and sat still. He observed what looked like a flat band that mimicked a sideways-laying projection reel, hovering just above the ground enough to disturb, but not rip up grass. It seemed to just pass through trees, bushes, and everything else in its path as if it was made up of a highly organized, materialized fog.

As this continued for another minute or so and the fog, screen, band thing approached Mark looked around in all three hundred and sixty degrees. It wasn't actually moving towards him, but it was shrinking in upon itself completely all around. When it stopped, just about ten feet from the edge of the carousel, it appeared to be exactly as he mused it was. It was, strangely enough, a film reel of a projection screen composed practically of a densely packed fog. Upon its settling, the one practically named after a Southern lawyer from a novel not actually about birds, but with one in the title, realized the breeze was still present, not diminished at all, but being filtered through the screen around him.

Suddenly, as if to cue a movie, the lights seemed to be turning down. His eyes darting back and forth, Mark could have sworn the fog film reel started turning with a slight click that was barely audible, but clearly there. It seemed to pick up a white noise-like clack as it picked up speed till it appeared no longer to be moving, but clearly was, as the optical illusion went. There was no shape or form of anything resembling the projector, odd as it was to imagine, as was suspect to come next, yet the screen began to flicker specks of dust that expanded into what precedes a picture show.

"Might as well sit back and see what happens next," Mark said out loud, trying to make out the image that was resolving on the fog film screen reel from somewhere, while he settled into his seat upon the carousel, that seemed to comprise the only ride of a very desolate, albeit beautiful, park in them middle of seemingly nowhere.

II

After the lights went down the stars went up, lighting up the sky like tiny candles. *I've got the place to myself,* he thought, *wherever this is.* Just above the somehow calming undertones of the clacking reel he heard crickets, jarred from their sunlight activities as they made the same sense of the sudden change of their environment. They seemed to adapt to their God-given natures and started up their song. As this was happening the words Mark had so passionately put down into his journals, from his younger years to his ever so dreadfully dramatic teenage years, came to mind. They shot directly into his mind, as if streamed, on an automatic timer, starting at this exact moment and no other.

On screen the murmur of voice began to become audible, but clipped and chopped up inarticulately from speakers that apparently needed no corporeal representation. It was coming from inside his head, however, just as he recalled the flow of words from his journals and visions from his memories were coming. Dust flecks expanded into skipping blotches of indistinct silhouettes that began to colorize and take on familiar forms. The first thing he recognized was resolving picture of himself - he couldn't remember what grade exactly - but it was the one where his parents, well-intentioned as they were, thought he looked so cute in those overalls he wore to early grade school, packed with other kids his age and height, all short.

He started out on the steps of his family's then front stoop, waiting for mom to emerge from the door to take him to school. She was a teacher and somehow just made it to her school on time, where she taught kids older than himself. He observed himself being swooped up by his mother, hand in hand, to the car, and being driven to school. The car pulled back down the driveway, everyone and everything they were carrying packed up, and headed to his school. He saw himself being dropped off at the door of his homeroom, crying from the shock of separation, but then just as quickly forgetting he was sad to settle into the school day with his classmates and friends. He remembered the times he was told that he had tried to strip those overalls off because they were uncomfortable. Apparently, even as a child, clothes that rode up on you in the most uncomfortable male places were bothersome.

Next, he saw brief flashes and clips of the usual preschool activities fade into a veritable this slide missing frame every so often, to jump forward a few years into third and into forth grade. The ride to school was the same, so were most of the friends and classmates, but he recognized the shift in his mindset, the lessons, and new emotions that developed. He saw himself in the classroom studying geography, spelling, math, social studies, English class, and more. He was amused to see each subtle change in school uniforms, school supplies, and the increasing difficulty of assignment, projects, and lessons.

In a solipsistic, dreamy haze, he took his primary attention off the on-screen scenery and took in the reality of the veritable reel to reel box of moving pictures, trip back down memory lane he was being entreated to. There was no door or exit to this box or theatre, whatever you wanted to call it. He was on the ride by himself, it seemed, and this was perfectly fine. He did feel strange, though, as if he was loitering somehow, in someway peering over someone else's shoulder, even though it was really his own.

Snapping back into focus upon the reel of past memories he observed a new theme to this part. He was shown on vacations in Florida, on the beach, on putt-putt golf courses, and there was grandma - now passed on - but there in full, living splendor. He was presented with shots of afterschool sports he'd been involved in, whether more or less actively, given his now realistic assessment of his rather minimal sporting abilities on the basketball court. Spliced in were scenes of around the house afternoons in the summer, beside and in the backyard pool with cousins and other family members upon annual visits, and evenings of dinners around the table. *How long has it been since we've all actually been around the table, together, not the TV,* he thought, *outside of the obligatory holidays?*

Musing on this, feeling a change coming on - something awfully prepubescent and even further into that awkward territory - to come upon the screen, he saw another this frame missing and similar pops and cracks upon the reel. The world he once knew was passing by all around him, on all sides, and it came rushing back - even if canned - to him more than he'd ever really let it before.

III

Next, he was witnessing himself as a young boy to becoming a pre-young man. This was the official preteen years, as far as he was concerned. This was the apex of his most awkward remembrances and he was glad he only had to watch them all over again, instead of having to relive them - which he had on occasion in his most unsettling dreams. *Interesting*, he thought on the matter, *I'm sure Freud or Jung would have something to say about that.* He guessed he was now in seventh or eight grade and was beginning to become beyond amused and making that gradual shift to that difficult, growing pain riddled area of preteen annoyed. As he watched himself in similar - on the surface - grade school scenes of classrooms, basketball courts, family vacations, afterschool homework, and dinner time sessions at home among other he even felt a little more uncomfortable inside, in his seat upon the carousel he'd almost forgotten about.

In his mind he was feeling the rush of new things, from head to toe, that he couldn't explain, but knew they gave way to the next epoch in his life that would somehow trump this. He knew it was all simply how he was reacting to the stream of emotions being beamed into his mind as he was being made to recall all of these memories, long stuffed down to only emerge even more explosively, like a veritable old fashioned colonial days' musket.

He could witness now, and recognize, the new sense of not quite dissatisfaction, but unsure mind that knew a significant shift toward a new wave of a lack of self confidence - that he'd gratefully shed many years ago - coming on. It was on his face in each scene that somehow mirrored, but somehow didn't even begin to tell the same story the images on screen almost harkened back to. Scenes of the ever so trying and will testing high school visits and admission tests began to emerge. Though he had viewed several frames of himself growing up, out, becoming more physically and factually fit - through library obtained books, more advancing school lessons, track and field, and other soul molding family visits and events - he was more than aware that the mind inside that body was screaming. That was the phase before his head would have truly started swirling into cyclones that seemed to dwarf the one Dorothy experienced, let alone the confusion Toto would have felt. That one had only thrown her into the world of Oz where every adventure - thought slightly threatening on the surface - was really just silly and much deeper learning experience for adults on a philosophical level. Marks's experience with his own personal cyclone was one that threw him down a dark hallway it seemed to take him a while to ascend from.

IV

He saw it coming a mile away and it did just as he expected. Scenes of high school came. Forget all those movies about aliens from outer space landing, having trouble getting acquainted to human life, and then emotionally imploding, to turn on the whole population en-masse, to take over their world. In his story Mark landed the same way, but upon self imploding he had to take it inside upon himself, with collateral damage occasionally spread all around him and in his path, unintentionally. He witnessed his first steps across the threshold of that highs school and cringed. *Here we go*, he thought, mustering all his bravery to witness what he remembered as an internal fiasco with only occasional external bright spots.

Here he was, on the screen, with an entire lack of social graces, making occasional friends - sympathetic and understanding, close to popular kids - who hovered on the outside of the primary cliché like loose electrons, but mostly with those who were more of the outsider mindset, like himself. He observed himself burning off the most dangerous, excessive steam in track and field, cross country, and first getting interested in the guitar and playing music. Wasn't that always the release the misunderstood ones found? He would, over the time of his high school days, find humor in the fact that his best sport was running - running from others, at your best, and towards to the finish line - so you could scamper off to be on your own, at peace, again.

He witnessed his keen mind for the artsy things making itself known more and more, as he begrudgingly muddled his way through high school math, social studies, history, and gym classes, and really dug into art class, playing chess with his running team buddies after school - waiting for their rides - and the occasional class project he could infuse a little of his offbeat musical, literature, and often misunderstood humor into. He cringed even more at his doomed from the start try-outs for sports you could actually get cut from - just around the time when the idea of cutthroat sporting performances and darker tinged versions of sportsmanship and competition creep their way into our lives. He could barely stand to watch his interactions with girls, as those were his most embarrassingly pathetic performances - still, even given everything he'd accomplished to this day - in his life.

And the raging emotions he knew his on screen persona was feeling - all the while the wind tunnel-like hurricane of distracted focus and thoughts in his head, on a daily basis - that were, even though to a lesser degree, being projected into his present mind didn't help. As if to mirror the pace and beat his heart and mind were usually paced at, throughout these years of his life, the film reel seemed to have picked up speed. He saw himself, however, as a comforting hand, show scenes of his victories getting dates at dances, coming close to truly excelling at track and field, and truly reaching what he could call friends who were actually, truly reaching back. Beyond the moments he cringe-worthily tried to desperately fit into this or that shape, when he was of a shape only Dr. Seuss could conjure up, he saw scenes of pool parties back at the house, parties he'd been invited to, and such.

Sensing another missing frame shot it came and went to flip over into his life outside of school. He saw himself, most poignantly, at his desk at home writing and writing and writing. He wrote tomes that resembled short plays, tomes that resembled short stories, and tomes that resembled the beginning of what he then called sappy poetry, but now was proud to be a progenitor of. He witnessed himself, as he had before, but now as a relatively older, taller, more mature version of himself going to church with the family, as he had been out of the practice, as of late. He saw the beginnings of his disenfranchisement with those peers of his own age, as he began to seek out the company of his superiors as colleagues - even down to several outside of school hour and day visits with one of the priests that would become a spiritual mentor, till time moved on and people did the same.

He witnessed himself more often seeking the company of his guitar and a pencil and pad, and eventually the family computer. In the moment of his persona on screen going to the movies and other usual hang outs with friends he clearly saw and internally sensed, in the present, seated position on the carousel, that he'd already decided those bonds wouldn't necessarily last. It wasn't anything personal, he just flitted here and there, scene to scene, too randomly to be able to attach other trains to his. Glad that the cyclones had slowed down to retreating in his head, he felt the calming - even though temporary - period of more resolved sanity that came with what stage came next.

V

Never having really had a clear idea or intentionality to his life, Mark had never
been one to stew on it. Rather, in hindsight, he realized he simply sampled what
he could, what was available at the time, and what seemed prudent - at least as
close to prudent as his mind could ever recognize - for best real world results.
Still, his fast and loose, creative mind had never let go of the steering wheel, and
it just seemed to take directions from backseat drivers at times - sometimes for
the worse or better. Most predominantly, however, he felt the next reel of
frames stirring up a newfound recognition of his being more comfortable,
confident, and sure of himself, whether it yielded a downpour or a parade.

He had entered into a new phase of life on screen. Life was getting more real
and the results of each of his steps had truly begun - as he had waited so long to
finally happen - to show results. College was by far the most interesting social
experiment he'd been involved in, whether voluntarily or by the pushing of
others. So many aspirations and dreams were floating around in his head, yet
even more proportionately lie on the side of road in graves left unmarked, along
the way, because he never had time to pay homage to the deceased, doomed
entrepreneurial ventures that were best left to die. He witnessed himself hiking
across stretches of sidewalks, between buildings, up and down even more
intimidating hallways, and sitting at desks staring at blackboards that professors
marched up and down before. There was an English class that he really liked,
there was that drama class that was really interesting, and there was that
sociology class that…well, let's just say he made when his spirit was able to
heave his body in the general direction of motivation for such things. He
witnessed scenes he thought he'd completely forgotten. There he was with a girl
from class, outside of the classroom, hanging out in the lunch hall. There he
was with another one, amazed that there even was another, honestly, and they
were hanging out off campus. He'd given her off campus church group
meetings a shot, but it didn't last. He did however get himself to go to that one
weeklong camp with the lake and the fellowship sessions with the live band,
among the other things he couldn't remember, to any avail. Spots like that in
the film were marked with dust-speckled flickers that seemed to blur the images
and action going on behind them.

Here, it seemed, the social life he'd been known to on and off, again, kick up had been most vibrant. In the department of personal tragedies he was experiencing a mind-blowing record few. He was out of the house and that nasty little X-factor that occasionally was able to be pin-pointed or wrestled down to be identified was making the least impact it could - and that was a good, to bordering upon, great thing. Stacks of books and backpacks, an occasional guitar case, and those occasional drama class project creations being carried over the aforementioned hikes, brought back strangely fond memories of braver times past. For all his momentary lapses in boldness and bravery, now and more recently, here he was boldly traversing the web work of a campus city and even the opposite sex.

In the present moment the thought that overcame him, now being streamed into his mind that was powering these projections, was that he was witnessing himself being let loose to discover, as a young man with greater visions and dreams of his own, that should have been obvious hints. He'd missed them in the moment, but in the next flash his likeness was just as readily and recklessly fast walking its way into its, as of yet unforeseen, but still not feared future. The undertones of consistent crackling and skipping record sounds in the background played on as the reel kept spinning and the gears kept white-noisily clacking.

Life, the stage he was finding himself in presently, before the carousel nap and awakening, would all have been much simpler if his corner of this sphere were still more like this. If he could only, at least, get back that innocent, proportionate bravado that heralded this part of his onscreen story. But it's never that easy and life is always changing, each moment to the next, as we evolve to the next thing in line that life gives us the right of way onto. We're left to consult our own veritable library of volumes to sort out the storylines, follow the threads we're given to pull at, and go deep into the rabbit hole as we allow ourselves - or are emotionally strong enough - to persevere toward.

The last scene he saw before the next missing frame was the sequence of himself playing at the coffee house. He had a drummer, on a small, jazz-like trap kit, backing him up. *Interesting*, he thought, as a smile broke the flat, studying look on his face.

VI

Knowing exactly what came next he saw it coming down the reel and took in all the sights and sounds it brought with it, as well as another version of himself. He was successfully calling back, on screen, reveries that seemed to re-enlighten himself to who he was and where he came from, as the pleasant grinding of invisible gears continued in the background. The picture show now pop, skipped, and leaped forward to show him as an adult. Allowing for himself to be tossed into this next adventure - as if he had any choice or say in the matter, otherwise - he watched on to view the life he'd already lived, but was somehow enjoying reliving all over again.

The frame started up showing him leaving the apartment, heading around the building via the neat, guiding hand of the sidewalk, to his car. He opened the driver side door and got in. Flash-forward to the next scene he was at work at the office. The phone rang and he answered it. He was pleasant enough and present enough in his frame of mind and was carried on by the support of his coworkers, some of whom he called acquaintances. In would come the tide of the next shift crowd as the tide of the shift getting off work was making its way out. He was part of this great migration in multiple scenes. Every step along the way, no matter how mundane, was a show of his life in full color and living shades. The scenes of the beginnings of his working days encapsulated the trek door to car, car to building, building to car, car to door, and back home to repeat this more than once more.

The best parts were the scenes of what transpired outside of this work. He observed himself pulling up to the house of the then boyfriend of his coworker, promoted to acquaintance. Entering the door the house was full of everyone who had parked their cars along, up and down the road, and around the house. He witnessed the card games and board games and drinks and homemade deserts and the games they played around the TV. He remembered this event and others similar to it, that also flashed by, only different by the date they occurred upon. He saw other scenes of himself out to eat with that same acquaintance, at her house to visit, there was another dust flicker, and then similar scenes carried on in similar resemblance, seemingly a few short years later.

Between these scenes there were the times with his friend outside of all of this, and as far he was concerned, who seemed to come entirely from out of left field.

This one, his name was Brian, he remembered, he'd met at another job. Just as he thought this flashes of the factory building came into clarity, he was on his line, and Brian was at his. At what point they started talking, became friends, discovered they both shared art and music as interests, and began that adventure in Mark's life he didn't' remember, but simply let the reel tell the story. There they were beside the lake in the park philophizing about nature, God, and life. Here they were at a diner discussing close to the same theme, but from a different angle. There they were at Brian's rented industrial garage loading in music equipment, playing something, and then leaving to go their separate way. Another scene passed by of them sitting in the same room, his apartment presumably, commenting on the movie they were watching, and then after another missing scene frame mirroring the same scene, but hinged upon the conversation about the newest Radiohead album they were listening to. Unfortunately, going their separate way down their own life's paths was the greater theme to that part of Mark's life.

Just as he was truly enjoying this part of the show he felt a jarring, slamming sensation. The reel that had been going full blast seemed to be slowing down. It didn't happen immediately, rather it was more like the process of a train with almost a hundred cars coming to a slow glide from a full charge, and it seemed dragged out to the last moment. As the picture show slowed down, brakes were being slammed on with clearly audible sound. As the reel eventually adopted a more slow and steady pace the white noise clack becoming more prominent and the invisible gears and brakes having chuffed out their last retort, to having been so intensely stepped on to to bring it to this pace, the film resumed.

Mark realized he had completely forgotten about his concern to know what brought him to this carousel in the first place. Just on point and tuned into his next thought - always a step ahead - the film showed him waking up on the carousel, his back feeling the bite of the iron handrail, and himself taking in the newest happening he discovered he was partaking in this moment in his life. He watched himself and the span of that past matter of minutes that had come to pass to shake him to the core, to simply pass on just as fast. Watching this scene he imagined that his soul was one of many, at a veritable bus station that buzzed with the thrum of the living. He imagined that each other spirit had a ticket to ride of their own, an existence to share with others of their own, and that their paths all crossed, somehow - or that they already had and everyone just didn't know about it, yet. They would all just figure it out soon enough.

Imagining this station in his head, though it didn't appear on the screen, as it apparently hadn't come to pass, yet, he saw and felt himself, and others, coming and going, leaving footprints, and even deeper memories. They were simply living them and leaving them all behind, equally and plainly, for others or themselves to discover later on. They each had their own baggage, going from terminal to terminal, and were following seemingly invisible lines toward their own destinations. As this was going through his mind the screen seemed to stop, as it had been - while he was daydreaming - in the process of gradually coming to a unpresumptuous stop the entire time.

VII

The grand finale of Mark's time on the carousel and his experience of having the best seat in the house for the viewing of his own life and times couldn't have been written better by Poe or directed better by Hitchcock. On the screen, now, making a whooshing and pulsing sound as it simply held its position, unmoving, showed Mark in real time. He watched his every move, as it was happening in his present, upon the screen - though not silver - through his eyes and that off a third person, neutral observer, at the same time. Waving his hand before his face, sitting up the carousel, his likeness did the same. As he stood up and walked toward the fog film screen to reach to touch it so did his likeness, as well. Only, when he was an inch from putting his hand, daringly and curiously, through the fog film screen, it began to peacefully, noiselessly, and uneventfully fade. As it did so the landscape all around him showed again, most prominently.

All around him the sun seemed to have come back out, the breeze - that at some point he didn't recall had become no longer evident - returned, and he suddenly realized luggage was sitting on the ground next to his feet. He hadn't remembered packing anything, but it was in fact luggage he did own. Somehow, even though he couldn't explain it he had felt that his soul had caught a bus, dropped him off here, and just as soon he was meant to be picked up, again. He had been brought here, to this seemingly not so well planned or thought out playground, and he was reunited with a familiar and resonant sound that hummed in his head. It was the language of his stories in his own words. Though they had never really been spoken of out loud to anyone by himself he'd been the gifted receiver of their visions projected out in the open, upon the film fog screen that was so real only a few seconds ago. That film real had aired out everything he once knew, but for him to see it from a completely different angle.

Feeling that his soul, now completely off the bus and clear of the station, and having already been taken on a walk for miles to kick up past dust, had an appointment to make. Looking up and over to his side - having sworn he just heard the most tender, gentle, easy-going sound of brakes any vehicle could ever make - he witnessed the taxi he was to take to the next destination. Right there, plain and simple, out in the open park field. It was to carry him up and over the threshold to where he was to take up his next residence. Closing and opening his eyes, and feeling the sun and the breeze, he bent down to pick up his luggage. The man in the driver seat unassumingly tipped his cap, reached back inside the cab to open the backseat, driver's side door for him, and then resumed his friendly of face, but focused, eternal stare forward.

If he'd stopped to turn around Mark would have seen the carousel not upon that ground anymore, for it disappeared to plant itself somewhere else it found it was destined to find breezy air and new rider. Mark entered the cab with his luggage, shut the door, and looked forward, as the ever faithful and vigilant driver did bade him to take him to his stop. The carousel, meanwhile, was meant to kick up old memories for another and become a personal theatre of this other's own, that they were to soon discover. As far as Mark was concerned this taxi was taking him further on down the road, at least once it got to the road beyond the park field.

The Viewpoint Of Time-Travelling Children
(2/22/2015)

I

Our viewpoint of the hustle and bustle, go go go, step by step, keep looking out ahead and in front of you, and by God keep moving or get out of the way world we call adulthood is something that, upon even the most brief period of study leaves children confused. This is perfectly as it very well should be, as well, as the viewpoint of children - still innocent, full of wonderment, an imagination filled with more fantastical content than the seas and oceans are teeming with aquatic life - is one that has not had its ties with the world beyond cut, yet. And it is those ties to a deeper, more understanding, patient, and open-minded world - where the connection that ties, but doesn't chain, us all together is still in tact - that makes the observations of children, in that completely free from a filter way they express themselves, something special to only children. It is exactly that critique that we must listen to sometimes and take heed to more than any and all of our empirical, categorized, and articulately defined conceptions of what it is to be alive in this world.

Not having a word of the above even remotely on his mind, as such intricately worded and thought out speech and elucidations would, as is fair, be beyond his mind until years down the road, there was a child who was simply passing through. His intent was to pass through, that is, but he then noticed something below that caught his attention. In all of his days and nights of playing real life with his friends, as all of the angelic, winged adults looked on with smiles they could hardly contain, this child - who for our categorical purposes was a little boy - never ceased to be amazed by the flurry of anthill-like activity that went on in the world below his. And for those of us who've passed on into the phase of adulthood, doomed to have to actually work at being a child again - who are absolutely itching to know the name of this boy, for categorization's sake - his name, in particular, was of no necessary importance. For our purposes, rather, it would be a distraction, as the messenger and prophet's name is not near as important as the message, or the greater name that message is passed forward for the sake of.

Having been given a pass to skip and flit about in self-discovery of the world all about and around him this boy decided to give the lower world another more than passing glance. Greatly curious to the point of bursting he decided to take a closer, childlike investigative look. Being a bit of space kid was in his nature - in both his ability to lose himself in daydreams, as well as focus so intently on whatever caught his fancy, that a telegram was necessary to invite him back to the reality of his peers - so this was regular fair for the boy. His angelic, adult-like peers would understand, at least, and beyond that probably even think him almost brilliantly and precociously curious in his odyssey to gain knowledge of the other worlds around his that he would eventually be called to watch over, when his day of age came. This having been more than decided upon, and having felt that the stars themselves practically dictated this mission, the boy descended to Earth - not knowing it, himself, but having had his mission plans overheard by one of the adult-like angels who put a protective aura about him, just in case. We could call it something, on Earth, similar to a significantly more effective backpack with a spare, light jacket, incase it started to rain or became mildly chilly upon the child's send off upon a play date or adventure outdoors.

Peering through tiny eyes, that somehow took in so much more and saw with a range far wider than any adult could ever even perceive, the child descended from his veritable, though minute, perch and stepped into our world. He was known by very many above, but by very few of any renown above or below anyone else, and was therefore softly and simply spoken. He was still, however, a miniature prince, as he had might as well taken a few small steps from a modest, humble throne, anyway. Having done so he walked set upon a path to walk among the crowds of those that even the adult-like angels of his world still misunderstood, on some level, but somehow managed to view with at least a little bit of reverence, sometimes deserved and sometimes gifted.

Not aware that he was still in his stately, but miniature version of, humble, yet still regal attire - as far as those of our lower, human world be concerned - he tromped forward. Standing at the height of a mere child among those of this corner of the world here he was dwarfed in size, upward and outward. He could tell, however, even without having the epiphany that only came with scrounging around for a while, first, that each face of those who traipsed around seemed to have a different, but distinct story to tell - if only they could be brought out of their shell - despite their similar physical forms and frames. They each had their own virtues to present to the world or hide as they sought to fit in so dearly, even if at the expense of their individuality.

Some of them were looking forward, glancing downward, peering side to side, and all around. Others were checking their pockets - a compartment of clothing that the boy had been told about, upon inquiring into what they were, greatly confused at their necessity - for something or other. Even more appeared to be dead-set focused on something in front of them that they apparently saw and everyone else was completely oblivious to. This was surely to be an interesting adventure that other children from above had been on before, as it was part of an initiation of sorts into the next step of learning how to consult on such matters as these beings partook of. Other children like him had come back with entirely new enlightenment and new ideas to rattle around in their head until they were formed into what the adult-like angels called philosophies, and he was intent on finding his own, as well.

II

Not aware that he was walking against the current, against the grain, he wouldn't have noticed - if it had been his prerogative to observe such a futile thing as this - and neither did his present company, albeit they were separated by the slightest veil of a curtain between worlds only their quantum mechanics could explain. From above one could have seen the course the boy was walking on as a track that had been seemingly cleared out both ahead and behind, as if a previously heavily trafficked and trodden path were worn into it. Reaching out the dynamically sparkling and crystal clear, but still slightly present veil - less seen than more felt - he reached his hand through it quite delicately and gingerly, and felt the atomic make-up of this material world, for real, in his hand. As if feeling a touch from something - not quite registered properly as that of an otherworldly, childlike angel from another parallel universe - a hand proceeded to swat away what it didn't understand, before even bothering to register it for the rare gift of contact that it was.

Looking above and about the boy noticed the significant difference in his height to theirs, for the most part, and observed that the sky - on a very clear, slightly cloudy, but nice, breezy, and just warm enough day - was almost blotted out as they passed by. The structures and buildings flanking them on each side, as well, seemed to pull off the same trick. *Funny*, thought the boy, *why would one want to put up such a thing that kept you from being able to see the sky all the time*? Musing on the above he then considered the below. The sidewalk - made of stone and brick, building materials he has been taught these humans used to erect structures to stand against the test of great lengths of time - echoed the footsteps of those around him. It was a clearly audible, flexible, and reflexive bouncing of sound.

Without feeling like he was interrupting anything of major importance, or something that required great focus and concentration - like the occasional studies of those adult-like angels of his world - the boy reach out to grab at something to see if he could do so quickly enough to be too fast to garner a human reaction. There were occasional glances of curiosity, intrigue, and sometimes perturbation from passers-bye, but nothing too evasive. He took notice of things that he had been taught they were known to have and use - shoes, pockets, belts, and socks, among other things - and he, if not for the safety track he was set upon, would have been knocked about, even though only reaching up to about their waist and knees. Following along with the crowd's pace, almost step by step and foot by foot, though for the most part two of his steps constituted one of theirs, he noticed the crowd slowing down to a gradual, for some, and more disturbed, halting stop for others. They apparently didn't notice the change in the group's pace, amidst their own thoughts and preoccupations.

At an intersection they all stopped, but it appeared to be for only a brief amount of time, however. Those who were either more careful or less daring looked side to side, watchful of what was coming from the other direction and exactly how much of it, also at what pace and rate of speed. Another similar mass of passengers, making their own perpendicular human train - mimicking the one he was in the middle of - moved across the intersection. Upon starting up, again, the centipede of legs started up - some more gracefully and inconspicuously, and other much the less - which would have tripped up the boy, if not for the track he was set upon. Bearing forward upon the path instituted, that constituted this part of these peoples' journey from one thing to another, the boy innocently and naively, free from fear or intimidation, carried on with them. His selective vision or bravery, whatever it was, bore him on toward what was coming next, along with the crowd.

In the near distance the boy sensed something, as only children can, that everyone else - seemingly oblivious to the importance of this paramount discovery - simply decided to overlook or just plain ignore. *How rude of them to not even be the least bit curious of what this feeling is*, the boy thought. He was taught by the adult-like angels of his world, in his upbringing as such the same way theirs was executed, that such revelations that could set your entire world on its end, and show you an entirely new and different path that could very well be where you were being lead, were it to be given the proper time of day and investigated. It was something you took the time to meditate on and really get to the root of, not just simply shoo away like a common housefly or other minor, disagreeable distraction.

Approaching him, ahead, was another like him. She was off his similar stature and ethereal quality. This little girl, potentially a little princess, had found her way to this plane of existence in much the same manner and by way of the same parental safety track that the little boy had. What the little boy felt was their two tracks joining as they came into such relatively close range. She - also of a name far too eloquent and angelic to be uttered on this human plane, which would be an equally distracting detail to only take away from the message she was to deliver, as well as the name it was to be delivered in - was moving his direction. She was of the same sweet, regal, but unknowing and completely oblivious, and inconspicuous of her level of divine, unquantifiable beauty. He felt she was the yin to his yang; a concept his adult-like angel counterparts had explained was the be all and end all of philosophy, that mattered at least, for the most part. It was the idea that she was the left to his right, the similar to his different, and the other piece to the puzzle as far as his experience in this, or their world above, was concerned.

III

Closing in upon the distance she raised her arm and waved to the boy with her delicate hand. It was an inviting, friendly way in which she called him over. And even though he didn't recall her lips moving, she seemed to speak to him in a voice that fluttered over and upon the congested air like a dove cooing, without any great cares or concerns. Seemingly defying the odds of physics within their shared physical space, and that they shared with those around them - this seemed to be a common theme both the little boy and girl were experiencing - the crowd didn't seemed to slow down or even acknowledge the spiritual gravity and import of their far less than chance meeting. Off in the distance - far, as perceived by those of this lower world, but much closer, as perceived by the little boy and girl - each of their adult-like, angelic parental counterparts had glanced over and down at them to make sure their safety tracks were in place.

As the little boy approached the little girl - not quite so much walking, as skipping, which children have been known to confidently and innocently do - the crowd just outside their tunnel of security flowed around them like pebbles in a river. The crowd had not sight, sense, or sound awareness of the two tiny, regal diplomats. The little girl stood patiently, smiling, as the little boy approached, and occasionally glanced around to acutely observe the people who were tussling about their shared current of filtered air.

"Where are they all going and what do they all do, is what you're wondering," spoke the little girl when the little boy had reached her, as if directly on cue from a stage left or right-side directorial prompt, "is that what I can assume?" The little girl began to speak to the boy, sensing he had many questions and queries she was glad to address.

"That is exactly, entirely what I was wondering, but I didn't even know where to begin," the boy resonated. The little girl seemed to fill in all the blanks of his mind and presence, down to her bright, open eyes. He had felt that she had either been down here before to view such things and therefore had a deeper understanding, already, or that she simply had that sympathetic and nurturing ability that only little girls who grow up into women do.

"You are observing the material coverings they are wearing," the little girl carried on, "those are their clothes. Some are dirtier or having been more worn in throughout the day, slightly or even much more than others. They work with their hands for a living, whether it may be inside, outside, or both." The prince observed, now, a difference of grit and kicked up debris on some of their pants, shirts, and sleeves.

"Those of clean, pressed, or just generally more taken care of coverings, or clothes," the little girl continued, "they work indoors and in a less physically industrious way, but more often have to use their mind and ability to relate to other people, person to person, over matters." The little girl looked up and around at the crowd of people, continuing to pass by, as the little boy did so, as well. She then turned her gaze back toward the boy, as he, feeling their conversation was to pick up, again, readied himself to take in everything she had previously observed or put together, so he could further understand, also.

IV

"There is another thing that happens down here. It is called age," the little girl imparted, "those with more wrinkles on their skin and face have lived longer in this place, as well as many other places." The little boy observed this. There were some that appeared to have an air of more experience about them and others that seemed to have an air of proportionately less. Then, he began to pick out the differences, in their faces and bodies and body language, that some were more feminine and some more masculine - similar to those adult-like angels in his world above.

"There are those who were created as women and those created as men, like us," the little girl confirmed, "but far beyond us in years, ahead." The little boy looked around, now seeing more facial and age-wise differences that he'd missed before. He observed their hair, that some of theirs was longer and some shorter, along with a few alternate styles that some of them - between their sexes - had seemingly traded. He also observed in their skin that some of them appeared to have tighter, smoother skin and some appeared more weathered and worn, having been around longer.

"There are some holding ones tinier than us, how we started out as, like a bundle," the little girl said, "and others just by the hand, to stand and walk on their own, beside them." She pointed them out as he turned his head to observe what she had just described.

"Those close to our stature are children, just like us, but some came before us or after us, in years," the little girl added to this, to qualify her previous statement. The little boy saw that those around were sometimes higher above and sometimes closer to his elevation. The little boy noticed, as well, paying closer attention and realizing it even more candidly, sensing more of a pull towards those he felt he could relate to more, called children, versus those he was told were called adults.

"Some of them are in a hurry, some of them feel worried about something, where others of them are at peace," the little girl said, "and others are a little bit of everything in between, which is also okay." The little girl was observing something deeper, in the eyes of the prince that he saw in their passing eyes. Upon this revelation's being uncovered the little boy felt he knew a little more about why they seemed to do what they did, at least as far as he could communicate that sentiment.

"Some of them are going home and some are going to or coming from work," the little girl explained, "and some of them are going to places of additional learning, or to acquire resources to maintain their life and comfortable shelter." This response explained the intuited feeling the little boy felt, a sort of deeper motive behind the way the taller ones locomoted to and fro and all around. He started to make connections in his mind that possibly even explained these people's more subtle thoughts that bounced around their minds as they went from here to there.

"There are those who, in the middle of all of this, are looking for or thinking of those they love," the little girl expanded upon her previous statement, "those who have gone somewhere else, for the time being, or are coming back." The little boy noticed the expressions on the people's faces. Some of them were looking around, dazed and almost missing, some wore smiles, others frowns, and even more had different combinations of these, as well other emotions in-between. The little boy thought he had an idea about them that he would, given time to let it all soak into his mind, come to understand further.

"There are people who always seem to be coming or going and others who take time to just reflect," the girl mused, "just as some have hearts that are warmer and other's seem to lose their glow." The little boy thought this out and realized that something deeper was always going on than upon their surface and what was just beneath it, more than he'd ever contemplated before.

"All of this is true, but it changes all the time, as well," the little girl shrugged as her mouth made a scrunched-up smile, "that's why they're always thinking, moving all over the place, and looking at things here and there. They're watching, knowing they're sensing something more, even if they can't figure out what it is, and reading further into it." She had elucidated everything the little boy has casually observed, but didn't quite have the key to unlock the door and explore further, let alone know how to communicate a desire to even do so.

"They have to have more on their mind, keeping everything in order for everyone else they've promised to take care of," the little girl seemed to be wrapping up her lesson in a tight, it really is this simple, but not quite package.

"There's a lot more to it than that, as everything changes day to day, and moment to moment," the little girl added, "but that is why they seem to appreciate slower moments to stop and think about it all. That's why they take time to themselves, sometimes, that we, as children, may not always understand." The little boy now understood why his adult-like angel parents and guardians were always going off by themselves, on occasion, to what they called their study, or spent so much time in silence just observing these people down here, or in personal meditation or prayer.

"You are starting to get it," said the little girl, smiling at the boy, having identified what the look on his focused, studying face meant, "you just have to pay closer attention to be able read into all their signs." With that the little boy smile and nodded acceptingly.

V

With that final caveat having been added the little boy's mind suddenly felt heavier, or denser, or more something, at least. He felt that feeling he usually did after a long, arduous, but meaningful lesson from his adult-like, angelic parents and guardians up in his world. The little boy knew he would be returning to his home to his guardians with a great tale to tell about this time down here, along with a final, deserved and earned request to come back another time. This next time he could, armed with an entirely new volume of understanding about these people be able to start really digging into their minds, sneaking a peak at their thoughts, take down notes about each and every interesting case for later reference, and then begin to put together a plan of how to help them. He'd have to get approval from his superiors above first, to actually interact with the people on a real, impactful scale - now beginning to understand the gravity of what such a thing could potentially do and mean - but he felt he was on his way.

With that both the little boy and little girl smiled, hugged, as innocent children do upon farewells, and skipped back along the way they had come to arrive at this point. The little boy thought to himself that he might, upon his next venture down here, eventually even be able to speak to a few. That would come with time, but he would slowly work up the courage and knowledge required to take that climb into their minds and confidently, bravely face the drop-off over the precipice to genuinely delve into their matters. Even his childish mind knew he could figure them out, even if they didn't realize it then or now. These people may be much deeper than their surface, and even just below their surface, emotions and physical tells may be known to give them away, but it was his calling to know them inside and out, even more than they knew themselves. Off in the distance, but closer than he knew, the little boy's guardians smiled, knowing he would be ready when his time came.

The Back Pages Of A History Book
(2/24/2015)

I

Whether or not we know the story we're after we will come to find that the
story seems to always have had a way of being after us. It called to us from
before we even heard its voice. We were being pulled toward it long before we
ever even felt the tug on the other end of the line, which we were apparently
holding onto without even knowing that, all along. Usually the writer of the
revelations held within these stories is someone who came long before us and
recalled a compilation of memories, stories, and times of a place long during
their times that others were trying to cover up or bury, for whatever reasons
they'd had. In all of these cases, however, all we have to do is simply research
the writer who came along before the sketchy details he recollected and we'll
have already begun to pull at the thread that unravels the entire pricker and
thorn-filled tapestry that was weaved as a result.

Arthur S. Larson, his press pass from the newspaper read, and the mayor of the
barely two or three-horse town - Arthur was giving it a little more credit than
that of a forgettable thumbtack on the map, but still being not much more, at
the same time - was glaring at it with ire. Arthur wondered if someone hadn't
snuck a playing card, like the one the Mad Hatter wore, into his hat as a joke of
some sort on the way here and he was to realize it later. He reached to feel the
brim and felt no such card, so he just shrugged off the mayor's disapproval of
outsiders as the old fashion story of small towns not liking outsiders. Rolling his
eyes at his excessively being studied by this no name mayor of such a no name
town Arthur though, *God help me if there's more of this local charm in store for
the rest of this trip.*

Arthur had been sent by the newspaper to research the story of a series of
strange events that had apparently been the precursors and backbone of this
town's coming into existence, as more than a rest stop along the way on the
great adventure out west, during the days of this countries' colonization. The
details of its growth from a watering hole with a general store and a hotel, that
was little more than a bed and breakfast, to becoming an official town in its
own respect were in his briefcase among his writing notebooks, newspaper

clippings, and other travel necessities. His first stop was with this charming representative of the town.

"Now what is it you're exactly a-lookin' for, Mr..." the mayor theatrically overacted, squinting to read the press pass, "Larson?" He looked up with a forced smile.

"Well, Mr. Mayor, I was sent here by the newspaper to get something to write a story about some of the small towns of this great state," Arthur said with no intended tact to hide his semi-confident feelings about the story's success, "and your town is one of those...mysteries." He was less than confident about the chances of there being much of interest in the history of the town of Stowell, a place that had never developed too much beyond that of the watering hole, general store, and micro-hotel that it had started out as. This was the general consensus of the general population among the larger cities around Stowell.

"Well, Mr...Larson," the mayor wasn't making any great effort to hide his lack of enthusiasm at there being an outsider with the intent to rummage around his town's history vaults and kick up age old dust, "you are free to find out what you will, but I doubt you'll find much, since the people of Stowell - as you must have already read about, I'm sure - have enjoyed being closed off from the rest the big cities. And they don't seem too quick to want to change that."

"I don't suspect they will, but I would still appreciate the opportunity to get a story of some sort," Arthur forced his foot into the veritable door, welcomed or not, "as I think some sort of recognition needs made of this town's addition to the state and its history. It only seems fair." He'd come this far, as intended, and as long as he was here to do the job he was going to come away with something.

"Alright then. Feel free to interview the people and get a taste of the local flavor, but I don't think you'll get much out of the local library and historical society," the mayor concluded, "as they haven't been kept up much, lately." Arthur didn't expect they would have, given the myths he'd heard about this town. He'd heard it was the Midwest's version of an old west ghost town, just with slightly more modern touches and fewer, if any, legends or ghost stories of relevance.

With that they shook hands, having seemed to have come to some sort respect - even if a short lived, temporary, contractual one - and went their separate ways.

The mayor hitched up his pants, dressed sort of like a town sheriff and mayor all in one package, and Arthur made his way towards micro-hotel to take lodging in one of its rooms. *Who knows*, he thought, *maybe because it's such a small place it'll be all the more comfortable for it, after all.*

As he made his way towards the Stowell Hotel, which did actually resemble an old west bed and breakfast in its design and architecture, only larger - luckily it didn't have a saloon as its central hub of entertainment - a few thoughts bounced around in his head. The lookout perched in his veritable crow's nest had long before yelled down to the captain on deck that something strange was up ahead. It wasn't exactly a well-explained or elucidated observation, but it was enough to go on for now.

He had sensed enough in the mayor, Stowell's requisite ambassador of sorts, of a showman that gave something, but it wasn't clear of what, away entirely. Soon enough, though, he'd feel out the town for what it was, what it wasn't, and figure out what the it was. He still felt like he had been sent into a circus of sorts, minus the tent, rings, and trapeze. There was, however, an air of mystery about the place that pulled him in its general direction.

II

After checking into his room - it was more like a motel than anything else in size, features, and amenities, if you could really call them that - he found that it was clean and comfortable enough. He'd lived in apartments that were smaller, before at points in his life, and felt comfortable enough there, so it was fine. The front desk and reception area were almost quaint and charming, as well, with a nice faux-tile floor, a good, solid sturdy front desk that was presentable enough for a workhorse that seemed to have lasted the test of time, a few decently comfortable, thought Spartan looking chairs, a few remotely recently dated magazines, and a cupboard behind the desk with compartments and room-keys for days. *Strange, for a place not that large*, he thought, *but whatever. So far so good.*

His first step outside the micro-hotel door was a collision into a small child, about nine or ten in appearance, who seemed to come from nowhere, other than directly into him.

"Whoa there," said Arthur, balancing himself so he didn't trip or fall, "watch where you're going, kid." He said it half laughing at the triviality of the entire trip and because it was only a kid after all. Dusting himself off and patting himself down, to make sure he hadn't dropped or lost anything, he looked at the child whose path he met head on.

"I'm sorry, sir," the boy noticed his press pass, "Mr. Arthur Larson…or rather, Mr. Arthur S. Larson." The boy was well spoken, polite, and seemed to have a soul much older than he gave away by appearance alone. Dressed in what looked like hand-me-downs he was still a perfect gentlemen, albeit a bit distracted or unfocused, given his directional prowess and spatially bull in a china shop introduction style.

"It's fine, it's okay," said Arthur, looking around, "I didn't see you come out from anywhere, either. It's like you just appeared out of nowhere."

"I have a tendency to do that, sir," the boy held out his hand, "Ernest. That's my name, sir."

"Good to meet you, Ernest," said Arthur, "Arthur, or I guess you already know mine." He casually flipped his press pass in the hand he received back from Ernest.

"You're looking around trying to figure out what's so interesting about this town, aren't you?" Ernest was spot on and seemed to be able to read into adults' minds and body language just as well as only kids could, just as much as adults have denied this throughout time.

"You've got that right," Arthur conceded, trusting his instinct in this boy's innocence, "I'm writing a story for the newspaper. This one…" he casually flipped his press pass, again. "It's about this how this town came to be from the days of the western expansion as an overrated rest stop to what it is, now….or so you probably already know." Arthur took his gaze from the panorama of the town to the boy's face.

"I do now," Ernest confirmed, "but I assure you there's more to it than you think." That was positive news. *Maybe I won't have to get overly creative with the filler for this article, then*, Arthur thought.

"No you won't," Ernest didn't miss a beat, as he looked around and saw the mayor headed their way, "well, I've got to be going, but I'll see you around, I'm certain." The boy spoke almost hurriedly, but politely. Having instinctually returned his gaze to the panorama, again, Arthur snapped back into focus to address the boy, but noticed he was gone just as soon as he'd come. *Where did he get off to so fast*, he wondered, and looked up to see the mayor. He waved politely and smiled, just as much, to the mayor, and the mayor did the same back to him as he himself kept on in the direction of the town historical society and library with a hurried, concerned look on his face.

"Wonder where he's going," Arthur said out loud, "and why he looks like he's hiding something all the time." Shrugging he resigned himself to the situation and wherever its breeze would blow him with a sigh. He then made his own way to the best place he could think of to get all the best gossip. As much he didn't really care for it personally it was like most local legends in that it was usually a good start and strangely, minus the fantastical parts, a fairly close resemblance in true form to the legend. With that frame of mind he headed to the local bar, or at least the closest one he could find.

On his way towards the local watering hole he found himself thinking about the boy and what he'd said, as well as how he seemed to be able to read him like only kids can see through adults, but better, somehow. *It was like he was reading my mind*, thought Arthur, *nah. That's impossible. I don't know who could even do that.* Still, there was something deeper to Ernest. He was a far less eloquent - on the surface of things - host, but on the same token a far more eloquent host in all other aspects. Ernest seemed to plant a seed of something in Arthur's mind, as if sprinkling rays of light upon shadows his first host had cast upon other landscapes.

III

At the local watering hole Arthur, who had rogue ways of going about his brand of journalism, and therefore always seemed to write the most interesting pieces with perspectives no one else could seem to get, went straight up the bartender.

"Hi, uhh...I'm..." he flipped his press pass, to which the friendly enough bartender nodded and half smiled, "yeah. Small town, you've already heard about me, probably."

"Yup," said the bartender, noncommittally, seemingly to avoid a long, drawn out conversation, "most people know who you are. Some are actually looking forward to talking to you and others, well they're the old fashioned kind who like to keep things about themselves and there own to themselves and there own." Arthur was on the fence about this one, as his face - stuck in a shape of mid-speech - had clearly spoken for him, wordlessly.

"Yeah. I kind of figured that. I'm glad you confirmed it, though." The bartender smiled at this. Breathing a sigh of relief he smiled himself and shook the bartender's extended hand.

"My real, birth name is boring and I don't even quite like it myself," said the bartender, amusingly, "but I still don't hold a grudge against my parents for it. They were from a different time, not too long after the one you're hoping to dig up something about. They call me Smiley, however, and that's a name I do like, much more." Arthur was now off the fence about this one and had decided he liked him.

"I like it, too," they each took their hand back as Arthur continued, "and you're right on to what I'm looking for. Anything you can tell me or are there possibly a few interesting characters in town you could lead me in the direction of, who can tell me a few things...interesting things, especially? I like to not only deliver a factually accurate news story, but also one with a good, rich coloring of local folktales from local folks."

"Then I know who you need to talk to, but just steer clear of the mayor," Smiley looked around, as if miming the severity of this sentiment, "it's been rumored he's got a distant relative of the man who shut up the mouth of that...well...person, who almost spilled all the beans about his relative who...I'll let them tell you. I'm no good at telling tales." Arthur, with his mouth gaping, was practically salivating at the potential story he was given an introductory, mysterious lead to. "Plus, I'm not overly informed on the details of it all, but I believe all of it. Here's who you want to talk to. I'm gonna' write it down so nobody bleats it to the mayor that I said anything, as I really don't like him all that much, and don't really need him on my back about it." With that Smiley wrote some names on a sheet of bar tab paper you'd manually write out a bill for purchased goods on.

"Thank you," said Arthur, taking the sheet of paper and directly pocketing it, "thank you, Smiley." He smiled, Smiley nodded, and they both went their own directions. Smiley got back to stacking a few last bar glasses and picked up a small guitar behind the counter that he started playing, as the bar wasn't too busy that hour of the day. Arthur stepped outside into the brighter light of day and read the note. He noticed Smiley gave him the name of three people and the locale they could usually be spotted at around town, as well as a reference to an article of clothing they usually wore or personally recognizable trademark that told on them. He headed off towards the first name on the list, as the time of day dictated they'd best be found at the nearest jog of a distance.

IV

Larhlam Daniels was the first name on this list. He was apparently, what Smiley the bartender has referred to as the town's general contractor, mister fix it, utility man, and garbage collection manager. *That's an interesting resume,* thought Arthur, *he sounds like an interesting character. He's got to have an interesting story to tell.*

"You bet he does, for sure," immediately, and again out of nowhere, spoke Ernest, who had just come from that place exactly, "you'll find him quite informative." Having jumped back about two feet Arthur was catching his breath, looking up over his note to find the kid standing right in front of him.

"How did you...where..." Arthur began to shake his head and look around, and then returned his look to Ernest, "you are something else, kid." Arthur smiled. He liked this kid and knew he was different, and special anyway, he just didn't know how. He trusted him, however. He let his amazement at the kid's apparent mind reading abilities just be what they were so as to not blow his mind, as he needed that part of him at its full capacity to see this now suddenly interesting journey through.

"Sorry for giving you the jump there," Ernest scrunched up a smile, and continued, "I just saw you there and figured you were on the trail of something.

No one starts up a conversation like that with Smiley unless they're up to something the mayor really wouldn't like." Ernest smiled and Arthur figured there were a few people who didn't like the mayor. He already liked those people.

"Yeah, I'm onto something," Arthur affirmed, "and it's apparently a lot more interesting than I thought, at first, too." There was something else about Ernest that kept coming up to make him more intriguing each time they ran into each other, and this was something else that Arthur would just chalk up to something he'd read in a book. People are like places, in that some shine and some don't. Ernest shined and he shined brightly.

"Just keep following the thread, no matter how weird it gets," the boy said, "you're sure to find something to make it all worth your while." *Interesting*, thought Arthur, as Ernest had just dropped even more seedlings to even deeper subject matter he wanted to see developed all the more, now. *How weird is it going to get and what is this all that I'm going to have to go through that will be worth it?* He was about to say something to the boy as he broke his musing reverie, to see the boy beginning to turn and bolt, as he also saw the mayor around the corner seemingly off on his way to be a weird, Scooby Doo-type protagonist somewhere else, now.

"I've got to go, Mr. Larson," the boy hurried as he turned to bolt, "I can't be seen here." Just as Arthur was about to say something, with his mouth mid-word, he closed it. *That's one interesting kid*, he thought. He gave him the benefit of the doubt, no matter what. Something about him just seemed just as right as everything seemed off about everything, and everyone, else.

"Hello, Mr...," Arthur's smile turned into a confused stare as he waved to the mayor, "mayor." The mayor stopped where he was, waved back with that same pensive look on his face, turned directions, and went off somewhere else to probably tell someone else they were meddling and if they hadn't done so they would never have found out about it. That thought made Arthur smile as he made his way into the general utility building and went up to the front desk.

"I'm here to see Larhlam Daniels," he said to the receptionist who didn't have a nametag or nameplate to identify herself, "I don't have an appointment, but I heard he was usually available around this time of day. I'm Arthur Larson, from the newspaper just outside of town." He second-naturedly flipped his press pass as he said this.

"I'll buzz his phone line to let him know someone's here to see him," she said, pleasantly enough to not look at him suspectly, but to make it seem as if this wasn't done often. She pressed a button on her phone, announced that there was a Mr. Larson from the so and so newspaper who was here, and nodded her head in the direction of the door behind her desk as it opened up on cue.

The man who stuck his head out of the door was friendly, but stoic, as general utility and mister fix it type engineers seem to be, and told him to come on in in a friendly enough way. Arthur nodded to the receptionist in thanks and went into the office. The secretary went back to her work on a novel she was reading. In the office of Larhlam Daniels, town engineer, Arthur went and they sat down to regard each other; Mr. Daniels, casually and comfortably back into his desk chair, and Mr. Larson at the spartan, slightly uncomfortable chair meant for once in a long while seen guests.

"I'm Mr. Daniels, but you can call me Larhlam," both misters shook hands and took their spots in their chairs, "I see you've come about a story on the town's history."

"Yes, and I've seemingly run into some equally interesting people, already," confirmed Arthur, "and some aren't so glad I'm here, I'm guessing."

"Nah," Larhlam waved his hand, "they're just old fashioned people who don't like new fashioned people and the ways of the world that they can't admit is changing. How can I help you, specifically? I have nothing to tell and from my experience this town has one hell of a bad, albeit underground, rap to shake." He got right down to the point.

"Well, I…" this tantalizing bit of information pulled Arthur into the story further, "I want to know how this town came to be, about its founder, and even more than facts I wanted some interesting stories from the locals, un-sanitized and full of all the colloquialisms I can handle." He would be forthright and to the point as well.

"I could tell you some of the same things that you can find right here," Larhlam pulled out a pamphlet about the town and its history, albeit a short and probably sanitized one, "keep it, by the way. I've got a bunch of 'em. I can also skip the boring facts and figures and names and dates and get right down to the interesting stuff...over a drink." He smiled. "It's alright. No catastrophes in plumbing, electric lines, sewage lines, or anything else - that separates us from cavemen and third world countries - has happened, or will, in a long time. I've got the utilities of this town running like a clock."

V

Next thing he knew Larhlam and himself were back the bar with a drink, on the city engineer's tab, and Larhlam had given him the quick rundown of the town's original settlers, spearheaded by the town founder named Elias Bounder - who it was noted was a distant relative of the mayor, for your information - and how his family and the town were both run under his stern and firm, but not quite fair enough, hand and sometimes fist. Maybe it was that the times were different and, like in the Old Testament, law needed to be laid down more firmly when you were indoctrinating rookie leaders into a first time establishment, and you couldn't afford to be soft or flexible about the rules of the book quite yet. Either way there were rumors of underground anti-prohibition rings, tax dodgers, and those trying to get away from the scenes of crimes, committed against lower classes of citizens of the times, from up to a few states over. All of this was apparently going on within a rogue group of untouchable-type castes of citizens that children were shunned away from and adults were just made for life to carry on otherwise, in about as much of a Christian way they could. There was a rumor that a whistle blower was about to tell on the mayor's own distant relative, since apparently some of such of the same activity was rumored to still go on, only in a modern time's version, but that was only to be taken as suspect rumor mill hogwash, which was the wording the town engineer used.

"Because there are so many other bright spots in the town's history as a result of a much greater number of citizens, that have been overlooked because of the stain of a much smaller-sized group," Larhlam continued, observing their drinks were about three quarters finished and he ordered another round, "and doesn't every town, city, or capital - for all I care - have a similar story, at least in general theme, to tell?"

"Yes, I believe it does," said Arthur, accepting his second drink and nodding to thank his beneficiary of said whistle wetting and stories, "and both are what I want to tell about." They continued talking about the details of the streams of wagons going west with vibrant, cheerful folks excited about the potential dreamed up lives they could have out west, those that settled here to have families to be raised up in Christian ways, as well as those few darker, shadowed wagons of anti-prohibition allies, their paraphernalia, and their goings on underground. He told of the law abiding families that planted themselves here and planted equally vast growing farms, the other industries that started up, the generations that carried on and developed the first general stores and bed and breakfasts, and addressed those that came to find refuge from criminal activities, whose black marks seemed to blot out the bright marks of everyone else.

"Well, I've got to be getting back to work, now," said Larhlam, not even showing any signs of having guzzled down two tall beers, extending a pack of gum to Arthur as he took a piece himself, "and that's so both us don't have to explain what we've been doing on my break and one of your hush hush work sessions." Arthur took the gum he was offered, they shook hands, parted ways, and Arthur checked his list to find out he could get a late lunch or early dinner - as he'd missed lunch over the time of their conversation - which had actually gone on much longer than it felt. Leaving the bar he looked around for the boy, half expecting him to run into him or for him to pop out from around a corner, or better yet from right out in front of him. Instead, as Arthur and Larhlam both exited the bar, making their last comments to each other to cap off their conversation, Arthur observed a couple of groups of ladies, dressed very nicely, and men, dressed casually and some nicely, looking at him suspectly.

"Remember what I said about them," Larhlam said, sensing the eyes on Arthur without even acknowledging them, "I keep out of the whole murky side of the business and just live my own damn life. I think it's good you're tryin' to tell the story of both sides, however. And remember to research that book. It's got even more stories and details than any of us have, but you'll have to track down the other two on that list of yours to find it."

As he heeded Larhlam's advice Arthur felt the heat of those passer-byes' glares. One group of them waited for him to pass by, as if to study him at a closer range, to try pick up something more about him.

"Leave it alone," one man said to him. Arthur turned to see who'd said it, but was immediately hit with another comment before he could follow the source of the voice or think of a comeback. "Let it be where it stands. You've got nothin' to do with it and that boy was nothin' but trouble," a lady's voice said. Unable to track the voices before the group walked on he noticed they'd turned their heads completely away from him and in the direction of their destination. They were guiding young kids, running around them in circles almost, on their direct route, as well. Shocked at all of this Arthur thought, *okay, that just made this even more interesting.*

VI

Next on the list was Charles Landers, the owner-operator and solely employed worker at the antique shop, other than his son and daughter. Stopping into the shop Arthur looked around. He could identify a few objects that appeared close to modern, but the rest looked old and even older. They were all from the town, as well, as the advertisement printed on the door had said. There were small, but packed in, sections and shelving for kitchenware, toys, books, smaller-sized industrial equipment and machines, other gizmos and gadgets that all looked dusty, and some practically ready to crumble from too rough of handling.

"And they're all authentically from this town's past glory days alone," Mr. Landers happily smiled and spoke up, noticing Arthur's press pass, his curiosity, and then the pamphlet in his back pocket, "and there's a lot more stories they could tell than that watered down, sterilized pamphlet. That dusty read has white-washed this town's history, the good and the bad, so much it's hardly got any local color left in it." His voice became disillusioned as he finished this statement.

"So I've heard, or at least something along those lines," Arthur snapped out of his musing and approached the checkout, having taken special interest in the book section, "the local bar tender and town engineer…" Arthur didn't know how to finish his sentence, but the kindly and apparently - as he would come to find out - informative Mr. Landers continued for him.

"Larhlam told me you were coming. He told me what Harold, or Smiley, as we call him, said, and what he himself added to it," the man looked around at his collection with deserved pride and then noticed Arthur glancing over at the book section, "and the book he referred to, it's not there."

Snapping his head, and himself, back into reality in Mr. Lander's direction Arthur seemed almost dejected. Smiling, Mr. Landers recognized this and continued.

"Don't worry though. I know where it was last said to be stored and have more to add to the account Larhlam gave you," he motioned for Arthur to follow him as he walked into his office and called out to someone, "Mary! Mark! Come tend to the store and the register! I've got a visitor!" He shouted this and surprised Arthur in the vitality of his voice and general energy overall. Mr. Landers looked to be in his seventies, but was moving quickly and was almost hard to keep up with. As they entered the office Arthur heard two pairs of hurrying foot steps come from the stairwell entrances around the checkout and the office door - one lead to a basement level or merchandise and the other to an upstairs level of the like. Both of them, one a teenage girl and the other a teenage boy, acknowledged him, addressing him as grandpa, ane obligingly agreed to keep shop for awhile.

Once in the office Mr. Landers sat down behind his desk, significantly smaller than Larhlam Daniels' desk, with a metal rack of file cases next it against the wall. Mr. Landers invited Arthur to sit down at a chair similar to the one Larhlam had offered him as well.

"They aren't the most comfortable chairs," he nodded to the one Arthur was sitting in, "but eventually you'll work your way up to this kind of cushy chair." Mr. Landers made a satisfied, comfortable sound as he sat in his cushy office chair.

"So you know more about the history of the farms, the underground anti-prohibition rings, the criminals on the run into hiding, and the families that started the general stores and motels?" Arthur opened up the conversation jumping right into what he hoped to find out.

"Yes I do. I can tell you all about them, especially the families my parents and grandparents knew," a smile alighted upon his face, "and even more about the booze peddlers. Hell, I'm a distant relative of them and even I enjoy a good, strong drink without any pencil pusher tellin' me when I can do so." He said this last statement with a smile, but an undertone showing he wasn't one to give into the authority that be, when it overstepped its bounds either. "Don't be frightened by me, though. I don't stand behind what the crooked and dangerous ones of that brood did. I was all for defending the rights of a man or woman to drink what he or she wanted to when their work day was done, or when no one was watching, as long they were decent people, and even some of those that fled the law to hide out here were innocent. Sure some of them were a little more than small town criminals and had been runnin' from being jailed for murder, but even more of them were in self-defense of their own families from muggers and bigger, more violent folks than your run of the mill pickpockets. Now their variety was definitely guilty, but I guess even they could've found God all over again, given the chance and a clean slate." With this said Mr. Landers paused and thought with a troubled look on his face.

"What is it, Mr. Landers?" Arthur asked. He had kind of figured not every accused criminal wasn't guilty or could at least change, if they were guilty, and that even then most crimes weren't horrendous or even much more than inconvenient in the end.

"Well, those that were escaping charges of helping slaves and Indians go free from crimes they were falsely accused of, those I had no problem with - either the ones I'd read about or their distant relatives. It was the other type," again he stopped and Arthur's interest was peaked, "it's just the ones in their slick business suits that came along, long descended from the more violent ones and the more crooked ones. Their ancestors wore less fancy clothes, almost country bumpkin clothes, but they were all the same. If you tried to even talk about those who'd attempted to rat on them before, those who'd disappeared more often than show up again with bruises and little less gusto to talk about anything anymore, you'd get real cautious around 'em." *So every town has its covered up secrets and skeletons in the closet*, thought Arthur, *and I'm about to hear about their ghosts, at least.*

Mr. Landers said he would get into that more, but first wanted to tell about the bright spots in the town's history, first, so Arthur didn't think the town was all bad. Mr. Landers got into detail about the Watkins family who started up the general store and kept it going for generations, moving from paper receipts and colonial goods and services into the post-colonial days when industrial mechanizations became more popular, and then into the early days of computerized technologies to organize business affairs and such. He talked about the Lindsey family who were the original farmers who kept up the trade throughout the generations, as well, married into the Smith family, and then on and on the family split off into other directions and automated technologies within the industry. He went about the father and mother and their fathers and mothers and the uncles and aunts. He talked about the times, as they flew through the eras of less enlightened viewpoints of slaves and black people, Indians, and other different nationalities, into the developments that came with new advancements in philosophical thought, literature's output of books about the great depressions, and beyond all up to the current.

"Back to the lesser gentlemanly and gentlewomanly folks, I was a kid mostly, and I don't remember all the dates and times and facts or figures as such, but I could sense something inhumane was happening," Mr. Landers continued his account, now going down the darker path, "just the way my parents would talk about how so and so who was the mum or dad of a friend I'd just made, who seemed to be the subject of a lot of rumors, weren't to be spoken of. Looking back, when I became a teenager and then a man, I figured out that my friends - who either moved away or lost their parents to unexplained deaths, or whom I just wasn't allowed to run around with anymore - well, they were the good ones. They were the ones defending those who defended the blacks, the Indians, and the immigrants. They protected them, so they could have an equal chance at the American dream. And they were also the ones whose ears pricked up at the rumors of underground dealings and gangsters, and the more violent anti-prohibition people who really, really didn't like what the authorities were doing, only they didn't take it with good humor, didn't have an innocently wily nature, and weren't afraid to kill to shut people up."

At this point Arthur thought they were toeing the line of information he wasn't quite ready to take in or take on, on top of everything else, and Mr. Landers - though he said he wasn't too keen in dates and times and facts and figures - started dropping quite a few names, the mayor's distant, and even not so distant, relatives, as well. They were talking a couple of hours and the sun had gone down. It had become time to close the store. A rap on the office door and the voices of his granddaughter and grandson told him they'd just closed up and had the collected sales tickets, receipts, and other business affairs wrapped into a tight little bundle, and were ready to go home.

Arthur and Mr. Landers had finally wrapped up their conversation, thankfully, as far as Arthur was concerned, and Mr. Landers sent him off with a few free of charge books on the history of the town, but not quite as notorious as the one he was to find tomorrow, at the library and historical society.

"Here's a few other books," said Mr. Landers, upon sending him off, "they're not quite the one you're looking for, but they are just as interesting in other areas of the town's lighter themed history. And you're welcome to come back to the Learned Owl's Perch anytime." He was sure that if his communiqué he had quickly written and put into the mail, to be picked up early in the morning - as he was one of the mailman's first stops, and the mailman was darn near fast as lightening, in Mr. Landers' words - he'd have no problem getting in on Hattie Sanders' good graces.

As Arthur had just left the store he was around the corner, with his mind sorting out the information he had just collected into its own sort of card catalogue, bins, boxes, and filing system. Forgetting, momentarily of the Ernest kid's ability to pop up at any time, he ran into him, literally, again.

"Whoa, there, Ernest," Arthur said, snapping back into reality and doing the same custom as last time, "you really do come of nowhere." His heart had started to slow down its racing pace, racing from the urgency of the situation, the intensity of the information he'd received, and the boy's physical and abrupt, as well as wordless, announcement of his presence.

"I do, and again, sorry," said Ernest, aware of his ninja-like ability to practically sneak up on somebody, "I just wanted to see how you were doing with your story." This struck Arthur as odd.

"Really? It's late, you're just a kid, and..." he lost track of this among other things spinning in his mind, "shouldn't you be at home, right now? I appreciate our visits, but..." Arthur genuinely did, but he was concerned about the boy, now, among many other things, and people in the town who had been quite forthright in not holding back information.

"As per my needing to be home, don't worry. It's...well, hard to explain," Ernest continued, as Arthur shrugged the word okay and mimed for him to go on, "I just wanted to tell you that while you were in there more talk has been going on between other townspeople about what you're doing. You need to move fast or it won't be there, by the time you get to Mrs. Sanders." *What, thought Arthur, with a cold streak running own his back, how did you know about...*

"Don't ask," hurried Ernest, rushing his words, "just go, first thing in the morning, to the library and historical society. The message will get there and based on the friends you've made so far, and those people don't usually make friends with others so easily, she'll trust you with it. I have to go now." And just as Arthur was, again, mid-word, let alone mid-sentence, Ernest was off.

VII

First thing in the morning Arthur was showered, dressed, and off to the combination library and historical society. He loved small towns like this that had such institutions combined, because of necessity and quaintness, and thought it only need a train and a bike and hike trail to be the perfect vacation destination - minus the apparent history of murders, cover-ups, and shady, long descendent characters, that was. On his way to the library and historical society he received glares from someone, or groups of someones, every other block. Men and women individually, in groups, and even kids looked up at their parents and then at Arthur, wondering what was so interesting or perturbing about him. Some looks were curious and innocent enough and others were viral, piercing, and locked onto him with laser frequency targeting force. Even the mayor opened his door, having seen Arthur coming around the corner from a caddy-cornered office window, and stepped outside to talk at him from his doorway.

"Having a nice day, Mr. Arthur S. Larson?" He tipped his cowboy hat, of course it had to be a cowboy hat, and spoke in the same tone his down the middle, but leaning a little to the south of nice, attitude undertoning it all. "You be careful, now, moving that fast-like." *That was a strange and creepy thing to say at this exact moment*, thought Arthur, not trying to see where this conversation could go.

"Yes, sir, Mr. Mayor," said Arthur, feeling suddenly warmer, now realizing he was physically walking faster to pass that block and its occupants, "yes I am, thank you." He didn't slow down or turn around to see the mayor close his door with contempt written all over his face. Nor did he take notice to any other eyes that more than may have been on him. He was driven on by a force that told him to heed the boy's words and hurry up, to be quick about it, and before it was no longer at his disposal. Once he reached the library and historical society he opened the door, stopped in the doorway, looked around quickly, and went in.

He went up to the front desk just as a woman, who looked about in her sixties, and very pretty for it, he thought, came out of an office behind the desk. She had a file folder in her hand, acknowledged his presence, looked down at the folder, and approached the desk. Politely smiling, she was still direct and to the point, a highly organized woman as such one must be to run an institution like this.

"Hello, how can I help you," Mrs. Hattie Sanders said, "even though I think I already know that." *News spreads fast in small towns*, thought Arthur, *but hopefully lynch mobs headed by easily irritated mayors don't*. Sensing his racing thoughts by the look on his face she nodded down towards his press pass and smile genuinely. "You have a press pass, which mean you're from a newspaper, and most likely the from the city. We don't have many other newspaper correspondences come around to these parts."

"Yes, I am, and thank you," said Arthur, relieved, but not sure what he was thanking her for, quite, yet, "I imagine you got the message from Mr. Landers, and you're Mrs. Hattie Sanders?" His eyes asked the question as much as his face.

"Yes, and the name sounds familiar because, as you'll find in most small towns, we're distant cousins down the line, a few generations back, and another left turn at the gas station on the corner," she smiled as Arthur laughed, knowing he'd been the recipient of her good graces, "and I was actually just putting together a collection of items for you...and your story." She looked down at the file in her hand.

"I think I'll give this to you now, to look at later," she looked back up at Arthur, who reached out to take it as she did so to give it to him, "and those are very sensitive articles and photographs, by the way. I did my research on you. There are quite a few, well-informed, good resources on the computer nowadays for inquisitive minds like my own in cases like these. Because of your glowing reputation and resume, as well your choice of friends and acquaintance in town, I trust you with them. You may keep them. They're only copies of the originals, anyway." Now, Hattie Sanders herself looked around, stepped out from behind her desk, looked out he window, and went to the door. She put up a sign in the window reading "Closed for a few minutes. Will be back as soon as possible." It had a picture of clock and two moveable arms to show a time, and she moved the hands to about one hour ahead of the actual time. *Oh*, thought Arthur, *I guess this, too, is going to be interesting.*

"Follow me. I have something to show you," Mrs. Sanders walked in the direction of the open area of the room beside the desk that lead to the library stacks and shelves, "I would like this to finally get out, on a personal note, as well. This town has had enough sideways glances from outsiders - other than those like yourselves, of course - and enough ill-informed rumors spread about it." Arthur followed her matter of factly, putting the file folder in his briefcase as he kept pace with the librarian, which was not easy, making sure to not drop or lose any of its apparently sensitive materials.

They passed shelves of local authors, fiction, the circulation desk - where a gentleman about Mrs. Sanders' age, dressed just as library and historical society professionally, looked up, acknowledged the head librarian and her guest - and then past the reference books, meeting rooms, graphic novels, and non-fiction section. They'd walked from end to end of the library, past the stairwells to the second floor of the building, and came to a door with a sign on it, next to a clear glass window the size of the door showing what the sign spoke of. It was the historical documents section and yes, he would first get the head librarian's permission to enter it, with her supervision, and be careful, as the documents were very old and personally valuable. Mrs. Sanders turned around to Arthur with a serious look on her face, with her hand firmly on the doorknob.

"What you're looking for is back here, hopefully," her face showed a sympathetic, scrunched up smile as she continued, and then became shrewd and rough, almost intimidating, "if certain local political figures haven't overstepped their bounds to get in the way of perfectly good, fair, and public knowledge, even though all of it may not be stories of rainbows, picnics, and happy, little butterfly farts." Arthur kept a serious face, given the access to the room, and potentially the book, he was being granted, but cracked a bit of smirk when she said the word farts.

"I know," said Mrs. Sanders, smirking a little, too, "even I have been known to speak as rough as Smiley and Mr. Daniels on occasion. We, however, won't be sharing a beer." With that her face went back to its serious position, as did her mental focus, and Arthur followed her example. "If it's still here it's all yours for indefinite loan until you get what you need out of it. It's full of the truthful, unsanitized history of this town with warts, shallow graves, and all." *Shallow graves*, shuddered Arthur, now understanding he was about to get his hands on the book they'd all been talking about as if it was a legend.

They walked down aisles of dusty, less impressively designed shelves, of industrial garage metal and make, with some documents in banker's boxes - marked with dates and the names of events any local would have recognized as important, landmark epochs in town history - and next to them stacks of archaic looking, and bound, books of sizes and dimensions larger than most typical dictionaries. Turning a corner, here and there, they passed through shadows where the overhead lamps' light didn't fill up the room completely, and then back into the light, again. They stopped at a shelf in the far corner of the room. Mrs. Sanders turned back to Arthur, in front of a shelf with a box labeled "Myths, Legends, and Cold Case Files" and a date that originated back over at least two hundred years.

"We don't loan this out, let alone allow it see the light of day," Mrs. Sanders spoke, cryptically, "it remains hidden from most eyes, as well, for good reason. Some people are more skeptical, some are just pulling off a hoax and their humor is beyond my patience and good nature, and others are trying to get it so they can destroy it for political or historical motive. It's sad really." She turned back to the shelf and picked up the box to take it down. Taking it down off the shelf she placed it on the floor. As she and Arthur were on their haunches beside it she looked up at Arthur with a look that said *let's see what we've got*. They both returned their gaze to the box and Mrs. Sanders lifted the banker's box lid.

VIII

At the front desk, the head librarian's station, the man who was at the circulation desk had taken up her post to concede his previous station to another worker at library from the upper floor's coordinating circulation desk. As he observed his workstation, for the time being, he saw the door thrown open and observed the mayor, accompanied by the sheriff, with his hand held close to the gun in its holster in a very obvious way. Both of them were wearing cowboy hats, which would have told Arthur to be very careful, on your guard, and ready to sound the alarms.

"Pardon me, Mr…" the mayor peered at the nameplate at the same time as looking down upon the librarian, whose name he feigned to not know, assuring himself he wasn't Mrs. Sanders, and carried on, "is the head librarian in? And did she have a guest with her? I won't ask twice." He nodded in the direction of the gun his sheriff had been primed and ready to reach for. The replacement librarian knew exactly what the situation was, having been given a run down of potential happenings and scenarios only half-expected today, given the book's sensitive nature.

"No, sir, and the gun isn't necessary. This is a place of higher learning," the brave replacement librarian stood his ground, "but how can I help you?" His bravery turned to fear as the mayor leaned forward and the sheriff put his hand, once hovering over the gun against his side, and unbuckled the latch holding it in the holster. The mayor smiled, but wasn't in an agreeable or pleasant mood.

"I said I wouldn't ask twice, so I'm going to just make my way back into the historical documents section, with or without your consent, and without your supervision," the mayor then pushed the air out of his way and bullied his way toward the entrance of the library, his lackey following, "this is a matter over your head and I am claiming jurisdiction over you and all of your books in this matter."

"You do not have a right to remove that book," the replacement librarian yelled, knowing he was defeated, but defending the eternally unwritten code of the freedom and importance of historical knowledge, "you can't just cover up history, or even dare throw it away!"

The mayor heard this in distance and laughed. The sheriff now held the gun in front of him as he escorted the mayor towards the historical documents section, bullying a few library visitors to leave, as this was none of their business, there was nothing to see here, and so on. Unknown to them, the replacement had sounded a silent alarm that went off equally silently, as well, in the form of a small, blinking overhead light in the back corner of the historical records room.

Having removed the lid to the banker's box that might as well have carried the town's version of the Ark of the Covenant, and having found the book, Mrs. Sanders and Arthur uttered a breathy sigh of guarded, careful relief.

"It's here," smiled Mrs. Sanders, carefully holding the book like a delicate, breakable vase, as a museum curator would, and held it out to Arthur, "there are secrets to this town's history certain career politicians, among others, would like to hide forever. Most of us here just live our lives, leaving it be where it may lie, so we can do this town a much better favor and write much brighter chapters for our grandchildren and their children to read in the future. So through our kids we can avenge what was done to that poor child, years ago." *What*, though, Arthur, as his face - once practically showing his inner giddiness at finally getting the book - went flat, white, and as he felt a great epiphany come over himself.

"Yes, we've made quite a great many excuses about why we don't loan it out, or why we just don't have it available, to certain people over the years," Mrs. Sanders said, addressing everything before the child's being killed, and then looked up at Arthur, "oh…" She paused. In that pause Arthur really began listening to what she would drop next on him.

"You've apparently met him, as have I, among others," Mrs. Sanders said, recognizing the change of the temperature in Arthur, "he was trying to make sure those stories and accounts didn't get destroyed and those with pure evil in their hearts did the worst thing they could, even for the them. They killed a child."

"How," said Arthur, amazed, "how…" He couldn't even decide whether to address the boy's appearing to people or the malicious hearts of his killers, and their descendants' willingness to cover it up, acting as if nothing happened and just carrying on with their lives in a business as usual way. Luckily he didn't have to.

The inaudible alarm went off and Mrs. Sanders and Arthur stood up quickly. She put the lid back on the banker's box, shot Arthur a glance and then a nod at the book and then to his briefcase, and Arthur carefully, but quickly stowed it away. They heard a commotion outside the door to the historical documents room and the proceeding pounding on the door.

"Let us in," the mayor roared, "you have something, and are doing something with it, that you should not be meddling in. I'm talking to both of you, Mrs. Hattie H. Sanders and Mr. Arthur S. Larson. I have a sheriff here with me. Open this door, now!" The door automatically locked with a magnetic mechanism and had prevented them from getting any further, so far, at least.

"No," shouted the vivacious, emboldened head librarian, "you didn't have intellectual or legal jurisdiction over this historical property before and you don't now!" She was both polite, well spoken, and aggressive, when need be. The wooden door shook on its hinges, as it was struck by the full force of the sheriff's body, and the mayor peered through the glass window and looked toward the far corner.

"I can see you in the corner," the mayor roared, even though he couldn't see that far into the room, but knew where the book was housed from having been denied access to it before, given his motives which all the librarians knew, "come to this door now and open it, immediately!" The head librarian looked at Arthur, then around towards another corner of the room, and back to Arthur, as if she suddenly had an idea.

"Go over there and turn down the short hallway," Mrs. Sanders nodded with her head, "there's a doorway to the back entrance to the building. The way the building was designed, initially, that's the only back entrance. I always thought it was ridiculous to have it lead right into this room, but now we can make use of that idiot engineer's less than genius building design." Arthur shot a glance in that direction, back to Mrs. Sanders, and nodded.

"But what about," he nodded to the door to the historical records room, "them, or what they'll do to you?" He was worried about the life of the librarian, given what past generations had apparently been willing to do to a mere boy.

"I'll be fine. They can't kill me. It's a different day in age," Mrs. Sanders spoke confidently, but with a bit of worry in her eyes, "plus, that alarm is rigged to set off another one at the police station at a desk of one of the sergeants that, like us, just lives to make better days to record in this town's history, and not simply bury the old ones, no matter what kind of scandal they could make for the mayor and his entire family line." Another bomb was dropped on the battlefield that was Arthur's mind.

"What!" Arthur nearly screamed, but caught himself, as he heard shouts from inside the regular library beyond the door. The head librarian didn't waste any time. She pushed him towards to the rear entrance.

"It's all in the book," she said as he headed towards the rear door and he towards the other door, "you'll read about it. For now, go!" She was brave and he, though he'd realize in later reflection upon this moment that he was as well, felt he was insane for what he was doing with the sensitive property he was trusted with. He, nevertheless, made for his given door, exited in a hurry as fast as his legs could carry him, and Mrs. Sanders went to her door, where she - upon opening the door and hearing other police sirens that both the mayor and his sheriff heard, as well - was bullied aside. Unbeknownst to Arthur, there was a second police car, other than the one the head librarian's friend in the department was driving, that was dispatched to make its way around the back of the building. This was done to ensure the safety of any people involved in the book's safekeeping and the safe entrance and exit of the police officers, as well, but this would now prove to be - even more to Arthur, given his current need - a way to get out of town quick and quicker.

IX

As he ran out of the backdoor, Arthur was prepping himself to not run full-tilt into the boy, again, and was good to do so. Almost on cue the boy appeared, but still surprised Arthur.

"You have it," Ernest smiled and glanced quickly aside at the briefcase, then back to Arthur, "Now go! I heard someone, a car coming around the other side of the building!" *Now what*, thought Arthur at these words, *now what*?

"You, kid," Arthur said, barely believing he was talking to a fully present ghost of a dead boy, "you are something special. And thank you." At this the boy shook his head repeatedly, as to hurry him along, and bade him to go on. Arthur did as he was told. Just as he made it around the corner of the building the mayor and his sheriff made it to the rear door, with Mrs. Sanders yelling that the book was not going to be destroyed by his family line anytime soon. As Arthur turned the corner he heard the police siren that he'd missed completely in the shock of continuing his conversation - that happened in part and parcel snippets here and there - with a dead boy named Ernest, who was also trying to prevent important history from being destroyed.

"Wonderful, just wonderful," said Arthur woefully as he saw the cop car before him, with a driver in his seat, not quite out of the car, yet, "what is with this book?" Arthur saw that the driver had a sympathetic look on his face and this quelled his fear a little. He saw the cop look up at him and reach over to open the door.

"You've got it, don't you," the officer said, "get in! I can get you out of here. I'm a friend of Mrs. Sanders and I can see by your press pass you're that newspaper guy. Now stop standing around like a deaf and dumb statue and get in. I can get you to the edge of town and into a taxi." *What now*, thought Arthur again, *what now*? Hearing enough to believe that Mrs. Sanders had been watching out for him, the book, and his mission to maintain Stowell's history he got in the car, sat down, and closed the door. The car drove off immediately, and just in time, as the mayor and the sheriff rounded the corner, only to hear a car having taken off and seen the dust it kicked up.

In the police car Arthur kept a tight hold onto his briefcase as the policeman was focused on the road, and speeding, with the siren and blinker lights going, occasionally glancing at the briefcase between looking at the road and Arthur.

"I'm Sergeant Sanders," he glanced briefly over at Arthur, to be polite, and extended his hand, which Arthur shook as he nodded, amazed at the entire situation, "Sergeant Mike Sanders. My aunt works at the library. You'll find the family lines represented well, and in some places not so well, all over town. I know about that book. I know about your newspaper article assignment and I'm going to get you out of town safely."

"Thank you," said Arthur, glancing at the book and then out ahead, "thank you, officer, I mean sergeant." He corrected himself out of politeness back to the officer who had potentially saved his life.

"Here," said the sergeant, reaching into the compartment between their seats and pulling out a cell phone he dropped into Arthur's lap, which Arthur stared at, "call for a taxi. The numbers are listed just underneath the mirror above you. Coming from my phone they'll be quick about it. Tell them to have a cab waiting at the town limits." The officer's focus remained ahead, on his mirrors, and on the road.

"Okay, will do," said Arthur, flipping down the mirror, figuring they had an unspoken code for where the town limits was, "don't have to tell me twice." He dialed the number he checked one more time on the rearview mirror and called for a cab.

"Hello, this is Arthur Larson, the newspaper guy everyone around here seems to know," he said, once the person on the other line picked up and announced they were with the town taxi service, where would you like a ride to, and where could you be picked up at, "and I know I'm on this officer, I mean sergeant's, phone, but he's here, too." At that the sergeant announced his name and badge ID to convince the taxi company representative. "I have sensitive materials on me and need picked up at the city limits to be taken away from this crazy town. Can you do that?" The taxi company representative said they could, they've taken people to and from the city before, and because it was at the sergeant's request there would be no charge. Arthur said thank you, signed off, and put the phone back in the compartment it had come from. He looked over at the sergeant, made a relieved sigh, and looked ahead at the road while he gently patted his briefcase to make sure the relic of a book was still in its place.

X

At the city limits the taxi was waiting. The police car stopped. It had turned off its siren and blinkers a while before, so as to not attract any more attention than to get people out of the way in the town's main drag. Opening his door and unbuckling his seatbelt, as he was the passenger of police officer after all, he turned to Sergeant Sanders.

"Thank you, again, Sergeant Sanders," Arthur said as he extended his hand, "for the ride, for your aunt being so brave, and everything." Sergeant Sanders shook his.

"No problem, Mr. Larson," the sergeant smiled, "you get that book out of town and off the mayor's radar as soon as possible. He's trying to erase history. That's just wrong." With that he sent Arthur off to the taxi, waved to the taxi driver, and watched to make sure Arthur was sent off and on his way out of that crazy town.

Arriving back in the city, far from any danger of the mayor's grasp and "jurisdiction", as he would have pompously stated, Arthur made his way to his humble, downtown apartment. He was just around the corner from the police station, a few blocks down from the fire station, and was already feeling more thankful for that, even if he did have to deal with the occasional middle of the night police car dispatching that woke him up, or the dispatching of a fire truck, whose clang that seemed to echo long after it approached and passed, disrupting his writing sessions' relative peace and quiet. He decided to distance himself from the contents of that file, the materials in the book, and the entire two days of insanity in Stowell for the night to pick it up again starting tomorrow morning. Tired beyond tired and having had his system shocked beyond anything ever experienced before he slept soundly, falling asleep as soon as his head hit the pillow.

The next morning, after his usual shower, coffee, and catching up on the newspaper headlines that jumped out at him the most - skipping the bulk of his usual reading, but at least catching up a little to get back into his normal flow of life - he went to over to his briefcase to dig up the beginnings of a story. After hours of flipping through the articles and clippings shoved into the file folder the head librarian had slipped him, he noticed they weren't copies at all, but the original clippings and articles themselves. *Apparently they were important enough to get outside of the town's borders, as well as the book,* Arthur thought before he had truly read the bulk of the content of the fairly large stack crammed into the file.

There were stories of railways being put in, general stores being put up, farms and the output of crops from different farming families, the building and operation of the micro-hotel, and the creation and subsequent goings on of other industries, as well as other institutional installments. There were references to the names that Larhlam Daniels, Charles Landers, and Hattie Sanders had mentioned. There were fluff pieces, as they were called in the industry, as well as articles on the controversial rumors of anti-prohibition activity, and the harboring and protection of those who helped, as well as those about the helped, black slaves, Indians, and immigrants. There were other articles that touched on the investigations into multiple murders and disappearances.

He'd taken a break for lunch to digest all of the information he had just taken in, as well as to construct a format for his article on the town. He would have to approach this one lightly, at first, and then get to the heavier parts, and finish on an upbeat note, maybe even referencing the good nature of Smiley the bartender, the neighborly banter with Larhlam Daniels, the old-folksy wisdom of Charles Landers, and Hattie Sanders' desire to - along with the rest of the good folks of the town - to simply live their lives in a way so they could write brighter chapters of Stowell town history. After his lunch there were still other clippings and articles to get through, but he felt interested in, and finally ready, to actually touch the book that so many wanted to get their hands to either save or destroy.

Picking up the dusty volume, much larger in dimension than modern, standard books and almanacs, he noticed the title and binding harkened back to days a couple hundred years ago, having been written about and over two hundred years ago. He flipped over a few pages, noticing the archaic printing and book organization method, along with the timelines, charts, and graphs. Intrigued, he was amazed to find the facts, figure, chart, and graph-based versions of the stories he'd read in the newspaper clippings and articles. Most interestingly enough, up to now at least, was the lineage he could trace back from those he had met. By his calculations there were less than a dozen different families behind the founding of the town from its beginnings, as well as those that continued to populate it to where it was now. *That's definitely a good way to set up some good old Hatfield and McCoy feuds*, thought Arthur as he turned over to the back page, *and who is this mysterious writer who was able to muddle through all this and collect this volume of information without going insane?*

Flipping to the back page, where the book's author and brief bio was printed, he saw the face and thought he had seen a familial resemblance to…Donovan

Landers. *That name sounds familiar,* though Arthur, *why didn't you mention that, Mr. Charles Landers?* He read the bio. The man, who must have been Charles Landers' great grandfather or great, great grandfather, was a journalist whose grandfather had started the first local newspaper - a mere leaflet issue once a week - for Donovan to expand it into an inserted magazine size volume, to a full-fledged newspaper. Reading on, not expecting any more surprises, he read that Donovan had a daughter named Virginia and a son…named Ernest.

At that last line Arthur stopped reading and froze. That was his ghost. It was the ghost of Ernest Landers and Charles Landers had not even mentioned anything about it. Thinking about this Arthur decided to have a quick lunch and get to work on the article. He called his editor immediately, told him everything that had happened, the materials he managed to collect, and that this story - sorry to tell you how the article for your paper is going to be done, since that's usually your job, but just go with me on this - would be in several installments. Arthur said he'd have the first installment on his boss' desk in a few days with a first draft of the next one and an idea how then next subsequent installments would progress. He got off the phone and ate lunch knowing he'd be at work for quite a while.

The Door That Nobody Else Saw
(2/25/2015)

I

Upon a walk beside oneself you can find out things about yourself you never
knew were possible. You can recollect memories long forgotten and revisit old
photos of yourself from picture books you'd never even known to exist - only to
have been witnessed by your scrapbooking mother or her cousin. As the
landscape drifts by and as the clouds paddle on upon the sea of the sky, lighter
than all other objects and atmosphere, they still remain anchored to the ground
and held below heaven for some reason. On such a walk one can feel similar to
that cloud - anchored here, but pushed down - for the time being, held down
from floating too high above just yet.

On just such a similar walk was a man who more than often stewed inside his
own head than lived in the world without him. We'll call him Samuel
Clementine, which was his name in fact, so it's just appropriate. Taking a break
from clacking away at his computer - merely a modern day version of the
typewriter his heroes of old had similarly come to know much better than their
human patrons of the their day, as well - he took a walk to clear his mind. De-
cluttering his head took too many dump trucks and one couldn't pack all the
ghosts of ideas of the past - or potential writings to come - into a single
cemetery, so he simply dropped the appropriate amount off by the wayside as
he walked on. It was the best way to stay sane and those who've walked dogs
know their animals had left worse things along the sidewalk and in the grass
than Samuel Clementine had.

Having passed through the suburban neighborhood that surrounded his
apartment building he came upon what was called downtown, the city-like part
of where he generally called home, outside of the walls, ceiling, and floor he
lived between. He went from passing by the occasional school, mom and pop
owned gas station, park, and dog walker or older couple out for a sweet, hand in
hand stroll, to passing by strip mall stores, parking lots, and significantly more
foot traffic. This served him fine, as well. There was a church up the way, which
was worth mentioning since it balanced out the levels of commercialism and
materialism to spirituality and religion just right.

Upon having made little eye contact with anyone, having nodded just enough to not look suspect or manic, he saw up ahead a shimmering something. What that something was he couldn't tell, but it appeared to be in the middle of the sidewalk, transparent and translucent, and set apart from the life and humanity buzzing all around and through it. Looking back down at the concrete in front of his moving feet he glanced up to see if it was still there. It seemed to have disappeared for the moment, but as he really looked deeper into the atmosphere before him - as one's eyes begin to make patterns of visual, 3-D picture puzzles - the fully dimensional shimmer returned. *Is anyone else seeing this*, he wondered to himself, looking around, and noticed that no one else was.

II

Having made a simple pass by the shimmering oval plate that seemed to have no physical body, but still required Samuel to squint his eyes as he walked by it so as to not have its light completely glaring into his eyes, he glanced back at it, now looking manic and being completely conscious of this. The glimmer was still there and no one else was acknowledging it. The crowd had not faded away completely, but become sparse as the lunch hour had come and they were all either at an eatery or at home. *This is the perfect time to investigate*, thought Samuel. As his body followed the direction his head and face held steady he met the shimmering oval face to shimmering oval the way he had before his first pass.

Samuel was a man not quite into his forties, but beyond his twenties and past the early years of his thirties. He was beyond the glances of those approaching and twenty year old women, to whose vapid company - unfortunately more than often he found their attention span and subject matter of discussion as such - he was glad to no longer appeal to. This being consciously on his mind, and his subconscious mind focusing upon the clear lake at noon-like reflective surface of the shimmer, he began to see a reflection. It was a shadow in the distance, within the distant depths of the tear in space and time, whose view the shimmer offered, that was. It was of more of a blob in definition, so no features could be read from its form.

Staring at it, however, the form seemed to approach, but not walk by walking. It seemed, at each occurrence of a blink in his eyes, to be then a step closer and gaining more definition, color hues, and contrast with each approaching baby step. With his intent, focused gaze upon this otherworldly view a small group of men and women - two middle-aged parents with their adult daughter and either her brother or boyfriend, to potentially become husband, possibly - came from the direction behind him. He heard their approach and snapped his head back at them to see them eyeing him with a look that said *pooh-pooh on you sir, I don't know what you're looking at, but you appear manic.* That was Samuel's translation, at least. He followed their eyes right back as he turned his head to watch them pass. They conceded in this game of downtown chicken to retain their sensible way forward and on toward the crowds of those not staring into nowhere, out in the open and middle of the sidewalk, looking manic.

Looking back to the shimmer Samuel saw it come into focus, again. *So no one else is seeing this, but me*, concluded its sole viewer. The monochromatic blob became a gray-scale blur with slight definition. It looked like a child's crayon drawing of a person that a parent would obligingly put up on the refrigerator. He still could not make out the features enough to place a recognized face upon it, nor a similarly identifiable body. It did seem, however, to be continually - even if in small steps and from an original great distance away - approaching closer and closer, inching its way along.

III

Now having realized that about almost a half hour had passed - as he studied the translucent, shimmering oval further - and the lunch crowds were returning, to make their way upon the same downtown sidewalk, Samuel prepared to face many more strange looks as he was intent upon discovering what this shimmer was trying to show him. On cue, as he thought it, the masses embarked upon their shuffle back onto the sidewalks, emerging from their homes and eateries to go wherever their day was taking them. The first group of this wave to come upon Samuel and the mysterious, seemingly enough nothing he was intently focused on was a couple in their twenties who stared at Samuel as if he wore the clothes of a homeless man and was standing upon a soapbox preaching in words that were more utterings with no syllabic or remotely English tint at all. Samuel gave them a passing, impatient glance to acknowledge that he knew what he was doing and was not manic, they went on their way thinking he was manic, and Samuel kept at his vigil.

The gray scale blur, with a slight child's drawing crayon level of definition, became a partially colored penciled hued sketch with rough features that appeared like an intermediary comic book artist's first draft rendering of a still frame. Wondering if he was in fact manic, however, Samuel though to test his theory. He shook his head, as if to dispel the shimmering as the madness the others, now an increasing crowd that glared at him - practically disapprovingly - en masse, had seen his apparent observation in the empty air to be. He made a second pass beyond the shimmer, twenty paces out, stopped, and glanced back over his shoulder as if he couldn't unlock his gaze from where the back end of the depth of the shimmer's cave-like hollows should have been. Shaking his head at his truly not only looking manic to others, since he was now feeling manic to himself, he returned - stomping impatiently - back to his own personal shimmer.

It was in fact there and the colored penciled hued sketch with rough features of an intermediary comic book artist's first draft was now closer up. It was now a more defined charcoal pencil and colored pencil drawn image of a person, casually dressed - like himself - that resembled, possibly, a peer of his, but from this other world behind the veil. Wondering if he could step into this veil he began to step forward - to all outward appearances making an exaggerated, almost comical mime-like routine step - potentially into the shimmer. He did not step into the shimmer, so much as he did so through it however, looked around sheepishly, and took a step back. His gaze returned back to the shimmer's sole existent being.

IV

Maybe, thought Samuel, *if I focus on it I can somehow project my mind or spirit into it.* That seemed as probably as anything else. And having decided this he put his arms out and up, as if in a Buddha-like meditation, but standing up. He closed his eyes, focused on the world within the shimmer, and imagined himself linking energies with the charcoal pencil outlined sketch person. Having felt that he'd sufficiently thrown enough spiritual energy into the shimmer to channel something he opened his eyes. Upon opening them, however, he had not projected himself into a gauzy, softly lit, fuzzy feeling alternate universe. He had only succeeded in now making the crowd that was passing around him want to avoid eye contact with the strange man miming out something they couldn't discern what it was and meditating in public, while staring intently at something in front of him none of them could see.

Attempting to make those whose eyes he did catch, upon darting in his direction to view the car crash without actually slowing down to catch the full carnage, he was moving his arms about in the direction of the shimmer and trying to make words come out to describe it, as if to defend his completely rational and empirical, scientific methodologized actions and motions. All that came out, however, was confused utterings that did in fact make him look manic and sound like a man, dressed as if he were homeless, preaching gibberish upon a soapbox. He just needed dirty clothes and a soapbox. Giving up on this, to save what little face and pride he could, he sighed and went back to the shimmer with even more focus.

I will figure you out, thought Samuel, *you're now an even more clearly defined, closer ranged, charcoal pencil outlined colored pencil sketch that's clearly my peer in age and general design, just from a different universe that I can see for some reason.* The man within the shimmer was now just about twenty feet out and approaching the precipice of the veritable line, the spot of the potential tear in the fabric that separated their worlds and realities. *I've got it*, smiled Samuel, thinking himself a genius, *I'll make you come to me, then.* If the image of Samuel suddenly becoming elated at a stroke of brilliance, or being in the middle of enjoying a joke only he understood, wasn't strange enough then his pacing back and forth - first with his back away from the shimmer, just to face and approach it again, in a small ovular rotation - his spaced out revolution around this fixed point of manic-ness was even stranger. People were now purposefully making wide sweeps around him to avoid catching, if he was in fact contagious with it, his manic-ness.

VI

Once he'd finished his manic, ablutional rotation as planet Samuel in his orbit, just before the shimmer, he refocused intently on the illusive image that was now a mere ten feet away from him. *Oh my*, Samuel's face became a jaw-dropped picture of one frozen in amazement at a vista only he could see, *I am becoming manic.* The crowd around him was now, for all intensive purposes, walking conspicuously faster around him, as if getting away from him faster would make this entire charade any less strange. Noticing the change in the crowd's reaction to his obviously challenging problem that he, and only, could solve - since he was the chosen one to do so - he shot a collective dirty, peeved look around at them all, as if to make a point that only, for all intents and purposes, made him appear even more manic.

Returning his now, if it was even possible - but yet it was - even more focused and intent, personally challenging glare at the shimmer he saw his own doppelganger, only from the other universe neighboring his own, staring back at him blandly as white milk and dry toast. With his own arms at his sides, slightly angered by this lack of any kind of reaction on his doppelganger's part, to acknowledge the massive importance of this moment on a global scale, Samuel was clearly shocked, amazed, and irritated all at once. Trying to make words, as if to speak to it, all that came out was utterances that sounded like the beginnings of words that never quite came to fruition.

Bringing him a soapbox to stand on and a dirtier set of clothes would have almost made him appear less manic, at this point, strangely enough. Thinking hard to himself Samuel knew he had to figure out a way to make contact with this doppelganger, whether it was in his world or this other world. He had to figure out how to somehow, at least, get a reaction out of this person. After all, the charcoal pencil outlined colored pencil sketch with clear definition, that was him, was a practically a mirror image of himself, in full clarity and definition. And all it was doing, for goodness' sake, was standing there oblivious to how monumental this moment was for both of them.

VII

With one more idea in mind, before he completely lost it and was beyond having already appeared to be manic, then confirming he was manic, to coming close to having men with butterfly nets and a long armed white coat for him to wear for a long, undefined time to come, he threw all of his energy into this. Eyeing the doppelganger with a look that was usually only used by old west cowboys in a good old Mexican stand-off, he gave it a look that could've burned a hole through anyone else, or at least won him a staring contest by merely weirding out his opponent, flat out. Then, in a complete about-face he regained a meditative composure, closed his eyes, put up his arms in Buddha-like fashion, mumbled a prayer, cleared his mind, and attempted to lock his energy, spirit, and aura onto the doppelganger.

Appearing to be in a trance from the outside and within the passing, now thinned-out wave of people - it having become late afternoon and early evening - Samuel stepped forward and put his arms out in front of himself. He motioned as if he was parting a shower curtain that split down the middle. Completely focused on the tear between their two universes, Samuel imagined himself spreading a curtain aside from the middle and stepping through it. And either he had a great imagination that could create physical, real world sensations - as quantum physics, he'd read before, had said that the observer always effected the outcome of the observed experience and did have an impact on the world around them, down to the atoms - he felt as if he was parting a curtain of velvet and heavy atmosphere that was at the same time sifting through his fingers.

Stunned, his eyes were bulging in amazement under their closed lids. Sensing that he'd pushed aside the curtains and stepped through, feeling a gentle swish of those curtains - something he'd never be able to explain in words ever in his life after that day - he stopped, gently dropped his arms to his sides, and opened his eyes. His heart was beating, he suddenly realized, at what felt like a million miles per hour. Standing before him was doppelganger in full human-like presence, but with a different glow about him physically. *Whoa,* though Samuel, *I did make it through.* Now, all of a sudden, it was the crowd's turn to be astonished, in that - those who were in the presently relative proximity to the manic man doing a strange mime act and series of meditative ablutions - they all suddenly slowed down to screeching halt, causing many a human pile-up, but without anyone minding the mild shoving around, given what they could swear they had just seen or now were no longer seeing as a result of it.

VIII

Welcome, projected Samuel's doppelganger, *I knew you'd figure it out soon enough.* He looked at Samuel with a look of sympathetic patience. Samuel noted this with an utterance of a word he couldn't finish from the shock of his newfound surroundings. It was the same landscape for the most part, but the edges and surfaces of everything were witnessed to appear as having been seen through a gauzy, soft, translucent, old timey movie filter. Focusing his gaze, having looked all around him, to observe this in sheer wonderment, and then back toward his doppelganger, Samuel noticed he had the same appearance and glow. Taking in his own features into account he noted that he himself had the same softened hues and edges, now, as his surroundings.

Now, it's time to go back to your apartment, the doppelganger projected. Stunned at the events that had just occurred Samuel watched and turned his entire body to follow and watch as his doppelganger walked towards the surface of the shimmer, only from his side, now, and walked through into Samuel's former universe. As his doppelganger stepped through the shimmer he turned back for a moment to nod and then headed towards Samuel's apartment in Samuel's own former world. Obediently following, as his doppelganger was doing going back down the exact path that Samuel had walked in what was now the other side of the shimmer - that he could see if he did focus enough to make it come to the surface, like a 3-D picture puzzle - Samuel made his way to his doppelganger's former apartment.

I guess this is where I live, now, thought Samuel, *I always did want a change of scenery.* With that thought in mind he was long past the strip mall stores, eateries, and church and marching past the occasional dog walker, older couple walking hand in hand, mom and pop owned gas station, and houses that surround his apartment building. Reaching the front door to the building he turned the knob, gently pushed the door open, walked in, and shut the door. He checked his mail and walked up the brief set of stairs - not big enough to constitute being referred to a case of stairs - and stood in front of his new apartment door, which was his doppelganger's former dwelling. With the same care and ease he opened his door and went in with the intention of continuing the story he'd left off writing.

Under The Tree
(2/28/2015)

I

Sometimes it is possible and entirely real that there is something to the inner
feeling we have about our impact upon the world around us, down to the atom
and particle, based on the theory that the observer is not at all detached from
the observed experiment. It can be said that life can sometimes be like a child
riding by on a bicycle and a grown adult getting lost in the rotational,
centrifugal motion of the wheel and all its parts, as well as the illusion the
system creates. Maybe, just maybe, it can be said that the faster we move the
slower we appear to be moving from an outside, neutral observer. It could also
even be possible that the life around us that has actually slowed down may need
for us to stand aside and allow it to pass us for the whole works to carry on.

He had come here to meditate. He had come to realize that - through all the
snows of winter, the rains of fall, and allergies of spring - came a great season
between spring and summer, as well as occasionally spectacular summer days
that harken back to spring. These days were mildly breezy, over top of a just
warm enough and just chilly enough in the shade, set of conditions that made
thinking outside in nature a great pastime. Also, since flitting back and forth
between New York and Ohio - for family, school, jobs, and personal ventures of
making his own life happen for real outside all bounds those pursuits corralled
in - he'd found truth to the statement that both states were known, more so
than others, for their bike and hike trails and parks. He had come to enjoy the
parks, especially, for this purpose.

Pulling into the parking lot in his reasonable, yet mid-career stylish, bachelor
sedan he found a parking spot near the large, wooden, recreation facility that
served as a public meeting hall out in nature and an indoor retreat for larger
groups of park-goers. Stepping out of car he took a deep breath of fresh, natural
park air and smiled. He looked around and saw the usual sights that a park, on
a nice day, will allow. He took them in and noted them all in mind, as he had
left the notebook and pencil at home for his trip - so he could best and simply
just focus on nature and not get distracted in writing down every thought that
popped into his mind. He wouldn't allow any interruptions to disturb his
continuous stream of consciousness today.

As he walked to his favorite spot in the park he passed the usual sunny day, cool in the shade and nice in the breeze views that such weather brings about. He saw a mother pushing a stroller along a paved sidewalk path that moved gently up and down the hills. He saw the tennis players on the court volleying back and forth. *They're actually pretty good*, he thought, *looks like a decent game to watch if I came here for that.* He saw elderly couples sitting on benches in the shade watching the younger parents of little children running around the open expanse of grass. He saw hikers with their official walking sticks in hand - usually outdoor exercise enthusiasts in their middle ages with a passport book of parks and trails walked stamped off sticking out of their back pockets - with their cargo shorts and durable hiking boots, ready to tackle the more difficult, near off-road and off the beaten path trails, that zigged and zagged through the woods. He saw the runners sweating it out, in their officially licensed workout clothes and shoes, having come from or headed to the more level trails that weaved in and out the woods and connected to other trails from nearby parks. He saw others, an entire demographic range of people usually, sitting on benches around the fire pit that came to life for those that fueled it if they stayed that late into the evening. He also saw parents and grandparents playing with the kids and grandkids by the swings, slides, and jungle gym equipment.

Watching the buzz of life, feeling like an outside observer that was invisible to everyone because he was there by himself, he felt like he was witnessing - upon closer, more focused attention on a single person or small group of people - that they seemed to slow down in speed. Almost like watching a bicycle wheel spinning so fast that it almost looks like it's not even moving, the spokes appear to not even be in motion, creating the visual trick the unfocused eye falls for. It was like he could almost hear their conversations or read their thoughts based on their body language, as well. He was always a sensitive person and people watching and meditation was interesting to him.

II

Making his way toward the path that looked like it jutted off into the woods deeper to the right he followed it to the left, where it took him on a short jog up and down over a few gently rolling hills. The path turned from mulch to dirt to where he followed it across a paved sidewalk trail that surrounded his favorite tree to sit under and meditate. Sometimes he really tried to actually meditate and other times he just sat under its shady branches, against its sturdy trunk, and relaxed while taking in the life around him. After he made the short walk from the sidewalk to his tree he took up his position. The buzz of activity was visible from here, and even passed by closely on the paved trail occasionally, but it was quieter in this spot. The groves of trees and forest seemed to soak up the excess sound that could interrupt his complete peace and calm.

Checking his sensitivity and sudden mental alertness in relation to those around him - being able to practically hear their conversations, read their feelings based on their body language, and feel the energy of their auras - he did feel like things slowed down when he really focused on just that one thing. At first he chalked it up to the sensation the mind creates when you mentally block out all other surrounding events and truly, intently throw yourself into that one focal point with complete singularity. Either way he was already becoming more and more at peace and in tune with everything around him - naturally, as in the natural preserve of the forest, hills, skittering animals heard or seen on occasion, and the weather elements, as well the people around him.

To test his feeling out he focused all of his energy on a mother pushing a stroller in the distance, along an easy paved trail. He focused on her, not too hard, but he observed her suddenly, albeit casually, look around her person, instead of straight ahead.

"Interesting," he said, "but maybe it was just coincidence." Turning his gaze, casually, but with a little more focus in his mind, he looked in the direction of an elderly couple sitting on bench in the shade. As if they got the message somehow both the man and woman suddenly turned their heads toward his general direction. It wasn't directly at him, or didn't look to be so, since there were more people coming and going in his general area, but they did apparently sense something. Taken aback by this, even slightly, he ramped up his focus and turned his gaze upon the tennis players - the one serving, specifically. The one serving was in mid-toss the ball up and serve it motion, but then stopped all of sudden. The one to receive the serve looked at him, patiently, but with a look that asked him what he was waiting for, as the one serving turned his head to look directly in the direction of the projected something.

"Whoa," he said, "I am really in tune today. I think I'll give it a rest for little while, since it clearly works." As he took his focus off the server the server returned his attention back to his game, served the ball, and just chalked it up to the feeling that, as they say, a goose had just walked over his grave.

Under his tree he decided to see if it really did feel like time was slowing down for some - as if his aura was an overbearing presence that was wrenching up the entire gears and works - and just observed intently, instead of throwing energy at anyone. *The runners*, he thought, *they're a good reference point.* Having seen a runner just pop out of the woods less then thirty feet from him he locked his gaze upon him. Nothing seemed different, to speed up, or slow down any more so than the runner adapted to the rolling of the hill. The runner, sensing that someone was observing him, looked in his direction and nodded a friendly hello and remained on course. It was casual enough of a glance and the runner hadn't though it anything more than a mere observation of a passing body having just emerged from the woods rustling leaves. But, as he saw the runner had his back to him, he noticed that as he focused deeper on him he did appear to slow down. Snapping his head out it, having momentarily been mesmerized by the effect, the runner seemed to speed up, like videotape speeding up to catch up to the present moment it was held back from while almost being paused.

"I have be careful," he said, "either there's a good amount of energy bouncing around here today or I am really tuned in."

III

After completing this little round of experiments he mused upon what he had truly felt like he had done to impact the world of atoms and particles and people around him. Curiously, he took in the scene of the entire park around him - from as close as the runner had been to as far as he could see in the direction he knew his car was parked. He saw the clock tower that was mounted atop the rec hall building hoping the comfortable ticking, tocking, and swaying hands would center him, again. As he kept his focus on them, however, they too appeared to be slowing down.

"No, no, no," he said, "I've got to snap out of this. Maybe I'm just feeling lightheaded or something from skipping lunch…or something else." But, to his dismay, as he shook his head and blinked his eyes, to reboot some sensory receptor in his head, his glance returned to a world around him that was in fact physically slowing down with a sound that was much like in a psychological thriller movie where a record is slowed gradually before you know it will come to a complete halt. With his eyes wide and his mouth agape he looked around as everything had in fact come to a complete stop. Shaking his head didn't change it. Blinking his head didn't render any different observation.

"This is weird," he was now thoroughly concerned, "what did I do? Or what is happening to everyone except me?" Thinking at about a million miles per hour ideas and theories flew around his brain faster than he could process them. He stood up immediately, not even thinking that if time had slowed down any fast motions on his part against the significantly slowed down pace of time and space could cause such friction as to tear him apart. It didn't however and he just looked oddly at his hands, held up in front of his face, as if they were a new development and then down to his feet.

Turning his gaze back forward and ahead, he sought to walk around to see if that could shed any light of discovery, realization, or maybe jolt his mind into thinking of something or anything. He walked past the sidewalk, the paved path the runner had moved on from, and found said runner in view - mid-stride and not a bit off balance or about to tip over for it. He looked towards the tennis courts and saw both players in mid-play. One had just hit the ball to the other side and the other was standing ready to receive it. The ball and net, as well, were frozen in the position they were before he - or something else - had decided to stop time. He observed the pair of grandparents, on the bench in the shade, frozen like statues as well, with the man motioning to something going on just in the distance and the woman following the man's guided gaze.

Heading back into the woods to the trail that dumped out into his spot under the tree he saw two hikers, in full on hiking gear and completely in the moment, frozen in a position of using their walking sticks to carry them forward and balance them over the uneven, dirt and root strewn path. He could see faintly through the wooded cover that the flag was somehow still blowing in the breeze. Now walking very fast, not quite in a sprint, but close, he ran toward the parking lot. Upon stepping out of the wooded path, and into the open air and sun, just below the parking lot he saw the woman who was pushing the stroller now standing like a statue as she was peering down over and into the it. Circling the stroller himself he saw the baby looking up with a glassy eyed, permanently fixed smile back at its mother. Walking on around the rec hall building he wanted to get a look at the swings and playground area. He saw the same scene there, as well. A grandmother was pushing a child on a swing, or she once was rather, and her arms were firmly unmoving, out in front, and aimed at the swing that was holding a rigid position forty five degrees in mid-air. The child was smiling and her face had a laugh stuck in place, as her hair was plastered in a motion of blowing back behind her.

"This is not good," he said, as he looked up into the sky for further proof of something or anything he could find out. The birds were just like the tennis ball. They were frozen in mid-motion in the air and appeared as if suspended by invisible strings. The clouds were still perambulating across the sky, slowly, along the breeze that was still blowing, but no leaves of branches were stirring. Looking around at the strange world surrounding him he closed up a little closer into himself, as if intimidated by something or everything, and stalked back to his spot under the tree to try to gather himself and his wits, again.

IV

Back under his tree - his safe place - he stared straight ahead, but more lost in a ten mile stare that looked through everything until it was one collective blur. Snapping out of it, knowing that he had to do something, to at least try something he thought of meditating as he had done before - in the full on lotus position. He'd done it before and no one at the park had ever shot him a strange glance or even took notice of anything strange going on over in his direction. This microcosm and part of the world was quite liberal and open minded, it seemed. Why not give it a shot? If it failed at least he could be at peace for a few minutes.

Getting into the lotus position, feeling the like the Buddha pre-epiphany, he cleared his mind and started the om chant. At first he didn't sense anything different happening around him, but did feel a little more at peace. After a few minutes he stopped and opened his eyes, having thought he heard a leaf or small animal skitter by, but no such luck was to be found. The world around was completely still. Getting back into his focused mindset - closing his eyes, holding his stance firm, and chanting again - he kept this up for a few more minutes before stopping, opening his eyes, and taking a look at the results. He could have sworn he heard a leaf rustle or someone move. Thinking of getting up to check it out he started to shift from his sitting position, but stopped and just looked over toward the tennis court. He could have sworn that just a moment ago the man serving was standing just a bit more to the right before and that the one receiving had shifted a little, too. Now, taking notice of the elderly couple on the bench, he observed the man had turned his head a little towards the woman, as she was now looking farther off into the direction he'd previously referenced her to do so in.

"Something's happening, just very slowly," he said as he observed these subtle, but promising changes in scenery.

Suddenly, he thought he heard a slight crackling or static hum of a frequency so low that you can't hear it unless your surroundings are near or absolutely silent. He focused his attention it its direction and was definitely hearing something. Now, slowly getting up he approached the spot on the ground. It was a leaf. It appeared to have a flicker of the same kind of static a TV losing or regaining reception has, but faintly. Shaking his head and blinking his eyes didn't even take that effect away from it or reboot anything. Without thinking he felt himself reach for it and was an inch from touching it till he snapped out of it.

"No," he yelled at himself audibly, "you don't know what will do. The butterfly effect, you idiot." Realizing something he hadn't before, upon focusing all of his psychic energy as best he could all around him in every direction, he could see the same flicking on everything in sight range and could just as well assume it was happening to things off in the distance. Back to the under tree safety spot he hurried.

Assuming the lotus position, again, clearing his mind, closing his eyes, and chanting, he began to meditate with as much focus as he had ever done so with before. After about fifteen minutes he heard the static buzz frequency pick up in volume, seemingly then snap off like someone had turned a dial, and then, while he continued chanting, opened one eye slightly to see everything around him - plant, animal, and human - crawling back to life and motion that he could see with his plain, naked eye.

"Good," he said, "this is alright and only getting better." Refocusing himself he began to chant louder, as if the power of his chant was fueling the change in the world around him by increasing degrees and intensity.

Stroller wheels started visibly turning and eyes and arms started to visibly flap around in joy, as the child looked up at its mother. The mother's smile seemed to morph into satisfaction as her gaze shifted forward and ahead. The elderly couple's heads seemed to turn toward each other, now. The tennis players began to locomote around the court in slow motion. The child and swing began to reach their maximum height and return to Earth again, as the grandmother retracted a bit to receive them. The hikers in the woods began to take slow motion steps over the dirt and branches as their walking sticks began to move up and down. Those around the fire pit area seemed to turn their heads toward each other as their lips started to move in a slow drawl again.

If he had been focused on the sound of life kicking back into gear again he would have heard a thrum of voices, flaps of bird wings, the echoes of children's laughter, the tap of the tennis ball, and the steps of different types of shoes on different types of ground. Since he was by now far deeper into his trance, however, he didn't quite acknowledge it, but he was aware of it as a sound in the far off background, as those in deep meditative states can seem to block out the entire world if they so feel the need to or take a mental close up of one single focal point. Feeling a stiffness, as if it was far off in the distance, but able to be felt this close up, as well - almost miles away - he passively shrugged it off and kept up his vigil.

V

If he could have witnessed his own transition - as if only he could have in an out of body experience, this deep into his trance - he would have observed that he was appearing to become stiffer and more solid, rigid from the inside out. And as if it were possible to become a living statue by merely willing it he was slowly turning into stone from his atoms and particles inside through to his shoes and clothes on the outside. So far he was petrified up to his shins. He was oblivious to this, in a direct manner of feeling it or feeling the need to respond to or address it, and kept on chanting. Life around him, however, seemed to go from moving at a crawl to speeding up faster than normal, as if to catch up for all the time that had been lost.

From the outside it was like watching everything in fast forward, only you as the observer weren't even aware of it, as those within the system were all on the same page, and on the same timetable, dead set to catch up to the present moment. The tennis ball was volleyed manically back and forth, the runners from the woods entered at one place and almost instantaneously exited from the woods at another spot, and the mother was strolling her child at a mad pace, now, beyond the rec hall building and making up ground toward the playground fast. The grandmother swinging her granddaughter was doing so at a speed that would be reckless, if not within this system, and the hikers were charging forward with what would have been reckless abandon if the world around them hadn't been keeping up with them. And those around the fire pit were shifting in their seats, some of them even getting up and returning to their seats split seconds later.

No one had noticed him under the tree, as the stone that overtook his features - cementing him in that seemingly peaceful position - advanced over his thighs, toward his waist, up his stomach, and into his shoulders and arms. It was crawling up around his neck. Nobody else noticed, however, since they were busy catching up to the present moment, and had been made to do so very quickly, given the time they'd lost. Under his tree, however, he was gone to the world around him, feeling that the world was returning to normal, enjoying that relief washing over his mind, and expecting himself to come to any moment, now. Starting to feel the pull of the world on his senses again, at least from his neck up, the world outside began to slow down to a normal speed.

VI

The hands on the clock tower no longer spun so rapidly that one would've feared they might fly off. The mother was now strolling her daughter at a less dangerous, hurried rate of speed. The grandmother was no longer hurling her granddaughter into the sky with reckless abandon. The elderly pair on the park bench in the shade and those around the fire fit weren't throwing their arms up and down in the air and talking so fast it was all garbled. The parents in the open grasses we no longer chasing after and running around their kids in an a fashion almost comical, like sped up old timey eight millimeter movies. The tennis players weren't going back and forth as if they'd just guzzled energizing, highly caffeinated drinks beyond the strength to give someone a heart attack. And the runners were no longer in a dead sprint. Kids were also no longer crawling all over jungle gym equipment like spiders, in a fast forwarded nature video, over prey they were attacking.

The sound of everything returning to normal pace was that of a movie being slowed down to regular speed, again. Voices were discernable from one another and specific, clear words and phrases could be picked out with ease, now. The pong of the tennis ball was now repeating every good one two three pong, one two three pong count. The feet of the runners and the boots of the hikers no longer crunched the ground underneath them, but rather padded along. The creaks of the metal joints on the playground were now coming and going at a good, steady pace. All the while, under his tree he was unaware of all of it.

A runner had entered the woods by the same path he had taken before - from the mulch, to dirt, to clearing the wooded path it picked up briefly, and crossed over onto the paved trail - and upon emerging from the forest entered the clearing to see and witness an amazing sight. The path ran off to the left out and around the entire park's outer grounds eventually, but the runner stopped in his tracks. He walked slowly to the tree where a man regularly visited this said spot a few times a week to just sit and relax or partake in amateur to intermediate level meditation. Not believing his eyes he saw a statue that practically looked exactly like him under the same tree, in the complete, full on lotus position. Now standing an inch from the new statue he reached out to touch it, but stopped when his hand was within a few inches, suddenly shuddering all over. He felt as if someone's eyes were on him, focused and intent, and he looked around to see where it could otherwise be coming from, but then turned back to the statue and felt that same feeling, again, but stronger. With that the runner shook his head, looked around to see if anyone else was seeing or sensing this, and returned again to his run.

The Philosopher And The Huckster

(3/1/2015)

I

There are those among us who, whether they are of Earthly years young, old, or in between, have naturally old souls from birth. They know, even though they cannot always elucidate it into so many words, the value of a life with proper balance between work and play, study and application, living out experiences, and storytelling or chronicling them. These types and varieties can smell out an imbalance between the two, where it's happening, to whom it's happening to, and whose perpetrating the misdeed. These types are the ones who, once they've become experienced enough in the ways of having made such imbalanced living mistakes, having learned to live with the right balance, and set that balance right when it begins to tilt one way or the other can even intuit when they need to step in to prevent tricksters from stirring up such imbalance on purpose.

There was a 21st century luddite, all matters of the truth to be told, who lived close to the center of town. He was their official, as well as beloved, poet and writer of stories, fables, sagas, and legends. He wore modern day casual pants, long hair for a man, glasses, and a sweater with patches at the elbows for a classic touch. His house was small, just the right the size for an eternal bachelor such as himself, with a small yard out front and back, surrounded by a humble fence and subtle gate on both fronts. Great trust was held between neighbors so fears of intrusion were minimal to near none. Upon speaking, though he was barely over thirty and less than forty, he told upon himself for having an older soul. His nature was, consequently, one that enjoyed peace, quiet, and a lack of - or absolute minimal amount of - confrontations, disruptions, or interruptions.

This man longed for the poetical musings found in leaves of grass and wished for the more free form stream of consciousness thoughts that come and go and eventually come back around again in some form or another similar to their last one. His mind drifted along with the clouds to usually set down for a spell along the tropics, whether they are of Cancer of Capricorn, to simply take off again and set down somewhere else it found fruitful. Being a small town kind of guy, who felt comfortable leaving the big city business to big city businessmen, was who he was and what he did best. Thinking about every minute detail that passed between the milliseconds, that he was surely missing everywhere and

every moment as they zoomed by at frightening speeds, was something he
didn't do and didn't lose sleep over.

His desires were to write for himself, to amuse the people, to constantly prove
his value as their residential dreamer, and he was more than willing to allow his
mind to dream a little extra for those who admittedly couldn't dream so well, or
vividly. The small, but substantial enough, paycheck that came in weekly was
good enough for a man of his single, more Spartan than not, stature of living
called for and was his comfort zone. He looked the part, played the part, wrote
the part, and lived the part every day of his life. It had been not too long ago, in
terms of larger sweeps of time, that he'd finally found himself in this perfect
place and state of mind for his talents, abilities, and level of being so
proportionately beloved. It had been quite a while and a long period of time,
measured in human years and the larger sweep of time on a higher plane that
had passed before he'd found himself and his calling, as well. Either way he was
planted here, his roots shown everywhere around his home, person, and around
town, and were even busting up through the grass and sidewalks around his
home, as if seeking out higher places, too.

He was just the right amount of confident. Excessive pride was not something
he found himself indulging in and, rather quite the opposite, found himself
passively returning the amounts of love he received - that he felt were too much
and overfilled his cup - back to the people so that they could pass it onto others
who needed it significantly, and genuinely, much more. The skills he possessed
to translate his, and the general townspeople's, musings into poems, stories,
sagas, articles, and legends were more than enough and still below the bar that
was set at a level that would have been too much. The voice on his pages spoke
for all of them and they didn't want to let him go, and he himself didn't feel like
a cage bird either, as he was happy to be wanted and never felt chained down at
any point in time since finding himself here.

For all these reasons our resident writer, whose mailbox label was decorated
with he plastic, capital marquee letters JSB, and stood for John S. Beck, was not
the least shaken when the provocateur - as he thought him to be - rolled into
town. It was heard off in the distance, and might as well have been accompanied
with all the bells, jingles, and jangles that could be strung from a passing circus
cart. The provocateur's mode of travel wasn't quite so much more the obvious
on the surface, but the overly dramatic and theatrical entrance he made might

as well have deemed it as such and as much. Still, it all started with the strangely joyous, but with undertones of a deceptively far too happy to swing into town and swindle everyone, calliope that left John S. Beck apprehensive and skeptical.

II

Off in the distance - his motorized cart shiny its the hubcaps, slick in its paint job, and bright in its color scheme - the man known as Jack "Cally" Hope was on his way towards the small town that was not so much sleepy as it was a smaller blip on the map than others around it. He was the type of person whose outward appearance of slicked back hair, shined shoes, the latest designs of a suit, and a stylish, fancy outing hat to top it all off gave the appearance that his kind seemed to flourish anywhere and everywhere. Behind the wheel he saw the town from the distance and was practicing his initial entrance speech, having already memorized his shtick in between from multiple other performances and stops along the way. It was only the ending of his presentation and the exit that was left to chance - whether it was a big finale finish or a cut and run, cut your losses, and move on with your tail between your legs job.

The entire way along the well paved road Jack "Cally" Hope felt a pair of eyes, singular and subjugating, set upon him. Being no stranger to such looks, and generally skeptical first impressions being burned onto him before, he had a tough, businessman's skin. That would normally have been well and good, but his tended to go deeper into that cutthroat, competitive, and nearing sneaky type underneath the eyes and skin of that of the presenter. That was what John S. Beck had read into him and what Jack "Cally" Hope hoped to break the other townspeople of, and rather leave them with a more exciting and edgy remembrance of him, if not a long lasting and completely trustworthy one, at least. Either way the shifty vehicle with an equally shift driver pushed on forward.

Entering the outskirts of the town, what passed for downtown, the strangely slick, city birthed vehicle drew its share of attention. Those out and about around the post office, the library, the family owned mom and pop eateries, the movie theatre, the banks, the police station, and the grocery stores all stopped to take a look at the passing visitor to at least catch a glance of what was in store for them if they caught his act later on. The authorities, being of small town nature and nurture, looked out their windows at the suspect vehicle and driver, but didn't stir too much or feel the need to investigate further. It all seemed innocent and public enough that no real deep seeded funny business appeared to be about to go on.

This all being part of the visitor's plan, he parked his city birthed vehicle on the side of the road and stepped out. Theatrically he took a deep breath of the small town air, with his entire face and upper body, and opened his eyes back up to look around the town. Holding his hands on his hips, he arched his back a bit, smiled and nodded at a few passersby, and mentally prepped the introductory words that would get the first stragglers to stand around to figure out what was going on. After that, once his introduction was done, he'd get into presenting the real meat and potatoes products, which would draw more people out based upon word of mouth. Once he really got into the full swing of his memorized act was when people usually trickled in more, really packed in the crowd, and made for a real audience. After that was for him to find out, in each city and town, whether they liked his act and closed in and around him to get what he had to offer or whether he left that particular town or city as a less than impressed crowd simply dispersed to go back to their homes. So far he'd never had a mob on his hands, at least, and that meant he knew, on some level, when and how to come close to a line and not blatantly cross it.

III

Opening up the lunch truck-like compartments around the rear of his miniature traveling circus cart-like city slick vehicle they showed printings of newspapers, magazines, and compiled volumes of stories. He was a one-man schlock and fanatical, fantastical journalism salesman and his vehicle housed many compartments that flipped, opened, and rolled out into racks of the reading material. As he flipped, opened, and rolled out these racks a small crowd stopped and those that seemed to slow down around them joined them, while a few stragglers continued to pick up their pace and head to where they were going. Their destination, that they'd set out for, would not be interrupted, not even by this slick, city birthed salesman. One of those not impressed, as well, though from a distance, was John S. Beck, who was writing at his desk by the window that faced towards the downtown landscape and had taken a moment from his work to make sure his town wasn't being too shaken up quite yet.

Of the small crowd that had gathered was, in attendance, the town librarian and postman. The librarian was running a library based errand and had a bag in her hand from one of the downtown shops and the postman had his bag of mail in hand, having completed most of his deliveries for the day, for the most part. The barber was standing in his doorway, caddy cornered to the action about to unfold, and was watching with enough interest to not be concerned about the breeze blowing in and out of this shop. The rest the crowd, so far, was made of a mix and match of different residential commoners - mom and pop families, single men and women, and grandparents, teenagers out on the town enjoying their temporary leave of absence from their parents, and so on. Meanwhile, John S. Beck had returned to the work he considered his own, but on behalf of the town as well.

Hearing the murmurs of conversations behind him as he set up for his presentation, Jack "Cally" Hope smiled practically ear to ear. It wasn't quite an evil smile, neither or nor one of genuine goodwill, either, but he was a businessman and travelling salesman of sorts, after all. He knew, gauging from the talk he overheard and the general appearance of the attendees representing this tack on the map, just how he would open up his spiel. Getting ready to go he theatrically opened the pressed front of his suit jacket, took a last theatrical deep breath of the small town air, settled himself, and turned around.

"Jack 'Cally' Hope is the name! I've travelled from California to Maine! I've sold fantastical stories, articles, and treatises of the big city and celebrity, and near unbelievable to dos from near and afar! I've come to you to show you and tell you of the latest, greatest, and hardly believable events of these, those, and thars!" He projected his voice loud and far and by the end of his little rhyme scheme he practically had his arms out wide with jazz hands on the end of each sleeve. With that same unpresumptuous, yet still hard, smile on his face he looked out at his audience. They were for the most part not stunned, yet, but some were a little more interested than not. On the inside Jack's face slumped a little as if to say *come on, people, don't you know a good pitch when you see one*?

Thinking he might need to try a different approach, as he saw others gathering to increase his crowd - phase two of the sparse crowd gathering was happening - he was ready to keep them coming and get them excited. He had become a fairly good cold reader of people, having been a salesman for quite a while - and believe it or not he hadn't been such a shifty one for as long as you'd think -

and had already found a few faces he liked and thought he could really lock in on. *Get them,* he thought, *you'll get the others to come along on board. They're just like undecided voters who need an exciting speech to get them to take a few first steps.* Having concluded his mental game plan, and having stood in theatrical grand entrance position long enough to get enough people's attention to now reel them in, he walked up to the first person, whose eyes looked left and right, as if silently looking to see if everyone else though this was perfectly fine and not too intrusive, as well.

IV

"You, ma'am," Jack 'Cally' Hope enthusiastically asked a middle-aged woman, who was with her leering husband, "and you too, sir, do you both like to read?" He addressed both of them and the husband stood aside again, sure enough this man wasn't a threat. Both of them nodded and said yes, why not, sure they did.

"Well, how often do you come across news that's happening on each of the coasts? And not just run of the mill political coverage and presidential doings, but actual adventures beyond the stock and trade headlines?" Jack Hope added, as both the husband and wife confirmed they didn't get to read much of that, not adding that they weren't really interested in that sort of thing from the start.

"Well, how would you," said Jack as he looked around at the others who had amassed around them, wide-eyed, curious, and listening, "like to read about scandalous activities of these public defenders behind closed doors? What about their carryings on with, dare I say, secret mistresses and under the table dealings with the criminal and mob variety of people?" With this Jack changed his face to show the expression he was trying to, and succeeding to do so, coax out of his audience. They looked on with the same expressions of shock, bewilderment, and awe - some with more gusto than others, but more were gathering and listening in.

By now the local town officials had come out of their offices and stood on the outskirts of the crowd. They weren't all too impressed by this offering of reading material, whether it be because of the suggestion they too were crooked, or because of the offense such activities brought to someone in such a position. Town merchants who were now off duty were gathering and those on duty watched and listened from their doorways and storefronts. There were more passing couples, teenagers, and everything in between, as well as others that glommed onto the crowd.

"Well, I offer you that juicy reading," Jack looked around at the crowd, and looked intensely at and through them, "but I also offer more." He waited for a moment to give those whom he hoped were now in shock at what more he could offer to gape in awe of such a possibility. "How about the political goings on of those overseas, and all of their juicy gossip and under the table dealings, as well? That's the real stuff of political journalism, not just the boring official tidbits! There's more than just the stock and trade!" Jack was looking around excitedly. Some faces were still skeptical - mostly those of the older generation and those who were with their children - but there were even more of the single, married, older, and in between ages looking on with wonder.

"And for those who like the lore of a good legend," Jack gauged the teenagers and those not quite middle-aged persons in attendance, "how about a good tale of the crypto-zoological, extinct, and once though mythological variety! Your bigfoots, chupacabra, man-beasts, Loch Nessies, and even other beasts of the land and water!" Jack observed the now interested look of the crowd, more so focusing on his words than before. There were the consistent skeptics, but those who harbored rogue fantasies and general interests in real life oddities were hanging on his words. As more people seemed to gather around, from the word of those in the crowd who'd left to return with others, as well as those curious of the new unscheduled development downtown, Jack continued to offer topics that he read off the headlines of his schlock magazines, horror stories, and supposed real life oddity journals.

Off in the distance, John S. Beck looked up casually from his writing and observed the crowd was getting larger and a booming voice was faintly heard through his cracked open window. His ears pricked up at the more prominent syllables and more pounding utterances of speech that he could not pick out the words of, but could pick up on the tone. He knew it was another travelling salesman or businessman hocking something in a circus barker or ringmaster-like tone, so he knew it was most likely not to be taken too seriously. He knew to never take a man or woman who had to speak only in booming, boisterous tones too seriously, as they were not usually saying anything near of the value of the man or woman who spoke in a natural tone of voice that didn't need to harangue everyone to get their attention. Still, he was interested in seeing how the townspeople were faring - whether they were being pulled into the apparent vacuum of tall tales and larger than life news and stories or not. He decided to take a break from his writing to see what all the commotion and vocal locomotion was about.

V

By the time John S. Beck was in the vicinity of Jack "Cally" Hope's revival of all sorts of rogue literature the ringmaster was in full swing. He was pulling all the tricks of conmen and con-women everywhere. First he was presenting a larger than life opportunity to get the dirtiest and most secretive details, challenging the general audience to react, and then zeroing in on the most gullible mark he could find first. Get the most undecided and gullible ones in on your sell, no matter how flimsy it was in truth, and you could pull in the others. Once you had enough dominoes falling you could even convince the rational ones - even if for a few moments - but hopefully not too long or enough for their own sake, however, to do irreparable intellectual and cultural damage.

"Like I said folks, there are facts and goings on about all of those big wigs you've only heard the names of and have simply accepted that they're just good old fashion, fine, and dandy folks," Jack said happily, but then theatrically put on a face full of warning, "and then there's their side you don't know. The nasty details that don't show up in the light, but that aren't quite locked behind closed doors. And there are stories of the extinct, crypto-zoological, and profoundly mythical legends that you aren't being told the whole of! Don't they say all legends and myths are based on truths?" The audience reflected the response Jack "Cally" Hope was projecting onto them from his face to theirs, from their faces back to his. It was a look of wonderment and curiosity with an insatiable craving for the dirtiest, most profane details, no matter how much against their normally rational, polite, and culturally intelligent natures it was. John S. Beck just watched with his arms crossed, an unimpressed look on his face, and a stare at the ringmaster at work.

"And even beyond that! What about secret societies? Did you know there are secret societies at work everywhere," Jack "Cally" Hope's face projected his riled up, shocked, and appalled face at the affront of such a thing onto the crowd's, "because there are! And they are setting in motion leviathans of butterfly affects that you can't even begin to understand what the consequences could be!" The crowd was responding with oohs and ahhs and ohs and oh nos that Jack was feeding off of. John S. Beck was, however, still unimpressed.

"Yes, sir, ma'am, woman, man, and child," Jack glared at them as he looked around his audience, now slithering like a snake from spot to spot to get a good lookout for his next one-on-one mark, "there conspiracy theories that are true! Not just hoaxes, but actually true! Stories of men from other planets, underground political parties and secret societies, and some of your own public defenders are hobnobbing with them! Maybe even as we speak!" Jack was getting the crowd whipped up into a frenzy that was not a violent, near riot yet, but one that had individual groups within the audience starting parallel and similar conversations of their own. They were along the same thread, usually parroting what Jack said and adding more to it, whether any of it was backed up with facts or firsthand knowledge, or just presumptuous guesses and grossly misplaced suspicions.

Having witnessed that there were a good number of his townsfolk not impressed by this huckster's frenzied speech, which was conspicuously devoid of clearly elucidated facts to back any of it up, John S. Beck was contented. It was those of the crowd who were riled up by such infantile accusations and even flimsier suppositions that concerned him. Standing back, outside the semicircle of an audience around the huckster's cart-like vehicle, John. S. Beck stood by his firm, rational, still imaginative, and dreamer's mind that - as he proudly would say he was raised to be such - held a firm grip on reality, still, to remain rational, reasonable, objective, and proportionally subjective in just the right amounts.

VI

As John S. Beck looked around the audience from outside Jack "Cally" Hope kept up his frenzied, worrying, tantric gospel of the book of ludicrousness and shadowy proofs. Beck saw many faces in the crowd. There was the librarian that knew what new books he'd like to read, the postman who dropped of his mail and packages, some off duty shopkeepers that knew him by name, and there was a teacher that he knew from the local middle school. Around the way were townspeople he passed by a couple times a week on his errands, who always asked how his new work was coming along and offered their constructively critical and praiseworthy responses to his latest published work. Here and there were others in the doorways of their storefronts and public officials, and some off and on duty officers here and there to make sure nothing got out of hand, as this sort of event wasn't an everyday happening.

Slowly, as the individual groups conversed in parallel along with the huckster's flamboyant and, honestly, impressive - from a standpoint of stamina - show, they began to notice their favorite, local, resident writer's presence. Their conversations parroting the huckster's boisterous speech, flimsy proofs, and wild offerings of stories that bordered on being profanely ridiculous - had the crowd had the advantage of hindsight in this moment - they turned to regard their resident poet, storyteller, article writer, and occasional correspondent in the local paper. After a few minutes Jack "Cally" Hope saw his hold on what he thought was his crowd fading and he too looked in the direction of their resident poet, short story writer, and occasional correspondent. With a sigh he acknowledged John S. Beck.

Not saying a word John S. Beck just looked around the crowd. His emergence from his writing studio and his small, humble home was always an event - as it was a welcomed and not too often occasion to get a glimpse into their favorite local non-celebrity's daily life. Not smiling or frowning, and not glaring, but not joyous either, John S. Beck was taking in the audience with interest. The crowd seemed to part as Jack "Cally" Hope was irritably stamping and stomping over to see what had broken up his steam engine-paced pitch that had been going so well. Jack Hope emerged from the parted sea of his audience and took in the modern, yet rustic look of his adversary.

"Ah yes, John S. Beck," Jack addressed him, politely on the surface, but not hiding his irritation underneath his tone too well, "local poet, short story writer, and occasional correspondent for the local paper. How nice to see you." *Yeah, nice*, thought John S. Beck as he chuffed out an amused snort of air and an amused smile.

"I was just offering these fine people some of the newest samplings of the news going on around the much bigger world around them," Jack spread out his arms to mime the larger than life meaning of his words, "that they may not have great access to here, all the time." Jack smiled that same shifty businessman smile that John S. Beck read like an open book.

"I heard," said Beck casually, "it sounds like you're all wind in a well made up bag blowing around leaves that were perfectly settled down." Beck had that same neutral, but well intended and kindly look on his face.

"Spoken like a true poet," said Jack Hope, "but there are things out there that people need to know that are hidden, covered up, and kept from them on purpose, by those with less than better intentions. I intend on letting them read and learn for themselves." Jack thought he made perfect sense, and in a drastic time and place he could have, but this was neither of the two. Beck simply chuffed that amused snort of air.

VII

"Ah yes," Beck's face showed his amusement he made no intention to hide, "I see we're now rationalizing insanity." A sudden hush fell upon the crowd as they observed Beck's con and latter to Jack "Cally" Hope's supposed pro and blatant former.

The crowd watched the duel of words and personalities, and even deeper moral and ethical afflictions between the two with awe. Their trance upon the possibility of possessing such a great, vast ocean of knowledge, facts, figures, and so on and so forth was broken, and they were now more intrigued by the words - rarely was Beck known to speak so much orally, rather so much more known to speak via words on a page - this being a sight not usually seen.

"I've heard your spiel," Beck said, now politely enough, "and I've heard the great, urgent gusto with which you speak. Unfortunately, you don't offer anything but flimsy speculation, conjecture, and a deeper, significantly darker hole than one anyone with a peaceful disposition and a happily lived place in life would want to go down. You don't offer enlightenment, but simply a heap and pile of facts, figures, conspiracies, and mythologies that are beyond what anyone reasonable would devote so much, or any, of their valuable time upon. Life is short and your distractions only add more adversity and division between the people." Beck paused to take a breath and take in the new mindset and attitude of the townspeople.

"Yes, yes, that's well and good," Jack mischievously added, trying to get what were, for a short time, his people back, "but what about their feeding their sense of curiosity, imagination, and their hunger for the real truth of…" Jack saw Beck flapping his hand at him with an air that said he wasn't impressed, that he had a rebuttal, and that Jack might as well stop because Beck wasn't listening, as he'd heard it all before.

"Let me explain things to you…Jack "Cally" Hope, is it," Beck said, respectfully enough for Jack's being a huckster, that is, "imagination is wonderful and feeding into one's curiosity is also wonderful. Let one dream and imagine all that could be, but not to the point that one entirely loses his or her grip on reality in the end. Just not to the point that one goes down such a dark path that they might not return the same person from it. And as far as knowing the truth, everyone has their own truth and a truth we all share, being that we all share this same world, have to get along, and in doing so allow each other to pursue their own dreams as long as they don't intrude upon the lives of everyone else destructively or negatively." Beck could see Jack miming like he was about to jump in.

"But information, Mr. Beck," Jack tried to defend himself, "people deserve to know what's going on. That's the truth of the matter. Knowledge is power, after all. I think even you could agree with that." He flashed that same shadowy businessman's smile that Beck read through and instead saw a snake's forked tongue flicking through.

"Yes, but there's enough information out there, already," Beck philosophized, "enough that we can hold onto and still live our lives happily and coexist with our neighbors in a healthy harmony. Then, again, there's such a s thing as too much information. That can be divisive, cause unnecessary rifts, and it's usually information that - until it was brought to the light - had existed of its own innocent way, and wasn't hurting anyone. Brought to the light, however, it divides us who were once friends, family, and community, once all together on the same general path, no matter what our own individual thoughts and ideas on the matters were. Take religion and politics, for example, when they're spoken of in the proper amount and with a goal of conversing and getting to know each other, to know how to accept each other. Too much talk of such things, like the mindless differences that never seemed to matter before, and we're suddenly taking different sides for no good reason." Beck, having made this point, Jack thought he had one more ace up his sleeve, and one was all it took sometimes to coax everyone back to even the shadowy side.

VIII

"Yes, but what about harmless stories of lore and legend," Jack strained for effect, to try to move the audience, "aren't stories of mythical beasts, monsters, and legends simply fun sometimes, whether or not they're true." Jack thought he could make Beck look old fashioned, stuffy, and prematurely curmudgeonly. Beck, however, read this and had a retort ready without even thinking, or having to do so.

"Those are well and good," Beck said neutrally, "as stories of entertainment to escape the real world, as we must do sometimes. They are even good material to teach morals and lessons in the form of stories for children and adults. I have possibly even written a few of my own. But, if you dwell on such things and delve too deeply into material that becomes too dark and profane, in the face of what is sacred, beyond the point of mere entertainment, you go too far. No one needs to add any darkness to their soul or take away any of the light that exists there." Expecting more from Beck Jack stood there, speechless, as the crowd's individual group's conversations - parallel, perpendicular, and all across the way - mirrored the sense they all collectively shared before the huckster had rolled into town.

"But, but," Jack, visibly struggling with having lost the audience completely, and having been shown for what he was, "where is everyone going? I...I..." In Beck's opinion Jack "Cally" Hope was sublimely flabbergasted. The crowd was now nodding in approval of the words their favorite local poet, short story writer, and occasional correspondent had spoken. They were all dispersing back to their embraced callings for that day, whether more humble and down to earth or, so appropriately as it was, more official and given fancy titles.

"You don't offer enlightenment or knowledge," Beck nailed his final point home into the coffin that was Jack's shallow above ground pool of a pitch, "you simply offer a burdensome load of distractions. A nice story here and there, some time to read the paper, and some time to share stories of each other's day - recounting their hopes, dreams, imaginings, or facts and figures - is great. Once it gets in the way of living the lives that create those stories and opportunities to tell of them the point is lost and all it lost along with it." With that Beck nodded in respect to the humanity, if nothing else, of Jack "Cally" Hope, and turned around. He headed back towards his small house to continue his writing session.

As John S. Beck left the scene of Jack "Cally" Hope's failed pitch so had most of the audience, and those that were perusing Jack's racks of literature out of mere curiosity - with no real or true interest underneath the sentiment - left, as well. Jack Hope was stunned and looking around with a completely silenced inability to only make indistinguishable, guttural utterances as he watched everyone carrying about with their daily errands, comings, and goings. He knew he was defeated, hung his head, and went to the work of closing up each compartment in the rear of his travelling sales wagon-like vehicle. Once this was done he opened the driver's side door, stepped inside behind the wheel, started up the engine, and looked around at the town. From his position back at his desk in his writing studio in his small house John S. Beck observed all of this and he sensed that Jack "Cally" Hope, on his way off to the next town, uttered and muttered words to himself to make himself feel better, at the expense of the town he had failed to pull one over on. Smiling and shaking head at the frivolity of the huckster's ploy Beck returned to his writing.

Mr. Devine's Roadside Attraction
(3/2/2015)

I

There are games of chance that you can lose and still lose - stay with me on this
one - and there are games of chance that you can win and still lose. There are
also those that, on occasion, if you're of a design that broke the mold of selfish
vanity, earthly desires, and other vainglorious attempts to hoist yourself up close
to anything near the self-touted title of a god, can overcome the odds. These
varieties of people have been known to beat the house. They've been known to
win and still win, even much to the chagrin of the dealer who was just doing his
job. But, however, what if that dealer had far less noble intentions all along.

Along a desolate, seemingly out in the middle of nowhere, lengthy stretch of
road there was a card table set up and man behind it. The card table itself was
innocent enough, the deck was of the standard variation, and the man looked to
be nothing more than a hippie, road worn, tropical tee shirt wearing Floridian
who travelled west and just stopped here to play a round with anyone who was
willing to stop along their way to the west or back home to the east. This table
turned out to be innocent, in and of itself, as did the deck of cards, but there
was something about the inside nature of the man and the look behind his eyes.
There was also something that reeked of an incantation placed upon the deck
that seemed to always stack it against the guest invited to the table.

As for the invitation to the table, it wasn't so simple. The chances of someone
driving along the highway, having been on the road for hours, and slowing
down to notice or seriously investigate the occurrence of a card table and a
dealer who was a little too willing to play for high-stakes odds was near to
nothing. The driver would most likely be road weary, dead set on getting to his
destination, and calling home to his family, parents, or friends - whoever was
his lean to source of support in his vocation. A diversion, however, would bring
crystal clear notice to his card table.

There were stories in the papers out west that occasionally made it to the
breadbasket of America, and on even fewer occasions made it to the Midwest or
east coast. These stories told of cars randomly breaking down on this stretch of
highway, usually with the intention of traversing the longer than normal

interstate on a cross-country trip, and disappearing. A few who made it through seemed to be a bit more depressed, less optimistic about life in general, they seemed to have lost their spunk and gusto, and acted more like ragged shells of men and women. They always told strange tales of meeting a road worn card player at a table in the middle of nowhere who they played a few hands with, then suddenly couldn't remember much for quite a few missing frames of memory, and then just listlessly stared off into space.

Those people were never taken seriously, having been told it was all delirium experienced from excessive travel on the highway, mirages, possible daydreams, or the result of bad sleep, overworking themselves, or an unhealthy diet of roadside diner food and coffee for too long. The strange thing was that those being accused of being guilty of the results of such blanket answers, that were all far from the truth as they could get, didn't even have the spirit or energy - or what some would call soul - to even speak on the matter at any more length to defend their case. They seemed to just accept it, or some other dark secret only they knew, even if they couldn't elucidate it into better words. All of this, however, was part of the plan that Mr. Devine - the roadside swindler - had set in place a long time ago, since when he'd gone by many other names like Scratch, Stitch, and others, since the title of devil just seemed too played out and overused. He needed a new identity like a man with a worn out coat from years of use in inclement weather needs a new one, so he made one.

II

Fifty years ago there was a story about a man, Charles Picket, who was a travelling salesmen in the time when his variety jetsetted around the states in their stylish suits, shiny cars, and peddled suitcases, briefcases, or crates of goods with a smile no one could ignore. It was said that he was bachelor from New York selling stocks and bonds, who also dealt in homemade articles of men's accessories - like neckties, belts, and such - that he made on the side, being more than a hobbyist in sewing and leatherworking, as well as a businessman. Per his agent back in the Big Apple his agent had reported that he was making record sales in the Midwest and in the breadbasket markets, and instead of turning around he found one last whirlwind push to try a few more stops out west. He was said to have stated that he was feeling lucky.

His luck, however, was to run out, as he called his agent at a gas station he'd said he'd walked for miles to get to, explaining that he'd broken down on the side of the road, but was getting help to get going again. His agent had noted a drastic change in his disposition over the phone, given his previous gusto and deserved pride in his recent sales numbers. His mother and father and brother, back home, had noticed a change in the same as well, having received letters and calls along his way telling of how much he looked forward to returning home once he conquered a few more markets. He was also looking forward to returning home to get a bonus, on top of his regular paycheck, that would allow him to get a couple fancy gifts for his brother and buy some necessary replacement appliances his parents had been wanting. He never made it home, though, and after a few weeks of searching the party was called off, declaring him and his car dead and missing. The news article never even made it into the Midwest states' papers.

There was another traveler, forty years, ago, along that road that had been married quite a few years, had never had children with his wife, but they both enjoyed travelling together, extensively. They were both successful in their careers of Mr. Stapleton's being an office manager for a supply chain and consulting company and Mrs. Stapleton's being a legal secretary. They were both travelling cross-country, from their home in Ohio, all the way to California. On the way they visited his brother in Arkansas and her sister in Nebraska. They shot down a ways into Texas to see some touristy attractions and then headed to California to spend some time on the coast, as well as in San Francisco. There life together had resolved each of their own past demons, but Mr. Devine - though he wasn't listed in the newspaper as doing such, or at all - had brought them to the surface, again, in snorting, kicking, full force.

After the car broke down the man made the same walk to the gas station, called back home to some friends of his and his wife's. The said they were delayed temporarily, but would be off to another adventure, defying those who said they didn't have such epic, magnanimous journeys in them anymore. Upon returning to the sight of the breakdown he spotted Mrs. Stapleton - a former, but recovered gambling addict - at a table fiercely playing a high stakes game with Mr. Devine. Confusion at the picture of such a thing at such a time faded fast as soon enough as a bottle of whiskey had surfaced, and Mr. Stapleton was drunk, getting a tongue lashing about his drinking, again, as he slurred his words contesting her gambling, again. Their car was found in the same spot by state troopers, with the unhappy couple near death from thirst and hunger, and all were brought to the nearest police station.

After returning home, the state trooper having helped them get turned around and headed back in the right direction, their lives were no better. Their old addictions came back, they distanced themselves from their friends and family, and their professional careers tumbled in the same way. Their attitudes and general moods were said to have become depressed, lackadaisical, and they seemed to just go through each day with no concern of a future for themselves or each other. They faded from the vivacious picture of life just as soon as their story printed in the paper, that made it to the Midwest news scene, but who would really believe what a newly un-reformed gambler and alcoholic, having fallen off the wagon, had to say.

Mr. Devine's game was one beyond a card table. It was one that carried over into and permeated people's lives. These were two cases of those who lost and still lost. The game was set up in such a way that this was one of a few possibilities of those who played. There were more possibilities, but those didn't leave the player to fare too much better, either.

Far off in the distance, having just left his hometown in Indiana, a man who'd made his way up the ladder at his office in quite a short period of time, was on a road trip to check up on the office's west coast branch. He had just made it beyond the Indiana border and was headed to California. His newlywed wife, who they'd heard was pregnant with a baby, supported him and told him - through all his fussing over her - that she would be find with her sister staying over the house in his temporary absence. Assenting to her well wishes on his trip he had started on his journey.

III

There was another tale of a writer, some twenty years ago, who was on a road trip, seeking muses of inspiration that could only be caught on the run or along the roadways, constantly being on the move. Jack Kearns had written travelogues for serial magazines and short stories. He'd also had an idea of a great cross-country novel idea that could only be truly and rightfully done by actually walking in the steps of his main character, along his journey. His main character played fast and loose, as did Jack, living with the mantra to get as much as he could out of every waking moment of every day. If a drink was necessary here, a mildly risqué outing with a friend or new acquaintance there, or juggling a few women he was between affairs with was what that called for it all was par for his course.

Upon his reaching Mr. Devine's station Jack Kearns was, instead of apprehensive and skeptical, quite amused and interested in what this experience could offer his book. His car hadn't broken down, since he'd been willing, in mind and spirit, to stop all along. Jack Kearns made small talk, big talk, and every kind of talk in between, and then eventually took up his strange host - who'd never, apparently, heard of the real estate motto and mantra that read location, location, location - for a card game. Sharing a drink with the card dealer Jack Kearns had played a few friendly hands, but then let it get serious. That was when his hand was up. Upon winning, we know this since it was well documented in his resulting book, Jack Kearns was off to pursue more adventures to fuel his book.

Unfortunately, his book was released posthumously, as Jack Kearns was said to have died of a heart attack and a gunshot wound. He had appeared on the scene in California and suddenly had taken on a few more mistresses, suddenly having even more charm, charisma, and personality than ever before, such that women found him absolutely impossible to resists. Cupid didn't even need to make an appearance for this writer to get the same results. The result Jack Kearns didn't expect was for one those women's husband to be man who owned many guns, had a jealous streak, and was just as convincingly personable of a friendly drinker and gambler to lure him into a night out just to end up shooting him, after giving Jack the scare of his life. The finished manuscript Jack Kearns had sent to his publisher, as he'd written the entire book in a flurry of creative energy, got there, but he didn't. The papers simply breezed over Jack's lesser qualities, as a human being given to temptations and passions that towered over his ability to coexist with them, and focused on his writing legacy.

Another story went that, just ten years ago, an entrepreneur was on his way to opening a west coast branch of the company he'd worked at for ten years. Mr. James Harding's plan was to get the office, who's building was already in place, staffed and operational. Once he started staffing the office and they started working with their first clients, who were already in line, as well, he would call home, have his wife of many years and their grade school age child come out to join him in the home they'd seen pictures of, and would be move-in ready by then. Till then Mr. Harding would spend long days and nights at the office or sleep at small motels, that would have been severely humbling to anyone else who wasn't already happy enough to do what he had to to create a better life for his family, that were well below his usual budget and style.

Having made it to Mr. Devine's spot on the side of the road Mr. Harding found that his car, which was brand new - purchased just for this road trip to break it in, as it would be the family's west coast car - had suddenly stalled. After calling home from the same gas station, which unfortunately went through too many different owners and staff to be able to notice a pattern developing from just down the road, he called home to Mrs. Harding and told her he'd hit a minor bump in the road, but that he'd called the office and they were okay to give him another day to arrive. Everything was still on track, ahead of schedule, and their new life was just around the corner. After setting up for a roadside service to come out to repair his car engine and get him back on the road Mr. Harding observed the card table and its dealer, and actually offered to help him to get where he needed to, because this desolate spot couldn't possibly be anything a but a breakdown point.

After some good natured conversation, as Mr. Devine, along with all of the greatest connivers in history, was quite skilled in this area, the two were playing and Mr. Harding had divulged his entire story to a complete stranger who was barely an acquaintance. Having started up a friendly card game they played till a friendly, but serious enough challenge was posed by Mr. Devine, which Mr. Harding took because he thought the dealer to be joking. Mr. Harding won the game and was off. His success in getting the office up and running was quicker than expected, and he became far richer than he expected, in just as little time as well. Unfortunately his mind became clouded by his new wealth and he completely forgot about his family. Even after multiple calls, which eventually lead to his wife pleading for him to come to his senses and reunite the family, he stopped answering her calls and lost his family. He was rich and successful, yes, but had lost the most valuable thing he'd earned even before that.

Mr. Devine's game was one that merely started out on the card table, but ended up in ways not even he could imagine. But, is it not true that the devil doesn't really need to do anything but simply suggest, and then sit back and watch as humanity shoots itself in the foot? Either way, the circumstances seemed to end up in his favor, which was all he asked for in the end. Mr. Devine had experienced his less than willing, who became intoxicated with the inhuman possibilities of his game, players lose and still lose. He had also witnessed them win, but still lose.

Having crossed into and over the breadbasket of America the office manager, just having been promoted to consultant to other branches, was making great time. At every rest stop he made sure to call his wife and then talk to the developing child in her stomach, with the receiver put up to her belly. Approaching the fated roadside attraction that few could resist and even fewer, if any, ever left better off, he was full of optimism. He'd had his own demons he'd defeated on his way to starting a family and promising career, and he was set on making an even better life for his coming child.

IV

Mr. Devine sat at his roadside card table. He studied each car as it approached, which was the first step in his game. If he deemed that person too strong of a personality for him to face, someone who was - God help him - faithful and of a religious bend, or was just someone who was already doomed by their own doing and humanity, he let them travel on. He would cloak his table and even his presence so that the passer-by saw nothing and was not even aware of his presence by that nagging, subconscious warning light that blinks on and off in the back of your head when you sense something is there, but you can't quite see it. He was quite skilled at cold reading these people at the surface and even better at straight up reading their mind, and what was written on their soul. It was a necessary evil, as those who don't put much stock into faith or religion of any kind, would say.

His game was simple, even before the real game. After centuries of watching these people from his place down below and here - which was still new and still took some getting used to occasionally, from being kicked out of his previous dwelling - he had figured them out. Give them something innocent enough to get into, appeal to what they already know and who they are, gain their confidence, and then ratchet up the competition in a fun way. Once you had them that far over the railing you could pull them completely into the abyss if you just nailed the next step. That next step was to play upon their deepest, darkest, most primeval and primal desire - to have anything they wanted for seemingly nothing.

His card table and card game ruse was simply a corporeal version of that. First, he attracted their attention - the hardest part - by being different, but interesting enough to make them want to figure him out. Then, he reeled them in. His card table was an innocent enough oddity on a roadside, such as this, so much that half of his victims offered to help him out of the roadside jam they thought he was in, by all appearances being what they seemed. The rules of his game were quite simple. The first few hands were for fun. He'd win some and they'd win a few more. Then, the stakes got riskier, as Mr. Devine made wages that they'd take only half seriously, given the rapport he'd build with them, and then when they were sucked into the game - their carnal pride having been put on the line and having the possibility of being awarded with any one thing they'd ever wanted - it was over. And who actually took him serious when he said the price, if you lost, however, was your soul? When he said it with that wink, smile, and nod you didn't know if he was serious, but you'd play on because you were already that far invested into the game to back out then.

The man who was travelling to California to consult on the branch's west coast office, having just been promoted from office manager and had a wife with a baby on the way at home in Indiana, was one, Mr. Walter Whit. He was a driven man, but was driven by the chance to make his family's new life the best it could possibly be. He was a proud man, but proportionately proud of the work he'd done to get where he was and he always touted that dedication, honest work, creativity, intelligence, and remaining faithful to your job and family was all he'd done, all along. He was as also a focused man who didn't allow many distractions to throw him off a mission once he'd taken it on, unless it was a detour that was part and parcel for the course.

Mr. Whit had also overcome adversity as well. In college he went through an alcoholic phase - as a result of the less than positively influential crowd he was with at the time - that he'd quit, soon enough, upon merely catching a glimpse of his future wife in a class they shared. It wasn't until a few weeks passed that he'd stopped drinking entirely and was taking the first steps to make a new group of friends, while awkwardly avoiding the old crew, that he even approached her. He'd even quit a short lived, but annoying enough, smoking habit for her. After college they settled into a small apartment while they served less than call home proud to mom and dad after getting your degree to work here, meaningless jobs, but then worked their way up to a condo after landing jobs within the scope of their degrees. Upon moving up in their perspective jobs they moved on up to the small, but cozy house they currently lived in. And now they were set to move into a house that would better suit their new family arrangement soon enough.

Mr. Whit was motoring along the stretch of desolate, seemingly endless highway with this thought as his motivation. He passed the gas station that others had made their last fateful calls from, being unaware of the history this fuel station had just as much as the current ownership and staff was. Approaching a bend he rounded he thought he saw a mirage of sorts off in the distance on the side of the road, but this was a long stretch of road of near nothing, so that was normal par for this course, most likely. Up ahead, though, Mr. Devine was letting down his veil. He'd sensed this one coming. He'd read his thoughts, read his past, read what was written on his soul, and then thought, *I like a challenge*, as he smiled a smile that had something behind it, something that was one of many things that got him kicked out of his original home in the first place.

As he rounded the bend he saw the mirage up ahead, as if it seemed to take form before his eyes from a distance, but he shrugged it off as mirage or the sun glaring off of something that had been there all along. His car started to sputter.

"Oh, come on," yelled out Mr. Whit, in retort, "we make it this far into this God forsaken terrain and now this." The car, other than being brand new, had run perfectly and without any of the minor, normal hiccups a car entering this kind of weather and landscape would be expected to, up to this point. As he punched the gas he steered the car as it drove forward on sheer momentum until it came to a stop. He'd steered it off onto the side of the road almost perfectly parallel with the road. Across the road and up about fifty feet he saw the card table and the man behind it. He looked like a road worn, older Floridian who'd broken down, by all obvious appearances, but by all less than obvious appearances was perfectly content with his feet up on the table.

"Having a little car trouble," inquired the oddly placed card dealer, as he put his shoed feet on the ground and addressed Walter Whit, "the name's Mr. Devine. How can I be of service to you, or would you like to play a game of cards while you wait for help to get you on the road again?" He lifted the brim of his hat to see Mr. Whit looking at him curiously, but shrug, and make his way over to him. On the outside Mr. Devine maintained a middle of the road look, but was smiling that smile on the inside as he pulled a deck of cards out of his pocket, said a mumbled incantation, and spread them out on the table.

V

Reaching Mr. Devine's card table, having taken in the surrounding landscape around them the entire short walk over, Mr. Whit was definitely intrigued.

"Strange place to play a few hands, isn't it," Whit said looking around as if to show the man what he may have overlooked, "out here in the middle of nowhere, that is? But I guess I'm glad someone else is out here, either way." There was folding chair in front of the card table that Whit nodded at, as if to ask if he could sit down, and Mr. Devine nodded in approval. Walter Whit sat down and noticed the cooler sitting next to the man behind the table.

"Have a seat," smiled Mr. Devine, "Mr…" He trailed off.

"Oh, sorry," said Walter Whit, "I already got your name. My name is Walter Whit. I'm on my way to California on a consulting job." The two men shook hands and the card dealer let Mr. Whit talk.

"I've got a wife back home with a baby on the way that I'm trying to get over to this coast soon as possible and even though this isn't the end of the world it is a little annoying," Whit didn't give his entire situation away, but wanted to make it known his stay would be no longer than it had to be, "I'd really like to be on my way. There was a gas station a short way back. I'm going to stop back there and call for triple A to get my car going, again." Getting ready to get up Walter took a look at the card dealer.

"You need anything…" Whit didn't know even where to start, given the strange scenario, "I don't know…" Whit didn't have the words to try to even begin to explain what he thought of Mr. Devine's setup or situation.

"No, I'm fine, thank you," Mr. Devine returned coolly, shuffling the deck as he talked, "I don't live too far away and I like to sit out here sometimes. It's not a bad view really and if I can be of service to anyone who might need me out here, here I am. I have this cooler here filled with cold drinks, just incase." It was a solid enough point. For all Whit knew people out west who really wanted to get away from it all - possibly this coast's equivalent of Midwestern country folk - did this sort of thing all the time.

"Okay," said Whit, getting up, "I'll be back, then." Whit began walking down the road toward the gas station. Passing by his car he shed his jacket, not needing it out here on this long walk. As he walked around the bend to go to the gas station to make his call Mr. Devine thought, *yes, do that, it'll be a good hour or two before they get out here, anyways, which will give us more than enough time.*

When Walter Whit returned to the card table he was sweaty and his pressed shirt no longer looked so nice or meeting ready. He sat down at the card table, as Mr. Devine looked up at him inquisitively, and looked around, then back to his strange acquaintance.

"So what brings you out here, other than the view and possibly helping a stranded driver," Whit was confused, "what even gave you the idea?" Why anyone would set up shop out here was strange, especially to a man who lived in the suburbs.

"I like the peace and quiet," Mr. Devine said, still shuffling the deck, "and I wouldn't expect you to understand beyond that, coming from the east coast…I saw your plates as you approached." He smiled and sounded like he made enough sense, but his sight had to be amazing to tell what they were from that distance. Or, maybe, he'd seen so many he could tell from that far what state they were from. That was entirely possible, as well…maybe.

"I guess that makes some sort of sense," Whit conceded, "so in the meantime, before triple A gets here, I see you have a cooler and a deck of cards. What do you play?" Mr. Devine smiled, successfully not doing so in a conspicuously weasely way.

"I thought you'd never ask," Mr. Devine said, perking up, "I play poker, find the card, old maid, gin rummy, war, and even solitaire when I'm bored. What's your game?" The deck shuffling stopped temporarily as he let Mr. Whit decide.

"How about poker," Walter suggested, "I'm not that good, but who really cares out here." Mr. Devine smiled at the suggested humor and at a darker, subtler meaning he derived from that statement.

"Yes, who cares who wins, out here," Mr. Devine, said in a mock genuine tone, "poker it is. A few hands for fun, but then we can possibly up the ante, still in a fun, sporting nature, however." This seemed well and good to Mr. Whit.

They played a few hands of friendly poker. The first game was a Mr. Devine's, as he had a straight and Mr. Whit had a pair. The second game was Mr. Devine's, as he had a flush, and Mr. Whit and a little better than a pair. The third game was closer, as Mr. Devine had three of a kind and Mr. Whit had the same, but of a lesser card. The fourth and fifth games, surprisingly, went to Mr. Whit, who achieved a straight and three of a kind. He was getting better, apparently, and Mr. Devine congratulated him.

"Nice game, Mr. Whit," said Mr. Devine, as he reached into the cooler for a drink for them both, "you're not a card shark are you?" Mr. Whit laughed at this. Mr. Devine smiled on the inside, as well, but in his case it was because he was successfully building a rapport with his newest player.

"Would you like a drink? A water...or a beer?" Mr. Devine waited to see what Mr. Whit, loosened up and having let down his guard a little, enough to be friendly, would say.

"Just a water," Mr. Whit said to Mr. Devine's disappointment, "I stopped drinking beer a long time ago. I used to get in trouble with it and gave it up so I could get my future wife to get on board with me." Mr. Devine smiled, nicely on the surface, but less than so underneath. *How sweet*, the dealer thought, *we have more time for a few more tests and temptations.*

"How about we change games," suggested Mr. Devine, "let's try find the card. It's quite simple. I just shuffle around three cards, using a bit of a slight of hand inspired shtick, and you find the queen." As he spoke he began to show how he could shuffle the three cards around, faster and faster, as he'd apparently had practice.

"Why not," conceded Mr. Whit, "looks like it'll pass time." As Mr. Devine shuffled the three cards around, with acute agility and nimbleness of fingers, Mr. Whit followed it has best he could. He missed the first few, but then started to guess the next few. He guessed one here, missed one there, and so on. They played this way for a while. They even started having a decent conversation - or rather Mr. Devine egged Mr. Whit on to talk about his life in detail - and even began to crack a few friendly jokes.

VI

After playing this way for a while and becoming better acquainted Mr. Devine felt he was in enough to start getting serious and start his real ruse on Mr. Whit. He began to feign like he was trying his hardest to trip up and trick Mr. Whit, but that Mr. Whit just kept on picking the right card.

"You are quite good at this," congratulated Mr. Devine, "or you're just catching on quite fast…I hope I'm not the one who's losing his touch." He smiled the friendly one on the outside.

"Oh no," said Walter, guzzling down some water, momentarily, "I'm just getting lucky, and lucky streaks tend to end quicker than you expect. I've come to learn that the easy way and hard way. That's why I don't gamble." Mr. Devine perked up at this. *Here's my challenge*, he thought.

"Very smart philosophy, indeed," Mr. Devine conceded, "but how about a friendly wager, not so much a gamble?" He gauged Mr. Whit's response. Mr. Whit appeared to be thinking about it and came around.

"Okay," Walter, said, "a small wager. Why not? We have to agree on it though." Mr. Devine liked where this was going.

"A small wager it is," Mr. Devine continued, "five bucks. You've got that in your pocket, don't you?" This was all to ease him into the next step and trap him into the last one. Mr. Whit, unaware, played on, still on guard to not get too chummy, however, and to remain a little distant.

"That works," Walter said, "that's hardly enough to call giving into a vice." With that they played find the card. The cards flitted over each other and under each other at a speed that showed that Mr. Devine was playing harder, now. It wasn't quite for real, but closer than it was before to such a thing. Mr. Whit picked the card and he celebrated a little. Being offered another round and another Mr. Whit played on.

"All right," conceded Mr. Whit, "we're about even now, so I think we can stop gambling." As he said gambling he threw air quotes up with his fingers and laughed. Mr. Devine however, had a look on his face that wasn't quite devious, but wasn't so free to let it go either. Mr. Whit's humor subsided at this.

"How about one last gamble, Mr. Whit," offered Mr. Devine, "and then we're done." Mr. Whit wasn't sure what he meant, but his eyes asked the question *and what are we betting, now?*

"How about one more round," Mr. Devine offered, "for your soul?" His smile turned and took a half serious, half joking tone upon itself as he reached out his hand to shake on it.

"Yeah, right," said Mr. Whit, reaching out his hand, thinking their good-natured antics were carrying on, "what are you, the devil, or something? Five more bucks it is." As Mr. Whit shook with Mr. Devine the dealer smiled, but Mr. Devine's smile turned crooked and his grip hardened. As he did Mr. Whit though he saw Mr. Devine's appearance flicker in and out between the version of him as a man and the version of him as a...devil? As he suddenly took on a face of horror Mr. Whit tried to pull his hand away, without even moving Mr. Devine's an inch.

"Why yes, I am," confirmed Mr. Devine, "and this wager, that you've agreed to, is for significantly more than five bucks." Mr. Devine's face remained a sneer, but he released Mr. Whit's hand - which Mr. Whit took back immediately - and did his air quotes of his own for the words five bucks. Mr. Whit was rattled, as the flickering between a red skin-toned, half human, demon form and easy going human form of Mr. Devine kept interchanging rapidly before his eyes. *This is no mirage*, thought Mr. Whit, and Mr. Devine smiled that internal, and infernal smile, on the outside having read this thought.

VII

122

"Fine," resolved Mr. Walter Whit, with a serious, focused look on his face, "but no tricks. No…spells or anything on the deck. If you are who you are, and I'm pretty convinced right now, as hard as it is for me believe what I'm hearing myself saying, than this will be done fairly." Mr. Whit began to utter a prayer inside his head and he saw Mr. Devine smile that sneering, evil inward smile on the outside at that exact moment. Mr. Whit knew that was exactly what he was responding to and that this was for real.

"Fine, as well," Mr. Devine sneered, now having stopped flickering between his true form and the man, settling upon the man, who was, now, equally frightening, "no incantations…is the word you were reaching for, I believe." Reaching toward the cooler he pulled up another deck that hadn't been touched the entire time in Mr. Whit's presence. He placed it on the table and read off the rules.

"My rules are such," dictated Mr. Devine, in a no nonsense fashion, "if you don't pick the queen I get your soul, eternally and forever. You're left to walk this earth like the other pathetic saps who've gone back home to ruin their lives and those of everyone around them…especially their loved ones. If you do pick the queen, however, you get one wish. You can wish for anything you've ever wanted in your entire life." His voice and face went from harsh and drill sergeant-like to dreamy and mesmerizing as he finished his statement. He was trying to put a drowse upon Mr. Whit to make his will weaker.

"Fine," Mr. Whit said, recognizing this, shook off the drowse, and finished the water off, "I want to see the three card first." Mr. Devine, genuinely amused at this, flipped up the three cards and mimed with his hands, as if to say *so you see, now?*

"Good, we're ready, now," Mr. Devine returned to sneering and leering, "but do know that even those who've won have lost in the end." He smiled at this, taking in Mr. Whit's faith in himself and something else, as well as his resolve. Mr. Devine returned to his sneer and leer and began to shuffle the three cards, now flipped back over face down, faster and with more agility than Mr. Whit though possible.

Meanwhile, off in the far distance, a police car with another vehicle, a triple A car, was headed in their direction. Taking his eyes of the cards that he still shuffled with deft accuracy, Mr. Devine acknowledged them. Mr. Whit didn't take his eyes of the cards, however.

"Your triple A vehicle is being accompanied by a police officer, just down the road that way," Mr. Devine nodded that direction, though Mr. Whit was unwavering, "and it will be at least fifteen minutes before they get here, just for your information." The sneer returned after a smile of teeth that suddenly were those of his true devil form. Mr. Whit didn't see this, but felt it and shuddered just the same.

"Fine, just do me a favor and shut up," Mr. Whit spoke boldly, which made even Mr. Devine do a momentary double take, "and keep on shuffling the damn cards." This amused Mr. Devine and he did so, obligingly.

VIII

After the cards had been shuffled for another minute Mr. Devine placed them each in their spot and sized up the cards, the table, and Mr. Whit. He looked up at Mr. Whit and smiled, with his hands folded on his side of the table. Mr. Whit spent another minute studying the cards, with his eyes flitting from one to the next, and then made his choice. He looked up at Mr. Devine. Mr. Devine's look was dead serious and so was Mr. Whit's.

"So which one will it be, Mr. Whit," spoke the dealer, "and make it quick. We don't have all day and I know whether or not you pick the queen you'll prove your feeble humanity. We both know that you will show, after all, that all I really have to do is merely make suggestions and your weakling race will walk yourself right off the cliff." He spoke viciously, chewing up and practically spitting out each word. Mr. Whit was staring right back at him.

"No," Walter Whit spoke more solemnly, now, "I won't prove that to you. You tricked me and if you win I will do whatever I have to do to make sure I don't hurt anyone else. And if I win I will still win and prove you wrong." He stared at Mr. Devine. Then, without saying a word he pointed to the middle card. Mr. Devine's face appeared to be a sneer, with a slight twinge of curiosity.

"You said we were to play fair and I have," Mr. Devine said, "I don't even know which one it is. But we will both find out, won't we?" With that he looked down at the cards and began to lift up the middle card, as Mr. Whit began to sweat a little, admittedly.

As the card lifted and showed a queen Mr. Devine's face wrapped up in rage and he did just the same out loud. As Mr. Whit saw the card, too, he released the deepest breath he'd ever taken - and would ever take - in years. His face broke into a weary smile and then took on a stone serious tone as he took in Mr. Devine. Mr. Devine, in a rage, slammed his fists down on the table and it tumbled to the ground, sending the cards flying, as a few legs of the already flimsy table snapped.

"How..." Mr. Devine's face was so full of rage he could barely contain himself, "how did you guess?" The devil, his true from, was coming to the surface as he spoke, emerging a little at a time. Mr. Whit noticed this and nodded.

"In college, during my drinking days," Walter Whit spoke calmly and coolly, partially from bravery and partially from shock, "my buddies and I would play this game. I had a friend, who, even drunk as he could possibly get, when he could barely walk, he could still shuffle that fast, too." Mr. Whit took in the sneer and the leer in Mr. Devine's face, and noticed he had completely taken on the form of his true self.

Mr. Devine roared in rage and looked over at the cars off in the distance, now having cleared half the distance since this last development. Mr. Whit noticed this as well.

"Seven minutes or so they'll be here," Mr. Walter Whit confirmed, "and I'll be on my way. First, however, I get that wish you owe me." Mr. Whit met the former Mr. Devine's look. Mr. Devine was scowling, enraged, and feeling even more so, having been defeated.

"What would you like," the former Mr. Devine, sneered, now a little less angry, having remembered how past mortals had squandered their wish, like clockwork, "wealth, for the your family to never have to work, again? Immediate success, so you can be loved by everyone for your genius and commanding prowess? Or something else even more juicy?" The former Mr. Devine thought he could still get Mr. Whit on the hook here.

"No, I don't want any of that" Mr. Whit said directly, setting the former Mr. Devine aback, "not from you. I'll work for it, as I have, already. I want you to disappear and go far from here to never return, again." Mr. Whit had, again, trumped the former Mr. Devine, and Mr. Whit saw the rage boil up again in his adversary's eyes.

"Fine," the devil barked at Mr. Walter Whit, "there will be others and there will be other places!" Shaking his body all over, the devil before Mr. Whit disappeared up into a ball of flame and was no more in front of him. Again, Mr. Whit released the second deepest breath he'd taken, or ever would, in his life. Looking down the road he saw the triple A car and the police car bound over the last hill after coming around the last bend. He went back toward his own car, sat in the driver's seat, set his head back, and closed his eyes. He was mentally and spiritually exhausted, said a little prayer, and a slight tear formed in the corner of each of his eyes.

IX

When the triple A car and the police car pulled up behind Mr. Walter Whit's he stepped out, having pulled himself together, and greeted the agent and officer approaching him.

"Thank you, you're a life saver," Mr. Whit said shaking their hands, "I was on my way to California and my car stalled." He nodded over to the car.

"Hmm," said the officer, observing the make, model, and condition of the car, "it looks almost brand new." He looked at the triple A agent and back to Mr. Whit. Mr. Whit just shrugged.

"Let me take a look under the hood, Mr. Whit," the triple A agent said, approaching the stalled car, "we'll get you on your way." All three men walked over to the car, following Mr. Whit. Once they reached the car Mr. Whit opened the driver's side door, popped the hood, the triple A agent rooted around the engine, and the police officer stepped aside to address Mr. Whit.

"You know, I've been an officer for quite a few years around these parts," the beyond middle-aged office confirmed, "and I've read about some strange things like this happening in this particular area for some years, now." He looked around the landscape, as if to see anything that could have been seen at that moment.

"I personally believe the stories, even though my colleague over here doesn't believe a lick of them," the officer nodded over to the triple A agent, who was moving around a hose here, looking at a fluid level there, and pulled a four in one screwdriver tool out of his pocket, "I'm just curious if you're familiar with any of those stories." As he studied Mr. Whit, Mr. Whit just shrugged.

"I don't know. I'm just on my way to California. In a few weeks my wife and baby will join me and we're starting a new life. That's all I know." He smiled thinking of them. Just then, after hearing a few bangs and hearing the car hood being lowered, Mr. Whit and the officer turned around as the triple A agent looked up at them. His shirt, arms, and hands were covered in a layer of grease.

"I had to tighten up a hose, check a few levels, align one of your belts, and even tightened up a few screws and bolts, just in case," confirmed the triple A agent, "but everything should be fine, now. I was a mechanic before taking this job. Plus, out here being a triple A agent means, if you want to save the company a lot of money and save the customer a few hours of delay time it helps to be a decent mechanic. Start her up and see what we've got." He stood at the back corner of the car with the officer. Mr. Whit opened the driver's side door, started up the car, and the motor rumbled softly to life. Mr. Walter Whit set his head back against the headrest, closed his eyes, and smiled. He was still going to make it California on time and ahead of schedule. Opening his eyes to see, in his driver's side mirror, he observed a car heading up and around the bend. *They will be safe, as well as countless others*, he thought, as he looked over at the bobble head Jesus stuck onto his dashboard and smiled.

Conrad Telley Ractor

(3/5/2015)

I

It is a far from uncommon thing to see the final product of an artist - be him or her a writer named Franz Kafka or Sylvia Plath, a painter or drawer named Pablo Picasso or M. C. Escher, a sculptor named Michelangelo or Rodin, or an architect named Frank Lloyd Wright - and marvel at their work, after the fact. It is even farther from uncommon for those, who are blessed with the opportunity to witness them in their craft creating such pieces, to be greatly confused, thrown for a loop, generally flabbergasted, or left not knowing what to even think about it. In these occurrences it best, and most open mindedly so, to give credit where it is due and extend your disbelief to simply marvel at someone being so taken up and in the moment by their muse. Why? Because these are the brilliant artists who break the mold - the mold that most of them will believe never had the right to made to be so constricting and bland in the first place.

Two children were approaching the plot of land on the street - the singular empty plot not having been built upon yet, for it was a well established street - with open grass and a for sale sign that had been removed in place of a sold sign. From the other direction came a truck, with the name C.T.R. Contractors painted across both of its sides and doors, headed towards this house. As there was no complete driveway to tell of yet the truck parked on the curb directly in front of the house. Out stepped a man, who was said to resemble a living, breathing, in the flesh Picasso painting in human form, and headed across the undeveloped driveway to fetch and remove the sign. Coming upon the sign, the two kids having seen the man emerge from the truck, they got a closer glimpse passing by the house, observing him and the property's intrigue.

"Hello, mister," said the girl, with a noble, knowing undertone, for a little kid, "hi!" Adaline waved at the contractor who turned to where he was addressed from and waved back, smiling not to big, but not small - rather, like he was not used to talking much to people. Seeing his moment to overtake his sister, the little boy picked up speed with a mischievous grin on his face.

"I bet I can beat you home, Adaline," the little boy spoke, as if he had a message of great import to get home before she could impart it, first, "I bet I can!" As he shot past her the little girl focused back on the trek home and caught up to him.

"I bet you won't, Christopher," the spunky girl challenged, in full on girl power mode, "I'll bet you won't!" They were off down the street as the builder was momentarily intrigued, but moved onto the sign, again, rather quickly. He plucked the sign from the ground, walked back over to the truck, and tossed it into the open back. He looked up the street, saw a larger truck - the one carrying the heavy load of building supplies beyond power tools, nails, measuring tapes, levels, and so on - and nodded in its direction to his associates. The two crew members, whose names were Mel and Charlie - known as the androgynous crew - stepped out of the cab and stood next to Conrad Telley Ractor, also known as the abstract builder. Mel and Charlie were said to at one glance resemble Grace Jones and at another resemble David Bowie.

The industrial supply truck pulled up to the curb in front of the house, on the other side of the undeveloped driveway, and two big, burly bulls of men stepped out of the cab around each side. One man came around the far side to unlock and open the backdoor of the trailer and the other man helped him pull up the door, and then set up the ramp. They stepped into the trailer and began to unload lumber, plywood, stone slabs, and other heavier materials. Conrad, Mel, and Charlie began to unload the trailer of their pickup truck and place their containers of cement mix, drywall compound, trowels, tool belts, power tools, saws, nails, and crown molding strips, and set it all under a temporary tent for their tools, relatively protected from the weather and elements.

As the men from the larger truck unloaded more and more lumber, plywood, and stone slabs and the men from C.T.R. Contractors unloaded their tools a neighbor opened her blinds, next door, to observe. Not looking up the androgynous crew and the abstract builder carried on with their work, as did the other two men. Mrs. Margaret Hartford, also known as the nosy neighbor, was beyond curious of the venture to fill in that last plot of land with a house and into the territory of feeling the urge to micromanage it from a distance. Her husband, Mr. Herman Hartford, would have much sooner just let bygones be bygones and left the neighbors - new or residents of many years - alone. He was known as the laissez faire neighbor.

"Huh," said Mrs. Hartford, already seemingly critical of their process, "let's see how long we have to put up with the noise of all that building." From her brief glance she didn't notice the otherwise, in a typical suburban neighborhood like this, atypical peculiarities about this particular crew.

"They're going to build a house, honey, and finally put something nice on that field of patchy grass," said Mr. Hartford, rationally and reasonably, "that's all. Just like some other construction company did for us when they made this house." He took a passing look up at his wife, still eschewing over a thought that had a good hold of her apparently, and he returned to his newspaper. The blinds were closed as the C.T.R. Construction crew finished unloading their equipment and began to help unload their raw materials from the larger truck. Soon enough the larger truck was unloaded, Conrad Telley Ractor signed off on the paperwork that he received the building materials, stowed his copy in the truck, and unloaded one last item from cab. It was a construction grade stereo radio. After this last item was unloaded they zipped their equipment tent up and returned to the truck. They drove off to return the next day.

II

The next day the androgynous crew, led by the abstract builder, began to work. They opened up the flaps of their equipment tent and turned on the radio, put a CD into the CD player on top, and turn it up so they could hear it over their work. It was a classical opera that Mr. Hartford would recognize. He'd been an avid listener of National Public Radio and was an equally ravenous reader of a bookshelf stocked full of books, as well. His wife, however, was an avid reader of the magazines in the grocery store checkout lanes that he called trashy and full of nothing but gossip. Her reading constituted, equally as one would guess, romance novels and the occasional book a talk show host would recommend at random.

"Well, there they go," Mrs. Hartford commented, with her eyes on the crew like a hawk, "let's see how loud this will be and how long we'll have to stand it. At least they're not playing that trashy rock and roll music." She observed them a little while longer as her husband had come into the living room, from the kitchen, with his tea - it was already too late in the morning, making its way into the afternoon, for coffee - and sat down into his chair. His newspaper was on the end table next to his chair.

"It's not that bad, and it will only be for a little while, dear," he reasonably spoke, and pricked up his ears to the music, "and that music is Hector Berlioz's 'Requiem'. It's a beautiful piece of music, an opera." He settled into his chair, took up his newspaper, and began to read over the random sound of the power saws, drills, and hammers off in the close, but far off enough, distance beyond the walls of their house.

"Well, I guess it's no so bad, for now," Mrs. Hartford conceded, and returned to her spot on the couch, "It is nice music, after all." She settled into her cup of tea and brunch as the TV played whatever talk show was on at this hour. The blinds were left open, as it was a nice day and early in the afternoon or late morning, however you defined it, and she peeked back a few times.

Outside, as the music played, Mr. Hartford would have recognized the movements of the opera as it played. As the Sanctus opened with graceful melodies following a gentle, angelic opening, the call and response of the male, and baritone choir, to the building woodwinds the table saws and power drills and hammers played along. At times they almost seemed to do so in time with Berlioz. The crew was putting up a roof planks and prepping weatherproofed, tacky, black tar covered pieces that they were nail gunning into place. Once this was done they pulled, from their large work tent, a couch and - as if walking on air - carried it over to a place in the middle of the first floor and set it down.

As the Sanctus had completed, with a female choir bolstering the male choir in call and response to the brass trombones and tubas, the momentum built up and passed over to the Introitus - the Requiem and Kyrie. Ominous strings, the male and female choir, and the sweeps across runs of scales gave way to the bold, strong singing that followed the melody line of the violins. From the tent was then heard the sound of a banister being made, with occasional power drill motor spinning noises and hammer pounds, and then set it place. It seemed to bridge the gap between the first and second floor primary staircase that hadn't been built, yet. Then, the androgynous crew came from the tent with buckets, cement mix, and larger, industrial size trowels and levels, to pour the basement floor. This was capped off with the introduction of a pipe organ, giving the image of a magical, mystical journey through potentially dangerous territory.

As the Introitus came to a close with music painting the picture of a hero being called to make a great sacrifice, and becoming stronger for it, a moody, darker line of music passed over to the next movement. The Dies Irae started with a bold brass section and a male and female choir going back and forth, in call and response fashion, as an introspective, thought evoking passage of melodies poured forth. Meanwhile, the crew brought in a bed, the frame, headboard, and a full set of sheets. This was placed seemingly where a bedroom would be built around it. On the basement floor, as Mel was finishing this up, Charlie and Conrad were at work setting up a series of support beams for a ceiling, whose other side would be a floor for the first level.

The music built up from a mystical, magical sweep of violins and male vocals to a sort of march, which gave way to a chaotic, energetic whirlwind seeming to pull its protagonist in many directions all at once. The abstract builder checked his blueprints, watched his androgynous crew go back and forth from the tent to their Penrose Stairs-like structure of a house under construction. Not able to quell her curiosity Mrs. Hartford popped over to the window at a commercial in her talk show that would soon again give way to what Mr. Hartford would have called an overly dramatized, far from real life experience, soap opera.

"Would you look at that," Mrs. Hartford exclaimed in great surprise, "that roof doesn't have a thing to hold it, but it stays up. There's a bannister with no stairs. A bed appears to be suspended in midair. All that makes sense to my eyes is the basement support columns." Between sentences she was looking back at her husband and the window, eyes wide in disbelief.

"However they choose to build their house is their choice," Mr. Hartford spoke calmly and coolly, half listening, "and apparently the family that bought the land trusts them enough to do so. And it can't be any harder to believe than those soaps of yours are overly dramatic. I've never found anyone I knew in that sort of situation ever in my life up to now, and don't see it happening to a sane person any time soon." His wife, unable to put words to her own guttural noises that almost resembled words and responses, kept her post at the window as the odd building continued.

"There's something strange about that crew, though, as well," his wife gained her words back, "they appear so alien and that contractor has a very strange appearance about him that I can't explain." She tried to make her case, but her words that could never quite explain what she was seeing were falling on filtered ears.

"They are just from a different town, that's all," Mr. Hartford tried to reconcile the case, "and everyone has something that makes them look different. Look at my family's nose and the way your side of the family scrunches their face up when they're in deep thought, to the point it looks like their faces will fold over upon themselves." He wasn't going to get pulled into this and had no interest in even considering what his wife was seeing, being raised a polite gentlemen who stayed out of the way when he wasn't needed, which was too long ingrained into him to be broken of it.

As Mrs. Hartford continued watch, and not be able to formulate words, the crew kept building. The Dies Irae came to a triumphant close with a marching beat of brass horns, rolled into strong male choir driven passages, and sing songy bounces of rhythm invoking discovery, as well as having moved on from a battle. The androgynous crew and abstract builder continued to construct their house every way but from the ground up. A couch was now dropped into place into another room, apparently segmented off as another communal living area. The sounds of power saws, power drills, and planks being transported from one place to another to be set into a staircase that went from the basement to a location on the first level that lacked a complete floor, carried on.

The crew built on as Mrs. Hartford, unable to believe the time and space-defying job she was seeing before her eyes, went back to her TV show, which seemed far more lodged in reality. She had no idea what the next day or even the rest of that day would bring. This would be an interesting process to watch and one that was so different from other rationalized circumstance, of which she defied anyone to label her as simply being a nosy neighbor for the sake of being that and nothing more.

III

The next day the androgynous crew of Mel and Charlie, under the guidance of their abstract builder named Conrad Telley Ractor, continued. By now, also, the amount of casual walks neighbors took in the neighborhood, passing by the house under construction, had increased greatly. Even those who hadn't taken to walking or jogging on occasion made time to stop and take a look, to watch the labyrinthine, mind-boggling methodology of C.T.R. Contractors, as well as its blatant defiance, structurally defying the commonly known laws of science.

Meanwhile, the crew built and didn't even take notice. The Requiem had, today, prominently featured a move into the Quid Sum. The male choir had stretched their voices from mid to high range as a feeling of tenderness and discovery was evoked. Violin sweeps, in small steps across the scale of musical notes, built to a personally challenging and thoughtful movement. As this happened musically pictures had begun to be hung from walls that had yet to be built. Still, the crew made sure they were level to a neutral observer. Pulling a large bin of PVC pipe, plastic containers of solvents and glues, and other brushes, towels, and assorted items from the tent they installed a sink that had no wall to be mounted to, but still somehow was.

"I honestly want to believe my eyes, but I can't believe what I'm seeing," Mrs. Hartford was still in disbelief, "I don't believe I've ever seen a house built this way...and still stand up." Mr. Hartford had still, as his upbringing had chiseled into his way of being, not intruded to rubberneck at the house next-door's building. He simply enjoyed his newspaper or book, his tea or coffee, and the music that was punctuated by power tools and hand tools.

"Leave them be, Margaret," he said patiently and as down the middle as anyone could, "they were hired to do a job and they're doing it. No matter how strange it may appear to you it's perfectly normal to them." Mrs. Hartford didn't think he'd be so nonchalant about it if he were seeing what she was.

"Yes, I understand that, but..." Mrs. Hartford, flabbergasted, mimed her arms to present the view outside the window, "but..." Words were lost upon her and made no impact on Mr. Hartford. She sighed, went back to her spot on the couch, and the two had their brunch. Those who were more than visibly and conspicuously passing by the house more than normal were in complete, even if it was nonverbal, agreement with Mrs. Hartford.

Next door, the Quid Sum gave way to the Rex Tremendae, with its strong jumps into jovial sing songy passages with a solid, low brass section being flown over by sweeping violins, and powerful male and female choirs. It resembled, sonically, a fall back to Earth from the imagination's musings to a joyous romp. This smoothly passed into a dramatic bounce back and forth between punctuated low and high range melodies. As this movement was going on musically, Mel and Charlie were each carrying a part of the combined end table and lamp that they set down on the nonexistent floor - the crew, still doing a midair walking act all this time - and plugged the lamp into an outlet not yet even wired. Conrad Telly Ractor finished it off by, for no reason that seemed odd to him at all, adding to this a cup of tea - he even set it upon a nice saucer - along with a book and light snack item on another saucer.

As the Quid Sum ended with a bold return to a passionate push of combined choirs and low brass section, evoking a joyous victory its protagonist had come to, it still maintained a philosophical tenderness. The Quarens Me Miser came in with a low male choir, followed by the female choir, and a pulsing violin. It evoked a mid journey push to build to a midway that lent itself over to a peaceful, sacred, and almost reflectively holy series of moments. All along Mel and Charlie were carrying a dinner table they placed where Conrad Telley Ractor, using blueprints, strangely enough, directed them to do so. The cutting of stone slabs and mixing of concrete paste had all lead to a stone walkway being set from the undeveloped driveway to where the front door was to go, one would have at least presumed. Mrs. Hartford, unable to curtail her curiosity any longer, even with the support of her nonintrusive husband, was back at the window.

"You will not believe what they are doing now," her voice matched her flabbergasted sentiment, "there's a stone walkway upon no yard. There's a dinner table with no chairs or dining room finished around it." Mr. Hartford was only half listening, as he was into a novel he was reading and patiently sighed.

"Really, Margaret, they apparently know what they're doing, enough, at least," he said patiently, having come to know how the dynamic of their marriage worked, and allowing it to work, thusly, "what they do is up to them, no matter how strange." He was still in nonintrusive, let bygones be bygones mode.

"But, really, this is both impossible and unbelievable," Mrs. Hartford pushed on, "it really is." She was looking back and forth between her husband and the oddity in progress next door.

"I'm sure it is, but everyone has their own methods unique to themselves," Mr. Harford thoughtfully said, "and that may be why they got this job." He hadn't flinched from his book. Mrs. Hartford was back to losing her words, sighed, and sat back down on the couch.

Next door the Quarens Me maintained a holy, sacred wave of sound, reflecting a feeling of meditative, prayerful downtime before larger action was to come. The androgynous crew and the abstract builder had begun to run power saws, power drills, and hammering as their crew leader assembled the cut boards into the shape of a gazebo set amidst an unfinished backyard. As if to defy the commonly known laws of physical science the crew continued to walk on midair as they laid tracks of handrails from the first floor to the second, like suspended train tracks, that were set in place onto walls that hadn't been put up yet. As they carried on with their work, consulting the strangest set of blueprints that had ever been written up and approved of, neighbors conspicuously walked by in both directions, having done so already - and again, repeatedly.

IV

The next day the crew carried on filling in gaps here and there, but still leaving obvious gaps of Earthly supports in place, to hold up the sparsely built odds and ends here and there, that seemed to stay upright and solid otherwise. The Requiem had today prominently begun with the Lacyrmosa; with bold upward and downward, in pitch and range, sweeps of vocal choirs. It evoked a flighty, high wire act spirit of joy and imaginative dancing. The sounds of power saws, power drills, and hammering continued to punctuate the opera, still, almost in time with the change of movements and rhythm of the music. The neighbors had continued to pass, not even bothering to try to mask their intentions, by the house under construction. Mrs. Hartford maintained her post at the window, as well.

"Alright, Herman, I have come to accept that I don't understand how all of it is even holding together," Mrs. Hartford conceded, "but I have no idea what kind of style they're going for. It doesn't look modern, standard by any means, futuristic, and it's surely not Victorian. It's not art nouveuax or anything else I can even guess what it's going to end up like." Mrs. Hartford had a degree in liberal arts and did enjoy the form and creativity of painting and sculpture, when she wasn't degenerating into a romance novel, tabloid magazine, talk show, or soap opera, and could speak knowledgably of this aspect of things.

"Well, maybe they're going for something different," Mr. Hartford intended to amend the confusion, "or we just won't be able to tell until they're finished." He was still unshaken, solid as a rock, and in ever vigilant live and let live - as long as it didn't hurt you or get in your way of doing so, as well - mode. Sighing in response to this Mrs. Hartford, completely blown away and amazed at what was happening next door, flipped the edge of opened curtain with her hand and took up her spot on the couch. Brunch had been served and they were both watching the news on TV.

Next door the Lacrymosa had passed though a moment of solace - with low range brass, baritone male choir, and high range female choir - to build back up to a mid range push of choirs and violins that swept over the pulse of the brass instruments. Adventurous, strong forward pushes evoked a battle, or foe being challenged and the protagonist overcoming it, with a drop off in intensity to a sweet, tender moment, just to rise up to glorious intensity, again. The Offertorium, the Domine Jesu Christe, began with violin sweeps over a low brass pulse and thump. Baritone male choir vocals accented by mid range female choir voice made for a tender passage of the protagonist amidst danger, still.

This was the point, from external viewing, that onlookers and rubberneckers could no longer even make sense of what they were seeing. Their sense of normalcy and understanding of commonly known laws of science, time, and space were bent and needed some thinking upon back at their own respective homes. Some understood, somehow, the creative bend of the androgynous crew and their abstract builder, in a reality and disbelief extending moment of conceding to what they were witness to. Others' minds were boggled, and their amazement - that penetrated body and soul, as well - left them mentally tired from trying to make sense of it, themselves unable to even comprehend a tree house, as done by this crew's design.

The Offertorium, the Domine Jesu Christe, progressed into a dramatic series of sweeps of mid and low range brass, trombone, tuba, and higher violin flybys on top, evoking a passionate sadness or fatefulness to come for its protagonist. This ominous passage gave way to a sense that its protagonist would have a sacrifice to make, though still maintaining steadfast bravery, capped off with strong, victorious moments of the reverent, sublime, and solemn variety. As the crew worked on there was a more scientifically minded bunch that had come along. This new crew of rubberneckers was one that didn't make their presence anything but boldly known, as if the situation required their attention to report upon - or even explain - the matter.

There were structural engineers, scientists, architects, and art enthusiasts in this new audience. The structural engineers couldn't understand how the structure was held in place and the scientists couldn't fathom how the laws of gravity and space were being broken, but the building still stood resolutely. The architects were cluelessly pondering what the style was the builder had in mind. The art enthusiasts, unlike the focused, contorted faced, and wide eyed scholastics of things physic and blueprint-based, were in their glory and reveled at the boldness. They were enamored by the process and its clear defiance of so many natural and physical laws, as well as its blithe and sheer abandonment of conventional, artistic approaches.

As this new scholastic crowd, punctuated by the deviant enthusiasts of this new and drastically different form of art, was observing this spectacle the Hostias had begun and carried on. With a reverent, solemn jumping off point of a mid range, collective choir, with punctuated brass undertoned by higher and wider sweeping violins, the image of a military march was evoked. With a feeling of sacred, reflective remembrance, and the acceptance of one's fate the protagonist's story was told. His story, the protagonist, was one of being under an ominous overtone of study from others, as he passed though it all with grace, dignity, and boldness.

"Oh, Herman, you should see the crowd gathered out front, now," Mrs. Hartford marveled, returning to her post at the window, "all the suits, notepads and pencils, and tweed jackets. It looks like all the local scientists and building intellectuals have come out." Mrs. Hartford took in the scientists, engineers, and architects as she noticed the hipster-looking crowd of art enthusiasts. She was thinking of a way to describe them to her husband.

"Well, maybe, they're interested in some sort of new method this builder is using," Mr. Hartford spoke reasonably and patiently, "maybe they see something or heard about something that is interesting to them. Who knows what would interest a group like that?" He hadn't looked up from his newspaper he was now scouring over.

"There's also a group of what appears to be post-graduate art degree students," Mrs. Hartford commented, "I could recognize that type a mile away, even not having been on a college campus in years." She was watching the artistic approach to the house with the same interest they were, only from a much more reality-jaded, older adult-like point of reference.

"Who knows what a group like that would find interesting, as well," responded her husband, "I appreciate a good piece of art, as well, obviously, but if what's going on over there is strange as you say it is then it's too much for my palate." Mr. Hartford had been confused over what more rogue branches of the art spectrum called and created, as part of a new movement, art. With that Mrs. Hartford took her spot on the couch. The work next door carried on.

V

The building of the house had wound down and Mrs. Hartford had become exhausted, mentally, trying to make sense of what kind of blueprints C.T.R. Contractors was following. As the final stages of their work were winding down the featured movement of the Requiem was the finale, the Agnus Dei. Punctuations of low brass and violin said that the danger had been passed by and a return to a solemn reverence of remembrance. The latest crowds of observers had come and gone and were even more sparse, to now being a passing, singular, studious looking representative of the scientific and architectural community at a time. They had their fill of Mel and Charlie, the androgynous crew, and Conrad Telley Ractor, the abstract builder.

Coming to a crescendo as they finished their final stages of their strange, bold, new approach to building, the music progressed into a mid range, collective, choral singing in call and response to a build of the music in fullness and volume. The image of a procession after a battle having been fought, with a hint of sadness or serene calm and holiness, was told in low range, respectful choirs singing in tones of remembrance and inflections of joy.

The house appeared to make all the sense of the Penrose Stairs and M.C. Escher's hand drawing another hand. It had the mystical, magical, and imaginative qualities of Salvador Dali and his persistence of memory. It was built, in part and parcel, with projections of structures hanging from seemingly nonexistent supports, but stood in tact, perfectly solid and strong. From a style standpoint it was impossible to tell what the final goal was, without walls, especially. Either way, the builder and his two-person crew stood back to view their work. Having done so, meeting each other's glances, nodding in approval, they began the task of packing up their tools, and everything else that was anyone's best guess, that was stashed under and within their work tent.

A crew of what appeared to be freelance and professional newspaper types came around, as well. Some had taken their own personal transportation, had their own personal equipment, and others had taken the company stamped vehicles and had professional company issue equipment. They had come late onto the scene, but were still no less dedicated to their due process of taking pictures, writing down any observations they could see, and had inquired of the straggling scientists, engineers, and architectures. They even dug for responses and statements from the new age of art enthusiasts that had gathered before, and were now visiting sparsely, individually, for their own curiosity's sake. Mrs. Hartford had made her final peeks through the window, as well.

"Well, it looks they're wrapping it up," she said to Mr. Hartford, "it's still a mystery to me and I don't think it looks anything near done, but they're packing it up. It doesn't seem to be getting that much attention from the neighbors or intellectual builder types. The newspaper people don't have too many eye witnesses to get a story from, having come this late, it seems." Mrs. Hartford made her own way to the couch for their usual brunch hour.

"It's all and well as it should be, then," confirmed Mr. Hartford, having kept up his vigil of minding himself and his own, "and that's probably a good thing." They both returned to their brunch over the TV news.

Next door the androgynous crew and the abstract builder had come to near being done packing up. As the tent was being taken down the Agnue Dei has progressed into a passage that evoked having broken through a melancholy moment, but was slowly, gradually building. A rise in strength of a collective - mid range male and higher ranging, sweeping female - chorus built up to a crescendo, accented by rumbling brass underneath, and violins amid and on top. It reached a joyful peak with sweeps of violin and brass, as well, telling of a return to a sense of solemn remembrance and mystical, magical, dreamy landscapes. As Conrad Telley Ractor, closer and closer, approached the construction grade stereo radio the music made its final build to a strong, passionate sound that evoked light streaming through clouds to illuminate the final stage of a grand event. Low drums punctuated the return of the prominent spirit of the protagonist figure.

As the abstract builder reached the radio the music returned to a solemn, holy amen of sorts that evoked the image of the protagonist having come through a struggle, worn, but strong. With the music coming to a close, bringing the builder to a contemplative pause before the radio all the while, he turned off the stereo radio and picked it up to pack it up into the truck. As he approached the truck, before his two-person crew, he placed it in the cab. At that moment the two children who had first greeted him, and who had been the only people the crew had collectively acknowledged from the first, rode by on their bikes. They hadn't been racing and were, rather, slowing down at the curb with intent to see the builder off in a way.

"Later, mister," said Adaline, in a noble and knowing manner, waving to the builder and glancing at his crew with a smile, as well, "I think it looks really awesome." She was half sitting on her bike and half standing on the ground, propping it and herself up. The builder and his crew waved back, smiling that same midway of the road smile of those who weren't entirely acquainted with too much vocal, or body language, interaction with others.

"I do, too," said Christopher, making sure to carry his portion of the conversion, as well, "it looks really cool." The builder and his crew flashed that smile at him, too, and then got into the truck. With that off went Adaline and Christopher. They challenged each other to a race back to their house, as competitive and innocently enough, rambunctious siblings have been known to do.

VI

After Conrad Telley Ractor, the abstract builder, and his two-person crew of Mel and Charlie, the androgynous crew, had left everything seemed to settle down and actually had done so in reality, as well. Fewer and fewer spectators came around to view the house - whether they were from the newspaper, were

141

engineers, scientists, architects, new modern art students and enthusiasts, or just neighbors walking by. On its own the house amalgamated its way into the neighborhood. Floors and walls, seemingly over the period of days and few weeks, and of themselves, had taken form to fill it out. Mrs. Hartford hadn't even been one to think about it too much anymore.

"You'd think before those floors and walls were put in that birds and animals would have gotten in, somehow," Mrs. Hartford recollected, "you really would have thought they would have." It was true that no creatures of land or sky had intruded inside the creation of C.T.R. Contractors, and better yet was the question of if they would've had to find a way of dealing with the lack of floors to walk on, or if they would have adapted like the strange crew. The Hartfords had been on vacation from the day after the strange crew had left, as well as two weeks after. Upon their return they saw the house completed and had assumed that another building company picked up where the previous one left off.

The house had taken on the feeling of the neighborhood, as well as the general style, for Mrs. Hartford's mind to be troubled no more by that pesky, ever just so far from the surface of things question. The realtor, who was no stranger than the normal realtor - unlike the builder and his crew who were far stranger from any other building company the Hartfords, among others, had seen - was no more in the know of the experience everyone else in the neighborhood had throughout its building. The house was shown to three different families and the third one had decided it was a perfect fit for them. On the day they moved in it was like any other move in day for a family into a new home. Mrs. Hartford peeked through the window to observe her and her husband's new neighbors. That seemed fairly normal enough for even Mr. Hartford to glance out as well.

"It looks like we have new neighbors," said Mr. Hartford, "and they look like the perfect family unit, don't they?" Mrs. Hartford met his glance, nodded, and they returned to watching the new family emerge from their family sized car that had parked in the paved, finished driveway.

The family was a not quite middle-aged mother and father and two kids - a preteen son and daughter. They walked to the garage, after it had opened from the genie in the car. The father talked to the mother about how he was going to use the garage for a workshop, when cars weren't parked in it, and to his son about how they would make the basement their media and general rec room. The mother talked to the father about she would design the kitchen, bedrooms, and bathrooms, and to her daughter about how the attic was perfectly finished and acoustically made to be a great music room for her to practice her violin.

"Can we put in a basketball hoop," asked the son, "there's enough room." He looked up at mom and dad optimistically.

"Sure," said the father, after checking the mother's reaction to be a positive smile and nod, "I...we don't see why not." They made their way into the house to look around.

"And with all that space up their for you to play all day and night you'll be able to learn the Requiem," the mother smiled at the daughter, who gave her shrug that said we'll see, "that is my favorite piece by Berlioz." With that the father, mother, son, and daughter explored their house to discuss further plans for each room.

A few towns over two children on bikes were approaching an undeveloped plot of land, the only one not with a house built on it and a family having been established at its residence. It, too, was a street that was, for the most part, developed with residents having established their permanence, for a long while as far as we're concerned. Upon its lawn, in the middle of the open grass, was a for sale sign that had been removed in place of a sold sign. Up the road came a truck, with the name C.T.R. Contractors painted across both its sides and doors, headed toward this house. As there was no complete driveway to tell of yet the truck parked on the curb directly in front of the house. Out stepped a man, who was said to resemble a living, breathing, in the flesh Picasso painting in human form, and headed across the undeveloped driveway to fetch and remove the sign.

Coming upon the sign, the two kids having seen the man emerge from the truck, they got a closer glimpse passing by the house, observed him and the property's intrigue. It was a boy and a girl. The boy and girl stopped their bikes at the curb and half sat on their seats and half stood up on the edge of the road.

"Hello, mister," said the girl, with a cheerful, confident undertone, for a little kid, "hi!" She waved at the contractor who turned to where he was addressed from and waved back, smiling not to big, but not small - rather like he was not used to talking much to people. Her brother looked on, good-natured, and also waved.

Jack Wick Pickering, The Ventriloquist
(3/11/2015)

I

Sometimes we find places and people that we are content with for being just fun
and kindly enough, and not only do we play along with the campy, seedy side of
the game that we know is part and parcel of the act and cost of the whole thing,
but we enjoy it all the more because of that element. There are many people of
such variety that fill that gap of varied, good old fashion family fun, and
macabre - under the surface - by creating such that scene at the carnival. Some
would say no place captures such a strange combination of inviting and
shadowy characteristics than the carnival. In this case it was exactly this that
made the entire scene, collectively, a landscape worth revisiting over and over
again.

Daniel Childress was an early thirty something who had been between hands
on, manufacturing, factory, and manual labor jobs - in between his attempts at
self starting a do it yourself writing career, of sorts - that he had loved because
of their nature. He liked the physicality of the work and the cathartic feeling it
gave him, the variety of people from the nice and kindly, the cool and collected,
the temperamental, the meticulous and micromanaging types, the kind that just
did the job and didn't think about it that deeply, the jokers, the serious ones, the
rule followers, those that flew by the seat of their pants, the well-spoken and
mannered, and the deliciously foul mouthed type. This created for the most
intriguing, interesting, and collectively best of all worlds functioning,
dysfunctional family environment he was most comfortable in. For this reason
he felt no feelings of wariness, concern, and sensed no innate affections of
creepiness or undertones of - even infinitesimal amounts of - underlying evil
intent at the carnival.

He had lived in the same town, Calloway Falls, for many years now and had no
intention of moving or moving on. He lived a short distance from the brief
stretch of more antique and antiquated shops along the river that ran through
the town proper, the boarded walkways along the river, the ornate water
fountain, and the clock tower that constituted its downtown area. He lived
walking distance from another part of town that offered another strip of
shopping, a movie theatre, and other modern amenities, balanced by the

presence of the church - one of a quite a few scattered about the town - across the way, as well. It was a small, middle class town that seemed to have laissez-faire attitude - even from the police department's standpoint. It was a little longer jog to the open fields that gave credence to the carnival every summer and fall.

He was familiar with the carnival for many years, now. Daniel had come to enjoy the simply amenities and guilty pleasures it offered. The food, it was like a campground version of soul food that was terrible for you health wise, but you had to allow yourself to indulge in the spirit of things. The games, sure you were set up to lose a few of them, but you played anyway because of the fun and the challenge of beating their system. The campy environment, it was the perfect blend of nefarious seediness and manic fun, and created many playground like memories for him, even into adulthood. The ferris wheel, it was the one ride that could unite the entire world upon one principle, at least for a single moment in time, even better than Coca Cola claimed its worldwide appeal could ever imagine to. And the merry go round, who didn't like a ride around the most childhood memory and adulthood memory inducing contraption every built - inciting both your greatest fear, nightmares, joys, and happiness, all at the same time?

As a kid he couldn't remember how many times he'd rode that merry go round and nearly, in an innocent and child like way, practically fought off other kids and maneuvered himself to lay claim to the tiger. He occasioned the smaller kiddie roller coaster, as a second favorite ride, once very young. Once he'd gotten over a childish fear of heights he enjoyed the ferris wheel's expansive view of the entire park and it was good for his teenage dating purposes, too. The bumper cars were great for being a snarky, wise guy, and playfully sticking it to his friends who beat him in every other game and sport they'd played together. The games were always a good distraction where everyone, who was toeing the line of becoming a little too old to enjoy the thrill of winning a less than amazing, but still pretty cool, stuffed animal for the fruits of their overcoming the game's odds, all played.

As an adult he came to enjoy the blend of personalities, the campiness of the acts, and the fact it was a great release from the real, outside world. It was like once you stepped passed the gates - having handed over a relatively small amount of money for the freedom to be a kid, if not just on the inside, again -

the outside world disappeared and you seemed to step into a different world or through the veil into another one. He had come to enjoy the juxtaposition of the thrill of beating the odds at the games, the peace of the contemplative ferris wheel's view, the small rush of the adult roller coaster, and the ridiculousness of the fortune teller's trick and trade game. Even the sideshow acts and the three ring circus were remembered for being pretty well arranged, for being small time versions, shadows of the philosophical larger versions - available at the big time carnivals - that us small town dwellers could have more readily available access to.

It was all like a more humble and less hoity-toity version of letting loose, in the style of F. Scott Fitzgerald's 1920's themed novels. There random characters, whose personalities took on every shape and variety and combination across the human spectrum, as well, made for an interesting human experience, too. The workers there were almost envied - even as on and off, cutthroat, and outside the normal bounds of what was considered a standard career - for being able to do, and excel in some cases, what they did for a their living. They were the, on the surface, underachievers who seemed to enjoy life more and have more freedom to pursue their passions - for better or worse - than others who settled for more conventional ways of life. They were in a class of workers in intriguing fields along with the writers, painters, adventurers, and philosophers of days gone past.

Daniel was making his way from the parking lot toward those magical, fabled gates where - upon receiving your ticket - you were granted access to worlds beyond where any standard key could take you. This ticket offered you the chance to not only unlock a door and settle in, while you could put your shoes here and coat there, but rather to unlock and unfilter your imagination in a way that required shoes, jackets, and anything else you could bring with you, comfortably, and that wouldn't weigh you down. He smiled on the inside as his face began to take on that same form, but the early thirty something version of that. He had heard they had brought in a new, outside act this year that it was promised to be something of an interesting venture, if not merely a very unique sideshow. He had some time off work for a while so he felt he'd make the best of it and go the carnival.

II

Having made his way past the gate Daniel felt the shift in his mind and body and he was in carnival goer mode. He had walked around most of the grounds and had taken a ride on the ferris wheel, and enjoyed the view across the entire park. On the merry go round he found that his coveted spot on the tiger was open and he didn't look out place, among the other adults on the ride with their kids, with their significant others, or by themselves. He played a few games - losing some, but winning more, as he was fairly experienced in their game beyond the one on the surface - and any stuffed animal prizes or anything else he won he was glad to offer to kids, after having first addressed their parents of his honest and sincere, kindly intentions, for them to have the pick of the litter. He partook of some of the carnie food - an elephant ear and a hotdog - as well, and made mental notes of the other sideshows to stop in at later on.

He passed by the kiddie roller coaster and noticed that the same carnie operator was there from the last three previous years. She was one of the random summer employees who went to college, otherwise, and was doing this as a temporary thing on the side. She now must have been close to earning her degree, this being her fourth summer here. Passing the miniature roller coast Daniel saw, overhead, the three-ring circus, in full swing of an afternoon show. The ringmaster, Trapper Van Dean, was outgoing, friendly, energetic, and had a flair for the dramatic - being both joyful and deliciously playful, but innocently hinting at the overdramatized danger in the circus act to play it up and make a good humored joke at its small-townness. He passed by the fortune teller, tarot card reader, palm reader, and astrologer tent - with its flaps open - and observed the same familiar, still youthful, but older tenant carnie operating the joint since he was kid - Madam Trappe. He always wondered if it was a reference to the ringmaster's name, if they were cousins, or whatever it meant. She was the intuitive, cold reading, but kindly, contemplative personality that tamed the ringmaster's over the top shtick.

Walking around the grounds, not having quite made it to the other polar side of the carnival, he was curious about the new act. Per the advertisement placards all around the grounds it was a ventriloquist act put on by Jack Wick Pickering and Zippo, his dummy. Interested, Daniel approached the tent and saw that the next show was in fifteen minutes, and still had a seat in the middle, back of the cluster of folding chairs that filled the large tent before the stage. He bought a ticket, entered the tent, took up a chair in his favorite general area of a seating arrangement, and soon enough the chairs were all full and the tent closed.

A cheap sounding, but adequate, public address system played fantastical, mystical music as Jack Wick Pickering stepped onto the stage from behind the curtain and introduced himself. He fashioned himself to appear in style of a Bella Lugosi-esque and Munter's era magician, with a Vincent Price flair. He spoke in a very haunting, but campy, charismatic, and yet deftly businessman getting down to work tone. He pulled out a dummy that looked like Edgar Bergen's Charlie McCarthy variety sidekick. They sat down on the chair on the stage and the show began as the music faded out into a less mystic, campier sounding instrumental track played on a constant loop.

"Welcome everyone, my name is Jack Wick Pickering," he looked out at the audience as he alluded to his dummy, who was doing the same, "and this is Zippo. Say hello, Zippo." *Here comes the line*, thought Daniel, who still found himself smiling in anticipation of it.

"Hello, Zippo," Zippo parroted, to an ice breaking crowd chuckle, "what, what it something I said?" The dummy looked around in a cheery way only a dummy can.

"Well folks, it's been a very interesting trip here. I saw many beautiful sights on the train ride here and had a chance to see your quaint, charming downtown," Pickering looked Zippo, who met his look, "I saw the lovely water fountain and walked along the river built into the cliff side. I also had the chance to meet a few locals." The dummy looked off to the side and back, with a sigh, and back to Pickering.

"Yeah, you had a nice trip here." Zippo responded with a sigh.

"Well, didn't you as well?" asked the ventriloquist in response.

"My ride was dark, bumpy, the view was terrible, and I could barely hear anybody else talking." The dummy lamented.

"Well that's terrible." Pickering sympathized.

"Yeah," Zippo responded, looking at him with a wry grin on his wooden face, "well, you're the one who shipped me here FedEx." He looked around at audience with an open mouthed I just made a funny look. The crowd laughed at this.

"Well, I think you made the trip and look very well, for having travelled so roughly." The ventriloquist assured him.

"Why thank you," Zippo eyed him, "I have a secret for maintaining my good looks." *Here it comes*, thought Daniel, smiling.

"What's that, Zippo?" The ventriloquist set up the punch line.

"A good coat of wood varnish every few months." The dummy looked around at the audience in another sweep, with that goofy, open mouthed look. The crowd laughed at this.

"Did I ever tell you about my cousin, who lived in a very old, gothic forest?" The dummy asked the ventriloquist about his cousin.

"No, tell me about him." Pickering said, with an interested look on his face, engaging the audience in a *this could be interesting* look and back to Zippo.

"Well, he scared easily and got scared of being out in the woods," the dummy carried on, "scared of shadows, noises, everything." Zippo explained his cousin's phobia.

"Well, that's not so strange," the ventriloquist sympathized, "people can be scared of strange things like that." The ventriloquist made his good point and gaged the audience's acceptance of it, and went back to Zippo.

"Yeah, but my cousin once got so scared he was petrified." Zippo gave the crowd the same open mouthed look and swept across their responding faces. They laughed at the reference to his cousin being a tree, as did Daniel.

"I did see an old friend, as we were walking around before, today." Zippo said, back to Pickering.

"That's great," confirmed the ventriloquist, cheerily, "that really is." He looked around at the audience, nodding, happy for his dummy.

"Good for me, but not much for him," Zippo said, as Pickering made a confused face and uttered a questioning vocalization, "he's a wooden bench, now." Zippo did his trademark facial response sweeping over the audience, as they laughed, and back to Pickering. *They're kind of good, actually,* thought Daniel, laughing.

The act carried on so, getting a good response from the audience and Daniel. They were pretty good. The dummy was animated and energetic. The ventriloquist addressed him as a real person as much as he could to play up the humor element and their buddy-buddy nature. Zippo was a good juxtaposed personality of dry wit and humor to Pickering's sympathetic, straight man, setting up the jokes. It was a good show, all things told.

"Well, let's give you a break, now." Pickering said as he intentioned to move the dummy, who looked at him almost shocked."

"What? You're not breaking me," Zippo comically protested, "I am made of balsa wood, after all." The crowd chuckled.

"No, that's not what I meant," sympathized the ventriloquist, "I mean that I'll give you a rest, a break, since you've worked hard and earned it." Zippo seemed okay with this.

"That's alright, then." Zippo confirmed. As soon as Pickering began moving to put the dummy into its box Zippo piped up, again. "No, don't put me in there! It's dark and scary! I'm claustrophobic," as Pickering smiled and shook his head in a consolatory manner, as Zippo was put away and his voice came in seemingly muffled, "at least crack the door. I can't breath in here." The crowd laughed at this banter.

"Okay," conceded the ventriloquist, "I will crack the lid." He left the lid to Zippo's carrying case cracked open.

"Whew," Zippo exclaimed, relieved, no longer muffled of voice, but slightly toned as if he was in a small, hollow space, "much better." The laugher died down as this part of the act came to a close

Daniel and the crowd thought that the act was very good. When it was over, after a few more gags, following the brief intermission of Zippo's portion of the show, was a talking portion by Pickering, reminiscent of Edgar Bergen and Charlie McCarthy. When the show was over, as people began to head off to other sideshows, the ventriloquist announced the time of his next act for the day. Daniel planned on coming back to see this, again, as he had time this week and this had amused him beyond what he thought it would.

That night Daniel dreamt. In the dream, that was preceded with an almost nightmarish sequence - which was strange, because he hadn't seemed to experience anything throughout the day to induce such a response, now - of a foggy, misty dissolve, and a watery, wishy-washy filter making all the sounds around him come in garbled and unsettling. In the dream, or nightmare, he had gone to the ferris wheel, merry go round, and other carnival attractions, and ended up at the ventriloquist tent. As he entered the tent, took his seat, he heard a faint voice that seemed to come from all around him at the same time, and it said "avoid the ventriloquist" in a tone that implied quiet, inconspicuous concern. Waking up, not quite sharply, he shrugged it off and went back to bed.

III

The next day Daniel returned to the carnival to catch another show by Jack Wick Pickering and Zippo. Upon entering the gates of the carnival grounds that same magical feeling came alive and he became a carnival goer sharing the collective feeling with everyone else. He went straight to the ventriloquist tent, bought his ticket, took his seat, and as he sat down thought he had felt another, more subtle, additional feeling upon having crossed the threshold into this tent. He shrugged it off as anticipation to see how this show would carry on.

Soon enough the tent flaps closed, the mystical music played through a workingman's quality public address system, the entrance of both ventriloquist and dummy was replicated, and the show began as the music faded back into the campy background music. Daniel saw many other similar faces in the crowd, as did the ventriloquist who addressed each face with something underneath the eyes, beneath the surface. *It's just the businessman side in him taking a mental roll call and crunching numbers in his head*, thought Daniel, *maybe*. As the dummy did his eyeball sweep of the crowd, seemingly observing the same thing, the show began.

"Welcome everyone to the show, and welcome everyone returning from yesterday's show," the ventriloquist began, "I am Jack Wick Pickering and this is Zippo, for those who don't already know." With that he addressed his dummy. "Speaking of yesterday's shows, which went over very well, I'd like to have a word with you." He seemed positively upbeat enough in this statement.

"That's fine with me, " the dummy met the ventriloquist's gaze, pleasantly enough, "because I can't really have one without you, can I?" Daniel smiled thinking *this shtick, again*, enjoying it deep down. The ice breaking chuckle spread across the audience.

"So far, I would say my favorite part of this carnival, outside of my show, is the ferris wheel. I've enjoyed it since I was a kid," Pickering reminisced, "I've made sure to go on a few rides between shows. What have you been doing with your time off, between shows, Zippo?" Zippo looked at Pickering with that permanently fixed goofy, cheery face.

"I've been taking good naps and reading." Zippo confirmed his off duty hobbies affirmatively.

"Really," said the ventriloquist in an interested tone, "and what do you prefer to read?" The ventriloquist set up the punch line in his trademark sympathetic, straight man style. *Here it comes*, thought a smiling Daniel.

"Oh, nothing too interesting," Zippo confirmed, "mostly just the label on the inside of my box." Zippo did his sweep of the audience's response with that open mouthed, goofy look on his face. As the collective audience laughter died down the dummy and ventriloquist addressed each other.

"So, we've been travelling quite a bit, lately," confirmed Pickering, "all across the U.S. We've been out west, on the east coast, and finally made it back to the Midwest." He did a sweep of the audience to gage their responses to their locale being mentioned and went back to addressing his dummy.

"I'm just glad we're not up north in the cold, anymore," affirmed Zippo, with no compunction about it.

"Why's that, Zippo," sympathized Pickering, "we spent some nice time around the fireplace in quite a few charming bed and breakfast communal rooms up north." Zippo's face didn't lose its straightforward impression.

"I know," affirmed Zippo, again, "I don't need anyone else getting the bright idea to use me as kindling." Laughter came as soon as that same goofy look and sweep of the audience's reaction. After the laughter subsided a bit the ventriloquist and dummy met each other's glances to continue their conversation.

"On one of my people watching walks I strolled by the roller coaster photo gallery where they show everyone's faces at the top of the first big hill," the ventriloquist story told, "and they all looked like they were having fun. I thought I'd give it another ride to catch my picture." The ventriloquist gaged the audience's faces, preparing for the punch line they knew was coming and went back to the dummy.

"Sounds like fun, for sure," said Zippo, sighing, "but I'm too short to get on roller coasters." The ventriloquist sympathetically considered this and Zippo continued. *Here it comes*, thought Daniel, grinning. "And the last time my picture was taken was when your carry on was checked at the last airport." Again, that goofy look and audience sweep was met with a laugh from the collective audience.

"I've got to say, Zippo, you've improved your part of our act a lot, lately," the ventriloquist commended a proudly grinning Zippo, "you've been practicing a lot lately, and it shows." Zippo beamed at Pickering.

"Well, what can I say," Zippo responded, "when your only alternative line of work is being firewood I guess it motivates you to be really good at your first choice." As the crowd laughed Zippo did his trademark move and then the two onstage returned to addressing one another.

"You know what I like about this line of work, Zippo?" Pickering asked his dummy, who looked at him, awaiting the answer.

"Uh-uh," Zippo shook his head, "what part?" Zippo considered what the answer could be.

"Well, I get to be creative and think outside of the box," confirmed the ventriloquist, "that's what I like about it." Zippo nodded at this.

"That's good for you, but I've always been more a philosopher type and thinker," Zippo responded, as his ventriloquist considered this with a *hm* vocalization, "yeah, it's kind of hard to think outside of the box when you spend most of your time in one." Laughter ran across the audience in a wave as the dummy did his post joke assessment of the audience, again.

"So," the ventriloquist carried on with Zippo, his attention returned to him, "you like philosophy? You must know all about the idea of the forest for the trees, then?" Zippo affirmatively nodded at this. Daniel grinned, seeing a response coming.

"I'd better. Seeing how I used to be one." The laughter still left over, not quite faded away from the first part of the joke, picked up again, and was followed by the same assessment of the crowd from the dummy.

"Well, we've had some great audiences here," Pickering inquired of his dummy, "haven't we, Zippo?" The dummy seemed to agree.

"Yes we have," Zippo said, apparently getting an idea, "and I have an idea. Why don't we invite one of them up onstage with us?" Seeing his ventriloquist consider this and positively nod Zippo scanned the audience, landing his gaze upon Daniel, somehow, throughout the entire crowd.

"That's a splendid idea," the ventriloquist confirmed, "and I see you've found someone you'd like to invite up, already." Pickering turned his attention to the Daniel, as well, which in turn made - for Daniel's introspective, privacy loving, passive nature was too much - more than enough heads in the audience do so. "How about you, sir," the ventriloquist picked up, "how would you like to?"

"No, no, but thank you," Daniel tried to avoid all the gazes in his direction, unsuccessfully, and conspicuously showing his shyness at being picked without any warning, "I'm enjoying the show from here." He said so in friendly manner.

"Are you sure, sir," the ventriloquist qualified his offer, "we'd love to have you as a guest." Upon seeing Daniel politely put up his hands and shake his head, with a genuinely appreciative - for the thought, and recognition, still - smile. Seeing this Pickering conceded, nodded, and shrugged as if to say, *so be it*. With this the audience, some who actually sighed a little, as if let down in a funny, but cordial way, returned attention to the act onstage.

"What do you mean, pal," Zippo badgered comically, looking at Pickering, "what's with that guy?" He said this to a kindly, sympathetic, shrugging ventriloquist.

"It's alright, Zippo," Pickering said, "it's alright. Not everyone likes to be put on the spot, in the moment, like that." Zippo looked back and forth Daniel and his ventriloquist, and then back to his ventriloquist.

"Huh," Zippo said, innocently and comically enough, "I personally think that guy needs to try something new and branch out a bit." With a collective laugh from the audience, including Daniel, the dummy assessed his audience with that same goofy face. As laugher died down the two onstage addressed each other, again.

"Well, I've had a lot of fun in this town with our audiences," Zippo confirmed, "but you know what I don't like?" Zippo said this with a wavering upon funny tone that meant a punch line was being set up.

"What's that, Zippo?" asked his ventriloquist. He put on a sympathetic face of interest.

"When people try to act like they're smarter than everyone else, especially me," the dummy confirmed, "I made a joke one time and a wise guy told me to make like a tree and leaf. I told him I already did that, before I got into show biz." With the laughter that followed the dummy assessed the audience, again, with his permanently fixed goofy expression.

With that joke having been concluded, however, the dummy seemed to turn its head and, again, look directly at Daniel, as if to try to project the thought, *you're not trying to act like you're smart than me, are you, you being coy and not participating and all?* This left Daniel feeling a bit strange, weirdly uncomfortable, and off put, having just been happily enjoying a seemingly innocent ventriloquist show. The rest of the show Daniel couldn't quite shake that sense of being studied by the dummy, or by the ventriloquist in a way vicariously through the dummy.

After getting home that night, again, Daniel was thinking about what transpired at the ventriloquist show. He wasn't angry or embarrassed by any means, since it was a carnival show and it took a wise guy - as Zippo had termed it - to be able to go up on stage and do that kind of show, but it left him thinking. It was all part of the show, but then again, it seemed like it was not part of the routine, but an addition on the fly by something with an ulterior motive, somehow. He didn't think too hard about it, but it was nonetheless quite an interesting conundrum to consider.

Daniel's sleep that night seemed to answer to his having not let it go. After the dream started out with that foggy atmosphere, that didn't get much clearer once he passed into the ventriloquist tent and the wishy-washy audio filter that garbled all distinct words, he was in his seat in the ventriloquist's tent. He was being stared at by all the members of the audience, as well as the two onstage, but none of the stares were inconspicuous, passing, sympathetic, or down the middle. They were all intent on glaring at him so hard they could have burned a hole through him and seen through it. The dummy, especially, but no less accompanied by the ventriloquist in the same spirit of things, was the most disturbing. The only phrase, though garbled like the rest, that he understood - simply from having heard it before and recognizing its intricacies and intonations - were the words "avoid the ventriloquist". It came now, however, in tones a little more urgent than passing concern, and in fact seemed a little more of a warning one would give, as if to say *you don't want to go down this path anymore, should just leave it be, and move on.*

At this point he woke up, shaken this time from uneasy and dreamless, rather nightmare filled, sleep. Tomorrow he would go back to the carnival and ask about this ventriloquist and he might even stop back in to see the show again, if for no other reason than to confirm or deny his mind's conclusions of what had happened. He needed to confirm a few things, or even better yet deny a few or more others, and he would then set his mind at rest, hopefully. He had always enjoyed the carnival, in all its combined personality, collectively and he'd even though the seedy, slightly nefarious side was merely created to give teenagers a reason, on the surface, to remain superficially brooding for their friends, and to merely maintain the appearance of such for their parents. Daniel decided to check it out again and see what it was all about or if it was simply all in his head.

IV

Returning to the carnival the next day Daniel didn't head directly to the ventriloquist tent. Instead he directed his way to the carnies, that he could get ahold of in person, and pick their minds for a background of some sort on Jack Wick Pickering and his dummy, Zippo. The first performance had been perfectly innocently, amusing, and funny, but the second one, even though it had started out the same, had ended on a much different note. His dream the first night after the show was a fluke of an overactive imagination having been plunged back into a potentially volatile setting for active imaginations - it had to be - but the second night, after the show, had stepped over the line into a nightmare. Whatever was happening had an explanation, as in any universe things that brought on these sorts of feelings and nighttime dreams and nightmares did.

First, Daniel approached and spoke with the ferris wheel operator. He wasn't wearing a nametag and Daniel didn't know him, so he inferred that he wouldn't even address that issue, and rather just get to the point of his case. This worked out well, however, because this man wasn't of a nature to talk much. His attitude was more down the middle of the road and he was of a kindly nature, however unsociable. Daniel had the same list of questions for everyone regarding Jack Wick Pickering's background, where they heard of him from, how he landed a spot - albeit for a short few weeks - at this carnival, if they'd heard about anything strange that found itself to be associated with the man and his dummy act, as well as anything else that seemed relevant based on what he found out.

During the conversation with the ferris wheel operator - the information he kindly, patiently enough wheedled out - of the man was that Jack Wick Pickering and his all too realistic in its, for lack of a better word, intuition was rumored to have been run out of other carnivals. Strange supernatural phenomena seemed to happen to and follow the man, the dummy, and the act around its travels across the country. Some carnivals welcomed the prestige of the macabre nature behind all of it and the intrigue, as well as the types it could bring to the carnival in droves, and other carnival companies that were more family centered either turned him down or kicked him out when they'd heard the same or when it got too strange. Even the more macabre loving travelling companies let him go on his way in a less then voluntary way when their workers or customers began to start reporting more and more potentially dangerous phenomena that could harm people or scare off more conservative would be customers. Exactly what the phenomena was seemed to be people hearing voices, feeling that they were almost hypnotized by the act, strange thoughts and dreams, and seeing visions that were never clarified by any media outlets or story passers-down.

Second, he spoke with Madame Trappe, the fortuneteller, astrologer, palm reader, and tarot card reader. She was quite mystic in her speech and aura. As per her own act she was said to know the ruse, but not to play it too over the top to be dangerous, but was known to push the limits when she read a personality that wanted to be shocked. She said that Pickering had taken her act and her person way too seriously for her liking. Pickering was rumored to have been beyond an amateur - and more of a journeyman - in his personal study of the dark arts, occult magic, and the more shadowy side of mysticism. She mentioned things out of H.P. Lovecraft and darker Edgar Allen Poe stories as a reference that she said merely peaked into the cracked doorway that was his world and depth of study.

Madame Trappe was very nice, cautious when speaking of darker things - crossing herself at intervals during the conversation when certain name of figures, acts, rituals, or references were made - but was very forthcoming in what she had heard. She said he made her feel ill at ease and very uncomfortable. Ms. Trappe compared him to a Vincent Price knock off that read too much Lovecraft and only the darker, and darkest, selections of Poe. She was convinced, based on a very eerie conversation with him, that he had in fact studied up on the more shadowy topics, but didn't believe that he - or anyone, for that matter - could actually pull of such tricks that defied God. It turned out that the resident, so called voodoo lady, was a Catholic who completely embraced the camp of her role and simply wanted to give people the fun they sought out, and very simply nothing more dangerous than that.

Third, he spoke with the bumper car operator, whose name he, also, was not in the know of. This conversation was rushed, given the nature of the slam, bang, and close call welcoming bumper car environment that gave such a simply, relatively short ride its charm and sway over even the most cautious - outside the carnival - of people. He was grumpy on the surface, which disheartened Daniel's hopes in getting any decent information about Pickering, but found he was almost charming overall for his nature. Though he didn't talk much, outside of the safety spiel for entering, during, and exiting the ride, he did hear similar things said about Pickering - that Ms. Trappe and the ferris wheel operator had confirmed - from more than a few sources whose distance and frequency apart said the same story was being told by many people.

Beyond this the bumper car operator said Pickering was aloof, to himself, mysterious, doesn't talk much outside of his tent, or act. Apparently the bumper car operator was the same, minus having an apparently controversial, in its aftereffect and under the surface, view of the ventriloquist act. He referred Daniel to get more and better information from nosier people or other carnies. Daniel took this information down, in the form of a note to self, and followed up on the leads he was given.

Fourth, he spoke with Charlee Stanton - it turned out that was her name, after all these years of knowing her by her role and personality, but not a name - who operated the small, kiddie roller coaster. She was friendly and outgoing, which was why she was placed in charge of the kiddie roller coaster and its kiddies, as well as smart from her psychology degree pursuance outside of this summer temp job. She confirmed that she'd heard what the others Daniel had spoken to before in bits and pieces, minus a few of the disturbing details, and had put together most of it herself. She had come to the conclusion - without needing her college degree in reading people's minds to do so - that Pickering, and especially his dummy, freaked her out in her wording. Needing to get back to her work, tending to naturally hyperactive children, and being around large, moving metal shells much heavier than the kids themselves, she sent him off.

Fifth, he spoke to the fireworks show operator. Not knowing his name and his not wearing a uniform or nametag, either, didn't assist Daniel. It didn't help, even further that the man was not wont to talk much at all. He simply said he kept out of other's business and therefore knew nothing about the man. He showed up to work in the field he loved, which happened to be, as he put it, entertainment explosives. If Daniel had been set upon a similarly driven information hunt for anything on this man he would've found that all the other seasoned carnies would have all been amazed he had culled this many words from the nice, but practically mute - by choice - fireworks show operator.

Sixth, Daniel spoke to the Trapper Van Dean, the three-ring master extraordinaire who had taken over for the original ringmaster, whom Daniel had been familiar with as a child. Trapper Van Dean was just as his persona had suggested he would be. He was outgoing, friendly, and had apparently perfected a flair for the dramatic - both the joyful and playful, but sometimes, only partial, hints at the innocently sinister or dangerous tricks played out within his three rings of commandeered ground. He displayed this friendly nature as he addressed children, men, and women as they passed by - in small snippets of miniature conversation - as he spoke with Daniel.

Trapper Van Dean had confirmed to having heard, and actually believing himself, what everyone else attested to having heard, with the others believing in different degrees and depths for all different reasons. This conversation wasn't long, but it was fruitful. Though Dean was off quickly to prepare for another three-ring show set to start in thirty minutes Daniel felt he'd affirmed the testimony of the others and that lead meant there was some credence to the reasons Daniel was being made to feel like he was post ventriloquist show. Van Dean had also saved Daniel time by assuring him he'd be wasting his time questioning the newer summer employees, only signed on for this summer, as they hadn't had the time to really get to know the situation and were rather - in their being so young and stunted in their perception of the world around them, still - clueless to all of it, somehow.

Daniel felt he'd gathered enough information to process as per putting together a background on the ventriloquist - and possible hypnotist and occultist - named Jack Wick Pickering. By association he felt that he knew the nature of the dummy, as well. Armed with this knowledge he felt the need to do a little more reporting, even if it was risky in what his mind was suggesting, after all of this just today, but he decided to check out the scene in the veritable lion's den that - even though he was the only one in crowds that came and went and apparently figured out - was such a dangerous scene. He needed to fill in a few blanks for himself. Heading toward the ventriloquist he prepared his mind, body, and spirit for anything.

V

Arriving at the ventriloquist tent, with its once inviting, but now threatening and tempting, flaps open Daniel checked the show times and purchased a ticket for the next one to start in a few minutes. He was in the process of coming to passing the threshold of the flaps as a man was beginning to close them, as if that could really hold in what was supposedly claimed to have been present within their confines, but he did so nonetheless. Receiving a polite scowl from the flap attendant, Daniel gave a similar, in spirit, response and took a seat in the middle back. The music had begun to play, the ventriloquist was beginning to take his place on the stage, and noticed Daniel's entrance. He gave a slightly perturbed - on the surface - facial flicker in reference to his being so late to settle into a seat, and gave an even more sinister smile on the inside.

The show began with the introductions Daniel knew well and he was now the only one in the audience not wearing a happy smile in anticipation of the act that was known to be funny and was only getting more and more attention and credence. Daniel was the wet blanket in the tent, he knew it, and upon becoming aware of his appearance to others around him - in odd glances at him, given the disparate difference between their outlook and his - Daniel amended this look to fit in better. It worked apparently, as no one else showed any sense of being put off by his difference of happiness and anticipation of the show. *On with the show,* thought Daniel.

"Now, now, Zippo, that's not what I meant to say," the ventriloquist had said to qualify a previous line in his opening joke, "you're putting words into my mouth, I fear." Pickering put a sympathetic look on his face.

"Well that's a first for this guy," the dummy completed the punch line and assessed the crowd with his open mouthed, goofy look, and then seeming to stop upon seeing Daniel, "if only someone would put interesting words into your mouth maybe you'd have more friends." And with that the dummy kept mugging for the audience. *What,* Daniel snapped even more into reality than he'd been already, *what was that? Did anybody else see or hear that?* Looking around the crowd reaction said they had not even heard it, as they were still laughing, as if nothing out of the ordinary had taken place.

"I thought I might spice up the act a bit," Zippo addressed Pickering, having returned his attention to him, "I thought I might try to write a joke." Pickering seemed to take this acceptingly, and nodded his approval.

"Well, that sounds like fun," Pickering approved, "it doesn't sound like a bad idea, at all." The next line opening was passed to Zippo to complete the punch line, a newer, more cynically approaching the act Daniel calculated.

"Yeah, I thought I'd try something new and do like my cousin, who's a tree," Zippo affirmed, "and maybe branch out a little." As the laughter whipped up the dummy took his post joke pose and assessed the crowd. He stopped, again, at Daniel, however. "Eventually maybe you can try to trunk-ate your own hack meat writing, too." Noticing that no one else acted as if the dummy had added a nasty wisecrack of a caveat to the end of the joke - albeit one only Daniel would understand - Daniel only stared forward. Back to his ventriloquist went the dummy's attention.

"I'd like to tell you a joke, now," Zippo said lightly and boldly to his handler. His handler approved in a nod.

"Alright, I'd like to hear one, then." With that Pickering seemed to be waiting with great interest at the joke his new writing partner would come up with.

"Well I would, but you keep putting words in my mouth," Zippo wisecracked, "man, it's like you think I'm some sort of dummy or something." With the laughter of the crowd Zippo mugged for the audience and then gave Daniel a less friendly, somehow - even though his face was permanently mugging - look as he continued their own personal aside. "Are youuuuuuuuuuuuu?" Zippo finished mugging and returned to Pickering. Daniel played it cool and watched in wonder, on the inside, as the rest of the audience seemed to not even be picking up on any of their personal asides.

"You know what I don't like," Zippo asked an interested Pickering, "other what I told you about yesterday?" Pickering was sympathetically attentive and interested in the answer to this.

"No," the ventriloquist conceded, "I don't. What?" He awaited the answer, setting up Zippo, again, as the straight man in the act.

"When people try to tell me what to do," Zippo wisecracked, again, "because, even though I'm made of wood and wires, no one pulls my strings, baby." Mugging for the audience, otherwise clueless to his other nature not so obviously presented to them, they laughed as Zippo tended to Daniel, again. "And who pulls yours, Danny boy?" Zippo returned his attention to Pickering.

After a few more jokes, with custom made and specialized caveats for Daniel, and Daniel alone, intermission was announced as Pickering did his mid show monologue. Daniel listened politely and bided his time to figure out the most inconspicuous, given the circumstances, opportunity to leave. He waited until Pickering announced he would bring Zippo back, as the crowd cheered, and Pickering turned his attention primarily to bringing out the dummy, again. He looked up deftly, however, and for the most part unnoticed - he was just that quick and secretive about it - to glare at Daniel's back, exiting the tent flaps, as Daniel didn't bother noticing the glare he received from the tent flap tenant, either.

Daniel found himself in the middle of another nightmare that night. It was the same entrance theme of foggy atmospheric conditions that never seemed to clear up, the wishy-washy filter in place, again, to garble the sounds that accompanied his entrance into the tent and taking a seat. This time the entire crowd was staring and glaring at him from the time he entered the tent to taking his seat. On stage the ventriloquist was standing at attention, wearing a scowl on his face, and the dummy in hand was wearing the same permanented facial expression with a deeper scowl underneath. The crowd was scolding him in phrases he couldn't quite make out the words of, but he heard that same, but now even more urgent and driving, call from a voice or vibration from beyond the veil into the next world, it seemed, for him to "avoid the ventriloquist".

Waking up dart upright Daniel considered his dream in a very calculated way. Something was calling to him at night, in his dreams, knowing that he was aware of the ventriloquist and his dummy's doings - even though Daniel had no idea what those doings were, in all actuality - and trying to get his attention. Daniel had come to the conclusion that he needed to somehow get more concrete evidence. He would go back, again, but this time with a camera and a pocket sized audio recording device. This would capture something and he was intent on doing so.

VI

Returning to the carnival the next day, crossing beyond the carnival ground gates, the feeling of passing over into a new, different world was punctuated with a feeling of driving, focused, intentioned anticipation to be hit with a barrage of more negative vibes from Jack Wick Pickering and Zippo. That was all right, though, because he had an audio recording device and camera with him. He would get something for sure and would figure out what it was. Maybe whatever was trying to communicate with him, what seemed to be calling out for help, would give him some clue as to how and what he could do to be of service, as well as make his own nightmares stop.

He walked, practically marching, in the most direct path to the ventriloquist tent, bought his ticket, and took his seat long before anyone else even entered the tent for that afternoon's show. He took a few pictures of the general space in the tent and put it away quickly when he heard a shuffling behind the stage curtain, as the audience started to collectively file and herd in. As the tent filled to its maximum occupancy, the tent flaps were closed, and the music cued the ventriloquist's entrance Daniel hit record on his audio recording device. The ventriloquist did the introductions, made a note to acknowledge Daniel's presence in passing, thought the receiver of the passing acknowledgment caught it, and the show began.

"Have I ever told you about where I grew up, Zippo," Pickering asked his attentive dummy, "about the house I grew up in?" Zippo responded in kind that he had not, by shaking his head, before he spoke.

"Nope," Zippo confirmed, "but do tell. I'm all ears." Zippo look sideways at the audience as an ice-breaking chuckle was made throughout, then back to his handler.

"It was a small house, but it had a big yard," Pickering seemed to be musing, "for me and brothers and sisters to play in." Zippo's body language read that he had a punch line for this set up.

"That's interesting," Zippo jumped in, in an amused tone, "because where I grew up we had a yard, too, but it was filled with lumber." Mugging for the audience as they laughed Zippo made his stop at Daniel's attention in his direction. "I bet you remember where you grew up? How long has it been since you've bothered to go back? And how's that relationship with your father coming along?" Daniel was expecting a deep rooted, harsh, and quite critical comment but this cut him deep. He felt a fluttering in his focus, but refocused. He played it cool and calm. The audience was completely oblivious of this retort, and all the others, as well.

"So, we've been at this carnival for a few days, now," the ventriloquist confirmed, "and I've enjoyed our time. How about you, Zippo?" Zippo appeared to acting as if he were considering this for a moment.

"Well, it's been fun and all," Zippo said, deep in thought, "but I don't think I can say." The ventriloquist handled this with trademark sympathy.

"Yes you can," Pickering confirmed all was okay, "please tell me." Zippo appeared to think it over and decided to say why.

"Well, I just don't like being in the same place for too long," the dummy explained, "I feel like I'll start growing roots." As the crowd laughed and Zippo mugged he returned to his favorite aside. "And maybe I'll bury you with me." Daniel had hardened himself for this, as this one, being a less then impressive - even for Zippo - cheap shot bounced right off of him.

"Remember the other day you were reading that book in the tent," Zippo returned his attention to Pickering, "in between shows, yesterday?" Pickering mimed like he was thinking and recollecting.

"Yes, I do," the ventriloquist confirmed, "I do in fact." Pickering mimed that it was a pleasant recollection.

"Well I picked up some books of my own," the dummy responded, "mostly just pulp novels." As the audience laughed the dummy mugged and returned to Daniel, while the crowd was apparently deliriously stupefied. "You know, the good old fashion kind with a murder in 'em." He finished mugging, as he finished this jab, and returned attention back to Pickering.

"And I took your advice, too," the dummy carried on, "to try to meet some new people." The ventriloquist seemed pleased at this.

"That's great," the ventriloquist beamed, "who did you meet?" Zippo took the set up and slammed it home.

"Well, I figured I should meet someone I can relate to," Zippo said as Pickering nodded, knowingly, "so I met a peg legged pirate. He could understand how hard it is to keep your limbs from rotting." Zippo mugged, the crowd laughed, and Zippo returned to his aside with Daniel while the crowd obliviously laughed on. "And how have you been doing lately in the friend department, pally?" Daniel knew, and he knew that Zippo - or Pickering - somehow knew, and let it slide off.

"I finally figured out who this Pinocchio you've been telling me all about is." Zippo said, back to addressing Pickering.

"Ah yes, the builder's wooden doll who comes to life," Pickering knowingly recalled, "and becomes his son." Zippo took the pass and carried it down the field a little more.

"Yeah, I heard about that," Zippo said, sounding less than impressed, "and I don't think it would work for me." Pickering responded with a sympathetic look.

"Why not, Zippo?" Pickering mimed like he was musing on the conundrum as he pondered all of the possible reasons.

"Well, I don't think my personality would carry over," Zippo confirmed, "my sense of humor's a little dry and my personality is a little wooden." Again, the crowd laughed, Zippo mugged, gave Daniel the same look, and carried on to no one else but themselves and Pickering. "Unfortunately it's more personality that you'll ever have. If you had half my personality you'd have more friends." He returned his attention to Pickering as Daniel stayed strong and kept the course.

"Did you know that the entertainment biz has been in my family for years," Zippo asked Pickering, "did you?" Pickering's contemplation mimed that he did not, in fact.

"No," the ventriloquist confirmed, "I did not. Who else in your family was an entertainer?" Pickering appeared interested in finding out this nugget of information.

"My father was a dummy, too," Zippo added, "in an act just like this." Zippo looked around, as if to see the faces of those expecting a one-liner right away, then back to Pickering.

"Really," Pickering said, interested to hear more, "so that's where you get it from?" Zippo had the clincher ready and loaded, and the crowd was anticipating it.

"Yeah, I'm a regular chip off the old block of wood, I guess." Zippo mugged, the crowd laughed, and Daniel's aside with him picked up. "But that doesn't make you any better than me and you'd do good to remember it." Returning to Pickering Zippo picked up the main act.

"So you have relatives in the entertainment biz?" Pickering dug for more.

"Yup," affirmed Zippo, "in the music biz, too." Zippo beamed, proudly of this, even if by mere association without actual accomplishment.

"That's great," Pickering pandered to the dummy some more, "how so?" Pickering mused inquisitively.

"Well, my cousin was made into an acoustic guitar," Zippo confirmed, "and my uncle was made into a piano." As the crowd again laughed Zippo again mugged, and Daniel and Zippo again had their exclusive aside. "And they've done more, already, than you'll ever do, you hack." Again, Zippo returned to the ventriloquist. Daniel stood his ground solidly and as intermission began he stood up, now to leave. He clicked the record button off on his audio recording device and at the tent, before stepping out of the opened flaps - courtesy of the obviously annoyed tent flap attendant - he snapped a series of quick pictures as the attendant complained about how no photography was allowed.

Daniel ignored this as he didn't even bother to watch the attendant close the tent flaps in a way that showed he was disgruntled as he could be, which made it all the sillier and more ridiculous, all said. He was off to the pharmacy and general store in one to get the pictures developed. He turned around and snapped a few more shots of the tent from the outside as the attendant huffily shut them. Going out the way he originally came into the gates of the carnival grounds Daniel still felt like he was in a different world, somehow, or at least more aware of the other world. This time it wasn't just the world of wonder the carnival seemed to spellbind carnival goers with.

VII

Daniel ended up paying extra for next day service on his pictures, requesting that they be done and ready for pick up first thing in the morning. Back at home, however, he had other material to scour over. He had half of a show's worth of audio, that was potentially nothing but a muffled recording of a distant stage act and closer up audience chatter, but also had the potential to be a muffled to clear recording of something otherworldly. Playing the recording back at his apartment he heard much more than just the muffled recordings of the ventriloquist's shtick.

Playing back his recorded case study Daniel was at first disheartened by the muffled shtick amidst occasional audience member conversations he'd picked up. Thinking it was most likely a wash, but he might as well carry on just in case, he fought his hopelessness and tiredness of hearing the act again, but was rewarded for his fighting through it. He suddenly began hearing a voice underneath what, at first pass, seemed drowned in static, but became clearer and more prominent. He couldn't make out all of the words, but the tone was one of clearly panicked urgency and nearly shouting at him, the words were intonated with such intensity.

He heard clear phrases like "help me" one minute, and the next he heard "you've got to help us" and he was beyond convinced of more things than he had planned on being convinced of that night. He then, as if his skin and ears weren't pricked up enough, already, heard that familiar phrase he had in his dreams - or nightmares, rather - but know spoken by many voices at once, saying "avoid the ventriloquist". At the end of the recordings he felt like he looked, which was pale, in shock, and ready to get those pictures first thing in the morning. He knew his dreams would be ratcheted up tonight, but to a level he wouldn't know till he was actually there.

His dream - or rather nightmare - opened with the same foggy atmosphere, but now it felt like something was behind it, just far enough away but close enough to make its presence felt. The sounds were still garbled through the wishy-washy filter, but he could make out utterances that mimicked those he'd recorded. Upon entering the tent the chairs were now knocked over, the crowd and the ventriloquist, as well as the dummy, all standing up and focused on him, as if intending to burn holes into him with their stare. They were now, suddenly, less human in appearance and more of flickering, ghostly transparencies over top of their human frames, and the ventriloquist finally looked like, on the outside, what Daniel thought he'd been like on the inside. Pickering had the look of a reptilian shroud over top of his human frame, skipping and jumping in and out of clarity.

The dummy - and this is what startled him from sleep - was now standing, however, of his own will and power. And if that wasn't frightening enough his transparent shroud, coming in and out of focus over his sinister Charlie McCarthy or Pinocchio-like frame, was that of a human, practically fleshed out. Immediately coming to, dart upright, more sober than anyone could ever imagine possible, and beyond, Daniel knew he had to do something, but what exactly it was he didn't know. He would take it one step at a time, since he'd come this far, and check out the pictures in the morning. That would dictate the next step. He had made it this far - only partially shaken, but not derailed - and would see it through. He had to approach the ventriloquist himself.

VIII

Daniel picked up his developed pictures first thing in the morning. As the first shift employee unlocked and opened the pharmacy and general store in one's doors he rushed passed toward the photo developing counter. Practically tearing the seal on the cardboard off Daniel knew something was there, simply in the way the person behind the counter stared at the cardboard package quizzically and suspectly after handing it to Daniel. Once opened he flipped through a few of the pictures, as he didn't have to go through too many to find what he was looking for, gaping in awe at the proof he had on film. He put them back into the cardboard package and headed over to the carnival.

On the way to the carnival he went over everything he saw in the pictures in his mind. There were orbs floating all around in the picture he took inside the tent once he stepped inside. Once he sat down, in the picture coordinating with that moment, the orbs appeared to all have closed in, around, and on him. There were translucent outlines that resembled lumpy, cloudy, post rubbed off chalk outlines still in tact. These figures seemed to be around the edges of the tent, as if unable to come through completely. The pictures following carried on this theme more and more intensely. The final pictures he'd taken on leaving the tent, and the one from the outside, showed wispy outlines of limbs and cloudy fog trying to escape the tent, but being unable to somehow.

He had no intention of catching an entire show, at least not the first half for sure. He would leave the ventriloquist and the dummy wondering where he was. *See if that throws off your act*, Daniel thought. He intended on giving the pictures to Trapper Van Dean after it was all over, but he felt the need to hold onto them for now. They might come in handy and he might need them. Either way, he bought his ticket for the ventriloquist show and proceeded to stand outside the tent, much to the confusion of the ticket vendor. Many times the ticket vendor mimed that Daniel could go in now and see the show, that it had started, but then gave up with a shrug after Daniel just turned his eyes to him, and back to the tent flaps.

Finally, when Daniel went in it was after intermission. Upon taking a spare seat, left open in the last row, Daniel's late entrance was acknowledged - as well as his presence outside the tent the entire first of the show was felt - by Pickering and Zippo in a single glance and a wink. The second half of the show carried on as Daniel merely ignored the looks he received from others, who had already been in attendance the entire time, at the arrival of a new person, strangely enough, this late into the show. It went on with the same tirade of jokes with personalized caveats with barbed, poisoned tips meant for Daniel, Zippo, and Pickering's own personal aside. Those were still exclusively their own moments in time. Daniel waited - as Pickering and Zippo knew he would - till the act was over and maintained his seat till the crowd dispersed out the tent flaps.

After the tent was cleared out, except for the tent flap attendant - who was just as glad to see him go as having seen him come - Daniel left and snuck back behind the main walk to where the attraction's temporary sleeping and living quarters, some tents and some trailers, were. Having misfired on a few, creeping around outside the tents to listen in incase someone was inside, if he heard nothing he entered and looked around. He found nothing that indicated the empty tents and trailers were the ventriloquists. After about a dozen more he listened and heard the ventriloquist talking. He was talking to someone, or something, who's voice sounded as if it were coming from a compartment with a door, or lid, partially shut, but partially open. He'd come this far and seen, and become a new believer in so many unexpected things - some welcomed and more unwelcomed - but still he couldn't believe this.

"That went well, Zippo," Pickering was heard to say, while he was shuffling through a drawer for something, "very well, indeed." The ventriloquist's voice was now very somber and subdued, without the stage sympathy, and all the straightforward business.

"Oh cut the Zippo, stuff, Jackie boy," the dummy, apparently formerly known as Zippo, was heard, viciously chiding Pickering, "call me by my real name, already." Pickering did as he was told.

"Alright then, Mr. Craft," Pickering fixed his phrasing, "I will. So what do we do with the guy, then? We can't keep egging him on forever. Eventually we have to deal with him or make him disappear, too, since he hasn't offed himself, yet." *Deal with me or make me disappear*, thought Daniel, *since I haven't offed myself, yet*, stepping forward silently as possible to hear better, approaching the tent doorway.

"He'll come to us. He can't help himself," Mr. Craft chided on, "we've reeled him in. You saw him today. He was biding his time and he's apparently planning some…wait a minute." Mr. Craft stopped talking when he heard the rustle of leaves Daniel had overlooked in his steps and froze, himself, when he heard it just as loud thunder, as well. "Check outside. He's here." On this command Pickering stepped outside the tent and saw Daniel standing his ground. He'd been heard and was now acknowledged. Now he would have his piece with the strange ventriloquist and his stranger dummy, which was apparently in charge.

"So now you know," Pickering said to Daniel, "so you might as well step inside and have the word you apparently want with me." Daniel followed him back inside the tent. Upon entering the tent he heard the chuckling of the dummy inside its carrying case with the lid cracked open.

"What's going on with your act," Daniel demanded to know, "I know what I've seen, I know what I've heard, and I have audio recordings and pictures, now, with…things popping up all over the place. Things from another plane of existence or world." Daniel was trying to communicate something he couldn't quite elucidate, but was already known, he realized, by Pickering and Mr. Craft. As he finished the dummy's laughing got louder.

"You ever heard of the dark arts," Mr. Craft chided on, as Pickering followed the conversation between his dummy, and master, and Daniel, "or voodoo? Let's just say you don't live as long, and as interesting I might add, a life as I have without it." Daniel was speechless as the lid to the carrying case was pushed open by a small arm and Mr. Craft stood up. It saw Daniel's eyes were wide open. "Oh come on, what did you expect? Anything less?" As the dummy stood up, it jumped onto the ground, propagating itself by its own will to stand next to Pickering.

"Hold on there, buddy," Pickering mocked sympathy and pulled a gun from his side that his stage jacket hid, "I wouldn't go anywhere if I were you." He smiled as he had caught Daniel, in a weak moment, instinctively moving as if to back up. Daniel stopped when he saw the gun. Pickering motioned toward Daniel with the gun as he nodded to Mr. Craft. "I've got you covered, in the case that he tries anything." With that Mr. Craft walked smoothly, as a wooden dummy can, towards Daniel to Daniel's horror.

"I know you've got pictures, so hand 'em over, wise guy," Mr. Craft motioned with a flick of his wrist, "unless you want to try my associate's aim with a gun at close range." The dummy stood looking up at Daniel impatiently, as Daniel reached into his jacket pocket to pull out the pictures.

"Here, here they are," Daniel said with a shaky hand dropping the cardboard package, sending pictures flying all over the ground, and Mr. Craft covering himself from the falling objects, "oh no. I didn't mean to…" He didn't have a chance to finish his sentence.

"Watch it, butterfingers, are you stupid or somethin'," Mr. Craft chided on, "let me see what you got here." Mr. Craft leaned over to pick up the picture with his wooden dummy hands, with surprisingly nimble fingers. Picking up a few more interesting ones he stood up straight and considered them. "You got some nice shots here. Not everyone captures the lost souls I've collected so well." He then threw them on the ground again and darted a glare back up at Daniel. "Pickering, get the pictures, and don't take your gun off its target, either." Mr. Craft considered Daniel cunningly.

As Mr. Craft commanded, Jack Wick Pickering moved toward the pictures on the ground.

"I have their voices, too, on my recorder," Daniel said boldly, "but you can't take that. I left that at home." Mr. Craft laughed briefly and roughly.

"I bet you do, just like every other amateur ghost hunter," Mr. Craft continued to chide, "so you know I'm no ordinary dummy, now. I might as well tell you." Pickering began to pick up the pictures on the ground with one hand, with his other hand holding the gun, as his glance darted ominously between the ground and Daniel. He held Daniel in his place.

IX

As Mr. Craft continued to monologue he hopped up on top of a chair next to his carrying case, closed the case after reaching in to pull out a gun that would have appeared miniature in Pickering's hand, but in perspective to Mr. Craft look just right and dangerous enough. He sat upon his carrying case and pointed the gun at Daniel.

"So I wake up in this body, about twenty years, and find myself on some sort of weird, ceremonial altar in the middle of a jungle," Mr. Craft story told, "there's candles lit all around me, weird lookin' Indian types - and I'm talkin' deep jungle natives - all around me bowing down, praying, doing ablutions of all sorts. I realize I've been transferred to a new body and take a look at it to see I'm in darn dummy. Then I look up and see Pickering here - he's actually quite the fan of dark lore, arts, magic, and voodoo - and he says he's raised me again to carry me on through this generation." Seeing Daniel's eyes darting around the room and settling on a bookshelf of old books with evil sounding, multisyllabic titles in Latin, he continued. "Those, oh yeah, Pickering does like to read, only his taste in books the Catholic church banned years ago and he's managed to hold onto for our sakes. You really didn't think the Illuminati and Freemasons were the only underground societies out there? Oh no, kid, they're not. And I call you kid because I'm a lot older than you'll ever know."

"Almost done, Mr. Craft," Pickering said as he was picking up the last of the pictures, distracted for a moment long enough for Daniel to instinctively react, "I've almost got them…" Pickering, as he looked back up to Mr. Craft, received a kick in the hand holding the gun and then the hand holding the pictures via the foot of Daniel. The gun skittered a few feet away and Daniel hit the deck in an attempt to avoid a gun shot from the dummy and to maybe even reach the other gun.

"No, you idiot," Mr. Craft chided Pickering, as Daniel, hitting the deck, avoided the shot that sailed over his body, flat on the ground, luckily, "darn it. Missed ya'." Mr. Craft had shot and missed, and before Pickering could get a look at Daniel he kicked him in head, scrambling for the human sized gun.

"Oh come on Pickering," chided Mr. Craft, "get him already. I can't do all the work around here." Pickering yelled out loudly in pain as he tried to get to his feet and prevent Daniel from getting the gun at the same time. Mr. Craft took another shot at Daniel and Daniel dove out of the way of Pickering's swinging arm and the gunshot. Landing next to the human sized gun he grabbed it and stood up.

"I've never shot anyone, but I know how to shoot these," Daniel spoke faux boldly, as he aimed the gun back and forth at the dummy and Pickering, who was now standing up slowly with his arms up and over his head, "stand over next the dummy." This made Mr. Craft laugh and take another shot at Daniel, who dove away from the shot.

"Get me in the box and get out of here," commanded Mr. Craft, as Pickering roughly stuffed Mr. Craft into his box, "don't be gentle, for cryin' out loud. Just get us out of here." Mr. Craft chided Pickering and Pickering moved quicker. As Daniel was struggling to get over shock of being shot at and being missed twice, to get up, and then take an overview of the scene as soon as possible as

Pickering snapped the carrying case shut, grabbed it by the handle and was off running. He pushed over a chair at Daniel on his way.

"Hey, where are you," Daniel stopped yelling as he knew they'd never stop to turn around and ask what he'd said, and then yelled out to anyone else who could help him, "help! Help! They're getting away!" As Daniel yelled he heard voices coming. First it was Trapper Van Dean, then the ferris wheel operator, and then the fireworks operator. They all seemed to speak up at once, even the ferris wheel operator and fireworks operator, but Van Dean continued for them.

"Are you okay, Daniel," Van Dean asked as he moved the chair off him and helped him to his feet, "what happened here?" He looked around and then saw the ferris wheel operator and fireworks operator kneeling down to look at the pictures on the ground. They were both in shock and awe as they flipped through each picture. Picking them up they then stood up and handed them to Trapper Van Dean.

"I have something else you might be interested in, too," Daniel said, throwing aside the gun he had in his hand, "I have voices I recorded during one of the ventriloquist acts, voices other than Pickering, Mr. Cra…Zippo, and the audience. Other peoples' voices from beyond."

Van Dean, the fireworks operator, and the ferris wheel operator were spellbound by the proof of the ventriloquist and the dummy's far less than even carnival hijinks' nefarious proceedings. As pairs of feet stamped the ground outside, and those not used to running so fast were breathing heavy, the bumper car operator, Charlee Stanton, and Madame Trappe were outside.

"What's going on," Charlee, being the only one not panting too hard to talk, asked, as the others nodded and motioned with their hands that they seconded the motion, "we heard gun shots and yelling…Daniel…Trapper…" She saw what they were looking at, as did the bumper car operator and Madame Trappe. Van Dean handed them the pictures his group of three were done with.

"Pickering and his dummy, and the rumors," Van Dean confirmed, as he looked up from his group of three's pictures to regard them seriously, "all of it was true. Daniel says he has voices on a handheld recording device, as well. Of other people than Pickering, Zippo, or the audience…other people." The newest three on the scene regarded the dead serious looks on the faces of the first three on the scene.

"They fled, Pickering and Zippo," Daniel confirmed, looking around at them all, "and the dummy's name is Mr. Craft, and he's no regular dummy. He's...he says he the raised soul of a much older occult leader...I'll tell you later, in Van Dean's office." Daniel cut it short, as he heard, finally, the footfalls of security officer shoes, the metallic clank of their guns bouncing slightly in their holsters, and the sound of police issue walkie-talkies rogering over and out and back and in. Beyond them was a small, but growing larger by the minute, group of summer temp employees - finally interested in something - and other carnival goers bold enough to step behind the main drag of tents and trailers, and into the much stranger world of carnies behind them.

"Let's go to my trailer, Daniel," Trapper Van Dean directed Daniel away from the scene as he commanded the security officers, "take care of...that, and call the cops. Tell them to see me. Everyone else get back to work. We don't need to panic anybody else. There's nothing else to see here." Van Dean lead Daniel to his trailer, where he locked the door behind them, and Daniel told him about his week. As he told him about his week the other seasoned carnies, who previously had their own ideas about the ventriloquist, name Jack Wick Pickering, and the dummy, who they realized was named Mr. Craft, came knocking at the door of their oldest esteemed colleague, as well as newest esteemed colleague. They each heard the story from where Daniel had left off and as they came in to different points in its telling.

Almost an hour later the seasoned carnies went back to their rides, booths, and tents of operation to get back to work. Van Dean stayed in his trailer as two police cruisers, which the carnival security cops had called onto the scene, were heard in the parking lot with their sirens on and wailing to the red, white, and blue lightshow on the car hoods. Daniel had been sent back to his apartment to get the recording device and come back as soon as possible. They would have a lot of explaining to do and they knew that would be the easiest part of it all. The hardest part would be first convincing them of the importance of tracking down a ventriloquist and his dummy, and secondly what to do upon finding them.

X

The next few months, as well as the next year, Daniel Childress overcame the urge to go to the carnival and renew that old flame and spirit that had loved the lore of its grounds. He managed to go without experiencing the awe inspiring ferris wheel views, the fantastic fireworks displays, the raucous bumper cars, the only partially rigged games, the faux mystical fortune tellers, and the indulgent carnival food. Daniel did so and he managed just fine. He'd read the newspapers to get all the information he would need. He had turned over his audio recording device and pictures to Trapper Van Dean, who had turned them over to the police, who then began a temporary investigation, but then one more focused on any possible criminal activity that may have been the catalyst to Pickering and Mr. Craft's consistent traveling, ditching, and leaving rumors behind.

Just as Daniel's interest in the carnival had faded so had any trail of anything the police could find that legitimized the case's going on any longer. Jack Wick Pickering and Mr. Craft, going by the much less sinister sounding name of Zippo and adopting a much less sinister attitude to match it, were off to rebuild whatever it was they were trying to do so somewhere else. All the seasoned carnies at the Calloway Falls carnival knew, however, to watch out for them and warned those they had a feeling would heed the warning the same. The rest of the summer and fall of just another disappearance of Pickering and Zippo, and another fresh batch of rumors to mingle with the rest, lead to the cancelling of the ventriloquist act, as well as the end of any consideration of one the next year.

The ferris wheel operator remained one to not talk much, but also remained kindly, and kept the wheel running properly, giving all a view of the whole park. Madame Trappe maintained the camp of her act, only playing it up for those she read as the type who wanted to be shocked. The bumper car operator maintained his stance of not talking much to anyone outside of the safety spiel. Charlee Stanton returned the next two years while she finished off a master's degree in psychology, while she made sure the kiddies enjoyed the kiddie roller coaster. The fireworks operator, much like the bumper car operator, maintained his stance of not getting involved in other people's business, but also maintaining a safe, constantly evolving fireworks shows. And Trapper Van Dean kept on amazing and amusing men, women, and children as the ringmaster of the second best show on earth.

Other than the seasoned carnies the summer temporary employees kept flowing in and out of the mix and the carnival carried on. The games still maintained being only slightly rigged and the food was still indulgent. Also, however, Daniel stayed away from the carnival just the same. The sound of it off in the distance didn't have the same allure or pull it once did. He went back to working in the industrial field of warehouses and factories he enjoyed and never looked back. He continued following his dream of writing and achieved local success, being published by a small, independent outfit, and was able to quit the work he liked to pursue the career he loved. In between being published by the small, local, independent outfit he worked as a part time correspondent for the larger of the local papers to fill in the time and money gaps. And despite all of Zippo's harsh indictments he did make more friends, fixed the familial relationships he'd put off for so long, and began to be a more regular presence at his parent's house.

As for Jack Wick Pickering and Zippo, or Mr. Craft, not much was known. There were occasional rumors of strange, supernatural, and just plain weird activity that occasionally made it into the oddity sections of local newspapers and was dramatized, and played up in the tabloids, as well. Larger and more damaging activities of theirs, to the likes of other people and souls alike, weren't brought up, as it had happened on even less of a spoken about level, which only Daniel and his new band of seasoned carnie acquaintances would ever truly be able to understand. Once and a while, however, as the newspaper had Daniel cover the local Calloway Falls carnival he felt that strange pull, thought he saw fog or mist or transparent figures out of the corner of his eye, and thought he heard the remnant of an otherworldly voice as he passed by the spot the ventriloquist tent occupied. And though he no longer had nightmares of the event he ended every one of his article with his trademark sign off - which his publishers never quite understood, but enjoyed it for the camp of it - which read, "and my final word…avoid the ventriloquist".

Let Me Sleep On It

(3/13/2015)

I

There are those characters in our history that are definitive and definitely qualified to be referred to as bad guys and good guys alike, however the distinctions can sometimes only be different based on what side they're viewed from. What's even trickier can be determining the intent and true personal nature of those generally agreed upon to bad guys, absolutely or for the most part, at least. Those assistants of these evil head honchos aren't always the villains we make them out to be, which is why we sometimes need to extend a little faith in humanity - even if it does stand on the other side of the tracks. Sometimes those in the number two commanding position on the ladder aren't climbing, but rather being stepped on and forced down, or into, something they don't quite revel in the doing of themselves.

Cole Dawson was a seasoned, but still youthful correspondent for local newspaper. He lived in town, had his apartment in suburbs, was single, in his thirties, and had a good writing career ahead of him. He a hardworking, diligent, and dedicated employee whose maxim was to get the details of the story - the large and the small - right and to make sure the context and sub context was correct and accurate. His focus was impeccable, except for when he wasn't sleeping well, which meant he only needed to rattle his brain back into focus with a good, wakeful shake of his head back to reality or a quick cup of tea or coffee. Still, even though he always had issues with being able to sleep well and consistently in long-term reference, and had adapted to being able to read when he was swinging even the slightest bit off of his routine, again, to get it back on track the process, in its entirety, was getting old.

He was in his editor's office, having submitted his latest piece for publication. Cole Dawson had written his usual quota of smaller scope articles that served as filler material to support this story, his larger scope article that had required - as they naturally did, to get it right and accurate - more time and energy to complete. It was, however, complete and ready to be turned into his editor, Jonah Murphy, as he stood ready to defend its content, character, and spirit, and assure that it upheld his own principles in journalism, as well. Murphy's eyes scanned over the words on the printed pages of the first draft of the story, approvingly, as he reclined in his chair. This took about two to three minutes, with occasional interjections of single word phrases such as *nice, good, excellent, alright,* and *positively.*

"Very nice work, Mr. Dawson," Murphy confirmed, sitting up straight in his chair and handing the small stack of papers back to a receiving Dawson, "as usual, it's very well written, to the facts, and even the grammar is near impeccable. A few minor spelling errors and a few minuscule mistakes in grammar, but I have faith you'll fix that up with a quick edit. Do that, get it back to me, I'll take one last run through it, and I'll pass it on to the typesetters." The typesetters would lay out his and the other stories in position of their rightful spaces on the page, figured out what page the continuing story would carry over on, and so on.

"Thank you, again, Mr. Murphy," Dawson proudly responded in kind, "I'll get it right back to you in a few minutes." Dawson left the office with his print in hand, as Murphy adjusted his glasses, and returned to paperwork of his own when his office phone rang and he took the call.

"You're done with that story on the town hall budget and tax policy changes," Amy Campbell, Dawson's colleague and coworker said, not really surprised at this, "already?" Dawson stopped at her desk as an excuse to take a break for a minute or two.

"It took a few extra hours of take home work," Dawson said, physically showing the extra hours at home, last night, around his eyes, ever so slightly, "but yes. Now I have a little more time to prep for the next assignment and possibly relax a bit." He smiled at the prospect. He was used to occasionally swinging out wide of the straight, consistent, steady path of getting a good night's sleep and the process of getting back on track, again. It was bothersome however.

"I can see that in your eyes and something more concerning underneath them," Amy said, handing Cole a photocopy of a clipping from the paper, "here. It's fresh off the presses, as they say. I got it from the guy working on the full article for the medical center." Dawson took the photocopy and read it as Amy looked on.

"Sleep study, huh," Cole read, and returned a glance at Amy, "thanks. I may just take you up on being a lab rat for this…Dr. Phillip Bergie." Dawson smiled, nodded, and walked on toward his desk as Amy smiled back.

"You do that," she called after him, "you could use it and you have vacation time coming up, anyway." She returned to her work.

Back at his desk Cole set down his print beside himself and sat at his laptop computer to do a quick edit of his first draft. With his hands on the keyboard he was about to type, but turned to look at the photocopy of the sleep study clipping. *I do have vacation time and I could use a break*, he though. With that he opened his e-mail and typed up a quick correspondence to Jonah Murphy, requesting time off for the duration of the sleep study, asking to use his accrued vacation time. He'd collected quite a bit of it, after all, as you don't get a reputation for being all over the place and on practically every beat and assignment by taking ample vacation or days off.

Throughout the rest of the afternoon he finished editing his copy. *There*, he thought, proudly looking at his work on the desktop, *no more spelling errors, typos, or grammar snafus*. He sent it off to his editor via e-mail and began to reorganize the arrangement of paperwork and random office supplies on this desk, as it usually, quickly devolved into a state of entropy while he dug deeper and deeper into a story. Upon having thoroughly improved the order of his desk, shifting in his desk chair to get up to head over to Murphy's office to ask about that time off request, his e-mail dinged on his desktop. Opening up his e-mail he came upon a response from his editor and opened it.

"Huh," Cole said, reading it aloud to himself, using his quiet inside voice, "you're approved for the time off, the entire, duration. Even though it would completely eat up your actual number of paid days off, sick days, and vacation time I will only deduct it from your vacation. I'll approve of the rest of it without affecting your other accrued paid days off and sick days. Get it figured out and come back even more refreshed. You've earned it." *Alright, I will*, he thought, and laughed at the thought of considering it a vacation. With that taken care of Cole finished that week and the next week, and then began the four weeklong sleep study.

II

"Hello everyone and welcome," a man in his late fifties to early sixties who, by his attire, appeared to be the head doctor of this study said, "I am Doctor Phillip Bergie. You are all here to participate in a sleep study that should not prove to be too highly intensive or demanding, but will leave us all quite more knowledgeable. We, as doctors, intend on leaving this study with significantly more information on the effect of our new therapy methods and newly authorized non-intensive medications. All of you, as patients, will leave with a better understanding of how to manage sleeping issues and most likely experience significantly more restful, consistent sleep routines." The doctor carried on in this manner explaining the schedule for morning wake up, breakfast, lunch, dinner, and general bedtimes. He covered, as he handed out individual folders of documents to each of the dozen or more participants, the general idea of how their scheduled group sessions and one-on-one meetings would work.

The sleep study would require all of its participants to remain at the medical center, on the premises, the entire time during actual patient study sessions, group meetings, and individual one-on-one sit-downs with the doctor to collect all the data necessary. During these sessions he would be asked how he was feeling overall, how were his moods, did he feel more focused, and other questions. There were regular guidelines - that were loose enough for the most part, but were strict on a few points - in regard to their diet of food and drinks consumed during the study, in regards to the therapy, medications, and other circumstance of the study. Other than that he, as well as the other participants, would be allowed to go out on occasional lunch visits with friends and family, as well as to get in a good walk or generally some good, fresh air.

Dr. Bergie explained that the therapy they were going to use was a mixture of sound therapy, the use of a mild sleep aid pill they called Sominex, and stressing certain breathing and physical exercises, among other things. He introduced the sleep study assistants, who were all recently partnered and certified medical doctors with degrees specializing in the area of general physical fitness, health and wellness maintenance habits, and sleep studies. There was Dr. Adrian Alger, Brody Jamison, and Clara Burton. Each of them got up and talked about their degrees and experiences before joining on for this study. They all seemed - albeit young in relation to their fields of study - smart, focused, prepared, and everyone was very well organized. None of it seemed, as advertised by the good doctor, too intrusive and or intensive and Cole was looking forward to this.

All of this and more was covered in the first meeting with all the sleep study participants, the assistants, and the doctors. Each participant signed waivers confirming any medications they were regularly taking before, allergies, any medical histories outside of the disturbed sleep that could be taken into account of their data collected, and other relative matters. After the lead doctor and each of his assistants was given their chance to monologue each of the dozen or so participants was given a few minutes to introduce themselves. They each gave their name, their field of work, named some hobbies of interest, and the nature of their sleep issue. Once everyone, including Cole, had done so there was a social of sorts as they all nonchalantly mingled for another half hour or so, during which Cole kept mostly distant and stayed to himself.

With everyone having gotten to know each other the participants were sent off to their rooms to set them up for their comfort for the next four weeks. *This is like college all over again*, Cole thought, *minus the bothersome token drunks and untamed miscreants that would always pop up.* Each participant had their own room, about the size of a college dorm room, there were in house shower and bathroom facilities, there was one wing for the men and one for the women, and group meeting and dining areas. There was the group session room and individual one-on-one sessions would be held in the head doctor's office. The assistants would administer the mild sleep aid at night, observe the group and individuals during the day, and assist Dr. Bergie in the group sessions, as well as the therapy sessions.

Cole Dawson set up his dorm room. He put his clothes in the dresser drawers, set a few books of his own bringing on the end table, took stock of the bed, the small personal TV, and set down a notebook and a handful of pens and pencils onto the desk. It was about as close to home as one could make it for a stay that would last longer than a usual hotel stay over, but not quite near prolonged as anything else beyond that. He was satisfied, however, that it suited his needs and purposes perfectly. As he looked around and thought to himself *well, that's about right* he heard a light knock at his open door. He looked around and saw the three assistants just outside his doorway. They smiled, getting his attention, and stepped into the room.

They each introduced themselves by name, again, and shook his hand. First was Dr. Adrian Algers, then Brody Jamison, and lastly Clara Burton. Dr. Algers said that they were glad to have him on board, as Cole's case was interesting in that it wasn't too severe, but was beyond something to be ignored like a minor sniffle, and was a good mid level bar to measure the issue by. Dr. Brody Jamison and Clara Burton seconded this notion. Dr. Brody Jamison picked up by explaining how either one of them would be by, at random, to administer the mild sleep aid, each night. Clara Burton finished off by explaining how that even though they each would be documenting their general and specific observations of the group and individuals throughout the four weeks it was not to be seen as a stress inducing intrusion or someone constantly watching them behind their backs. It was all perfectly transparent, part of the study, and they were there to learn just as much as the participants, as well.

Cole Dawson assured them he was fine with all of this, swept over what he said during his own personal introduction to the group before, with a little more personal detail, and the three assistants were headed next door onto another personal meet and greet with another participant. They were making every effort to make this all go as calmly as possible. Cole checked his schedule for the day, as it was still early in the afternoon, and saw that he was, next, set up for a session with the lead researcher, Dr. Bergie, and that he was to be personally escorted to the individual appointment room by the lead doctor himself. He saw that he had a good fifteen minutes still, so Cole began to write what was on his mind in the notebook he brought with him, taking a seat at the desk.

"Mr. Cole Dawson," the lead doctor spoke kindly, as he knocked lightly on Cole's door, and Cole looked up from his writing, "ah, I see the dutiful writer is ever vigilantly at work. Even on vacation." Cole regarded Dr. Bergie's genuine kindly nature and sense of good humor as such.

"Yeah, I figured it would do me good to finally write about something I've never bothered to, before at least," affirmed Cole, noticing the lead doctor's face asking the question of *what would that be*, "me. Myself. I've always put myself out of the equation, as rather being simply an objective participant, and maybe it could make for an interesting story, or possibly an epiphany, if I kept a journal as a subjective participant." Dr. Bergie nodded, acceptingly.

"That is perfectly within reason and quite sound judgment if you ask me," the lead doctor confirmed, "as long it doesn't publish anything specific to our methods or step by step processes and procedures. If it's all simply subjective and explains enough for readers to better understand the study, without giving out trademarked information or methods." Cole had closed up the notebook, put his writing tools into the single desk drawer, and stood up to make his way toward the doctor.

"I'll make sure to comply with that," Cole honestly conceded, "I've always taken my brand of journalism honestly and openly." Dr. Bergie smiled, nodded at this, and mimed for Cole to follow him to the individual meeting room for their first one-on-one session. On the way to the one-on-one room Cole noticed the door with name placard that read "Dr. Joseph Warner". The door was cracked open and Cole made to try to peek inside, in passing, to get a look at anything that was worth seeing. Dr. Bergie noticed this, glancing back quickly, but carried on forward toward the one-on-one room.

"That's the office of Dr. Warner," the lead doctor confirmed, "he's what we call the third shift doctor. He is to take over my duties when my shift is over. I have the late morning to early evening shift and he has the late evening through on into the early morning shift. He was mentioned in the meet and greet pow wow this morning, in passing, but still mentioned nonetheless." Dr. Bergie glanced back to see that this answer fulfilled Cole's curiosity and they carried on toward the one-on-one room. At the appointed room the lead doctor opened the door, held it open, and invited Cole in. Cole entered first, the doctor followed, and the door was closed behind them as their session started.

III

The first week at the sleep study was routine. Cole had two one-on-one sessions a week with Dr. Bergie where they discussed his more personal feelings about work, outside of work, and how he carried on his life at work and outside of it. They discussed his exercise regimen, his diet, his relations with his friends and family, and how this impacted his mind's inner workings. The first one-on-one was simply to get a background of Cole, but the successive meetings gave way to more focus on questions and answers and the sound wave therapy, as well as keeping track of his feelings, moods, and general outlook as the days carried on. Dr. Bergie probed into how the one person sitting down with another person and talking therapy, the sound wave therapy, and the mild sleep aids were impacting all of this.

In each meeting as the first two weeks passed Cole confirmed he did feel calmer, more collected, more focused, and was noticing that where he usually felt a wide, chaotic out swing that usually broke up his steadier, more consistent sleep he didn't feel it quite as extreme. It didn't feel quite so wide or chaotic and, rather, felt like a minor stumble off onto the berm of the road, to simply coast back into his lane, again. Dr. Bergie was satisfied with this. Cole was active in the group meetings in confirming his general improvements, pointing out where his sleep issues seemed to share common themes with others, and where they all seemed to be helping each other to understand how they could all get themselves back into their own lane, again. The three assistants continued to randomly float around with their clipboards and take focused, slightly face contorting - while in moments of great focus to find the right words - contemplation, when they weren't passing by and greeting each participant with a smile and nod.

"It's going very well, actually," Cole confirmed to Amy, upon meeting for their scheduled and approved of lunch outside the facility, "it doesn't feel like you're under a microscope, being treated with kid gloves, or being pandered to and around." Amy had asked him, jokingly, if he felt like the Irish protagonist or the broom pushing Indian in *One Flew Over the Cuckoo's Nest*, yet, and confirmed that she had genuinely noticed an improvement worn upon his external expression and impression.

"You don't look so tired," Amy confirmed positively, "and this is usually when one of your wide, chaotic swings out, as you put it, happens." She added to this that the office was slightly less organized and less ahead of thing without him, but they were carrying on well enough, however.

"That's good to hear," Cole said, "and Murphy's still okay with it all, now that it's actually happened, and is happening?" Cole considered that he didn't expect things to fall apart in his absence, since he was one of a cast of worker bees at the paper, but still considered it.

"Yup, he's still peachy," Amy affirmed, "everything's running smooth. So how's the journal you said you're keeping coming along? Any really interesting op-ed observations we can turn into a perspective piece in response to the study, from an insider's point of view, once it's all said and done of course?" The editor had, once Amy told him what Cole said about keeping a journal for the sake of his own entertainment, but finding out from Dr. Bergie that he just may be allowed to publish his observations without breaking any privacy or secrecy laws within the study, that it would make a good caveat to the story.

"It's coming along well," Cole assured her of his progress and revelations, "I'm taking down very thought provoking perspectives of my own personal results, leaving out trademarked or sensitive information, and it's turning out to be an interesting read, actually, from a psychological standpoint. There is one thing…" Cole trailed off, in deep thought.

"What," Amy noticed, "what thing?" She was interested in hearing what the but wait there's more to this comment could be.

"Eh, it's probably nothing," Cole resolved, for most part, at least, for the moment, "he's a third shifter and those types have always been known to be a bit more interesting of personalities than first or second shifters. There's a third shift doctor at the study who seems to always be in and out all the time, like he's trying to be quick about something so he doesn't get caught. I'm thinking it's just me and that he's just a doctor who has a lot of work to do by himself." Cole shrugged it off and their lunch carried on. Before their corresponding lunch breaks came to a close Amy said their editor wanted to meet him for lunch in two weeks, the same time and place, and Cole said he'd contact her once he got it approved.

Over the next few weeks Cole's marked improvement continued. He didn't feel any of the wide out swings off the road, of his good sleep routine, and was quite relieved to not have to spend that energy pushing the car back onto the road, again. Rather, he was spending the time doing a good deal of writing down his experiences, thought provoking ideas, and other items in response to his sleep study time in his journal. As he wrote more Dr. Bergie had him bring his journal into their one-on-one sessions, as the doctor confirmed they were the most honest, personal forms of confessions of our feelings and moods, in the end. He confirmed keeping journals was great for us to more freely, honestly, and nakedly state our real feelings in a safe place we knew no one else could intrude upon. With his feelings and moods and sleep being confirmed as markedly improved, so did the other participants', as noted in the group meetings.

There were, however, a few stragglers who managed to start acting weird and, as the days and weeks went on, weirder. It was only a handful of the group in general, so it was deemed as coming along successfully, all in all, but those stragglers were seen less and less in group, and as of late only seen in passing - by those who were improving - upon their going to and from one-on-ones or other functions. The lead doctor and assistant doctors confirmed that there were always a small few that seemed to not take to some therapies, or allowed stress to cause them to degrade before they got better, especially in more interesting and closed off studies like these, but also that they were being taken care of. Cole was leery, though, of the third shift doctor.

Dr. Joseph Warner, though seeming to follow the same routine as Dr. Bergie, only during the night shift hours instead of during the day, seemed to be more frantic and popping in and out more often. He had been interested in all of the patient's files and histories, and seemed to be double-checking the medications of some participants more than others. He'd checked on Cole's medications, more interested than normal, on one occasion, and Cole realized that was just before his less wide swings off onto the side of the road. Cole also thought that the third shift doctor seemed to lose interest in certain patients - mostly those who were improving as Cole was - but focusing more intently on the ones who were degrading, slowly and then more rapidly. It was interesting to ponder whether that was the effect or if he was the cause.

Either way, Cole's approved lunch outside the facility with his editor, Jonah Murphy, had come along and Cole looked forward to it. Cole had been approved by the lead doctor to show his editor the notebook he'd been journaling in, the lead doctor thinking this could be a good advertisement and press for other's involvement in the next sleep study. *Yeah, that and funding,* thought Cole, but it was all in good and proper enough order for his understanding, at least. He trusted the process, didn't feel the presence of too much strange activity to set off his internal alarm system, and he felt that the assistants - being approachable, kindly, and still maintaining their observational and assistance roles - were a good measure of the study's genuineness. If only the third shift doctor hadn't set off the less panic inducing triggers of curiosity in Cole's mind, by his strange behavior, all would have been perfectly normal.

IV

The lunch with his editor, the same time and place as with his colleague and coworker, was another nice, air refreshing, temporary escape from the sleep study that was coming to an end. Cole was relieved there was only one week left, as he was getting antsy, as one usually became upon seeing the light at the tunnel, while finding yourself still in the tunnel. He was looking forward to getting back to work and was excited about the prospect of turning his experience into an article for the newspaper. His editor arriver right on time, on his corresponding scheduled lunchtime, as well, and they caught each other up on what was happening in each of their worlds they'd been supplanted in.

"So, you've got some interesting material apparently," Jonah Murphy inquired, "Amy told me about how your journal's been progressing." He had been in contact with the medical boards behind the sleep study to get authorization to publish Cole's experience and was close to getting it officially.

"Absolutely, sir," Cole confirmed, "not just stuff related to the study, but also very introspective biographical kind of stuff that more than a few psychological magazines would be interested in reading, and possibly publishing, as well." Cole had filled up a good portion of his journal notebook with his observations, feelings, and general thoughts along the way, as well as the sights and sounds around him, and his own.

"Great, and we're looking forward to getting you back," his editor said welcomingly, "we've had our usual freelance guy filling in for you and he's starting to get worn down by your average workload." Cole did have an overachiever attitude that bled over into and through everything he did, whether at work or outside of work.

"I've been getting antsy to get back, as well," Cole affirmed, "it's like when you know you've gotten out of something what you're going to and you know you have to finish it off, but you're ready to get back to what you knew before." As he said this he remembered the journal and passed it over his editor, with one of those *oh yeah* looks,

"So this is it," the editor eyed the journal and handled it as if it was fragile, "I'll let you tell me all about when you get back next week." He pushed the notebook back toward Cole, as Cole began thinking about the third shift doctor again.

"Yeah, it's been great and all, as Amy has probably told you already…" Cole trailed off, seeming to ponder something just beyond his grasp, trying to reel it in.

"As I can see from the lack of bags under your eyes for one," the editor jumped in, to avoid the situation's getting awkwardly silent, "and from your distinct lack of, how do you put it, swinging out wide off the road." Cole, seeming as if he'd caught what he was reeling in, was given the chance to continue by Murphy.

"Yeah, good sleep, better focus, clearer thought, but there's one interesting character," Cole said carefully, "the third shift doctor, Dr. Warner. At first he seemed to just be going about Dr. Bergie's duties, only on night shift, but then he started to seem to be too busy. He was checking and double-checking and now triple-checking certain patient's meds. And it seems the ones that got better are the ones he leaves alone and the ones that got worse are the ones he checks in on more often." Cole appeared to be in thought at this, still.

"Maybe it's because of their cases," Murphy said, not quite convinced, but convinced enough for now, at least, "that he's reacting that way." Cole was partially appeased by this, but not completely.

"Yeah, I considered that," Cole confirmed, "but I can't help but wonder if he's the cause, and that his increased attention isn't just the effect." The lunch ended on a better, more upbeat note as they talked about the new assignments coming down the pipe, just waiting for Cole's journalistic touch.

They both went their separate ways after their corresponding lunchtimes came to being nearer and nearer to over. Jonah Murphy went back to the newspaper and his office. Cole went back to the facility and his one-on-one with Dr. Bergie, where he once again covered what he'd entered into his journal, and was said to be a gem of a patient in the sleep study. Upon the completion of his one-on-one he was kindly acknowledged by the assistants, that seemed to be all over the place, making their observations and writing down their notes onto the corresponding patient's paperwork on their clipboards. That night Cole made sure to try to watch over and observe Dr. Warner as much as he could, without being noticed, from a distance and the safety of his room, group sessions, and other required appointments while following his schedule to a tee.

That last week came and went quickly, much to Cole's appreciation, as he was ready to sprout wings and fly out of the building come the day those released - all but the handful who seemed to degrade and get worse, significantly so - signed forms of all varieties. Those being released were made to sign consent forms, release forms, privacy of sensitive information forms, and so on forms. The worst part for Cole was waiting for the lead doctor and assistants to process the forms and approve him to go. Soon enough, however, he was approved of and sent off. He got into his car and drove to his apartment and unpacked all of his personal belongings, to put them back where they went in his truly comfortable space of living.

As per the third shift doctor, his behavior had not ratcheted up in strange and odd ways or events, but carried on. Cole had many discussions about his observations, likewise, with Dr. Bergie in their one-on-ones and in the end the lead doctor agreed to take special interest in seeing that those stragglers were tended to. He also confirmed he'd make sure that nothing fishy was being allowed to happen, otherwise, as well. This didn't really settle Cole's mind at ease, but did let him know his part was done and he could no more do anything to help those stragglers, but interfere and get in the way, not truly knowing what he'd do, or what to do, anyway. This decided, he let it go and returned to his normal life, again.

V

Cole Dawson, back at his apartment, and now armed with a notebook full of journal thoughts, reflected back upon the month. It had been a nice four weeks, overall, and he did genuinely feel more relaxed, focused, and hadn't felt his mind or sleep routine swing wide out into the side of the road in a while. All of this settled his mind at ease at the entirety of the thing, even though the nagging thought of the stragglers and the third shift doctor still persisted in floating back up to the surface. He let it float aside, however, trusting it and the entire case of the stragglers, to be resolved, by leaving it in the capable hands of Dr. Bergie.

Cole reflected upon the first week, his cautious, but open-minded approach and willingness to take part of it all, the thing having been set in motion. He didn't see it as a vacation; not quite so much as the strangest voluntary leave of absence ever conceived of, at that point, but went with the flow. He remembered the kindly and patient explanation of the entire sleep study's proceedings by Dr. Bergie, as the three assistants - later to be known as Dr. Adrian Alger, Brody Jamison, and Clara Burton - filed in. Even then they had their clipboards, paperwork, writing utensils, and game faces on - all from the start.

As he read his journal he recalled this first week and on. He made it past the first week, past the introductory and softball one-on-one and group sessions, and read on as they turned into more regimented hardball one-on-one and group sessions. He read back his reflections upon the sound wave therapy. That seemed to stick out so much more than the simply talking therapy or mild sleep aids. He looked in the general direction of his bathroom, where his two weeks worth of as needed sleep aids to go were stored, and back to the journal. He read about how he came to trust, and almost like, the three assistants. There was that section, however, about his first impression - and not a good one, either - of the third shift doctor, even though Dr. Bergie, with his good nature, supervised him, as well as the entire study.

Next he came to the section of his lunch meeting with Amy Campbell, his favorite coworker and colleague at the paper. They had discussed his improved and marked increase in positive vital signs, focus, and more consistent attitude and outlook, overall. She was in good spirits about Cole being in good, and even better, spirits, and confirmed their editor's interest in the piece as a possible story. He recalled her kindly send off that Jonah Murphy had wanted to discuss the piece's potential further - not the material in the journal, quite yet - but its potential. He read about his own further improvement and the notebook being used in his one-on-ones with Dr. Bergie.

Cole read on about how he had begun to regard the third shift doctor in a leery, untrustworthy way. He noted his entries that focused on his observations of the late night doctor's interest, increased interest, and then almost fanatical, micromanaging interest in the pills and dosages of the patients that were doing well, and then those who began to straggle. He read his uncensored, in the moment, thoughts after observing the doctor spending more time with those who were getting worse, whereas he seemed to leave the participants showing improvement - drastic or not - alone. He'd started by leaving them only partially alone at first, regarding them at a semi-interested distance, but then completely disregarded them to obsess over the stragglers, now truly plummeting down the tubes.

He came to the part about his lunch with his editor, where he'd elucidated a little more about his previously mixed feelings about the third shift doctor, those now completely devolved into complete and total distrust. Cole read into his own words, passionately honest, forthright, and raw as they could be - having been written in the moment - that he wanted to trust that the doctor was on the level, and that he himself wasn't a doctor, but still there was something about it. Cole finished the section about his lunch with the editor leaving them both off at a point of anticipation, about having a rejuvenated Cole Dawson back to work to take back over for the already exhausted freelance part-timer who'd been trying to fill his shoes in his absence.

Cole read, lastly, about the final week where he was told he was the gem of the sleep study, by Dr. Bergie himself, and that Dr. Bergie would see to the stragglers, as Cole had referred to them, as well as seeing to Dr. Warner's activities. Whatever it was that seeing to it meant was not clear to Cole, but Dr. Bergie had shown himself to be trusted, as did his three assistant doctors. It was just the question mark of Dr. Warner that Cole had to put out of his mind for now, to let the lead doctor finish the work that was his, not Cole's. Cole breezed over the section about his anticipation to pack up, do the bureaucracy shuffle - completing the release forms - and then return home. Now home, and finding only a few pages unfilled in the notebook, he filled up those last few pages with his reflections on his having returned home. It felt like a good finish to the journal.

That night he went to sleep right away, but began having a weird dream. It started out in a dorm room on the facility that looked like his in overall theme, but was personalized by someone else's taste in carry on luggage and clothes. This person was not as neat and tidy and Cole, but they seemed to be trying, at least. This part was fast-forwarded through to sessions he was familiar with, both one-on-ones with Dr. Bergie and then in a collective group. He even saw himself; apparently this was through someone else's eyes, still, and then a flash-forward, again. The montage seemed to zip past what this person had deemed irrelevant and repetitive, but stopped again. It stopped at a point where a doctor, with a facial expression that was unclear - having either put down a clipboard or having nudged it to read what was written on its pages - was checking on them and giving them their medications.

Sitting upright in bed, shaken awake, Cole wondered what that was all about. The doctor seemed friendly enough and the patient's visions seemed lucid enough, but the time of day was still something that left itself to be discovered. No clock was seen in the passing day-to-day movement, the fast-forwarded parts or the regular speed ones, so that was left open, still. This was unsettling, but he thought maybe his mind was playing tricks on himself. He went to the bathroom, took one of the mild sleep aids with water, checked his appearance out for overall normalcy, gave it a thumbs up grade of passing, and went back to bed. He fell asleep immediately. He slept soundly all night and woke up without experiencing any oncoming notion - not even a sense of anything coming down the pipe from a distance off - of swinging wide into the side of the road.

Waking up he thought about the dream. It was strange, but then again he did experience an interesting four weeklong stay, on site, as part of a sleep study. That was something he had never done before and he had just finished reading his entire opus about the adventure. He realized he wasn't a doctor, that Dr. Bergie was on the level, as were his three associates, and that he didn't speak ill of Dr. Warner, and felt he should let it go. He was, after all, one of those who proved to be gems of the sleep study and had come out of it remarkably better. Dr. Joseph Warner seemed a bit odd, but Cole tried, and succeeded for the moment, to explain it off that maybe it was because all third shift workers seemed to be a bit more interesting of character.

VI

Cole Dawson returned to work that Monday and was welcomed by his colleagues and coworkers, but mostly Amy Campbell and Jonah Murphy. They'd left their desk and office to come to his desk to see Cole Dawson getting it organized and set up to dive back into work again. He didn't see them coming, as he was not overly, but slightly, miffed that his general desktop items had been shifted around just a bit and felt the need to set them right, again.

Once that was done he took a seat in his chair, leaned back, closed his eyes, opened them, sat upright, and saw them both headed in his direction.

"You're back and ready to go, I see," Jonah Murphy said welcomingly, "we let the freelancer use your desk." He looked at Amy, as if to confirm she agreed to it as well, and then back to Cole. *I noticed that*, thought Cole, but he resisted from saying anything.

"We made sure to lock your desk drawers and laptop, however," Amy reassured Cole, "so all that he used was your pencils and pens and your workspace." She smiled at this, letting Cole know this was all completely okay, and Cole laughed mildly.

"It's fine," Cole assured them, "it's all set aright and back in its proper place. I figured you two would look out for me." He turned to Murphy at this. "Any new assignments for me to get into?" Murphy seemed taken by surprise at this request coming so quickly.

"I'll let you two get back to work, then," Amy smiled and began to turn to head towards her desk, "I see you're ready to dive right back into the pool." She left them at this, kindly and conceding, as such, in a friendly manner, having known Cole to be a worker that was just so dedicated.

"Well, we do have a story that will require a few days of researching and reporting," Murphy said, "and one or two more small ones that can be knocked out in a single day each. I'll bring you the files for them." His editor began to turn to head back to his office, but Cole got up.

"I'll go with you and get them," Cole saw that Murphy conceded to this, "I'll walk with you. I could use the exercise." They both went back to the editor's office, making small talk on the way, and at his office Cole picked up his work to then return to his own desk.

He immediately began going through his work for the week. The two smaller stories were on site interviews. One was with the mayor about the unveiling of plans for the new shopping development, to be installed downtown, and the other was with a representative of the water department about temporary maintenance being done to the water lines in one spot on the grid. The larger story that would take a few days was one that required multiple interviews, each with different people, all of whom were owners who had businesses going up in the projected shopping center. He began to plan his week, do some initial Internet research, read up further on the documentation he was given on the subjects, and before he knew it the end of the day had come.

That evening he did his exercises - breathing, meditative, and physical - finished off his evening with a good dinner, and read a little from the book he was currently into. After this he got ready for bed and went to said sleeping arrangement for another good sleep. He fell asleep right away, didn't feel the remotest inclination of wide swing out and off the road coming, and was deep into good, restful REM sleep when it started, again. He felt himself stir on the inside, but was still coming off of being out enough to where he couldn't - as he sometimes found the ability to be able to do - shake himself to waking from such a dream.

He was in another dorm room on the facility, but this was neither the one he'd occupied, nor the previous one. This person was blatantly messy and hadn't bothered to do more than throw their clothes in the corner of the room. It appeared, by the more delicate surroundings and more personal items - a bare bones make-up stand and a variety of things, along with a few framed pictures of family members - to be a woman's room. It started on into the same theme as the first dream like it, with the fast-forwarding to and through the one-on-one and group meetings. This person was more introverted and shy, so when it slowed down to one of the group meetings her hand wasn't raised and she didn't voluntarily speak so much as she was called upon. She did however speak and respond in full, and in complete obligatory and cooperative manner. This sped up to pass through scenes of walking to and from different functions, to slow down on a one-on-one.

At this one-on-one Dr. Bergie seemed more concerned, based on the stressed, slightly twisted look of his facial features that said so. This one was apparently not getting better. Flashing forward the scenes seemed deleted and went black to return to light - which Cole took to mean nights passed and days began - and the same theme carried on. It stopped at moments of passing the three assistants, acknowledging them, and his host being acknowledged, as well. It slowed down upon apparently more urgent one-on-ones. It ended with a doctor, who's face wasn't clear, again, moving around the clipboard - Cole still wasn't sure if it had been placed or nudged by him - and suggesting she take her medications. This time it was a little more urgent than the first dream ended.

Sitting upright Cole took in the difference between this dream and the first. Apparently the first had been someone who was fine, improving, or in a slower state of degrading. The second was someone in a steadier course of degrading. He decided he'd consult his more level headed and down the middle about things colleague, Amy, in the morning, however, not now. He went back to sleep after taking one of the sleep aids, not having connected them to any bad side effects, or any side effects at all for that matter, and fell back into restful REM sleep. He made a mental note to bring this up to Amy in the morning.

"Wow, that's weird," Amy affirmed, setting Cole's mind at ease that someone else thought so as well, "and you're still taking those sleep pills?" She thought maybe they were causing it.

"They never caused this sort of thing the entire four weeks at the facility," Cole began deducing, "so I don't know why they would, now." He was confused and hoped this conversation, and consultation, both wrapped up into one interaction, would lead to some idea of where to start unraveling the mystery from.

"Well, if it was me I'd stop taking them," Amy suggested, plain and simply, "what's the worst that can happen? You came out the study otherwise not only perfectly fine, but better." Cole considered this.

"Okay, I think I'll try that," Cole agreed that this sounded logical, "I will. I'll monitor what happens." Cole decided to stop taking the sleep aids for real, not just to appease her. It was worth the experiment.

"And start writing down your dreams," Amy suggested, plainly, "you may see some connected themes and images, or connect dots or something, by seeing it written out on paper." That seemed like a good continuance of what he thought was the end of the sleep study adventure notebook, his back home portion.

"I will, I will do that," Cole spoke like an excited, driven man, set upon a new mission and directive, "and I think I'll consult a psychiatrist or something. I could do that after work." Cole nodded, with his thoughts off into the air as he planned his next steps, and he turned, about to head back to his desk.

"You do that," Amy called after him, "you go see a psychiatrist. There's no shame in that. It just may be useful after having done the sleep study lab rat thing." Cole stopped to seriously regard Amy, heard her out, nodded his acceptance of this idea, and went back to his desk.

Back to his desk he immediately pulled out an empty notebook from his desk drawers, now routinely unlocked, again, and wrote down both night's dreams under their corresponding dates. That being done he then did a quick Internet search and found a local psychiatrist. He made a call, spoke with a very pleasant secretary named Daliah, and scheduled an appointment for the next day after work. He wrote it down in his weekly planner and pushed on forward with his interview with the mayor that day. Tomorrow was his interview with the water department. He also made a mental note to start research on the big story once he got back from this first interview.

VII

Cole Dawson, after the next day's interview with the water department, as well as a few brief interviews of a few owners of stores in the new downtown development, headed to the psychiatrist. He went directly to the office, did not pass go, did not collect $200, and did not stop at the apartment. In his messenger bag, which Cole carried around when doing his job, because he was a bit of an old school throwback and accessorized as such, was his sleep study notebook and his newly begun dream journal. Arriving at the building he parked right up front, by the door marked with the address number he was looking for, and went in. He spoke with Daliah, the receptionist - whose full name, voluntarily given, was Daliah Hill.

"You are right on time, Mr. Dawson," Daliah said, handing him a clipboard with paperwork on it, "fill these out and Dr. Messier will be with you momentarily. Cole took the clipboard - as a shiver ran down his spine at his immediate mental association of the clipboard - and took a waiting room seat to do the bureaucracy shuffle. He finished the shuffle quickly enough and was at the receptionist's desk again to hand it back to Daliah, as she took them with one hand, smiled, and then spoke into a phone system to Dr. Messier, stating that his next appointment was here and ready.

"Hello, Mr. Dawson," an older than middle-aged man, but not quite in his sixties, came out of his office doorway, "I am Dr. Messier. The spelling of my name looks like I'm terribly disorganized, but I assure you I'm not, as it is pronounced mess-eeh-ay." He smiled, reached out his hand to shake with Cole, and Cole responded likewise to do so.

"Thank you for seeing me on such short notice," Cole said, and the organized, despite his namesake, doctor lead him into the office and shut the door, "I'm the one with the sleep study notebook, rather journal, and another one, a dream journal, for you to scour and tell me what's going on in my head." Cole sat down and handed him to the notebooks from his messenger bag.

"Why thank you," Dr. Messier took the notebooks, sitting down on the chair before the couch that Cole naturally gravitated to, "I know Dr. Bergie from medical school and another practice after that, before he went to the hospital and I came here. He said this was how your best sessions went with him during your one-on-one visits during the sleep study." Seeing Cole's surprised face, as he was about to say this same thing, so as to expedite this process, the doctor responded. "I research any lead my patients give me, so I can have all the necessary information I need to be the most helpful. We didn't discuss anything private or specific to the study, just the methods of your individual meetings that were so productive." Cole's face said this was all on the level, relaxed into the couch, and the doctor skimmed his pages.

"I didn't have any of these dreams until after the sleep study," Cole confirmed, "and I'd been taking the sleep aids they gave out the entire time there, so I doubt it's them causing the dreams." As Cole said this the doctor looked up, nodded in agreement, and read on.

"I believe that, as well," Dr. Messier agreed, putting down the notebook and addressing Cole completely, now, "you should have been having them long before being released from the study otherwise. But do tell me a brief version of yourself before the study, skim over the parts at the study, and tell me even more about yourself after the study." Dr. Messier smiled in a receptive, kindly manner, and then resumed his serious, kindly face, as the session began.

Cole covered the entire before the study portion and made it into the beginning of the sleep study portion of his life. At this point the doctor asked to hold onto the sleep study journal, to read it at his leisure at home, so he could be even more in the loop for their next visit. Cole assented to this request and then scheduled another appointment a few days out, as the doctor was heartily interested in this case, and he said it was a favor for his friend, Dr. Bergie, and anyone who Dr. Bergie spoke well of. This was all well and good with Cole, as he did not feel that he could wait another week or two. He felt he would burst from the inside if these dreams kept coming and building up inside of him without a release.

After his dinner he went right to bed, not having time to read his book, and fell right asleep. He didn't take the sleep aid, as part of his personal experiment - that even Dr. Messier agreed with his and Amy's intuition on - but still fell into deep, dreaming, restful REM sleep. That was the perfect circumstance and environment for the dreams to come. As he expected the dream did come and this time it was the third installment of the series of how many, only someone much higher up than Cole, Dr. Bergie, doctors Alger, Jamison, Burton, or Dr. Messier could ever know. Cole didn't count Dr. Warner in the mix because he was still leery about him and his jury was still out on any deliberations regarding him any further.

In this dream it all started up the same way, but in a third room. This one was about Cole's temperament of cleanliness, but was apparently a different adult male. He based this on the resident's version of getting comfortable and his pictures on the stock supplied mantle, of which he had to be one of the people in them. It carried Cole through the fast-forwarded and regular timed portions. He saw, through this patient's eyes, that the Dr. Bergie - in their one-on-one - started out like he had with Cole, but gradually became more concerned by the look on his face. In the group sessions this one was not quite outgoing, but did voluntarily jump in and add something to these sessions, if only to attempt to show that he was fine and in normal spirits. Back to the next few one-on-ones, after skipped scenes and black frames between days and nights, the doctor appeared to have a brow that furrowed even more, as though concerned, but not quite as he was with the female patient. This one seemed to be midway between Cole's personality and nature, and that of the woman's.

As the dream fast-forwarded through more one-on-ones and group sessions, among other interactions with the three assistants, Cole saw the end of the line coming on this installment in the series. He saw the patient getting up to answer the door, still not sure of the time of day as the lighting was strange and indefinite in the these dreams, and heard the voice of the same unclearly-faced doctor. This time, upon answering the door, the doctor seemed less forceful than with the almost panicking woman, but was still forceful in suggesting the aforementioned meds. Cole saw the tail end of the doctor's glancing over at the clipboard, again. He hoped these dreams, that appeared to be skipping around - if only to add to the mystery of figuring it all out, once he put them in order of escalation and time frame - would make sense and connect more dots, sooner than later, however.

Waking upright again Cole grabbed his dream journal, now stationed next to his bed, and proceeded to write it down. *Amy would be proud,* he thought, *I'm taking her advice and it seems to be helping everything along, as well.* After he had documented every last detail he wondered where Dr. Messier was at in his sleep study journal. *What week is he up to, now,* through Cole, *and is he finding anything in there a neutral third party would, something that I missed?* Having settled his mind on the fact that Dr. Messier was as far into the reading as he needed to be Cole went back to bed and back to deep REM sleep, this time minus the strange dream. That would have to wait until another night, apparently. He, however, had more interviews to do with storeowners of businesses in the new downtown development and other smaller pieces to complete tomorrow - as he looked at his clock - which was technically later on this early morning.

VIII

That morning Cole worked on writing up the complete and filled out versions of his story outlines. Since it was easy work for him, that being his usual method and one that he was now a fast, quick pro at, he began to check his schedule of interviews for the rest of the day. There were only three quick ones, but the driving in between and brief documenting of their most important bits, for his purposes of writing the final story, were the most time consuming portions of this process. This in mind Cole gathered up his necessary audio recording device, notebook, pens, loaded up his messenger bag, and was off.

"Hey, Clark Kent," Amy kindly chided him, "you're seeming more distracted, again. Not quite as bad as before the sleep study, but not quite as focused as when you returned." Cole was not quite by her desk when she stopped to address this with him.

"Wow," Cole said, surprised, "that was very succinct and to the point of you. I'm impressed. I will take the hint." Amy was pleased with herself at this compliment.

"I've been working on being succinct, lately," Amy beamed, then regarded Cole seriously, "and I figured you kept on having those dreams. You've been going to the psychiatrist, also, haven't you?" Amy checked up on Cole from time to time and was doing so now, as well.

"Yes I have to the dreams," Cole hurried, "and to the head shrinker, also. It's helping to make some sense of things, as far as easing my mind a bit, for now. At the moment I'm off to get a few interviews knocked out, come back, and make my notes. I have a doctor appointment after that. Later." Cole was off and running quick as he was before, and Amy returned to her work, shaking her head and laughing at Cole's entire lack of an ability to do anything but zip around.

That day Cole completed three interviews. The drive between them turned out to be most time consuming parts, as he expected. When he got back from that day's work he saw Amy, still at her desk, working out the right wording for one of her bigger stories, she was just this close to being done with. He regarded her with a passing glance, went immediately to his desk, and unloaded his day's work materials. Filling up a few sheets of paper, in a much shorter amount of time than he realized he'd done so in, he loaded his messenger bag with his dream journal and a few other things he felt necessary. He then headed off by way of passing by Amy's desk.

"You'd be proud of me," Cole opened, upon reaching Amy's desk and seeing her look up to regard him, "I did three more interviews today, on top of the three yesterday, and am almost done with the field work. And now I'm off to unload the contents of my head." Cole said all of this very quickly and succinctly, and Amy simply looked on, amused.

"Well you go do that," Amy affirmed, "I have to finish this piece. It's just about ready to be dropped off with Jonah. I'll hear about your trip to the psych tomorrow." With that Cole was off and Amy went back to work.

At Dr. Messier's office Cole was prepared with his dream journal containing his latest installment in the series. Before even getting into where he left off, at the beginning of the sleep study period of his whole story, Dr. Messier read the dream entry, gave Cole a *that's quite interesting* look, and with that they began their session. Cole read the message clear and was set at ease that someone else was feeling his confusion at all of it too. Dr. Messier had the sleep study journal on his desk and his bookmark - a new addition to it - showed that he was almost all the way though the book. It was apparently a very interesting and gripping read to him, as well.

"So we shall pick up from just after the beginning of the sleep study," Dr. Messier began, "I believe that's where we left off last time. And, based on your look just now, I can confirm that yes I have been reading the sleep study journal, I am that far into it, and I would love to hear what exactly transpired that you're so emphatic about in it." Cole was impressed and immediately began.

From the point that Cole began at he carried on to the end of the sleep study. He didn't need to fill in most of the details that would have taken the most time, as Dr. Messier had read them in the journal. At some point into this session Cole passed the point that Dr. Messier had read up to and the doctor consulted the journal as Cole spoke of this. He made it to the end of the story of the sleep study period, right up the day of the recovered and improved patient's mass release and exodus back into the world. Dr. Messier handed back Cole's notebook and asked to see his dream journal.

"I will say it's all very interesting," the doctor spoke, curiously, "and I see why you've ben slightly distracted lately, not horribly unfocused, but not sharp as I imagine you can be either." Cole was not surprised to hear this critique. He'd heard it once already today and was convinced he was showing it on the outside.

"Yeah, I've been hearing that lately," Cole confirmed, "and you are right why it's so. I think you're up to the third dream, so far, based on what I can see and tell." Dr. Messier looked up from the notebook, not surprised, as he too had been showing his feelings on the outside. They both projected their most nagging, itching feelings outward.

Their session ended with them covering Cole's movement from his focus being on and off before the sleep study to an improved focused after the study, to wavering off then, and to now. Cole confirmed he felt it as well, as the doctor said he'd try to figure out if there were any dots that could be connected. Cole felt he was on the edge of figuring something out, as Dr. Messier conferred that he was as well. As Cole and the doctor left his session office they scheduled again for another few days out. The favor, due apparently because Dr. Bergie had put Cole Dawson in his good graces, was still operative.

That night Cole prepared himself. These dreams seemed to come every few days or so and he was up to three by now. Four, and however many more, had to be coming down the pipe, as well. The good news was that he hadn't taken a single sleep aid since he'd quit them and hadn't felt any remote urge to swing wide out of this lane. This told him, for the better, that he was still one of the improved patients, but also that, for the worse, he didn't know why these dreams were coming, or what was bringing them about. He waited for this night's occurring dream to come to answer that.

As the dream came, amidst a restful REM sleep, Cole woke up in another person's body, at least camped out, undetected somehow, behind their eyes, and in the room of another patient. This was another woman's room, based on the clothing style and design, the pictures set up, the make-up supplies, the feminine products, and this time a clean and organized home-making technique. The fast-forwards and regular speed intervals passed and stopped, and came and went. Her one-on-one sessions seemed to start out like Cole's, in that they were regular with no big to-dos or drastic shifts, but then, as witnessed in her interactions at the group sessions, she started to panic. Her conversion, based on reading the faces Dr. Bergie made in the individual sessions and those of the three assistants in passing, as well as in the group sessions - on top of her seeming to dart her glance here and there rapidly - seemed to show that she was losing her grip hard and fast. This dream ended in the same style of the clipboard being glanced at by fuzzy faced doctor suggesting she take her medications - this time in a calm tone, but a weasely, coaxing, dark of undertone voice that suggested the *or else* caveat.

Upon waking up Cole wrote this down immediately. Before he was even upright he was reaching over to the end table, had the notebook in hand, had felt around for the pen, and upon opening his eyes flipped to the next open page and wrote. The progression seemed to make sense in a way that showed some patients progressing less than others, some falling prey to something or someone sooner and more intensely than others, and the unclear-faced doctor demanding that they take their pills. For some reason Cole knew this doctor was acting out the part of the effect, but wasn't sure if he was the cause. He felt in his gut that the next few installments, if not the next one, would unravel the mystery. He knew it like he used to be able to feel those swings wide off the side of the road coming, when they used to come.

IX

Cole finished up his piece on the store owners of businesses to be developed downtown, put together common threads between them, and submitted it to his editor, who said it was great and as soon as he fixed a few spelling and grammar errors, upon a second pass at it, could submit it. Then he could pass it on to the typesetters. Cole, having worked quite hard on this story, was ready to move on to the next series of small one-day stories and the next big story that required a couple days, like this one, of research. He had the story edited, changed the angle a little bit, and had it on his editors desk. Jonah Murphy said it was great, he loved the new angle even better, and after a quick pass over it would send it on down the line. After he received confirmation it was good he'd drop off Cole's next assignments.

That night Cole had a feeling a dream was coming. All of the elements were just right and lined up properly, like planets on strange solstices, and he prepped himself for what he hoped was the capper of the mystery. Like other stories and events in his life he felt he had a good run with it, but wanted to move on to the next thing. That was why he liked the newspaper writing business. It allowed him to work in the same building, in the same job, and at the same desk, but to still be able to move on to next thing all the same. Having done his exercises, meditative routine, eaten dinner, read a bit, and laid down in bed he prepared for the dream he felt coming like the wide outward turns off the roads of before.

This dream came quickly and steadily as the others. Immediately after he fell into another deep, restful, sleep aid-less REM sleep he awoke behind the eyelids of another patient in another room. This one was a man based on the décor style of his choice and the clothes he was putting into drawers. Expecting a little more time before the next phase Cole was jerked into the fast forward motion, jarred a little - even in the dream - carried into the group intro, and then quickly into the one-on-one session. He started out, based upon Dr. Bergie's facial reactions and tone of words, calm as Cole, but something deeper in the doctor's eyes seemed worried. Flash-forward to the group meeting the man seemed manic to be involved in responding and giving material for others to respond to. Flash-forward again to the next passages in the halls, black screen frames, the next days, and the next individual meetings with Dr. Bergie it all got more herky-jerky, like an older, but still operating wooden roller coaster.

The next one-on-one the man was manic to respond and be responded to, just as he was in the group meeting, but even more so. He was escalating quickly. Dr. Bergie was suggesting the man be taken out of the study, but a knock on the door - at the perfect time apparently - one of the night doctor, Dr. Warner, called Dr. Bergie aside. In an uncomfortable chat, based on Dr. Bergie's face, the night doctor - this man's one-on-ones were the last of the day shift doctor's, Cole guessed - Warner suggested they keep on observing him and see if they couldn't just wean him off the study. Flash-forward to what - in a time of day frame and setting, based on the lack of light out the window the patient was looking - a pounding was heard on the door and the patient seemed hesitant to answer it. He did, however, after significant, aggressive verbal coaxing from the voice at the door. Cole recognized this portion of the dream as the part that had been the not quite revealing reveal, as the face in the glass in the door - of the doctor - was blurry. It wasn't until the door was opened, however, as the aggressive voice demanded he take his medicine, that the face was perfectly clear.

This time Cole woke up bolt upright and grabbed the notebook and pen, writing a flurry of words with a passion he'd never felt before. He saw the face, still, in his mind, as he wrote down every detail. *The doctor will have a field day with this*, Cole felt his heart pounding as he wrote, from having woken up from such a revelation so intensely, but felt it slowing down to a calmer rate as he expelled the words onto the pages. He filled up two pages with this entry and it was a good one. It was the one that capped off the dreams and connected the dots. He was right to be suspicious of the night shift doctor. He had apparently been doing an inside, double-agent sort of test of his own on patients. He'd been isolating the ones that were exhibiting the responses he'd been looking for more and more all along, until it was reminiscent of one little, two little, three little Indians. Those last Indians - far from the one that fled the cuckoo's nest - were ending up like the Irish protagonist of that particular story.

Cole, upon seeing that he still had a few hours to get a bit more sleep, laid back down immediately, tired out from the intense rush. He did it without sleep aids, as usual, but had predicted this version of a wide swing outward off the road. This time, however, he'd witnessed someone else's swing off the road, but they were still in the high grasses and weeds alongside the road, and this he just felt he knew even though he had no idea why. After waking up, as he usually would for work, he was glad he took the sleep he could, as he felt he would need it for this day - needing to be sharper than sharp and more focused than normally focused to communicate this to Dr. Messier - and he was glad that their appointment was scheduled for today.

All day at work Cole was thinking about the last dream and the appointment he had with Dr. Messier later that day. He received his next bundle of assignments and knocked out the interview that day with another city utility company representative. He got to work outlining his story format, the most interesting points of the interview, and then got to fleshing out the story in its entirety. He dropped this onto his editor's desk and Jonah Murphy asked him if he had already done his second edit and rewrite. Cole confirmed he had and Murphy confirmed it looked like it, and that it would be sent down to typesetting, as well. The rest of Cole's day was spent scheduling interviews for his bigger story, for the next day, and reading up on the specs for his remaining small story - a one-day interview and quick write-up. After this he headed right over to the psychiatrist's office. He passed by Amy's desk. She was impressed by his alertness and quickness today.

"You, sir, are on fire today, Mr. Dawson," Amy said, impressed, as Cole came to a quick stop at her desk, "you're attention is a mile down the road and you are making a beeline to it, apparently." She was smiling, but turned serious, as Cole regarded her.

"Yeah, I'm feeling that way," Cole spoke, hurriedly, "I had a fifth dream last night. I know the link, now. I'll tell you later, but I think I'll need the good doctor to intervene on this one." Amy could tell Cole was in a hurry and let him go.

"You will call and tell me, thought," she said to Cole, as he was on his way out, "I'll hear it then. Go, intervene, and connect dots and such." With that Cole was off to the psychiatrist's for their appointment.

At the psychiatrist's office they did their usual first five minutes of catching up with where they were each at in the mystery. Cole filled him in on the rest of the story, covering when the dreams started, and then told him about them all, down to the final one.

"Dr. Joseph Warner," Dr. Messier said, befuddled, "I didn't think he could do it. So you surmise that based upon your observations of his checking people's charts, whittling down his clientele list to his favorites, his odd sneaking around, and your favorite catchphrase - the capper to each of these dreams - that he was doing his own alternative experiment?" Dr. Messier didn't pose it as a question so much as he was reiterating it out loud for himself to connect the dots, in between dots and others in between other dots, subconsciously, which he did.

"Yes, I do," confirmed Cole in a cold tone, "and I believe you do, too." His gaze was straightforward at the doctor, now no longer musing upon the words while staring off into space, but meeting Cole's gaze, with his shocked, befuddled look.

"And I believe it," the doctor confirmed, "it all seems to make sense and fit together based upon your day by day description of the sleep study, your emotional responses to each event in the journal, and the dreams just seem to prove it." Dr. Messier looked tired for a moment, but Cole realized it was disappointment. "I'd heard Dr. Warner talk about the potentiality of doing human trials on that drug, but didn't think he'd actually do it, but then again there was that look in his eyes. I should have known." Dr. Messier's look became serious.

"What drug," Cole asked, urgently, "it wasn't what I took, because I'm fine." Cole knew that much and the doctor stood up to go over to his desk.

"This drug, Sominex X," the doctor handed him an informational print-out, "I was on the board, along with Dr. Bergie, to not include it in the sleep studies we projected doing - which were planned for years out after much research was done on each of the drugs - and we both knew the X version was too potent, based on monkey trials." The doctor paused and Cole read the sheet. "What happened to those monkeys, psychologically and reactively, was a tragedy, but it seems Warner never let it go. You already know about Sominex, so you can figure out what I figured out about the X version." Their eyes met straight on.

"If I'm reading this correctly, it's practically poisonous," Cole said, shocked, "that's what made some of those, who ended up being released with me at the end of those four weeks, backslide a little. But when Dr. Warner whittled down his clientele to those reacting the way he wanted them to, and let the others go to get better, he really pushed the others on forward with his own agenda." Cole put it together into words and Dr. Messier nodded that he had it right.

"I need to contact Dr. Bergie and tell him what's happened," Dr. Messier moved to get behind his desk, "and you need to go home. Be here the first thing in the morning when we open. I have calls to make. I want to get a jump on this, but to go chasing anything now is foolish. I need leads and I'll get them." Cole nodded and packed up his dream notebook.

"I'll be here first thing the office opens tomorrow morning," Cole said, and Dr. Messier nodded, as he went through drawers in his desk for business cards with phone numbers on them, uttering swears under his breath as he did so, "I'll see you then." With that Cole left and Dr. Messier kept up his search. He found a business card for Dr. Bergie and was heard on the phone talking as Cole left the office, with the doctor's session office door shut, to go home and take it all in.

X

That next morning Cole Dawson was at Dr. Messier's office first thing in the morning when it opened and the doctor cleared the entire day. Cole had done the same thing by taking a sick day. He called Amy to tell her he was getting to the bottom of the weird dreams, that it had a connection to the sleep study story, and that he'd call her to tell her later on, but had to go. Dr. Messier, holding a sheet of paper, with three addresses and three phone numbers written on it, as well, was rushing him off the phone. Cole got off the phone right way and they sat down in the doctor's office with the door shut. It seemed that much was a force of habit. The doctor told him of his calls after Cole left the evening before.

"I called my old friend Dr. Phillip Bergie, you know him," Dr. Messier said, "and we did some digging. We're, all three of us, wrapped up in this business, to a degree. After college Dr. Bergie and I served for a spell at a medical center, along with Dr. Joseph Warner, a class behind us, but he was there a year after we started. We were there for a while, and then Dr. Bergie and I split off on our own separate ways. I made a few small stops along the way, as did Phillip. He ended up in his hospital research department and I ended here at this practice. Dr. Warner followed Phillip to his next gig, but didn't last long, as Warner was fanatical about studying the effects of a drug that predated Sominex, intended for something else, but become Sominex X, the more potent version Warner was apt to want to peddle around to humans. Phillip, before Warner was let to go somewhere else because he wouldn't give it up, told him to not work on the drug that predated Sominex X, because Phillip concluded it was too dangerous just on the details Warner gave him." Cole followed along, even as Messier, bounced around a bit.

"So this drug that predated Sominex and Sominex X," Cole proved he was following along, "what was it called and what was it for, Dr. Messier?" Dr. Messier put up hands to wave off the salutation.

"Heinrich, call me that," Dr. Messier said, "this whole formal salutation thing will get old fast. I can't remember what it was called, but Phillip - Dr. Bergie's new, familiar name we're calling him, now - would, but it was even more potent. It was a hallucinogen that was meant to calm your nerves, but the specific combinations of other drugs in it were volatile together and made it a super-hallucinogen. It was dangerous in how it caused the brain to spasm and deteriorate, as well as cause the patient to hallucinate in a most intense, frightening way. Philip made sure Warner was kicked out of that research group so he could be cut off from access to the drugs and chemicals, incase he wanted to do any extracurricular work, if you know what I mean." Dr. Messier was now the one connecting the dots for Cole.

"I do," Cole affirmed, "do go on." Cole's eyes were intently focused and his mind was taking everything in that his ears heard.

"Well, Phillip had Warner kicked out of the group, but damn Warner found a new group," Dr. Messier was visually perturbed by this, even after all these years, "and they had no problem carrying on with his studies. He picked up where he left off. Not even reporting Warner to the FDA could stop him. Years later, after Philip quit that group to move onto the hospital research ward - he's been there for a while, now - Warner was brought back. Phillip protested it, but couldn't overrule the hiring board. He knew Warner had been sneaky about keeping his research up, but didn't know just how sneaky. Phillip was, by now, working with the much less potent, far milder and safely usable Sominex. Phillip allowed Warner to be on the research team only as long Warner was kept in check and Phillip kept in charge. It looks like Warner found a crack in the system and getting in on third shift, on a laxly regulated team - outside of Phillip's efforts - caused him to have access to all the guinea pigs he wanted." Dr. Messier wrapped it up.

"Aright, that explains his involvement at the sleep study," Cole surmised correctly, as Messier nodded approvingly, "and that's why he didn't so much as acknowledge Warner in the meet and greet." Cole had it.

"Exactly," Messier affirmed, "and I have, here, the last three known buildings he's worked out of. Maybe we can find something at one of these." Cole understood in his tone that they needed to work fast.

"Let's go then," Cole read Messier's mind, as Messier followed Cole out of the office, "I'll drive. You guide." Cole got in the driver's seat and Messier got in the passenger seat.

Dr. Messier guided them down the main street and a few side streets that Cole recognized, and even more that he didn't, and it looked like this first location was on the bad side of town. They pulled up to the first location, after passing by how many trashy looking convenient stores, cell phone stores, gas stations, drive through beer and cigarette places, bars, and run down houses, and the place looked like it hadn't been maintained for years.

"Here, this is where he started out," Dr. Messier confirmed, "he figured in a bad neighborhood who'd look. God knows why the others in his group went along with him when he showed them the place, but that's why he signed on with them, I guess." They both looked at the run down factory building with broken windows, a decrepit fence all the way around, and a serious padlock on the fence dangling below a sign that spelled the end for many buildings' livelihoods.

"I can see why this place is condemned," Cole stated the obvious, "and why Warner would pick this place. If that drug was potent and lethal as street drugs I see why he'd have no problem fitting in here, and if he was crazy as he sounds I see why even these people weren't rough enough to mess with him." Cole and Messier regarded the building, defeated.

"Bergie told me it was closed up, but I was hoping we'd get something out of it," Messier said, "hoping maybe we'd catch a vibe off of something." He looked around at the property from inside the car.

"We did," Cole confirmed, looking around the same, "we got the drug company name. It's on the sign on the building in the distance. It says Warner, Smith, and Hoolihan Chemicals Inc." Cole turned to look at Messier, who was squinting at the building, but then met Cole's eyes.

"You can read that," Messsier marveled, "wow. Well, we have a name to discuss with him, now, when we track him down. Onto the next exotic locale, however."

With that they were off to the next location. This one winded out of the area of a few side streets of the sketchy neighborhood, into the main side streets, and back onto the main drag. After a few minutes they turned onto the first side street they came to and then one more at the next intersection. They pulled up to a nicer, but still unmaintained for few years - by many less, however - building. Weeds grew up in what were once maintained, miniature gardens out front beside the front doors. This looked like a corporate office plaza that hadn't been rented out for a while. This place, too, was chained shut. It had a closed sign dangling from the door.

"Really," Cole said, exasperated, with his head, then raised it up to look around, "what are you getting out of this, Dr…I mean Heinrich?" Cole looked around and so did Heinrich. Cole observed nothing interesting, but Heinrich did.

"I found a sign this time," he was smiling at Cole, "it's closer to the ground, not quite knocked, over on my side of the car. That's why you didn't see it." This turned Cole's face of tired exasperation to *okay, what do we have then?* It says S&H Inc. They dropped the Warner and the Chemical. They kept the Smith and Hoolihan, but shortened it." They were onto something.

"Maybe they wanted Warner out and they also went bankrupt," Cole put it together, "or they needed to rebrand to escape being searched for by the old name, the one that could have been ambiguous at first, but then became uniquely inescapable." They met each other's *we've got this, now* look.

"On to the next exotic locale, Watson," Heinrich sounded good naturedly, but with an edge to his voice that said they were on the trail to something less than pleasant, hopefully, "go left at the next street." Cole followed his directions.

XI

Cole drove around the neighborhood of a nice looking, well groomed, and maintained corporate doctor's office plaza. This had to be the place. They both read the posting on the large, painted address board out by the road and followed it back to the spot. It said J.W. Associates Inc. Both sleuths met each other's glance and then went back to the sign. This was the place and they knew it. Dr. Joseph Warner had, not too creatively, but enough to his feeling of safety, rebranded and picked up his craft, whatever it was he was doing there, under this new name. Getting out the car from both sides Cole and Heinrich closed their corresponding doors and walked up to the main door of this building.

"This is the last listing Phillip gave me," Dr. Messier said, "so he's got to be here, associated with something here, or have something to do with it." Cole heard the hope, not faded, but on the edge of falling off of a cliff.

"It has to be," Cole opened the door for Heinrich, who walked in first, "it has to be, but we won't know unless we go in." Cole followed Heinrich.

They followed the signposts with removable letters neatly arranged to tell who was on what floor. They followed the direction for J.W. Associate's Inc. to the second floor, of which the entire level belonged to Dr. Joseph Warner. On the way up, however, they saw white powder and residue, what appeared to mud and dirt from outside, and other random bits of debris leaving a trail up to the door marked J.W. Associate's Inc. The glass around the door on each side was broken, with shattered, prismatic shards in the hall, as if it had been broken outward. The door was cracked badly, barely on its hinges, and dangling open. Cole and Heinrich ran to the door.

"Woah," Cole said, shocked at the absolutely destroyed medical looking office reception area inside, giving a clear shot into equally destroyed and rummaged through offices, "he apparently made enemies." Messier followed Cole into the office reception room and gaped at the mess.

"Yes, he did," Heinrich said, failing at pretending to be calm and cool, "Phillip and I told him if he got into this stuff and it got into wrong hands this would happen. We…" Heinrich stopped, thinking he heard something or someone moaning or in trouble. Cole and Heinrich walked around the room, stepping over busted up wood, office supplies and equipment thrown everywhere, and marveled at the holes kicked into the plaster-showing walls.

"I heard it, too," Cole said, "someone's in here and barely made it." They both started looking into the individual office rooms, pushing aside planks, debris, busted stuff everywhere, and looked up at the drop ceiling that was broken up all over place, with panels on the ground at random landing places. The human moan became audibly louder.

"Over here," said Cole, in one of the back offices, hunched over the side of a very badly beaten man, about Heinrich's age, partially covered by drop ceiling panels and random debris, "over here, Heinrich." At this name the man that appeared barely alive sparked to life.

"Heinrich…Heinrich Messier! Over here," the man was panicking, but calling for Heinrich, as Cole tried to calm him down and remove debris off of him, "over here!" Cole had uncovered him enough to be able to start helping the man to his feet. Heinrich entered the room and his face looked as if he was feeling partially sympathetic, then sad, then angry, but finally shocked, and rushed to help him stand on the other side. He mowed through debris.

"Joseph Warner, is that you," Heinrich called out, rushing towards the man, as Cole looked on confused, "what happened here? What did you do? What did you get into?" Heinrich motioned for Cole to help him move the man outside to the main room, what could have formerly been a reception area.

"Are they gone, yet," the man fought their forward motion, as he yelled out in a panic, "if not, don't take me out there!" As they made it to the main reception, the man stopped panicking, resigned himself to what had happened, and shook off their support. Hanging his head he turned to Cole, recognizing him. "Thank you for being here, and I'm sorry for what I put you and the other's through." He turned to Heinrich. "I'm sorry for not listening when I could have gone clean and found myself in a practice like yours or Phillip's."

"This is the guy, isn't he," Cole put it together, it all finally settling in, "this is Dr. Joseph Warner." Cole was partially sympathetic and angry at the same time. It felt strange to feel both of those things simultaneously.

"Yes, it is," Joseph Warner spoke before Heinrich could, and Joseph waved him off, "I will explain. Once I sit down." They all moved over to a spot where debris was covering three chairs, cleared it off, and sat down.

"Explain, Joseph," Heinrich spoke, coldly, but with a blunted, softened edge that said he was willing to listen, "as if I don't know what happened, already." He didn't take his eyes off Warner, as Cole didn't either. Both were regarding him with a chilly demeanor.

"I will…and I can," Warner said, pathetically, "about what happened after I was kicked out the medical clinic, what came after, and my involvement in the sleep study." He looked back and forth between the two, hung his head, shook it, uttered a weak, but agonizing guttural moan, and continued.

XII

Cole was about to call the cops, almost having pulled out his phone, looking at the destruction all around them. Their having found the man behind the horrible chemical turned drug, that both good doctors had warned him about, but who had continued to work on it, and then test on patients at the sleep study, he was in their clutches. They could make sure that justice was paid due for the patients Cole witnessed going mad in person at the study, the one's who's dreams he was in using their bodies as a host to share their point of view, and all those who came in between the blank spaces Dr. Heinrich Messier and Phillip Bergie couldn't fill in.

"We've got to call the cops," Cole said, with the phone out of his pocket and in his hand, "we've got him and they need to search the crime scene." Dr. Messier stayed his call off with a hand wave.

"No, and I can't believe I'm saying this," Heinrich spoke, sympathetically, "but we must hear him out. I believe this is deeper than we know. Go Joseph, tell us what happened and why I'm not having my friend here have you arrested." Joseph Warner pathetically raised his head up straight, regarded both of them, and stared straight ahead to speak of his tale.

"What didn't have a name before it became Sominex X was dangerous, extremely potent, and poisonous for the brain and mind," Warner addressed Heinrich first, "you were right about that and that it would get me into trouble with bad people, either the drug element, as you put it, or the government. It turns out I avoided the government, but all the while piggybacking off the drug element - just one made up of other doctors like myself, back then, and their muscle - and that's what ended up doing this. After Phillip was working with us at the medical center, and I started discovering what became Sominex X, I had noble plans to neutralize it or use it, strong as it was, for good somehow. I really did." He paused at this.

"Really," Cole said, "how exactly, if I'm to believe how dangerous that drug was, and seeing how Sominex X did in that many people at the study, so badly, especially?" Heinrich stayed off Cole's questions, but went back to regarding Warner with a less then sympathetic, but still patient look.

"I thought if I studied it I could figure it out and learn how to make sort of an antidote from itself," Warner continued, "but all I did was end up getting addicted to it, at first, then trying to make it stronger and stronger. I tried it in small doses because I had no other human trial subjects and no court would have held back from throwing me in jail for endangering humans. I met up with the group of scientists and businessmen you and Phillip warned me about. They had muscle, hit men, goons - you know they type - but I should have seen what they were, instead of believing they were simply hired security. I wanted to figure out how to neutralize it at first, when I was far nobler, but addicted to it, still. I was threatened all the time by their so-called hired security and was forced to make it stronger. They used it to drug, kill, drive insane, and frame their enemies - business, personal, you name it." Cole still regarded Warner with distrust and venom, and Heinrich began to look at him sympathetically. He waved off a comment he saw coming from Cole.

"That was Warner, Smith, and Hoolihan Chemicals Inc.," Heinrich confirmed, "wasn't it?" At this Joseph's face became pained and he hung his head, but regained himself and raised his head to continue.

"Even then part of me regretted ever getting involved with them in the first place," Warner pathetically continued, but seemed to be getting his strength and composure back slowly, "that's when their physical enforcement to maintain loyalty began. After years with them police started to get closer and closer. We thought our hiding in the middle of that run-down dump of a neglected town could hide us, but their eyes all over the place saw the cops - even undercover - snooping around. They tracked shipments of chemicals in and out. We had to rebrand, move into where we wouldn't be so obvious, and could hide in plain sight. That's when their businessmen broke up the company and created S&H Inc. Even then I wanted out, but was blackmailed to stay on the team, even though I wanted to go clean and get into practicing medicine or doing medical research again, but was instead forced to continue making the drug for them. With Warner, Smith, and Hoolihan Chemicals Inc. they only threatened me, but with S&H Inc. they threatened to hurt my family and friends…and even former colleagues." Warner turned his head to Heinrich to search for sympathy, as he glanced over at Cole and was getting none, yet.

"I see, and know you see it, too, even if it's too late," Heinrich said, sympathetically, "then what happened? How did you end up with Sominex X and the sleep study?" Cole became quite interested at this part.

"For years S&H Inc. operated and no one suspected anything," Warner continued, "we technically operated a clean business just creating the drug. The businessmen legitimately sold it to illegitimate people, who set up their enemies to the business by using the muscle to make the drug find its way into their drinks, forced into their mouths, and you can figure out what else they did as well as I can. This went on for years. My handlers wanted to see how far they could take the drug, so the businessmen classified it with a medically sound and professional name Sominex X, only they declined to sell it to any legitimate medical company. They cheated the system, I don't know how, but did, because they knew it would never be approved and that it would link them all the way back to Warner, Smith, and Hoolihan Chemicals Inc." Cole knew this was linked to the sleep study and Sominex, but didn't know how.

"How does that lead to the sleep study," Cole said, not demandingly, but quite coldly, "and Sominex. Most patients were actually helped by that drug." Heinrich let him carry on, as this interested him, and Cole wasn't being too rough.

"I will tell you, Cole Dawson," Warned looked at a completely aware, intently listening Cole, and then straight ahead, again, "yes, I remember you, by the way. They needed a cover for the Sominex X, so they had me create a far less potent version that could actually do what I always thought it could…either help people with drug addiction, to wean themselves off drugs, help with depression, or calm the brain down, like a mild, mild hallucinogen. I made Sominex, which took a while, but it kept the police, the FDA, and the government off of us, and this drug kept them off our trail to Sominex X. Plain Sominex, after we tested it on monkeys, was what it was now being called. The businessmen bought me a complete lab to work with and create the tame version. Meanwhile they were killing their enemies with violent version, hypocritically enough. The monkeys all showed the signs of relaxed nerves, perfectly normal brain function, and acute, improved awareness and focus. It worked. That legitimate drug was cheated in to the system, sold, and Sominex X was forgotten about. Some of the muscle thought it would be funny to switch a couple doses of the violent drug with the potent one, the animals they truly were, and that's where the rumors of tragic results from monkey testing came from. I figured what they were doing and put an end to their little joke, as they called it, right away."

XIII

"How come…" Joseph waved off Cole's question, but Cole persisted, "Sominex X was used on those patients in the sleep study, still. Explain." Cole hurried his speech and Warner heard it loud and clear.

"I was allowed out on a bit longer of a leash, and found out about Phillip's research group," Warner addressed Cole, "remember I was with S&H Inc. for many years. Because of Sominex, the generic company name, and shady, but genius businessmen - along with killing all of their enemies and paying off the right allies - we remained under the radar. They took my best years, however, but even the old man you see before you, I could enter Phillip's study and do some good with Sominex. Once I proved I was clean again and showed I helped people I could report to S&H Inc. and not spend my life in jail. The businessmen paid the right people, the muscle killed the ones who got in the way and asked too many questions, and my credentials were faked to be squeaky clean, even though Phillip could intuit that they were far from it. I wanted to trick S&H Inc. into thinking I was doing their human trials, myself knowing that no sane board of reviews would allow such a thing, with Sominex X, but I was really using Sominex." Cole wasn't satisfied with this.

"How did Sominex X get involved then," Cole impatiently chilled Warner, "how?" Even Heinrich was chilled at this and let it play out.

"The businessmen had the muscle convince people hired by S&H Inc. to switch out the good, mild drug for the bad, violent drug, but only a little at a time and slowly," Cole saw it all coming together now, and realized the doctors he thought merely to be kind observers were inside S&H Inc. hired hands, "and it was snuck in by recent college medical student graduates who were still prone to doing anything to get ahead, or make a few extra bucks on the side, as long they didn't get caught." Warner noticed the realization on Cole's face. "Yes, Dr. Adrian, Brody, and Clara. They are real doctors, but they are on the S&H Inc. payroll. I was fanatical about what was happening when I figured it out, but didn't say anything. I thought the night shift and their lax security would let me get one over on them and sneak Sominex back in to everyone's dosage, but they were always a step ahead and switched my distribution trays with Sominex X pills." Cole began to become furious again, but now it was at people who weren't even here. Heinrich spoke for him.

"So you mean to say you were trying to save them, but you were inadvertently poisoning them," Heinrich couldn't believe it all, even as he said it and saw the whole ball of yarn unravel before him, "and they were making you look like the guilty one to toss to the wolves." Cole suddenly became sympathetic for Warner and met his gaze to say *I'm sorry* with little to no voice, too shocked to make his throat speak it out loud or audibly.

"No, it was my fault," Warner said, "I was crazed and passionately doing everything I could and - unbeknownst to myself - everything they set me up to do for them. At this point I had to disappear, so I created J.W. Inc., a shell corporation that on the surface was advertised as a medical consulting firm, using my good - but ill-gotten by cheating - credentials, but actually did nothing but hide. I haven't been here for more than a few months after escaping S&H Inc. after the sleep study fiasco. But they found me here, did what you see all around you, and have threatened to destroy my credentials and turn me in, blaming me for being behind all of it all along, if I report them. Now you see why I tried to disappear. I lived here at this office because my own home was no longer safe from S&H Inc.'s hired muscle." Warner looked at Cole and then at Heinrich pitifully, then back at the ground.

"Call the cops, Cole," Heinrich said, staying off Warner's shocked expression, "but only once Warner's out of here. They can find it like this with him here and S&H Inc.'s eyes all around. We can report that we've been here, we found it, and rummaged through the rubble to sit down and take it in while we called them. That will explain enough."

This was how Cole Dawson and Heinrich left Warner and his situation behind them. Warner expressed his desire to run and wasn't to be stopped, and being involved in the S&H Inc. crime family - and toxic environment - wasn't what Warner wanted for Cole or Heinrich. So Cole and Heinrich stayed at the scene and gave Warner fifteen minutes to leave, whereupon they were to call the cops, follow the story Heinrich created, and meet up at a later time, if and when Warner felt it safe to contact Heinrich, again. The cops arrived, viewed the damage, bought the story on account of Cole Dawson's credibility and character witness - arrived at by contacting his editor at the newspaper - and Heinrich's work record and lack of anything but a history of proper, genuine medical work.

Dr. Heinrich Messier agreed to, doing a completely independent investigation of his own from the inside, to use his contacts with Dr. Phillip Bergie and his connections, as well, to get Dr. Adrian Alger, Brody Jamison, and Clara Burton investigated. Cole would use all of his journalistic connections and access to the local and larger papers - he occasionally would do a freelance job for - to put out articles to blow the entire thing wide open when Heinrich gave him enough information and the time was right. Cole Dawson called Amy Campbell and explained everything to her, so she was informed, and he wasn't suspected of anything criminal or, even worse, not keeping her in the loop and forgetting to call her back as promised. Jonah Murphy was proud of Cole's boldness and his journalistic beat on the story of the J.W. Inc. building break in. Lastly Dr. Joseph Warner had disappeared and was somewhere biding his time until it was right to give his former college friend - and at one time in life potential colleague - the call that would set up the downfall of the S&H Inc. crime family, once and for all, whether or not he himself fell with it.

Visitors To The White Oak
(3/21/2015)

I

It is known and known far and wide, as well as popularly held to be true, that inspiration and direction is the hardest thing to find. That is one of the few surface-level conceptions that the entire world, as well all other worlds around, can agree upon, and that is where the communal empathy seems to end. Beyond that everyone has their own take upon things of the daily, weekly, monthly, yearly, and longer-scaled frames of time one and all of us have to carry on and through with in our lives. Others will intervene and drop their own acorns, leaves, twigs, and low - as well as high - hanging fruits of learned, experiential knowledge and wisdom, as they know. Sometimes, they even may have a new approach, a different vision, and straight out of left field observation that we may have missed, but seemed to know all the more so illusively right in plain sight in front of us, all along. It is these interactions - the civil and conversational ones, however - that we must never forget and that we must remember forever, which may seem redundant to say, but upon further reflection shows just how much we have forgotten and need to remember all over again.

Wesley Fitzgerald was a man who was in his own head too much and too often. The number of times he was told, and had believed it to be true himself and still find himself there, that it was the most dangerous place a man or woman could spend their time was beyond counting. He was a thinker who thought himself to craziness, a doer who did himself in until he had no fuel left in the tank, and he was a giver who gave of himself until he had become the one in need. He was a liver who had experienced so much that he felt the need to run from that vantage point of the world and find a new one for the sake of sanity, starting over, and hopefully getting it right every new "this time" that came along. His life, times, and existence was a nasty, vicious-looking learning curve when it was charted and plotted along a graph, and showed all the telltale signs of manic highs, more moderate highs, neutral midlines, being in a little more want than having, and panic-inducing lows. All told, honestly and more forthright, consistency and just going with the universal flow was not his greatest asset or ability.

He was a self-touted Jena Paul Sartre, Edmund Husserl, and Soren Kierkegaard rolled up into one singular embodiment. Wesley held onto all of the self-paralyzing fears, trembling, imbalanced worldview, confusion of how he himself fit into it all, desire to feel he could control a bit of his destiny somehow and at the same time, and all of the tenets that held shaky ground, constantly in flux, together. The path of his life was one of the usual, modern day thirty year old whose fragile, dreamer's mind - that was always on the move, seeking more and more, and deeper and deeper - had been thrown into the real world in a day in age that valued numbers, statistics, distractions, and busy-work over the real stuff of life that past societies held guarded and dear. To Wesley there was no question as to why the older generation looked at his, and other proceeding generations, with discontent, at a distance, mistrust, and yet still with sympathy and empathy. He was the black sheep in his own generation, had few friends - in a sheer numbers game - to show for this, didn't buy into ignorantly blissful distractions, and chose to rather do as the boxer who may not have been a champion, but loved the game. He chose to take all the hits - both the small and massive blows - and reveled in the fact he could feel and appreciate how it felt, even at the gradual self-destruction of his mind, body, and well being.

Wesley Fitzgerald was the best candidate for an existentialist and carried it proudly. He boldly, and profoundly, feared and trembled his way through every day as a man driven to figure this life out even, if, and when it finally - by the time that time came - killed him. Joy was a fleeting thing for him, Kafka-esque nervousness was a daily routine, and a face that projected his every thought, feeling, and emotion that was his stock and trade. None-the-less were his personal accomplishments in beyond amateurish arts of writing, reading of his predecessor's literature output, musical abilities, and overall ability to read the world and all it was peopled, and animaled, by. None-the-more were his surface accomplishments - which this newer, colder, crueler world reveled in only - of marital, parental or business-regarded status, paper printed degree, renowned name, position, title, exclusive office or parking space occupancy, or anything that followed this string of thought. This line - he felt - was a bumper-to-bumper stock and feed line of sad, sorry, career candles that burned out from both ends on more often than not regular occasions.

As much as he could elaborate, into written words, the greatest throws and sweeps of his imagination, daydreams, visions, hopes, wishes, and goals he was cripplingly limited in his ability to carry on conversations of any length or communicate such internal epiphanies as these to any more than a scant, one-decimal-place percentage of people. He had always felt he was on the brink of a realization that would change his world and everyone else's by association. At the same time he felt that he was either a step behind, ahead, or had simply overlooked that realization from being distracted, looking in the wrong direction at just the wrong time, or some other coincidental, monumental, or fleeting period of a few seconds. It was these moments and seconds that filled his thoughts, which was why he was always the epitome of the modern day thinker, mental tinkerer, and philosopher in the making who just needed discovered, as well as guided at times.

Where the four basic tenets - as he saw them to be in his own personal study and observation of human nature and humanity's general, overarching experiences in total - of education, occupation, happiness, meaning he was not, on paper, as most this new world's existence seemed to solely lived upon and comprised of, the pinnacle of success. He never quite knew what his future held, as neither did his contemporaries or historical likenesses seem to have in common either, but he knew it wouldn't ever be quite the whiz, bang, or pow excitement of every passing, temporary, and temporal bumper sticker, few second slogan, or generalization. His was something deeper than that which passed off as explanations for everything that was too far of an epiphany-inducing journey into the cave of self-realization for his generation's remote understanding, capacity, or willingness to face head-on, lest it mess up their own blissful view of the world as it flew by too fast to really see what was going on.

All of this was what specifically had brought him to this tree, in the vicinity of the middle of the city park, upon this day that felt like spring but wanted to be summer, had known it would become fall, and accepted the eventual winter to come. He had recently come into possession of the most valued commodity of someone of his mindset, which was time off from the real world, stressful life, strenuous demands, and pulls in every direction other than the one he was most intent upon investigating, venturing down, and discovering. He let his mind become a blank pallet, an empty canvas, and a jar that was ready to be filled to near brimming over with fireflies that lit up, sparked imaginative ideas, and sparkled throughout the nighttime for everyone - who had that specific talent of vision - to see. His goal was to take in nature like the most devoted churchgoers took in every Sunday. He would sit back and listen with the hope of seeing and hearing a new revelation that rivaled the Bible's own in intensity and grandiosity, but on a smaller scale. To others his pursuit would not have made sense, least of all the explanation, but it made perfect sense to Wesley Fitzgerald.

II

Wesley Fitzgerald, partly reclining and partly sitting with his back up against the white oak, had just awoken from, by a brief glance at his watch's face, a half-hour nap he had been the recent recipient of. Among all of the city parks in and around his neck of the woods, and world - with their scattered cottonwood, sycamore, silver maple, bitternut hickory, box elder, red elm, crack and black willows - was this white oak. This miniature part of the forest, set within the middle portion of the park, had a great diversity of canopy trees, with flowers popping up around each tree. This one was a good, solid, shade-providing tree that was perfect for reflection and writing. He was armed with his faux-leather portmanteau, pencil, a fresh legal pad of paper, and a mind that had begun to feel the beautiful calm of the oncoming storm of creative energy and ideas that stir up concepts into life. To get to this spot the trail passed around and through ravines, over streams, and wound up and around similar nature trail walk scenes. Sure they were miniature versions of state park's claims of such things, but they were just right in Wesley's frame of mind, reference, and proportion.

Upon waking he took in the light in the sky, for it was that interesting changing of the guard between late morning and early afternoon, and thought it appeared as if a great, universal filter was removed somewhere. The breeze felt more alive, the trees looked to be more animated, the branches and leaves seemed to waver about with a slight bit less refusal of their mother tree's resistance to hold them back from, normally, and the sky seemed a little clearer. It was as if something above had decided it needed a clearer look at Wesley Fitzgerald for one reason or another. As he contemplated this two ravens from off in the distance, which seemed to not be following the passing migration routes of the other birds, were all but inattentive and oblivious of his presence here. They seemed to be following a beeline straight to his location under this white oak tree and as he stared harder and focused more intently on them they seemed to nod their head, each of them, at Wesley in return. This gesture landed its intended response on Wesley and threw him for a momentary, confused, and mind-blowing loop he came to from immediately.

"Hello, hello, my name Hugin," the first raven spoke, as the two were in the process of landing and approaching in front of Wesley, "and I am the brother." With this both ravens landed, shook off their travel-worn wings, and began to strut toward Wesley.

"I am Mugin," spoke the second raven, "and I am the sister. I've seen that look before and we get it every time, for the first, we meet someone." Wesley remained speechless as the apparently intelligent birds filled in the blanks to questions he couldn't form the words to.

"We fly all over the world and bring information to those who seem to be quite thirsty for it," Hugin spoke, "and we are known for being quite to the point about things. You are a man with many questions and unfortunately don't know what to ask…at least by your silence, I am to assume such." Both ravens met each other's glance and went back to regarding Wesley.

Wesley was thinking many things, rather fast, and completely taking in even fewer, as the ravens chattered back and forth to each other under their breath, solely for themselves, and not Wesley to hear, apparently, for the moment. Before, Wesley had felt like a John Steinbeck character - in real life - in the world with the constantly evolving philosophies and outlooks of an F. Scott Fitzgerald character that was now living out Franz Kafka story. He had for a long time wished he could commit to the outsider mentality, as Walt Whitman could, and simply embrace the innocence and pleasure, the good nature, and charmed outlook of the simple life of a Charles Dickens' character, but currently felt like his had landed in L. Frank Baum's land of Oz.

"He appears to be in deep though, this one," Mugin stated the obvious, "his eyes have the quick, darting, back and forth flitter the bipeds have when they're tied up of the tongue." Hugin seemed to agree with this.

"Yes, yes, and he seems to be in a temporary state of shock that we can speak, and intellectually at that," Hugin kept up the singular track of dialogue the two carried on, "and I see nothing's changed with the bipeds, in regard to us, since the 13th century." Mugin began to step backward and forth, and settle in position, again.

"Yes, nothing has," Mugin carried on, "only the characters that respond to the role call." Both ravens regarded each other, quite amused at this, then back to Wesley.

"I'm sure you speak, Wesley Fitzgerald, and yes we know your name," Hugin stated quite directly, "I would expect you to speak much more intelligently, as well, than the other bird-folk we passed on our way, simply from experience." Wesley's eyes were following each raven as they spoke and passed the veritable, invisible speaking feather back and forth.

"I would expect he would, too," Mugin added, "significantly much more than the red-winged blackbirds, pied-billed grebe, red-necked goose, red-tailed hawk, cardinal, and red-necked grebe. And much more politely than that militaristic hawks, especially." The militant hawk must have made them uncomfortable, collectively, as the ravens shook themselves off at its mention. Then they returned to Wesley, whose silent lips began to move and eventually caused words to come out.

III

"You startled me, that's all," Wesley began, "I was just thinking about…things….and I not only saw you two coming off in the distance, but felt you were going to come over here, as well. And you did. You startled me…that startled me…that's all."

"Yes, there's no more a startled biped than one that's been caught napping," Hugin confirmed, "and you apparently can see deeper than others, to have caught our message, even though it was sent silently and wordless." Hugin cocked his head to the side and then back for a moment to take Wesley in.

"Yes, I come out here to think," Wesley said, miming to his portmanteau, "and to possibly write, should I be put in the right mood to do so. I enjoy writing and find I'm much better at communicating with most through writing than talking, unless they're my own kind of people." The ravens considered this momentarily.

"And yet you find you still don't even reach everyone, after all," Mugin continued, "not even all of those like yourself and by far even fewer of those unlike yourself." The ravens had come to learn to read people well in their time and experience.

"Yes, but we have known many bipedal shamans, like you," Hugin carried on, "who bring a certain life out of words and concepts that, understood or not by those he's writing for, he must do so because it's just what he does." Both ravens nodded at this.

"I like that idea, but my work hasn't seemed to really become what I wanted it to, yet," Wesley confirmed, realistically and with sympathy for himself, "I'm trying to do what I finally realized I love doing all along, after years of jumping around from this job to that that job, and here to there…it hasn't quite worked out, yet, though." Both ravens considered this.

"Just as well, not even a king, Odin or any of the string of prominent pre-Christians," Mugin added, "those thought to be mythological or not, real or not, and believed to be such or the other not all, had or have it all together, either." Hugin's eyes showed him to be in thought at this comment's mentioning and the next line of reasoning it brought to his part of their singular track of thought.

"Yes, it's just as such with other bipeds throughout history, long before you," Hugin continued, "their actions and words were, and are, like banners. Some are of greater size, strength, and meaning. Some flutter violently in the air, some softly and gently, and yet others fall flat and dead to earth. It's a mystery, truly, which ones will leave any lasting impact upon those that discover it in the air or on the ground." Wesley thought about this for a moment.

"Yeah, I guess I'm like them, somehow, if you say so, even," Wesley thought, "I feel like for everything I've tried to learn and do I haven't quite stumbled upon the bit that lets me say I really get it, now. I don't seem to quite…" As he spoke Mugin strained her eyes and shook her head.

"Bah, all the listing of details of books of history that bipeds like to iterate for some reason," Mugin returned a thoughtful look at Wesley, "you must always be in the pursuit of doing something or else you will never realize what you are to become, as if you are doing nothing to realize it for yourself you are doing, even less for others, to realize what you are meant to become to them and for them." Now it was Hugin's turn for his eyes to flash with the next continuance of their singular track of thought split up onto two parallel rails of cars moving at the same speed.

"We have seen many of your kind, bipeds that is, and many others of your kind, self proclaimed and well-intentioned philosophers, that is, as well," Hugin kept on, "and we have taken many different forms ourselves, but whether it was the 13th century men later were touted as Norse, 9th century pre-Christians, and the 20th century's final offering of noble thinkers, writers, leaders, and doers they have all had to be discovered while in the middle of doing something else, meanwhile." Wesley considered this and received the next line from Mugin, as he expected Hugin to pass it on between them.

"As for everyone else in between, we've simply lost track," Mugin admitted, "we never really were the type to ledger journals and document records for keeping, as we simply pass on our collected knowledge we're meant to keep in the old steel, rattle trap." Both birds mimed with their wings, referencing to their heads at the same time, amusing Wesley.

"Yes, and we are now here for you, Wesley Fitzgerald," Hugin confirmed, "and there are those who have called upon us and our presence, omens of good fortune, but mostly it's just our words guiding on those whose fortune is a mere reflection of their own already-received good fortunes, for them to realize their own hopes, to use their own already-forged talents and abilities." Wesley instinctually turned to Mugin.

"And our being guardian spirits to descend upon such bipeds," Mugin continued, "is merely dependent upon just how much of a guardian, or guiding hand, or voice they need. We will be that for them, however." Wesley took this in and the ravens continued down the track, onto another subject and matter at hand.

"Just like you, in all that you've done and said, as well," Hugin affirmed, "we too, Mugin and myself, have been the recipients of different judgments, castes, and wives tales from 9th century pre-Christians, 13th century Norse, those 20th century last bastions of wisdom, and everyone else in between. Oh, even the scores of gods who didn't live up to their titles, whereas mortal bipeds seemed to trump them in effort, and successes - both every day and occasionally - of great spirit, and gusto." As Hugin finished this statement Mugin's eyes flashed on cue.

"As even a centuries old, one-eyed king is, once in a while, placed on the same level as men and women," Mugin amusedly confirmed, "mortal or not, and whether you're considering mortality deemed by one's actions, legacy, being, living, or having died." Both ravens twitched a moment and shook off the latest breeze that blew. Taking into account the look of trust and newfound calm in Wesley, at their presence and words, both ravens gently lifted off the ground and perched, one on each of Wesley's shoulders.

"Sometimes, through it all," Mugin carried on, "Hugin and myself have even questioned whether or not to return to our current master or masters, but in the end decided it was in the best interest of ourselves, as well as them, to do so." Wesley calmly regarded both ravens on his shoulders with interest and intrigue.

"It seems to always be the best decision, no matter what age or era you've been born into," Hugin finished, "as it is always a good matter of policy, and minding to one's own heart of the matter, to return to where one came from to figure out where one is going." With that both ravens regarded each other, quickly flapped their wings to lift off of Wesley's shoulders, and hovered in front of him.

"I would suggest that instead of walking on the straight and familiar, or narrow, path," Mugin said, "you try to learn to fly and spread your wings a littler more. You bipeds and your straight, comfortable lines have always eternally confused us." The ravens seemed even more mesmerizing as they flapped their wings gently to maintain their position in front of Wesley.

"Focus on the journey and reflect upon where it takes you," Hugin continued, "for the mere sake of the journey and the reflection, and take continued survival - and the chance to share with others how to do so - as a success in and of itself." Hugin turned his head to Mugin, as if cueing that it was time to be off.

"Also, consider this, student of Husserl, Sartre, and Kierkegaard," Mugin concluded, "think more about being a singular part of a greater scheme where all of our lives, experiences, and everything else you bipeds focus so intently on, are intermingled for better or worse. And realize that you make it, for the better or worse, based upon what you decide it should be." With that both ravens regarded each other, took off toward the sky, and headed off into the great distance beyond.

Upon his entire search, up to this point, muddling - as Hugin and Mugin would have referred to it, as bipeds loved to do - through history books and endless stacks of this and that to find bits of knowledge and wisdom, to find themselves at their own I get it now, moment, he'd overlooked the most important thing. He'd forgotten all about the moments within the time, spent sifting through page after page, and especially about the lives lived in between such ventures through biped's collected histories. Wesley found that his education - as he had dictated it as such - was dictated, up to now, by the words and wisdom and experiences of others, strictly so. To truly find, and not merely stumble upon, his own personal I get it now moment he would have to live and experience and learn of his own power, and take all of his book-learned information, statistics, facts, and figures out into the real world for a test drive to see what fell off the wagon by the wayside, as well as what stayed along for the ride.

For all of his focus on intentionality being the hallmark of all consciousness, Wesley hadn't considered that there was the possibility of just living and going along with the flow at a certain point. At that point he thought that letting go of the reigns and following the direction he'd set himself off upon could be more eye-opening than micro-managing every step along the way. This seemed to allow for him to come to even further realizations without rigorously logical, analytical, and step-by-step driven, stodgy, stuffy timelines of history that were recorded by those who - upon reflection later on - would realize they could recount all of it from databases of texts, but couldn't truly tell the stories of their own interesting history. Wesley wanted to experience and learn where and how he fit it, but didn't want to be so aggressive about it that he forgot how enlightening it was to be passive for a spell, and allow life to show you how it's lived on occasion.

IV

Once the two ravens, Hugin and Mugin, who had shared a single track of thought together, had flown off there was rustling of a few straggling leaves that lay fallen on the ground. Looking in the direction of the gentlest disruption of nature, towards the creek at the edge of the clearing of the forest, Wesley observed a large, white stag taking a drink. As if to acknowledge Wesley, but to also show a level of sophistication and confidence that was unshakable, the stag slowly raised its head up to Wesley and kept its eyes upon his. The deer trotted along gently toward the white oak. Having reached the white oak the stag stopped a few feet before him and nodded to acknowledge.

"My name is Cornucopia," the white stag introduced itself, "this color is not normal for my kind, so that makes me stand out as different, as you feel you do yourself, but for different reasons." The white stag responded to Wesley's captivation at his coat's coloration.

"It doesn't seem too common," Wesley confirmed, "coming across a white stag, especially around here." The stag considered this.

"I am not from around here, nor am I from this when," Cornucopia answered, "and my coloring is natural. It is a reflection of my inner spirit and energy penetrating outward, whether or not the world appreciates it. I am a messenger, as the Celts of old thought me to prominently be so." Wesley thought this was in line with most recent events.

"A messenger," Wesley thought, "interesting. And what message have you been sent to tell me. I did come out here to think and find something, after all." He genuinely was curious at the arrival of such a tamed wild animal. Even at the most recent departure of the two ravens he was still amazed by this series of happenings.

"Normally my presence is preceded, and called forth, by one who is finding themselves in some sort of trouble," the stag considered, "but then again my presence is also called forth and preceded by one doing a good deed, as well. It all depends on whom I'm being called to, but I see nothing of either sort here. So I am not sure what the message is, exactly, but like all good messengers who find themselves tasked somewhere I will figure out what it is I am to tell you." The stag seemed to think this was all good and well enough, so too Wesley did, as well.

"Being that my specific message for you has not been made clear to me," Cornucopia said, "but knowing that there is always a message for someone, we will consider what it is and come to it. Either way you have most probably passed the same moderately more difficult nature trail, the one your bipedal kind hasn't completely torn out my nature to create, along the cliffs that follows the river to get here." The stag perked up his ears to take in the sounds around him and then returned a calm demeanor to Wesley.

"Yes, I like that one," Wesley confirmed, "I find it makes me feel like I'm more back to nature than on the other ones." He thought about the view of the river from the trail.

"A noble thing, being back to nature," Cornucopia said, "that river cut into the land and cliff sides over a period of hundred and thousands of years, all told. I've witnessed its progress and it's truly a miracle to watch a force of nature, like water, and know that not even bipedal machines can completely capture or control it, especially not forever, without quite a bit of work. Like myself, I've managed to evade men's capture as long as I can remember. And it's not because of man's ignorance or my kind's sheer brilliance and deftness, but mostly because of bipedal man's inability to commit, subconsciously, to what they would do once they caught us." The white stage took a moment to take in Wesley's intrigued reaction.

"It is also part of the thrill of the chase," Cornucopia carried on, "the joy of a good old fashion chase has called to bipedal men's hearts as much as the catch. But you or your kind will never catch me simply because I do not want you to, in my case, and I am rather needed to be free to be a messenger for all those who need me to be such."

"Interesting," Wesley's mind began to grip onto a theme to what the stag's message was, "I've sort of been contemplating how I fit into it all, how I can contribute to my world, as well." The stag saw that Wesley saw something underneath all their banter that tied it together somehow.

"Well, we are in fact realizing the message I have come to deliver," Cornucopia affirmed, "as we, myself and those who I'm sent to, always do. You may be seeing something. My presence, influence, and mere being has sometimes been the catalyst for many a Christian martyr to be converted into such a role as mine, and they have even, on occasion, at least with St. Eustace, been known to see a vision in my horns. Tell me, Wesley - a good messenger always knows the name of his recipient - do you see anything in my horns?" The stag waited a moment for Wesley to consider this, as Wesley, currently not seeing anything, thought he could if he willed himself to.

"No, I don't," Wesley sounded disappointed, "I don't. I'm trying to, but I really don't." The deer considered him sympathetically.

"That is perfectly all right, as well," Cornucopia comforted Wesley, "not all bipedal men do. But the way you moved to find yourself here, taking the more difficult nature trail, you were springing forward and upward, and keeping a keen eye out all around you." The stag saw Wesley's attention peak up a little.

"There's a lot of roots that push up under the dirt," Wesley confirmed, "and rocks in the path, let alone the stones and boulders built into the ledge on the cliff side that make up that stairway when the river turns. You actually saw me?" Wesley was more amazed at the stag's observation and instinct than thinking he was being spied on or watched by a stealthy, sinuous, or malevolent being with likewise intentions.

"I observed you were quite stealthy," Cornucopia commended Wesley's trail and tracking skills, "and my kind, are also known to spring forward, upward, and keep a keen eye out. It's the true spirit of scouting that leads us to do so and that same spirit is in you, as well. It is the spirit that leads oneself onward to leap over difficulties, to face new adventures in your active pursuits of higher aims. That could be a part of the message as well." Cornucopia's cheerful voice signified that he thought their banter was getting somewhere, closer to revealing the message, in its complete fullness that he had for Wesley.

V

"That definitely sounds like something relevant to where I'm at right now," Wesley confirmed, "I have been on the look-out for something and it tells me I'm doing something right in my search of what it is." He considered that the stag might drop even more nuggets of wisdom into his lap and read deeper into what the stag continued to say.

"Good, good," the stag considered cheerily, "then how about this to carry on. My kind, we are a symbol of purity. We see only with eyes of goodness and honesty and can suggest such things to the recipients of our messages. There is a purity inside you that has called me to you. You find yourself in the company of yourself, and a small number of others sensitive to such things as yourself, avoiding the impurities of the rest of the world as best you can." The stag saw understanding in Wesley's eyes and continued.

"We are a symbol of otherworldliness, as well," Cornucopia said, "I cross between many different parallel worlds regularly and routinely. I have seen them all and can tell you they are no better or worse, but only different. It is the world above ours, however, and no other parallel world, that is better and different entirely. As to your fear of your purity being threatened you must be strong, as I am when I enter into a new world." The stag saw a smile on Wesley's face.

"Now that definitely sounds like a clear cut and direct message for me," Wesley said, "I do feel I need to show that I can be bolder and stronger than I allow myself to be." The stag was pleased with this.

"My kind is also a symbol of peace or truce," the stag continued, "which is why we come into and out of bipedal men's sight and elude most others. We do not act as aggressors. We merely get one's attention in a subtle, but direct enough way, and we stay out of the way until we're called to deliver a message. I sense a desire to keep peace within yourself as well, and a sense to act in a such a way to avoid the need of disastrous confrontations, but the need to step in yourself, when you or yours needs you to, as well." The stage observed Wesley face acknowledging that he did in fact have a pacifist spirit, but a hint of a look behind his eyes that said he'd do what he had to, so as to maintain that peace and resolve of the world around him, should someone try to disturb it.

"Lastly, my kind, when caught by bipedal men," the stag carried on, "have been known to grant a wish for anything, of any kind, that men desire, but only when we're caught. And unfortunately, Wesley, you have not caught me, as I have rather allowed myself to maintain rapt by your attention for this appointment…but I can see, too, that you neither require one or would ask for it, otherwise." The stag was pleased with this and saw a stronger resolve and courage in Wesley that his message had very possibly brought out.

"No, I won't be needing one," Wesley confirmed, "I've found that anything my family, myself, or a greater power can't see as necessary for me probably isn't as such." The stag knew he had delivered the message he and Wesley had revealed, for both exactly what is was and what it meant.

"I would suggest that you think more with your heart than with your mind, as you do enough thinking with your mind. Do and act simply to do the right thing - whatever it may be for yourself or others - without concern of ends or means. We are all ingrained with purity and peace and an intuition that we are born with. This unites all of the facts and figures you bipeds seem to be so obsessed with, as well as the religious communing of all natural things. This will help you with your scouting and searching, as well." The stag carried on.

"I would also suggest that you move forward, and move on, with less concern and more awareness of your natural instincts and vision ahead as you go on from here to there and feel motivated to do so," the stag concluded, "and focus on being a beacon of hope, light, vision, and honesty. Enjoy the thrill of the chase and always be in pursuit of goodness, integrity, and to be as a living example for others, especially when you find yourself called into uncomfortable places and must face adversity and confrontation."

"With my work done here I must be going," Cornucopia said, "I have lead others to and out of real and supposedly fictional lands - to the limited minds of non-believing bipedal men - and I believe I have done so for you, as well. I am now off to find out for myself what the next message is that I must deliver and to whom I must deliver it to." The stag's ears perked up, he became momentarily alert, but then maintained a calm resolve as he concluded with Wesley.

Up to now Wesley had felt that he wanted to be able to be blissfully happy as a Charles Dickens' character, but felt he was - by virtue of circumstance and situation - quite similar to another one in a story that took place in a completely different season, but similar enough as such. He'd found that his approach to finding active employment - professional or personal - to contribute to the world, was noble enough and he was simply scouting his way to next place he was needed. There were spots, he could now see with a newfound clarity, where he could have better sought to find out why he, upon finding himself somewhere else with an unclear sense of purpose, was called to land there and what message he was meant to give. Wesley could remember many instances where he'd missed the opportunity to simply enjoy the thrill of chasing down a job and task he could really get into, where he could be something to somebody, and just enjoy the little victories of coming closer each time.

He felt a strengthening in his belief that one could base realizations and belief systems upon what was seen, sensed, and witnessed to occur all around him, but to hone it by seeing it with honest, pure eyes and find the message it was telling him underneath it all. Wesley felt he better understood, from the calm and resolve of Cornucopia, just how - on the other side of things - anxiety, meaninglessness, and a loss of focus can afflict those in and around that sphere of happenings in that world, and that he should be the beacon of hope with a different message. He knew he needed to fear less, not tremble at all, be unafraid to show a graceful spirit, even in the most graceless of times and places, specifically those he had been avoiding at all cost. Most importantly he felt another opportunity to be the bearer, firsthand, of another entirely new and interesting experience that few had the openness of mind and heart to be invited into being the recipient of, as he heard another stirring in the bushes just a little ways off.

VI

Looking in the direction of the stirring he observed two foxes, each with nine tails, approaching him. He could hear them talking, or rather mildly arguing with each other as a brother and sister in blood or spirit would, as they came closer.

"Oh, now why did you have to go and do that, Huxian," the other fox said, "why must you play tricks like that?" Wesley was intrigued at the dialogue that carried on from this.

"Oh, you never break the rules, or even bend them, Huli Jing," said Huxian, "you're always going on about how this is bad, that's not good, and why I can't have just a little fun." Wesley was amused by the fact that his next two visitors seemed to have a little more spirit of a kind he recognized growing up with his siblings.

"I do to have fun, sometimes," Huli Jing defended himself, "I just don't like playing tricks, that's all. Not even like yours, even as innocent and less deceitful, than lighthearted, as they may be." Huli Jing was what Wesley remembered was called a goody-two-shoes in grade school.

"And that's all it is, I say," Huxian defended herself, "a little fun that doesn't hurt anyone but makes someone laugh a little and have a bit of good, sporting fun. It leaves the tricked one a little more on their toes, is all." Huxian must have been the prankster of the two.

"And look now," Huli Jing said, a bit disappointed, "our arguing has up and completely, utterly ruined our mystical and magical entrance we'd planned." He looked up to see Wesley's amusement at the two.

"Now we could do it all over again," Huxian resolved, ready to turn tails back into the woods and redo it, "we could, now." Huli Jing just shook his head and Huxian followed his lead towards Wesley.

"Sorry about all that, Wesley, but I am Huli Jing," the male fox introduced himself properly, "the good, honest spirit, and this is Huxian." Huxian jumped in to complete her introduction.

"I am Huxian," she added, "and I'm what Huli Jing calls a bit of a trickster and prankster, but I'm not really bad. I just come close to getting carried away sometimes. And we really do get along quite well, you will find." Huli Jing nodded in approval of this, and then began to smell the ground around them.

"I smell a bird…no…a raven, specifically," Huli Jing said, "and…a deer, no…something like a deer…" Huxian sighed.

"A white stag, Huli Jing," Huxian confirmed, "I tried to lay an innocent little trip-up for one in the woods once, hid a good distance away to watch it all, and all the thing did was stop in front of it, smell the air, look in my direction, and shake its head at me as it leaped right over it." Huli Jing looked on with a *serves you right* look.

"Well I guess it was all and good then," Huli Jing said, "no one was hurt or made a fool of. But getting back to why we're here, again, Huxian…" Both foxes turned to regard Wesley.

"It was a pair of ravens, Hugin and Mugin," Wesley confirmed, "and Cornucopia, the white stag. I'm getting quite a few interesting visitors today." The two foxes considered this momentarily.

"Well that makes perfect sense why we don't seem to surprise you," Huli Jing said, "being able to speak to you, and all. You can assume we are here for much the same thing, then. But we do have quite a bit to say about it." These two were like Hugin and Mugin, but with two different tracks of thought and what seemed like a friendly sibling rivalry, and friendship happening at the same time as well.

"And no tricks either," assured Huxian, "you have my word on that. And even the word of a trickster counts for something." Wesley prepared himself for the next lesson in life from another set of the more interesting, far off, magical, and mystical characters in life and time's cast that had lived it longer than him and seen much more, as well.

VII

"We have been know to take on different physical forms, human ones like your kind, specifically," Huli Jing confirmed, "but there's something about you that tells us you're a little more open to us being ourselves. And we are happier as ourselves, as well." Huxian nodded her head in accordance with this notion.

"I've been know to take the form of a beautiful woman, being a lady of course," Huxian said, "and to give the mortals a reason to have their safe and secure stereotype of them, so to not divide them or make them have to think too much. It's also quite a trick, as well." Huli Jing sighed at Huxian's love of tricks, especially those played on the bipedal human mortals.

"As I have taken the form a male of your kind," Huli Jing said, "as we have used our magic to intervene, to whatever extremity and capacity, when we felt it necessary." He said this with a *what can you do* look, with eyes directed at Huxian.

"But we didn't this time, with you, because we didn't think you needed it," Huxian added, "other than your will, drive, determination, and imagination to guide you through this otherwise utterly boring, rigid, materialistic and surface-level world. I don't know how your kind make it through, sometimes, through all the aggressive, noisy, and attention grabbing muddle the other bipedal mortals like to create, as if they can't handle what's really underneath it all." Wesley had always felt like an outsider and now didn't feel strange, but rather special because it.

"You don't lack imagination or an appreciation of mystical things," Huli Jing said, "unlike the other rigid, strict, excessively rational ones of your kind. Your kind of energy is what we spirits and immortals thrive one, but have no fear however. The energy we take from you is created eternally by something inside you that will never stop replenishing its supply. It keeps multiplying itself all the time." Wesley had not realized they did this before, but was relieved to find that it hadn't been adversely affecting him or his kind, all at the same time.

"You see we're really not dangerous, to good people," Huxian affirmed, "just a bit of tricksters on occasion, for some of us, and on more occasions for others of us. To those who are truly wicked the tricks needs to be of an extremity to make them think to change their ways, that's all. We're more misunderstood, a bit like yourself, than anything else." Huli Jing confirmed this sentiment.

"To give an example, it's like being given what you need, not what you want," Huli Jing explained, "and how mortal human bipeds can construe and misconstrue there lives away, which results in things like vanity, materialism, and weakness…among a few other traits and things we won't mention here." Wesley was seeing an underlying theme and message to their banter that was on a level of what he came out here to listen for.

"There are more of those who don't understand us, like the monks, lovers, Buddhists, and Christians to name a few, just as there are more of those that don't understand you," Huxian said, "but there are enough who do understand us, as Huli Jing understands that I'm also good, deep down, as well, and that is enough for us." Huli Jing nodded at this mention.

"Yes, we are a misunderstood variety, even more so as the ages and civilizations carry on so, as they have been know to do," Huli Jing affirmed, "why take this for example. Your reasons for taking the more difficult, but scenic route, with a historic significance, all to it to get to this spot is something others wouldn't understand. Why not just take the easy path, the paved one that doesn't cut through and beside the wildest of the forest? Why feel the need to pass by the cave with its history, harkening back to the frontier days of the French, the Indians, the intra-cultural war, and the river that once passed through it all in the 1760's?" Huli Jing perked up his ears and cocked his head to the side to add to his sentiment.

"Why? Because we enjoy it and it has a completely different vibration of life running through it," Huxian added, "we feel like something was lived here and we are drawn to its energy, the energy of life that we sense and feel, simply because we're open to receive that energy."

"Even after all that we've said we don't understand what we've been sent to tell you," Huli Jing said, "but the white stag said you're a different one, a more feeling and intuiting one who will get it, either way." Huxian seconded this notion by nodding. Both foxes considered Wesley for a moment and then regarded each other.

"Right then, dear Huli Jing, we must be off," said Huxian, as Huli Jing nodded, "you'll get what it is we said, meant for you, underneath all of that." Wesley was already putting together what he had been pondering in his head and how their banter had filled in many blanks.

"Before we go, lastly, Wesley," Huli Jing began to conclude, "I suggest you try simply being what you need to be for those that need you to be such, especially when it's necessary for yourself or them. Be a source of energy to strengthen others and create a little magic of your own once in a while." Huxian added to this.

"Don't be afraid to toe the line of right and wrong, as long as the best of intentions are held at heart," Huxian said, "trickery is sometimes a good tool to lead those, who are hopelessly defiant, to reach the end that they don't even know is for their best." Huli Jing agreed with this sentiment.

"Focus on being a little more easy going, energetic, and less stuck on pure, rigid, moral dogmas," Huli Jing affirmed, "act more along the lines of good will in action and doing what needs done, even if it toes the lines that biped are so fond of…must be because they have the ability to stand up and make such straight lines, that they're so careful to not walk on them and smude them." Huxian's eyes lit up as a final idea came to her.

"And eat, drink, and be merry," Huxian concluded, "all in good measure and in brotherly and sisterly nature, of course, but do so, still." With that the two foxes were back off to the woods.

Wesley did understand what they meant to say and how it was meant to relate to him. In his own personal quest for happiness, the truest and deepest happiness, that pervades all situations and circumstances in life, he was missing something. These two foxes showed him an energy and sprite-like cheer and happiness that seemed to make every otherwise dull, dismal, and far less than happy moment - to whatever extremity and capacity it was such - slide off of them. Huli Jing and Huxian had a less dogmatic and more sacred approach to life, but it was still one of respect and one brimming with the living essence of what made life brim within it. Wesley knew for sure that the additional message they conveyed, without saying the actual words to deliver it, was to think less, live more, and have a joy that seems to take the better and worse natures of everyone alike in stride, and still stand by them, especially if they're family or close enough to be held as such.

His previously prominent idea that existence precedes essence was being lived by these foxes without them even trying to put words to it. Huli Jing and Huxian simply accepted the fact of what they were meant for and why it was that they existed. They also took it further - being philosophers without even knowing it - to live and thrive, simply because they existed among others whom they wanted to do the same, as well. There was in fact being and nothingness, and these foxes were truly actively involved and aware, and they were far from even allowing a void between themselves and the world around them to exist. When it came to the decision of the philosophy of decisions, freedom from fate, and about being in the world, they simply decided to be and were. They didn't even consider fate in how they simply lived and acted without fear of living, and were a true sharer of the world's energy. The white stag was right in that Wesley would see what even the foxes didn't know the message was they were sent to deliver to him.

VIII

As the two foxes entered the woods again, at the same spot in the bushes they had come from, Wesley heard a low growl - followed by the quick scamper of a trickster fox, and then the cheerful reproving of her more thoughtful counterpart of a fox - from another spot along the edge of where the forest clearing and creek met the heavier, denser woods. From the same spot where the white stag had drunk from the creek a large, black panther entered the clearing. It sniffed at where the stag had been, considered it a second, and then approached Wesley in a slow, nonthreatening quadrapedal walk.

"My name is Panterra and you are right to not fear me, Wesley Fitzgerald," the panther calmly and soothingly spoke, noticing that Wesley did, in fact, not show any sign of fear, "others however, with less noble spirits and intentions, had best fear me, but not you." This last part told Wesley that she was still all panther deep down, but with even more to it than just that, having been chosen to be one of his animal spirit guides.

"I've been told I'm a bit of a different biped than all of you are used to seeing," Wesley said, "and to think, all along, I just thought I was strange not to be able to relate to many other bipeds, as all of you have been calling us." Wesley was amused by this, rather than offended.

"You have had other visitors," Panterra confirmed, "the two ravens, the white stag, and the two foxes. I can smell them. I've been around quite a while, as you can surmise based upon your previous guests." Panterra regarded Wesley nobly and lounged on the ground before him, as she looked around again before regarding Wesley, alone.

"My nature is stereotyped far and wide, and though partially true," Panterra continued, "it's far from the compete story. It is both biblical and infernal, as both Christ and Dante have something to say about it, based upon experience." Wesley, though otherwise now used to wild animals as spirit guides, was a bit in awe at the panther that lay before him.

"My kind have struck fear into many hearts as ferocious beasts, yes," the panther spoke, "but part of that has been a great misunderstanding of our calm and collectedness, to be able to wait. To those that were of less noble spirit and intention however, it was all ferocity and nothing less. But my kind, especially myself, have made our rounds and visitations in our time. I have visited the likes of Christ, Dionysus when in his glory days and during his downfall, and I've passed between the worlds of the living and the dead. I've found, not strangely at all, however, that it was with the Native Americans I felt most accepted and revered." Panterra looked around at the scenery Wesley chose to take as a vantage point of his rest.

"It is a nice view," Wesley said, noticing, "I like to come here and write sometimes, and just to sit in silence other times." The panther growled a low growl that seemed soothing, understanding, and seconded the spot's appeal for such an activity.

"Like the others I may or may not know what it is I'm meant to tell you," Panterra confirmed, "but I will nonetheless tell you what I know and let you figure out what it means for yourself. That's usually how this works best, at least, as I've come to find." The panther's tail flipped gently on the ground behind her.

"All of the heraldic tales and claims about myself and my kind are true," the panther continued on theme, "the sweet and incensed breathe Christ experienced, the signified and dignified fierceness and fury, impetuosity, and remorselessness, in moments, but they're all one and the same, and misunderstood. The simply come as a result of doing what we must from commands of a higher force than nature."

"So you witnessed Christ alive," Wesley spoke in a low and sacred tone of voice, "you must have been around for a while, then." Panterra nodded slowly at this, to confirm that yes she did and yes she had.

"Being immortal has its more interesting moments," the panther confirmed, "like that, as well as watching the natural world change. Like the ground around us only a few minutes' walk away. I witnessed, step by step, the retreat of glaciers that carved out ravines and valleys over a period of ten thousand years. I've watched the different species of plants and trees grow naturally, watched the seasonal birds and hawks come and go, and even witnessed your kind plant a tree here and there. Usually it was the children in scouts of modern times, as well as their more archaic equivalents, but quite a few naturalists and others, also appreciative of nature." Panterra thoughtfully considered this.

"Christ to Dionysus to Dante," Wesley marveled, "to girl scouts. The world has changed quite a bit since then to now." Panterra growled what sounded like a panther's version of an amused laugh and continued her story.

"I do have a labyrinthine knowledge that has come with time, that even Pan himself couldn't come to understand," Panterra carried on, "but I did try to pass it on to him. After all I'm not all beast and am rather not all-anything for that matter. And even as much as Christ's typesetters - most significantly Jeremiah, Hosea, Solomon, Habakuk, Isaiah, and Paul - have been most flattering of me and my kind in their accounts, I do still appreciate it." Something close to an amused smile came to Panterra's face, recalling this memory.

IX

"I have been the sign, when making my presence known to your kind, of the overcoming of lower desires," the panther carried on the story, "just ask St. Augustine. And though your lower desires aren't so primal I am here to tell you, even if just as a side note, to jettison your lesser wants and distractions aside for your true needs, as well as those of others who need you. To tell the stories you've been contracted and covenanted to you must focus and find your genuine muse, and then you will understand the language in which you are to tell those stories. After all, what doesn't kill you only makes you stronger."

"Me," Wesley was greatly surprised at this, "tell amazing stories? Well, that's all right then. I guess I've got some work to do, as long as I've got the time." Panterra nodded at this and growled that acknowledging, nonthreatening growl.

"I have been the same muse of others before," she continued, "the one that awakens the unconscious urges and abilities, once shut down, in those who muse upon me and my kind. It's not in vanity that I say this, that no one is an early onset visionary, but rather that they must return to inspired places and beings to find it, and so birth the creations they were meant to." Panterra paused to take in the scenery again as her tail swayed gently back and forth, and then settled.

"Your own personal time of immanent awakening has been signaled, as a matter of fact" Panterra said, to Wesley's calmly registered, but still, astonishment, "and I am the bell tolling to tell you of this in person. Not in loud rings, however, but subtle, more prominent tones that need no such volume or force behind them, just as your works shall be."

"Me," Wesley, again, could hardly believe what he was hearing, "as long as there's time for me to realize it and be able to do it." Panterra nodded.

"You humans, mortal and bipedal and so lacking in faith," Panterra spoke, "you don't know the power you have, even that over my kind - for both better and worse - when it's collectively united as one." Panterra seemed to consider this for a moment before continuing again.

"I have contested with, and among, horses and bears, and can tell you this," Panterra continued her story, "other than the horse's riders, myself, and my kind will be those left, as the later-most existing viewers to what will happen, after all is said done. Also, as it is being said and done, and till it can no longer be spoken of when it's done." Panterra observed as Wesley took this bit of apocalyptic offering in.

"I am the dark mother, the dark of the moon, the symbol for life and power of the night," the panther carried on, "as well as the symbol of feminine energies manifest upon the earth. We are strong and not to be contested, but rather respected. I am the symbol of darkness, death, and rebirth from out of it." Wesley considered the timeline of events that Panterra had confirmed she lived and observed, and didn't doubt this.

"I am here to be the encapsulation of the fear of the dark and death," Panterra carried on, "as well as that of overcoming it and breathing into it new life. It all just depends upon where the one using myself, or my kind, as their muse is at that time in their life. I am here to help those understand the dark and death, and the inherent powers of them, and that by acknowledging them they can eliminate their fears and learn to use that power." Wesley thought about this for a moment.

"There is a fear of the unknown in you, Wesley," Panterra confirmed, "but if you acknowledge it, face what's there in the dark, and eliminate the unknown you can use that power to embrace what's in the unknown and no longer fear it." Panterra watched at Wesley put together pieces of his life behind his eyes, right before her.

"Fears of darkness and death are misguided steps that lead to falling into traps of their own making," the panther concluded her story, "the fear of the wrong choice, the one that potentially goes against destiny, but you mustn't worry so much. Instead, keep on moving forward and getting sharper, more focused, and smarter all the time."

"I think I get it," Wesley said, appearing quite tired out at the sheer amount of epiphanies that he'd heard in the short span of the day, "gradually, but I think I'm finally getting it." Panterra saw this and nodded that she saw this in him.

"I suggest you allow yourself to see that what doesn't kill you makes you stronger," Panterra confirmed, "for yourself and everyone else around you, so you can inspire your actions and words by its understanding. Allow higher spiritual and universal desires, and needs, to take over the lower, temporal, human, and strictly self serving desires." Panterra's gaze was locked onto Wesley, as she came to the culminating points of her visitation, and she stood up on all fours again.

"Pick and choose your battles," Panterra said, "the ones you can compete in, and never intervene unless you know you can leave standing up afterward, no matter what happens in between, for better or worse." Panterra's tail began to sway back and forth.

"Focus on concerning yourself with what's going on in your own head and heart, how and what you feel about yourself, and not with the conceptions the world around you has for you," the panther carried on, "for they will either come around to realize it as you do or they never will at all, simply because they never wanted to in the first place." Wesley found the train cars in his mind to be clicking into place as he began to recall multiple times when he allowed other's views of himself to get in the way of his doing and being better, for himself and others.

"Try a new philosophy of remembering that home is where the heart is, being there for those that need you, and indulge in those moments to yourself, but only when they're available," the panther looked around at the landscape that was Wesley's time and place of epiphany, "sacrifice otherwise, see the joy of giving of yourself, and enjoy it all the more when you're being given to." As if to signify that was the crescendo of her visitation Panterra gave a low growl to show her respect for Wesley, turned back to forest, and crossed the creek and beyond the last edge of the clearing.

Wesley had understood what had just happened. He thought about how he had been meditating on his search for a life of meaning and value to himself and others. Fear had held him back from taking small steps forward, let alone great leaps, simply because it was the unknown that lie ahead. His lack of experience was one thing, but it could have been overcome by fearlessness, and the calm and collectedness Panterra saw inside of him, and had been beckoned to come out and play, finally. She had experienced her heraldic tales because she had been bold enough to live them and this, as well as the respect she paid towards him - to his amazement at his worthiness of it from such a being as her - told him he was allowed to live out his own tales of equal measure. The stories he was to tell, that he was not only contracted to write, but also covenanted to do so, he was now bound and determined to uncover from inside himself.

Wesley reflected upon his long held standard that the truth is finding you are free, but free in a prison, and that men run from their true freedom toward constraints. This was done to feel, on the surface at least, safer and more structured, but was self defeating. He realized that his freedom was outside with the true animals of his kind, to discover those like himself amongst them, and to learn to live among the others. His so-called safe and secure zone was the thing with a constricting hold, with bars, keeping them out, and also holding himself in. And then there was the classic tenet that someone who deceives himself is himself exhibiting bad faith. As for how he had exhibited bad faith he didn't know, but figured it had been happening for a while, at least. Knowing now that he had been doing so he would no longer, however.

X

Upon this last realization Wesley could hear a faint, watery, distant, but getting closer voice, and felt a poking on his shoulder. Opening his eyes he noticed that it was dark outside. He checked his watch and saw that is was early evening, just about the time the park closed for the period of time that came before the true night. He looked up and a saw a park ranger standing in front of him, leaning over toward him, and gently, but gradually more and more firmly, waking him up. Wesley came to completely and looked around at the edge of the clearing, and on the ground around his white oak tree.

"You alright, there, guy," the park ranger asked, "you were out cold, asleep. I don't see any bottles around you, can't smell anything on you, and you look to me like an intellectual type - with the notebook, backpack, and pen - so I'm going to go with that." Wesley finally spoke.

"I came here to just sort of sit back and relax," Wesley confirmed, "and reflect. You know, sort of meditate on life, as weird as that must sound. Then I fell asleep and had a really interesting dream…really vivid." Wesley began to lose himself in trying to understand just how vivid it was, but then snapped back into reality.

"Yeah, it must have been one of those dreams that really grabs you and won't let you go," the park ranger confirmed, "I've had those. And this here is nice spot to just sort of sit and reflect, I guess, so I don't think that's weird at all. Here." The ranger offered his hand to pull up Wesley, who was starting to get up and gather his things.

"Thank you," Wesley said, as he bent over and gathered up his things into his bag, "I guess I'm off to go home, now, then." Once Wesley packed his bag he nodded to the range, who nodded back, as he walked off toward the path that took him back to the parking lot while there was still enough light outside to maneuver the trail he planned on taking.

"Well, that's the darndest thing," the park ranger said as he shined his flashlight onto the ground, to augment the natural light still left, but fading, "are those animal tracks?" He shined the light around the tree and outward and saw six different sets of tracks. He got on his walkie-talkie and called it in to the other park ranger on duty, who was now currently sweeping the other trails for stragglers still at the park.

"Hey, Freddy," said the park ranger, "it's nothing major, but it's strange enough. You know that spot at the tree in the clearing, darn near dead center of the park?" There was click from the other walkie-talkie responding to his call.

"Yeah, what about it, Mattie," Fred asked, "all the trails, picnic areas, playground, and everything else look clear on this side. What's nothing major, but strange enough?" Matt paused a second to take in what he saw.

"There's six sets of animal tracks around this tree, where I just found another writer, new age type - notebook, pen, bag, and all, asleep," Matt confirmed, "I woke him up and he's on his way, but the same kind of tracks we've seen before, are back again." There was the click and then Fred continued.

"Really," Fred said, with a surprised tone, "again? The same six sets?" Matt was now shining the flashlight around the wooded area surrounding the clearing and the oak tree.

"Yes, siree," Matt confirmed, "the same two raven prints, the deer prints, the two fox prints, and the panther prints. No one hurt out here, however, and no signs of wildlife hunted or killed. It's the weirdest thing." He was shining his light around the area as he said this and waited for the click that told him Fred would wrap up their conversation and final check of the park before they closed it down for the night.

"Well, as long as no one's hurt and no wildlife's been killed I'd say we're fine," Fred confirmed, "just head back to the car and we'll report it back at the station, again, after we close up the park." With that Matt shined his flashlight on the trail he was to return to the parking lot by.

"Alright, then," Matt said, "I'm on my way back." As he was off onto the trail Wesley had found his way to the parking lot, reflecting upon his newest gems of Buddhist, German moralist, Epicurean, and good old fashion paternal philosophy he had picked up from a pair of ravens named Hugin and Mugin, a whit stag named Cornucopia, a pair of foxes named Huli Jing and Huxian, and a black panther named Panterra. He knew he had some work ahead of him and was ready to start getting down to it, and the first item was chronicling this enchanted visitation by the oak tree.

If This Seat Isn't Taken, Of Course
(4/3/2015)

I

To tell good stories that are remembered throughout and down through the
ages, as time and culture march on, one must give of themselves in a way that's
personal, spiritual, and leaves one quite vulnerable. The best writers are most
often susceptible to finding themselves tossed around by the riptides and
pushed around by the waves of the world they're immersed in, the worlds they
write about, and the world of people outside those worlds that they present their
stories to. To tell good stories one must have an interesting, active imagination,
an interesting background and life story, have lived an interesting, multicultural,
experienced life, and have sought out good stories where they've been lived.
Often, as is usually the case, this mean the most interesting and offbeat
characters seem to be the tellers of the tales and spinners of stories we find most
enchanting long after even those authors of characters are dead and gone.

Paul Spiegle, a great appreciator of the works of such dedicated writers, and
equally greater products of their work and toil for hours each day for years of
their lives, was at the coffee shop with his book. The theme of this shop was a
dog tweaked on the stimulant-laced drink peeking over the top of what looked
like something between a larger teacup and a small mug. This was his favorite
spot, when he wasn't working his third shift factory job or trying to carve out
his earned bookshelf space for his writing in local bookstores and independently
operated libraries, where he came to divulge writing ideas from murky shadows
in the ether to bring them to the light. Then, they could be deciphered for the
introverted, deeply philosophical, and meaningful symbolism they utilized - that
either mirrored or showed society in a better image - to tell great stories
through.

The time was the gray area of late morning and early afternoon where the calm
before the storm of the lunch hour was beautifully quiet, made for the best
meditative environment, outside of one's own head to take in and feed off of,
and let him get his favorite spot. This spot was a location beside the windows
with a view of the city courthouse, a hotel, and a hospital off in the distance on
this side of road and a large, corporate apartment complex flanked by two small
strip malls of eateries and boutiques, with a gas station beside the road that split

them. There were two hard-backed, but padded, and straight-gaited sitting chairs with wooden arms - both of the same design, that was delightfully British tea room-esque - with a dark wood stained, square, humble table between them that required you to lean over just enough to set down or pick up your chosen coffee, tea drink, sandwich, or bakery item.

Having settled down with the coffee of the day - today, almond something or other, which was always good, so he just ordered it and enjoyed it - along with his scone and biscotti. As he began to read the author's life and times bio he heard and felt the place starting to pack in as if on cue. He observed the usual businessmen, trendy socialites, and other random groups of all ages that frequented this cultural little space that called out to just such an intellectual, ever young and vivacious crowd on a daily basis. The place had an energy that he loved. More so than anyone else Paul Spiegle noticed one man in particular as he made his entrance from the parking lot. He didn't see him emerge from a vehicle, but saw him approach the front door, almost nervously and hesitantly, but with an a friendly enough and outgoing air about him, that he seemed to not realize he had exuded, that overcame and overshadowed his nervous, introverted side.

The man was intriguing to Paul Spiegle from head to toe. His personality, even from a distance, showed a good and friendly, outgoing nature that sought to take in all that life had to offer him, with an edge of nervous energy that seemed to tell of a conversation between many cross-talking voices in his own head, of differing thought processes, his conscience, and other moral compasses, all talking at once. Paul was used to this however, as he thought all creative minds had this sort of mentality about them. There was also the way the man was dressed. It was as if he was outside of modern time almost, but on purpose as a result of his being a bold external show of a personal character and style that was far more interesting that the other more modern, pedestrian, repetitive, and trend-sailing copycats of coffee bar patrons.

The man who had just entered the establishment's front door was wearing what looked like a frock coat with a shirt collar, bound tight and together at the neck by a tie, that was slightly over the collar of the jacket. His pants matched the suit jacket, whose material was not of the most modern, chic, and breathable variety of the updated clothing fashions. The cuffs of his dressy white shirt stuck out slightly, as in a long-scale type of dress shirt, from his jacket sleeves, and his hair was slickly parted down the middle on top. His eyes spoke of a hawk, only one tending towards a self-aware nervousness, taking in the scene he had just emerged upon. Looking down at his book, so as to not seem like he was spying on the man for any secretive, ambivalent, or any other reason than veneration of his spirit and exuded energy, Paul observed the man head over to the chair across from himself. This made sense, as the spot was quite the spot for musing and seating was being gobbled up by the minute.

"Hello, my name in Anschel," a less than confident, but far from fearful and rather quite bold voice said to Paul, "and I was wondering if I might sit down here, across from you, if this seat isn't taken, of course." Paul looked up from his book and observed the austere, charming, quiet, and cool appearance of the man.

"It's not taken at all," Paul said, "feel free to take the seat. It's my favorite spot in the house." Paul observed as Anschel took his seat, politely noticed the book he had in his hand, and took in the view Paul recommended.

"Thank you," Anschel said, "the place seems to be filling up, and I didn't want to take up an entire table, as I came by myself." Anschel regarded Paul.

"It usually does around this time," Paul said, "my name's Paul. Nice to meet you Anschel."

Paul thought that Anschel looked of the strange, offbeat, intriguing variety of others who come and go. He reminded him of a writer and figured Anschel was somehow aware of it in his style, nature, person, and work in general and overall.

"I was taking some time off today from my work and getting out of my sister's house," Anschel said, "I live with her because it seems to work out for both of us this way, and I thought this place looked interesting." Anschel took in the scene's visuals of different subcultures of patrons represented, the noises of combined conversations and culinary preparation, and the world outside the coffee shop's fishbowl glass walls and windows.

"Me too," Paul conferred, "I'm taking time off my work, that is, and I find this a good place that has an interesting energy to it." Anschel seconded this, by Paul's observation of Anschel's miming that he had felt it, too.

II

At first the conversation started out a little sporadic, stop and start, and sputtered in and out, but it began to pick up. Paul, sitting across from Anschel, had put down his book, to rather engage in conversation with the interesting character, and Anschel had noticed that his stepping into Paul's sphere of attention and space of a comfort zone was a welcome one, not an inconvenience or bungling intrusion. Paul could pick up on the telltale signs that Anschel had a sense of not being from around there and was a type that was not usually found there, but he was glad he was there and felt he fit in perfectly. In fact, Paul though Anschel made the place more interesting, merely by his presence. Anschel seemed to notice, even though the conversation didn't seem to drift toward any context about it, Paul's book of choice and regarded it - as well as Paul's choice to have chosen it - as a intriguing, interesting, and intellectually cultured reading selection. The conversation, with droplets of Anschel's dry humor here and there, took stride upon Anschel's guiding it toward discussion of his life and family. Paul Spiegle was perfectly happy to observe, listen, and respond as necessary when it seemed a good addition of recognition of where Anschel was in his story.

"I was originally born in Prague," Anschel said, "which is why I seem like I'm not from around here. In fact I usually speak German, even though - as my name suggests - I'm of Jewish descent. We were encouraged to speak German, so it was, myself and my two brothers and three sisters."

"Big family," Paul confirmed, "I just have the one brother. He's the one with the wife and kids and I'm the prospective artistic mind pursuing writing while I work the daily grind Monday through Friday." Anschel nodded as he had known how working to pay bills had to be done while pursuing one's own personal dreams, writing or whatever else it was.

"As I was saying about my father and mother," Anschel carried on to Paul's interest, "he started out as a traveling salesman and eventually owned and operated a store of fancy goods and clothes with fifteen employees. The store logo was what was once referred to as a jackdaw - a European bird known for being opportunistic in it's meals, living simply, and living in small groups with complex social organizations in farmland, woodland, coastal cliffs, as well as urban areas. A nod to the range of terrain my father covered probably."

"My mother was the daughter of well-to-do retail merchant parents," Anschel added, "and understood my father's business well, usually helping out with the daily operations. She had a bit more college education than he did, but so it goes. She was quite shy and quite. He, however, was a shrewd, overbearing, larger than life businessman and did well for that reason, but was quite difficult to live with at home, away from the business, but I digress." Anschel may have claimed to have digressed, but Paul could sense that his father's personality had influenced Anschel's overly polite, quiet, and introverted nature that peaked at times.

"As business became better and better we moved to a bigger family apartment," Anschel said, "but my sisters moved out to go with their military husbands. They eventually moved back to the family apartment during the war, but I was given their apartment and that was officially my own first apartment." Anschel appeared to be in his thirties and spoke of this event as having been quite recent and Paul knew about blossoming late in regards to the term the world saw as blossoming.

Throughout the icebreaking portion of their conversation Paul noticed, most prominently, a couple at a table nearby looking over their way occasionally. He couldn't quite read their faces or what it implied - whether it was recognition of overhearing something more interesting than what their own conversation offered or if it carried judgment - but Paul chalked it up to intrigue at Anschel's interesting story. There was also, even though Paul was a bit biased in this matter, the overall more cultured, intellectual, and interestingly brooding and introverted nature of Anschel's demeanor, his clothing style that set him apart from others who were less externally bold, and his personality that exuded writer down to his core. *Let them acknowledge this man*, Paul though, *since he is quite interesting.*

III

The conversation had switched gears to Anschel's education - worldly and beyond. The later lunch crowd didn't maintain it's gusto so much as it seemed to see its participants begin to slowly straggle out of the coffee shop, but the place was still fairly packed in. As Paul was working on his coffee, scone, and biscotti Anschel carried on telling his story, to which Paul was glad to listen to and add his own yeas, nays, smatterings of his own experience to the relevant points in the story, and mostly observe and take it all in.

"Even though I was born Jewish my official Jewish education splintered off with my Bar Mitzvah," Anschel continued, "at which point I was enrolled into a German elementary school for boys. Being immersed in the German culture I didn't really enjoy attending synagogue and my father and mother went only on the four high holidays of the year." Paul smiled at this and noticing Anschel's studying face, at this, explained his amusement.

"Yeah, I know what that's like," Paul confirmed, "sort of like of your Easter and Christmas service Catholics." Anschel picked up on Paul's drift, found the amusement in how Paul related to his own story, and mimed that he understood as he carried on.

"After this I was enrolled into a secondary school," Anschel picked up, "that was quite rigorous in their approach to the classic German education system. I studied there for eight years, speaking and writing Czech. Though I never felt fluent enough in it I was told I spoke it quite well and received good marks the entire time." Paul was impressed at anyone who was multi-lingual and could see the beginnings of what made Anschel such worldly person, which was why it seemed Anschel didn't need to work to exude the sentiment of being such.

"I then went on to the University of Prague," Anschel said, "where I studied chemistry, but changed majors. I began studying law, German studies, art history, and started a student club. It was called The Reading and Lecture Hall of the German, which is a mouthful, but really just means that we organized literature-based events and other similar activities. It was in this group I met my longtime and closest friend Max. We read Plato, Flaubert, and found Dostoyevsky, Flaubert, Franz Grillzparzer, and Heinrich von Kleist to be - as the saying going - speaking our sort of language. I began to become quite interested in Czech literature and first became interested in Goethe."

"I recognize a few those names," Paul said, proud of himself, "and I can add to that list that I've found Henry Miller, Kenneth Patchen, Jack Kerouac, Hunter S. Thompson, and Bob Dylan, among other offbeat writers that I've found quite interesting." Anschel regarded this with interest.

"I believe your Henry Miller, Kenneth Patchen, and Bob Dylan give mention to Goethe," Anschel added, "and his name as a muse for their work, as well." Anschel felt a kinship to the literary spirit and the spirit that found peace, solace, and enjoyment in the classics, as well as the offbeat and deeper down in the veritable philosophic hole of writers, along with Paul Spiegle.

"Having completed my time at university," Anschel finished this chapter of his story, "I received my degree as a Doctor of Law and spent a year, in what I understand is called an internship, as clerk for the civil and criminal courts. This was not my lifelong dream of course, but it takes us down that road, now." Anschel concluded this chapter of his story as Paul took it in and thought about the concept of going down that road, and how he'd still been on his own road.

Throughout their conversation they caught more looks from another, a different couple at a table a few placements over, which Paul Spiegle read as intrigued, slightly confused, but interested nonetheless. This seemed all on par for the subject matter Anschel and Paul had been conversing about so far, as well as where it seemed to be leading to, additionally. *If only your conversation partner was as interesting,* Paul thought to himself, quite amused, *you wouldn't have to keep on trying to sidestep your conversation to pick up tidbits from ours.* Not only did Paul's conversation partner dress the part as an intriguing character, Anschel had the backstory to really explain it all, as well. And whereas others seemed to be posing, when it came to their self-proclaimed flair for being culturally and intellectually more interesting, or simply on another level, Anschel simply was, by merely being himself.

IV

As Paul was finishing his scone and biscotti, and as his coffee was near the bottom of his mug, Anschel turned the conversation to his employment. The later afternoon crowd had thinned out and evolved into the gray area of the late afternoon and early evening lull. Paul offered to buy Anschel a sandwich, but he politely declined, so Paul ordered one for himself and let Anschel simply carry on telling his tale. Paul was glad to listen and be intrigued, and Anschel was glad to tell and intrigue.

"After that year, as a legal intern, I took a job as an insurance agent in the Mediterranean," Anschel continued, "and even though the views, the sights, and the sounds of Italy were nice I was unhappy working the typical eight to six, Monday through Friday. I, like yourself, found it difficult to really concentrate on my writing working those hours, so I lasted a year at that job before I resigned." Anschel saw Paul regard this and second this notion.

"I've been there," Paul conferred, "I always felt that a job like that really has to be your dream job, or else you really don't have much of yourself, or relative time, left at the end of the day to pursue your real dreams." Anschel nodded at this. "That's why I don't mind my third shift factory job. Come the weekends, when I've really organized my writing ideas all week, I'm ready to let loose on the laptop and get down to some serious hours of writing, when my brain is really alive, at night." Anschel nodded at this, too, and carried on where Paul left him off.

"A few weeks later I found something else that, like yourself, allowed me to do the same," Anschel smiled and carried on, "I began a job at a worker's accident insurance company for the state, where I investigated and assessed compensation for industrial worker's accidents on the job. It paid the bills and, though I sometimes despised the work, it did allow me to get off of work with time to spend writing for hours a day. My father expected me to take over for the family business, but I had enough to deal with between often too occasional illnesses preventing me from working at my job, as well as writing." Paul tried to consider what illness this seemingly health man could suffer from, other than his occasional coughs - some that seemed heavier than others - that seemed to make an appearance here and there between tidbits of his story.

"I still had my writing group," Anschel said, happily and musingly, "we called ourselves The Close Prague Circle. But, I soon became partners with my sister's husband at a factory, where I liked the work at first, but then began to, again, dislike how it interrupted my writing time. Writing, which I can tell you feel as well, is very important to me. It is a form of prayer and meditation, and I preferably can only do it in peace and quiet, in order to do it the justice and give it the focus it deserves." Paul consented to seconding this notion with a vocalized uh-huh and a nod.

"The tremendous world I have in my head," Anschel confirmed, "but how to free myself and free them without ripping apart. And a thousand times rather tear in me they hold back or buried. For this I'm here, that's quite clear to me. For man cannot live without trust in something indestructible within himself, though both that indestructible something and his own trust in it may remain permanently concealed from him." Paul was impressed with the passion Anschel had in his tone and voice as he exclaimed this maxim of tortured artists.

"I did find enjoyment and entertainment in Yiddish theatre, at this time," Anschel continued, "somewhat returning to my Jewish roots. This was the beginning of my exploration of my Jewish heritage. I even became a vegetarian." Anschel said this with an air of *well, what do you know,* to it.

"And I don't know how you feel about military service," Anschel spoke carefully, "but I avoided drafted service in the war, barely, because my work was considered important government service in and of itself. I did attempt to join the military later, but my recurring illnesses prevented me from being accepted, and I spent my time on pension from work in and out of hospitals recovering." Paul was again intrigued at the mention of health issues from this seemingly healthy conversation partner, other than his occasional coughs - some light and passing, and a once in a while cough who's intensity would have incited a nearby party to glance over at them.

"I did have other hobbies, as well," Anschel said, "like a personal study of alternative medicines, research into modern education systems and Montessori schools, airplanes, and film." Paul was taking this in as he thought about his own personal hobbies of studying guitar and music theory, catching up on literature classics, a personal interest in varied fields of philosophical, and sociological studies, as well.

The coffee place had well cleared out and was ready to slowly, but gradually fill up again for the evening crowd to cap their evening off with the scenery, coffee or tea, and sandwiches or bakery the coffee shop offered. He noticed that Anschel and himself had been talking for a while and that neither of them had lost any bit of attentiveness or interest in their conversation. Anschel's story was quite interesting, Paul found, and he appreciated Paul's related input at relevant points, as a sign that they shared a kinship on some level. Paul noticed that the bulk of the patronage of the coffee bar, at the current time, was himself, Anschel, and the two working behind the counter - who looked over at him as he looked up, regarded each other with faces and observations he couldn't read from his seat, and then returned to work.

V

As the coffee place began to fill up again, slowly, with a crowd that filtered in gradually and in gentle waves, Paul and Anschel carried on their epic conversation. The topic matter had shifted to Anschel's personal life. Paul had near finished his sandwich and had finished off his coffee meanwhile. Anschel, intending to carry on his story, did so as he returned to the new topic, as Paul was genuinely ready to begin listening, again.

"I don't know how much you got into athletics, but I wasn't interested much in them as a child," Anschel began, "but I did, later on, enjoy riding horses, swimming, rowing, and going on hikes with friends. Activities where you're out in nature and nature is brought out of yourself." Paul nodded at this notion.

"I wasn't the best athlete as a kid, or near the best," Paul confirmed, "but I do enjoy a good walk on the trails, as well. It's nice to get out into nature once in a while. It's good for reenergizing the mind, body, and soul, I find." Paul saw Anschel agree with this and allowed him to continue.

"I did, and do, like the ladies, however," Anschel perked up, mischievously, to Paul's amusement, "let me tell you, and I can see you can understand. We are men, after all. Some of it was innocent and some of it wasn't, but we've all grown up and evolved, haven't we?" Paul nodded at his, conceding without words that he too had grown up and evolved in the matter.

"There was Felice, a relative of my friend Max," Anschel mused, "she worked in Berlin as representative of a Dictaphone company. We communicated back and forth through many letters - I do love writing a good letter, and do so quite often - and we were engaged after. Those letters were found to be so interesting to others they were even published - my end of the conversation in the letters, at least. Felice's were lost." Anschel amused *well, what do you know* facial response to the letters being published at the public's interest was replaced with a *well, what can you do about it* facial response at the word of Felice's being lost.

"After Felice I was engaged to Julie," Anschel mused, again, "a less well-off and less educated hotel chambermaid. We lived together in an apartment, but were never officially married." Anschel's mood took a less lively and whimsical tone to be replaced with a darker, sadder tone.

"My father objected to the marriage due to her Zionist beliefs," Anschel continued, "and I gave into his inevitability of it not working out and moved on to someone else. I wasn't feeling so self-confident, was turned off by the physical aspect of it, and was shy. I did, however, use that experience as inspiration to write a story about a couple whose marriage was frowned upon by such a fatherly figure." Anschel brightened up about the aspect of finding a muse and writing about it, but was less than happy as per the color of the mood that had invoked the muse and the writing. Paul began to mime that he was sorry for this turn of events, but Anschel waved it off as he continued, and Paul gladly listened to the captivating tale.

"This was when I began to experience my medical issues," Anschel pushed on, "and moved to my brother-in-law's farm to work, while I recovered. It was the best time of my life. There were no major responsibilities, I had time to write - a very interesting collection of reflections on sin, hope, suffering, and the true way - not to get too Zen or Buddhist, however." Anschel perked up as he mused on this time.

"I then began an intense relationship with a Czech journalist and writer," Anschel said, "and then I met - on vacation to the Mediterranean, the Baltic Sea specifically - a kindergarten teacher from an Orthodox Jewish family. We went off to live in Berlin - even though briefly - so I could focus on writing outside of the shadow of my family. She inspired me to pursue an interest in the Talmud with more vigor and I wrote four more stories I prepared to be published." Paul considered this with interest as he finished off his coffee and mimed to one of the workers behind the counter to get a drink, not more coffee, but water.

"Yes, I did prefer the art of letter writing in communicating with family and close female friends," Anschel continued, "like my father, my once fiancé Felice, and my younger sister, Ottla." Anschel mused upon this for a moment.

"You know, I haven't written an actual pen on paper letter in a long time," Paul meditated on the matter, "not since I was a little kid, writing thank you notes for birthday or Christmas presents, or, now, the occasional scribble in a greeting card." Anschel observed Paul's revelation, and musing on the topic, and carried on.

"I have felt burdened by some aspects of my life, that you've heard, so far," Anschel seriously considered, "like the strange relationship with my father and my conflicted feelings that, even though I am Jewish, it has quite little to do with me, if I may say." Anschel mused on this as Paul thought of something.

"I've had issues truly getting into my own born and raised Catholicism, as well," Paul confirmed, "and I've had some difficult periods of my life where I didn't quite get along so well with my dad, either. I understand you completely on that. And as per girlfriends, I guess I've had my share, without really having found a serious one, yet." Paul shrugged as Anschel regarded his relating to his story.

"There are those who say these things factor into my work, my writing that is," Anschel continued, "as it may into yours as well, you may come to find, but I don't really see it in my own, myself. I'm not married, yet, either, but I do hold marriage and kids in high esteem. I'm told I've shown signs of depression and related physical signs of this, as well." Paul regarded Anschel in an *I've been there, too* sort of way.

"I've also found myself, as spirituality and religion are concerned, of an atheist bend, myself," Anschel added, "and politically I've found myself, and it may also be connected somehow, a socialist. However that all turned out I'm sure it plays a part in it all." Anschel now returned a likewise and such *what can you do about it* mime gesture back at Paul.

As Paul and Anschel were collectively musing on this topic Paul noticed the two working behind the counter looking over at them suspect. As they found themselves to have been found out the two behind the counter quickly returned to their work and some, what appeared to be, minor revelations to themselves alone. Paul chalked this up to the conversation having taken an emotional turn that, unless you were involved in it from the start, it seemed too heavy for two people who had just met a few hours ago to be sharing life stories and experiences about. *Whatever*, thought Paul, *those on the outside looking in, who really and truly wish they were able to have someone to have this sort of conversation with seem, to act that way when others find someone else and the ability to do so.* As he let this passing event with the two behind the counter roll off he noticed the place begin to fill up again for the early evening crowd.

VI

As the coffee place had once again filled up with the evening wave Anschel's story drifted, with a clearly guided hand, however, into the territory of his religious belief system and how it regarded his view of life, likewise. Paul had enjoyed Anschel's story and Anschel had been very forthright in his offering of his story. Paul found Anschel, for all the characters he seemed to have in his head and for all his melancholy sways in personality - based on where he was in his story - to be a good natured, kindly, and interesting conversational person. So, likewise, and such the conversation carried on.

"So I grew up in Prague and a German-speaking Jewish boy, becoming a man," Anschel carried on, "and even though I was intrigued by the intensity of the spirituality of the Eastern block Jewish community, versus the West, I simply felt outside of it all. I felt what have I in common with Jews? I have hardly anything in common with myself and should stand very quietly in a corner, content that I can breathe." Anschel watched for a moment as Paul took in this philosophical viewpoint of the situation.

"I was so bold, therefore," Anschel confirmed, "that I, in my mere adolescent years, declared myself an atheist. I was not aware of myself incorporating Jewish character, culture, or themes into my work writing, but others see them in there, somehow, in a way I cannot, myself." Anschel puzzled upon this for a second in his head and then continued.

"I did, however, even if later in life," Anschel continued, "study Hebrew while living in Berlin. I hired a friend of Max's from Palestine to tutor me while I attended classes in Jewish faith and studies of Judaism. I even sent a postcard to a friend in Tel Aviv to announce my intention to immigrate to Palestine, but they refused to host me because they had young children and were afraid of exposing them to the medical issues I was recovering from." On cue Anschel coughed gently, but waved off Paul's offering of getting him a glass of water.

At this cough Paul noticed a group of friends a table over glance back at himself and Anschel. Paul simply shrugged it off, thinking that it was a minor cough if anything, and followed the example of Anschel in completely ignoring it otherwise. Paul thought that Anschel was a very quiet, cool, and genuine personality and when you found yourself in the fortunate place and time to have such an interesting conversation with someone like them you simply let others not understand. All he was concerned with was hearing more of the story he could tell that Anschel was brimming to full to tell.

VII

As the evening carried on the conversation took the turn of going off into the direction of stories and books Anschel had written. Paul had begun this turn by telling Anschel about his own two self-published books of poetry and the book of short stories he was in the process of writing and editing, to then have three books of material he had faith in to begin approaching real, major editors and agents with. Anschel, showing genuine interest and being genuinely interested, turned the discussion in this direction.

"My first published work was a collection of eight stories," Anschel said, "in a literary journal, and then there was a story I wrote about two men having a very intriguing conversation themselves, almost like us just now. There was then the story I wrote about a marriage that the father figure protested against, which was a complete opening of body and soul of a story that evolved as a true birth, covered with filth and slime." Paul contemplated on the depth of the description Anschel gave to the intensity of the material and the clues to his personal attachment to his subject matter.

"I then wrote a story about the transformation of man, a travelling salesman," Anschel continued, "into a creature of detested abomination, despite himself, and how his family reacts to it. People seemed to like this story the most of all of my work." Anschel shrugged at this, considering, himself, why they would be interested in this piece more than any of his other work.

"Let's see, the next story was about an elaborate torture and execution device," Anschel said, "and the penal colony official who oversaw it. The meaning was to talk about the state of the prison system and those that meted out punishment." Anschel thought about this for a moment and regarded Paul's considering the depth of such a concept.

"Then came a story about a victimized protagonist," Ancschel added, "who experiences a decline in the appreciation of his strange, carnival craft of starving himself for extended periods. And then a story about a singer of hymns and songs in the community. Both of these were about the relationship between artists and their audience." Paul's interest was peaked at the drastically different range and spectrum of characters Anschel talked of having written about.

"As per full-length novels, which I believe you said you hadn't quite delved into, yet," Anschel added the caveat of yet, motivating Paul to do so, "I wrote one based upon the experiences of my own relatives, of the Jewish community, who emigrated to America. It had a surprisingly happy ending." Anschel mused equally and surprisingly gleefully, for the moment, at this concept of one of his books or stories ending happily, which amused Paul.

"Next, in another attempt to address the legal system," Anschel said, "I wrote about a man arrested, and prosecuted by a remote authority, whose crime is not mentioned or even alluded to, to the victim's demise. This was, deep down, about Felice. I tried to tell an emotional tale of emotional suffocation and shifting power while still allowing for moments of ardor and delight." Anschel's face was one of intrigued contemplation with an upbeat feeling, but an edge of melancholy.

"After that I wrote about a protagonist who tried to gain access to the authorities of a castle in a village," Anschel carried on, "about alienation, beauracracy, and the frustrations of one man standing against an entire system. In a way, the futile and fruitless pursuit of an unobtainable goal. His legal claim to live in the village was not valid, yet, taking certain auxiliary circumstances into account, he was permitted to work in it, however." Paul thought about this for a moment and Anschel, noticing this, waited a moment while he did so.

"Heavy material," Paul confirmed, to Anschel's nod, "but interesting and very deep. The kind of socio-political stuff someone's got to write about." Anschel smiled at the fact that Paul had understood his message and intentions, and not - as the critics had done - merely questioned his political affiliations and nationalistic allegiance.

"Just as you said," Anschel confirmed in response, "that was my intention, but instead the higher authorities merely questioned my political views and allegiances. I was, however, a regular attendee at meetings of anarchist, anti-militant, and anti-clerical organizations. I was and am a socialist at heart. I guess I have something in common with the philosopher Marx, but not entirely."

"I can sort of see that," Paul confirmed, "but can also see that there's much more to it, as well." Anschel regarded Paul's understanding.

As Paul said this he noticed two things about the one of two coffee place workers who was leaving for the night. They were leaving, first, which meant it was that time of the evening that precluded the last slow period of the coffee place for the day, and second, that the employee seemed to be giving Paul and Anschel a confused look on his way out. It was hardly masked and Paul picked up on it, but brushed it off, as before, as if merely to back up Anschel's stance of not even acknowledging such looks. If the content and context of their conversation was too much then they simply should just have a conversation of their own with someone else.

VIII

As the evening slowdown began to come on full force, and the place emptied - to what might as well have been the company of the last lone employee, Paul, and Anschel - the conversation took upon the subject of material Anschel actually had published. This was of interest to Paul, being that he had yet to have major publishing, or representation, behind him and his own work. This could offer insight into his own work and at the very least be a continuance of a really interesting conversation with Anschel.

"As I said before, my first works to be published were in literary periodicals," Anschel continued, "and that was, in different times of publication, the first eight stories. The one I told you about the very interesting conversation, except this one has an almost combative element to it, between two people, was included here." Anschel thought for a second and then carried on.

"On a trip to Italy with my friend, Max," Anschel carried on, "I wrote a story about an airplane show. This was part of a greater collection that included, more popularly, a story about a man who, in writing a letter to tell his friend in Russia that he's to be engaged, his father questions the mere existence of this friend of his, accusing his son of selfishness, among other twists. I meant to really delve into the psyche on that one." Paul contemplated this and thought it was quite interesting to really study the mind of man on such a deep level.

"There was another collection of stories," Anschel said, "that was published between a few different literary periodicals and journals of renown, whatever that means. But the first dedicated book of my own was the collection of stories I mentioned before in our conversation. It was dedicated to my dear friend Max."

"Max sounds like he took an interest in your writing," Paul said, "one beyond that of a friend and more of someone really helping to push your career along. I've got a few people close to something like that." Anschel nodded his happy approval of the fact that Paul had someone like his own Max, as he felt everyone should be so blessed.

"Then, the story about the man's transformation into a detestable creature, despite himself," Anschel continued, "was printed in another literary magazine. This was followed by the story of a doctor who travels into the country for a patient, which was dedicated to my father. After that came another collection of stories, including the one about the artist who starved himself for great periods of time, which was in the process of being published." Paul thought to himself, *what about all the other stories and books you just mentioned a little bit ago*, and Anschel read this in his eyes.

"As to the other stacks of stories and books, which I believe you were ruminating upon," Anschel smiled, at his own personal deftness and ability to read people, "I really would rather they be burned, if anything else. Some say my reaction to my devotion to my work, to be perfected before it is read by an audience, is a bit extreme, but I stand by it all the same." At first this struck

Paul by surprise, as his eyes showed his shock at such a statement from a man who'd spent so much time telling so many stories, let alone having agonized over so many of them. This reaction was abated, however, when Anschel smiled, shrugged that *what can you do about it* shrug, and Paul was again charmed by the man's personality.

"Well, a man's art is his art," Paul conceded, "and as amazing as it would be, if the rest of your material is as good as others think it is, even though there are many who think it would be a great loss to literature, it's your call." Anschel maintained a steady, personable face.

"Yes," Anschel confirmed, "that is how I feel about it. But I must be going now. I came here for some unknown inspiration that I knew not how it would come or what it would be, but it has come, and I must go, now. I have work to do." With a friendly, personable, albeit slightly nervous and introverted retreat, Anschel left Paul with a nod and went on his way. Last, but not least, Paul noticed Anschel take one last glance at the book Paul had brought with him - with the original intent to read before this most interesting conversation graciously improved his afternoon and evening - with interest, before he left.

Paul was about to observe Anschel's exit, to see from where he had come, if for no other reason than to be the perfect ending to the chapter of the story that was his life that day of his interaction with Anschel, but was distracted before doing so, completely. He noticed that the place was empty, that the lone worker of the coffee place was looking at Paul, and then looking around the coffee house. Paul, however, had decided to shrug it off as he had done so before, if for nothing more than to honor the dignity Anschel had done so with, having been of a character that Paul thought to be far more interesting that the usual fare of patrons here in a while. That was so until the employee approached him with a face and body language that implied he was curious about something.

"Hey, Paul," the lone coffee place worker remaining for the night said, upon making his way to the table as Paul began to gather his things and leave, "I...I don't mean to sound strange or anything, or to bother you, because we all know you and like you around here..." Paul was slightly confused.

"But…", Paul mimed, curiously and quite cheerily amused, "but what?" Paul had gathered up his things and was ready to go, once he had addressed the night shift closer's inquiry.

"Who were you talking to all night," the worker asked, with a face that was serious and stone sobering, "because you were talking to someone, that's for sure." The worker stood before him as Paul, confused, began to try to make sense of things.

"Anschel," Paul inquired, with a questioning, but pleasant enough tone, "he just left. He had the most interesting story about his life. I meant to read my book, but his story was just captivating." Paul held up his book.

"Huh," the coffee place employee said, regarding the book and then Paul, "but I didn't see anybody leave just now and I didn't see anyone sitting there the entire time. I don't know…" He left off nodding in the direction of the chair across from where Paul had been sitting.

Paul tried to get a word out, but didn't even know where to begin. He began to get the beginning of a word out, but then only made the guttural sound of vocal utterance that didn't end up sounding like a word, after all. He looked around the place, as if to find something to latch onto, but found nothing. Anschel had already left and made his way off with the same deftness as the way he arrived. As the night shift closer regarded Paul he shrugged, picked up Paul's dishes, and headed back behind the counter. Paul was dumbfounded and confused, took a final look at the copy of the book in his hand that he had originally intended to read, before the conversation that enraptured him all afternoon and evening - *Kafka: The Complete Stories* - and left feeling in such a way he wouldn't have been able to put words to it had you asked him to do so.

Thanks and Credits:

To my family for their continued and lifelong support of my writing ventures, be it music, poetry, short stories, and anything else I decide to take on in the future.

To the local libraries and independently owned bookstores for carrying my books and giving my work a chance to make it into the public sphere of readership on the first level.

To my friend Fred, his wife, Julie, and, even if just by association, their kids - Vince, Hannah, and Ruby - for their constant support of my music and literature ventures.

To Walt Whitman, Stephen King, Franz Kafka, John Steinbeck, Antoine De Saint-Exupery, Ray Bradbury, Nathanial Hawthorne, Johann Wolfgang Von Goethe, and all the other writers like them that came before to inspire these particular short stories, as well as myself.

To God for giving me the abilities and talents to do what I do, as well as supply me with the words, phrases, the sparks of ideas, and will power to work them out, from rough, into final drafts.

NOTES

Michael DeBenedictis is a twice self-published author of the poetry books *Mr. Swan's Poems* (October 2014) and *After The Flight* (March 2015). *Beyond And Between The Veil* represents his first collection of original short stories. He is 33 years old, and lives in Cuyahoga Falls, OH. When he's not working a day job to pay the bills he pursues a do it yourself, self-starter writing career.

To date his published and distributed works are comprised of multiple albums of original music (from 2009 to 2014), his first book of poetry, *Mr. Swan's Poems* (October 2014), his second book of poetry, *After The Flight* (March 2015), and this book.

NOTES

Beyond And Between
The Veil

A Collection of 15 Original Short Stories

By Michael DeBenedictis